ASPEN TRILOGY

ASPEN TRILOGY

By Cindy Stark

Published By

C. Nielsen

www.cindystark.com

ISBN: 1500913340
ISBN 13: 9781500913342

ALSO BY CINDY STARK

ASPEN SERIES
Wounded
Relentless
Lawless
Cowboys and Angels
Come Back to Me
Surrender
Reckless

RETRIBUTION NOVELS
Branded
Hunted
Banished

Whispers (An Argent Springs Novel)

Moonlight and Margaritas

Sweet Vengeance

RELENTLESS

(Aspen Series #1)

CHAPTER ONE

From the corner of her eye, Lily Chandler caught a blur of black as it dashed into the road. She slammed on the brakes. The tires on her little white Honda screamed as she swung off the pavement and onto the grassy area at the side of the road, narrowly missing a ditch.

When the car had come to a standstill, she plastered a hand against her chest, trying to slow her racing heart. "What the hell was that?"

Hannah eyed her as though she'd lost her mind. "I was going to ask you the same thing. Are you trying to kill us?"

"No." Lily glanced across the isolated two-lane highway, searching for the critter that almost lost its life. "There was something in the road. Didn't you see it?"

"Uh...no." Her friend looked around. "It was probably a skunk or raccoon. We have those out here, you know," she said with a tinge of sarcasm.

Lily narrowed her eyes. "I know that." Actually, she had no idea what she'd find in the small town of Aspen, Utah, but she wasn't about to admit it. She scanned the surrounding green pastures one more time for the little beast who'd stolen a year of her life.

"Can we go now?"

Lily sighed as she pulled out onto the never-ending stretch of blacktop. Her bug-spattered windshield showcased nothing but farmland alive with early summer grass. Occasionally, a house had popped up on the horizon, but not often enough for Lily's comfort. Somewhere up ahead was Hannah's brother hauling a good portion of their possessions in Hannah's truck. Everything else had been left in a storage shed in Salt Lake with the hopes that she and Hannah would be returning soon. "I'm starting to wonder if this was a good idea."

"Are you kidding?" Her friend tilted her head, the action making her auburn ponytail shake. "Don't second guess this now. When I left home seven years ago, I swore I'd never move back. I'm only going now because you begged."

"I didn't beg." She hadn't. But moving in with Hannah's family seemed preferable to being home-less. Two weeks ago, they'd both been fired from their respective jobs at a local newspaper in Salt Lake City, all because their boss hadn't been able to keep his zipper zipped. His wife had found out, and now the paper was slowly disintegrating from all the bad press and soon to be split assets. If it hadn't cost her a job, Lily would have been happy the jerk had been found out. She could totally commiserate with her boss's wife. She'd dealt with similar humiliation and pain when she'd caught her fiancé cheating with her sister.

Hannah folded her arms. "This was your idea. No complaining. I warned you my family lived in a rural area."

"Rural?" Lily let go a nervous laugh. "To an L.A. girl, rural is like…subdivisions. Like the outskirts of

4

Salt Lake. Places where people still live. Not this... vast emptiness." She gestured to the hills that didn't stop until they touched the sky. "If a person got lost out here, they may never be found."

"Ain't that the truth," Hannah said with a laugh. "Let me rephrase then. My parents live in a backward, podunk, God-forsaken town." Her friend pretended to shudder. "And look. We're here." Hannah pointed to a sign stating, Aspen, population: 250. "Welcome to my version of hell."

Only 250 people? There had to be that many living on their block in downtown SLC. Lily forced a smile and slowed as the speed limit dropped considerably. What if the people here didn't like her or couldn't relate to her? She was a city girl through and through.

The little town was cute, though. Baskets of pink and purple petunias swung from streetlamps, and all of the buildings were in good repair. It was like going back in time fifty years.

"Sorry to postpone our arrival. Mom asked if I could pick up a couple of things before we head out to their place." Hannah nodded toward a building with Andersen's Grocery painted on the side. "Do you mind if we stop?"

"Not at all." Lily cruised into the small parking lot, grateful to have arrived. "I'd like to look around the place I'm going to be calling home anyway."

Hannah snorted. "Don't get too excited."

Her friend seemed really down on her hometown, but Lily hoped it wouldn't be that bad. More than that, she hoped they'd both have new jobs before long and be headed back to civilized Salt Lake. Lily shouldered her purse and headed down the short street as Hannah went inside the store.

The air was fresh, if a bit cooler than it had been in the city. She inhaled again. Like *really* fresh. Like it almost had a sweet taste to it. That was certainly a nice change her lungs would appreciate during her morning runs.

In the same parking lot as the grocery store, stood a small strip mall with a pizza parlor, a beauty salon, and Betty Johnson Real Estate. A small "help wanted" sign tucked into the corner of a window near the door of the real estate office snagged her attention. She'd be headed there first thing after they got settled in.

A gas station took up space on the other side of the strip mall, and a bit farther down was a bigger building with the words Swallow's Bar and Grill. The other side of the street housed a cute little bakery and coffee shop. The town's version of Starbucks, perhaps? She'd definitely check it out later. Ahead of her was Randall's Western Outfitters that apparently carried clothing, tools and more. Everything a girl could want, all in a few short steps. It would certainly provide a different shopping experience than Rodeo Drive.

The door to the western outfitters store swung open in front of her, and she had to stop short to avoid running into it.

"So sorry, Miss," said the older guy in a worn cowboy hat when he realized he'd almost plowed the door into her face. He totally looked the rancher part with short, grizzled whiskers, accompanying denim jacket, and carrying a large bag of something over his shoulder.

Lily shook her head. "It's fine. You couldn't have known I was here."

The wrinkles around his grass green eyes creased when he smiled. "Still, I apologize."

She was about to respond when another man came out right behind him, carrying two identical bags.

"Dad—"

The younger guy stopped short when he saw Lily. "Well, hello."

He was a taller version of his father, with the same beautiful green eyes. His biceps bulged beneath his dark blue T-shirt from holding the weight of the two bags, and an interesting tattoo peeked out from beneath one of his sleeves. A hint of short brown hair hung below a khaki-colored ballcap, and she was surprised to find he wore small, thick silver hoops in his ears. Apparently, the small towns of the world were finally catching up with everyone else.

"Um…hi." She felt silly now, impeding him and his dad.

"Did you want something, Luke?" his father asked.

He hesitated. "I'll tell you in the truck." He nodded toward a big black pickup, and Lily couldn't help but feel he'd just dismissed his dad.

The older man seemed to pick up his cue as well. He winked at Lily, nodded and headed toward the vehicle.

"You're new in town." The younger guy smiled, making Lily feel slightly giddy inside. She wasn't quite sure what to make of him. Hannah had been dead wrong in her assessment of the men in this town if this guy was any indication of who she'd find here.

"I just arrived. I'm going to be staying with my friend's family for a while." A soft breeze blew several blond curls into her face, making them stick to her lip gloss. She tried several times to remove them, but kept missing some. He reached out, holding the weight of his load with one hand, and pulled the last hairs away from her lips.

"Thanks." She tugged her long tresses to one side, away from the breeze, to keep them under control. The attraction she felt for this guy was awkward, surprising, and a little exhilarating.

"What's your name?" He continued to stand there as though the heavy weight he carried meant nothing to him.

"Lily. Lily Chandler."

"I'm Luke Winchester. It's nice to meet you." His lips tilted into a grin, and she couldn't stop herself from mirroring the gesture. "Who are the friends you're staying with?"

"The Morgan family. Do you know them?"

"Of course."

At her puzzled expression, he continued. "You're obviously not from a small town, 'cause here everybody knows everybody."

"Lily?" Hannah yelled from down the street. "Let's go."

Luke turned his gaze to her friend, his demeanor cooling. "Hey, Hannah. Welcome back," he called out.

Hannah sent him a heated look and then got in the car, slamming her door.

Lily raised her brows. "Ouch. You and Hannah have some sort of history?"

He shook his head, a disappointed look hovering in his eyes. "A slight misunderstanding. She'll get over it one of these days. In the meantime, promise me you won't believe everything she tells you."

Interesting. She couldn't wait to hear Hannah's side of the story. "Okay." She would give Luke the benefit of the doubt. For now.

"It was a pleasure to meet you, Lily Chandler. I'm sure I'll run into you again."

He held out a hand, and she took it. His fingers were strong and warm, and they sent a fascinating spike of energy coursing through her. "Nice to meet you, too."

She let go of his hand and turned, walking toward her Honda. She desperately wanted to look back at him, but she was certain he still watched her. She could feel the almost physical touch of his gaze. When she reached down to open the car door, she dared a glance in his direction. A swift current whipped through her when their gazes connected. He nodded as though affirming they'd meet again and turned.

Lily blew out a slow breath and slipped into her car, trying to pretend Luke Winchester hadn't shoved her pulse into overdrive.

CHAPTER TWO

"What did he want?" Hannah's usual pleasant demeanor had vanished.

Lily shrugged. "I don't know. I nearly collided with his dad as they came out of that store. I guess he just wanted to introduce himself."

"Of course he did. Cute new girl in town. Fresh meat for him." The anger in Hannah's voice surprised her.

"Whoa. What's with all the hating?"

Her friend narrowed her eyes as Lily put the car in reverse. "He's like the biggest jerk in Aspen. You think your ex was bad for cheating with your sister? This guy is ten times worse. He's the biggest player in town, and he's broken every heart in the valley."

Lily raised her brows. "That bad?" He was certainly cute enough to break a million hearts.

Hannah nodded, visually upset.

"I'm guessing you were one of those victims?"

"I should have known better, you know? He'd already dated most of the girls in the county before he asked me out. I'm a couple years younger than him. But he finally noticed me, and when Luke Winchester has his sights on something or someone, he's relentless in his pursuit. But I didn't mind. I'd convinced myself all those other women weren't

10

right for him. I would be the one he'd fall for." She snorted, flinging her hand. "Nope. I was just another conquest."

"He sounds like a real jerk." Which disappointed her. "Did you sleep with him?"

"No." Her friend shook her head. "But only because I was smart enough not to. I'm pretty sure he's been with just about everyone else. He's the screw 'em and leave 'em type."

"Wow." Those were some pretty strong words, and she hated people who took advantage of others. "I wonder how he'd like it if someone did that to him. Maybe he deserves a taste of his own medicine."

Hannah drew her brows together in a frown. "He'd certainly deserve it, Lily, but not from you. It's better if you stay away from him."

"Yeah." She sighed. "Probably so." It's not like she would have actually followed through with her threat anyway. Getting a new job was her priority for now. She stared out the window, a gray cloud of emotion settling over her as the small town faded away and they were swallowed by more fields and barbwire fences. She'd experienced some major chemistry with Luke, but from what Hannah said, it seemed he had a way of bringing about that feeling in a number of women. Figures.

As cute as he was, Luke Winchester had just been added to the "do not touch" list.

Luke watched until Lily Chandler's Honda Civic disappeared from sight, a fresh spark of hope growing in his chest. Here, he'd thought there would never be another woman in the small town of Aspen that might give him a chance. Not after how Hannah Morgan had shredded his reputation. But he'd caught the look of interest in Lily's deep brown eyes. She'd taken a long look at him, and apparently, she'd liked what she'd seen. He hadn't realized how much he missed flirting with a woman who didn't regard him with wariness.

He'd enjoyed looking at her, too, with her soft blond curls reaching past her shoulders, and those smoldering brown eyes. Damn. He hitched the bags higher on his shoulder and headed for his truck. Today was a good day.

Now, he had to figure out a way to see her again before Hannah could damage any chance he might have with Lily.

Lily's spirits lifted as Hannah directed her to turn off the main road and onto a gravel-paved lane that wound toward a small, red brick house flanked by weeping willows and a sprawling two-story white home that lay beyond. Near the big house stood a large, wooden barn, with several farming implements off to the side.

"Home sweet home," Hannah announced, as Lily's car bumped over the rough road.

"The big house or the little one?" Lily asked. If they were staying in the smaller house with her brother and parents, things were going to be very cozy.

Hannah laughed. "We'll stay in the little one, but everyone else is in the main house."

"We get our own place?" That was a nice surprise. It wouldn't feel like she was intruding so much that way.

"We lucked out. My cousin and his wife had been living there until a month ago, but now they have their own home. And this way, I won't be forced to live under my father's thumb and my mother's ever-present criticism."

Lily frowned. Hannah's mom had always seemed so nice on the phone the few times she'd talked with her. Coming home seemed to bring out her friend's dark side. "I'm okay with whatever. I'm just glad to have a place to stay."

"That's what I'm hoping for, too. This place has zero nightlife. Stay here too long and it will choke the life right out of you."

Lily parked next to Hannah's old blue truck that was piled high with all of her friend's belongings and some of Lily's. On the other side of her vehicle sat a newer model Mazda. Lily wondered who it belonged to. The sporty little car looked out of place in the small farming town, which was exactly how Lily felt. But she supposed if the sports car could fit in, so could she.

"The place is kind of small," Hannah said as she led the way inside.

Lily walked into what would be her home for the next little while and was met with a quaint, homey feeling. "It's adorable." She loved the old-fashioned, hand-carved shelving built into the walls. The lace curtains blowing with the afternoon breeze bespoke tranquility. Maybe that's what she really needed at this point in her life. A chance to regroup before she moved forward. "Besides, I think it has more room than our apartment."

"I do believe you're right." Hannah dropped her purse on a worn brown couch. "This is the living room. The kitchen's behind it, with two bedrooms to the side. The bathroom is at the back of the house. It was added on after the house was built."

"Seriously?" The house really was from another period, but it had character.

They found Hannah's mom putting away towels in the bathroom. She was exactly how Lily had pictured her. A little overweight, strong hands, and a warm smile that matched her fading auburn hair. Not at all the difficult person Hannah had described.

"You poor girls." She hugged Hannah, but after a second, her friend pulled away. A hurt look flashed in her mother's eyes, but she quickly buried it behind a couple of blinks. "Both of you losing your jobs like that. It's a shame the way people live their lives. Do they not realize their choices affect others besides themselves?"

Hannah rolled her eyes. "Don't worry about it, Mom. We're fine. We won't be here long enough to bother you."

Her mother frowned then. "You know it's not a bother."

Lily stepped forward, wanting to diffuse the uncomfortable undercurrents. "Nice to finally meet you, Mrs. Morgan. Thank you so much for allowing me to stay with you."

Hannah's mom shooed away her thanks, a pleasant look settling on her face. "Please, call me Sondra, and don't even worry about it. Despite what Hannah thinks, I'm glad she's home, and any friends of hers are always welcome here." She lifted a stack of sheets sitting on the counter. "I brought down fresh bedding from the house. I figured you'd both probably packed yours and might not get to it right away."

"You didn't have to do that," Hannah answered. "We can take care of ourselves."

Lily didn't know what had spouted her friend's unkind attitude, but it wasn't typical of the Hannah she knew. She took the stack of sheets. "Thank you. This is very kind."

"No problem." Sondra smiled at Lily. "I'll let you get to unpacking. Tyler left your truck here, Hannah, and went up to the house to get some lunch. He'll be down later to move any unwanted boxes and extra furniture into the barn. I put some sandwiches in the fridge for you."

Lily followed her out into the living room with Hannah coming up right behind her. "Before you go, Sondra, I wanted to ask Hannah's and your opinion. I saw a help wanted sign back in town, and I was thinking of applying. It's at the real estate office, but I'm not sure if I'm qualified."

"Oh, yes, that's right. Betty *is* looking for a part-time receptionist to handle calls in the afternoons and on Saturdays. I doubt she'll be able to pay what you were making in Salt Lake."

"That's okay." It was more than okay at this point. "I'd just like to be earning some kind of a wage while I search for something more in the marketing field."

Hannah gave her a sideways glance. "You could take a little break first, you know."

"No." Lily shook her head. "I insist on paying my way while I'm here, and if I can save a little too, that's even better."

"Smart girl." Mrs. Morgan opened the door, letting in sharp rays of afternoon sun. "If you'd like, I can call Betty and give you a good reference."

"That would be wonderful. She might be hesitant to hire someone who isn't local. Thank you so much." Already things were looking up.

By the time Lily and Hannah had eaten the required dinner with the family, Hannah had progressed from irritated to agitated. She and Lily had returned to their house and unpacked a few more things, but it was obvious something was wrong.

"You okay, Hannah?"

"Ugh." Hannah haphazardly tossed silverware into a kitchen drawer. "I'd forgotten how stifling this town can be. No wonder I left."

"It's not that bad." Sure, things moved at a slower pace, but the air was fresh and the people seemed nice.

"That's because you didn't grow up here. I spent the first eighteen years of my life not knowing what the real world was like."

"In case you haven't noticed, the real world isn't all that great either. People, noise, pollution."

Hannah rolled her eyes. "Like I said, I'll give you two weeks, and then you'll understand."

"Your parents seem like great people."

"Of course. Everyone loves them. But they drive me insane with talk of husbands and babies. There's more to life than that."

Lily didn't know what to say. Her parents *had* asked Hannah when she intended to settle down, so Lily could understand her friend's irritation. But Lily could also see how much her parents loved Hannah and wanted to see her happy. Hannah apparently did not share her viewpoint.

She'd seen her friend in this kind of restless state before. Only in the past, it had resulted in a major shoe shopping spree or a wild night on the town. Both of those didn't seem to be an option here. Maybe getting out of the house would help. "We could go check out that outfitter store."

"Ha, ha." Hannah leveled a piercing gaze at Lily. "You and I are going downtown to get a drink."

"Downtown?" There really wasn't much of a downtown in Aspen. Okay, there was none at all. "Where?"

"Sparrows." She grinned. "It ain't much, but us two city girls are going to show this town how to party."

Lily laughed at her friend's sudden jovial mood. "I don't want to spoil the moment, but in case you've forgotten, we're pretty much broke."

"Doesn't matter." Her friend waved away her excuse. "Up here in the back country, the men aren't afraid to buy a lady a drink."

The thought of letting off a little steam appealed to Lily, but she wasn't sure she wanted to make her mark on this town quite the way Hannah seemed to. "I don't know if this is the best idea. I might not be from a small town, but I'm pretty sure if we go in there guns blazing like we've been known to do in Salt Lake, people are going to talk."

"Don't worry, Lily. This town could use some good gossip, and it's not like we're staying for long." She navigated her way between packing boxes and headed toward her bedroom. "I'd suggest a short skirt and some high, high heels, honey."

CHAPTER THREE

In the end, Lily hadn't worn her shortest skirt, but Hannah had. However, Lily had redeemed herself in her friend's eyes by wearing her signature hot pink high heels. Together, they looked like they were going clubbing, not heading for the local bar and grill. Lily couldn't escape the sinking feeling Hannah's plan had disaster written all over it. But this was her friend's town. She knew the people and what was acceptable, so she'd let her make the call.

Lily insisted on driving, knowing there was a good chance Hannah would overindulge. When they arrived at Sparrow's, the parking lot was full. That didn't say much though, because the gravel lot held thirty cars max.

Lily had to be careful that her heels didn't sink into the gravel as they made their way to the front door. Just outside the doors, two men in their fifties stood smoking and drinking bottles of beer. That wasn't a sight she'd find in Salt Lake. The smoking, yes, but public drinking would certainly mean a ticket or a night in jail, depending on how intoxicated a person was.

Just as Hannah reached for the door, one of the men whistled his appreciation.

"Are you kidding me?" she whispered to Lily. "Give me a second."

She approached the men. "Hey, your last name is James, isn't it?"

"Sure is pretty lady. Do I know you?" He shifted his stance, glancing at his friend with a grin.

"I think so. I'm Hannah Morgan. Remember me? I went to school with your *daughter*."

The other man choked on his beer as the cocky grin dropped from Mr. James's lips. "Hannah?" He wiped his mouth, looking guiltier than sin. "I'm sorry. I didn't realize you were so grown up."

She smirked. "I'm the same age as Kaylee, old man. And much too young for you." Hannah swiveled and stalked toward the front door. Lily was sure she'd swung her hips a little more than was necessary.

"*Really?* Perverts," Hannah said as they walked inside together.

Lily wanted to remind her they probably looked more like hookers than young women as far as the residents were concerned, but apparently Hannah had something to prove to the town that had raised her. All Lily could do was support her.

Inside, there were more people than Lily had seen all day. It seemed this was a work hard, play hard kind of town. The lights had been dimmed, and a row of customers filled the barstools. Eighties rock music blared from a hidden stereo system.

Most of the tables were taken. Some of the customers had burgers or steaks in front of them, but everyone else was happily consuming tankards of beer along with shots of whiskey.

Lily followed Hannah, who still continued to over-shake her booty, to a wide table occupied by her brother and two other guys, one with blond hair and a big smile, the other with dark hair and somewhat of a seductive, interested look.

Hannah stole an empty chair from a nearby table and squished her way between her brother and the blond guy wearing a Steeler's t-shirt. "Who's buying us our first drinks?"

All three of the men seemed a little shell-shocked by her attitude, but the blond found his tongue first. "Hey, Hannah. I'd love to buy you a drink." His startlingly blue-eyed gaze slid down her body before returning to her face. "You're looking pretty hot these days."

Tyler lifted his chin. "Watch it, Milo. That's my sister you're talking about."

Hannah ignored her brother's comment. "Thank you, Milo. For the drink and the compliment." She gave him a flirtatious wink as the dark-haired guy scooted over and pulled up a chair for Lily. She thanked him and sat down.

"Has Mom seen what you're wearing?" Tyler raised parental eyebrows.

"I'm twenty-five years old. I don't need my mother's approval on what I wear or what I do. Got it?"

"Shit." He laughed. "You know she's going to hear about it."

"I don't care."

Lily had to wonder if this was more about proving something to the town or to Hannah's parents. She really hoped it wasn't a family thing. Her mom and dad had been so nice and welcoming.

The waitress came, and Hannah ordered them both a shot of tequila. Lily cringed. Tequila nights were never mellow.

"Are you going to introduce your friend, Hannah?" the dark-haired guy sitting next to Lily asked.

"Sorry, boys. I forgot my manners." She grinned at Lily. "This is my best friend, Lily. We shared an apartment and worked together in Salt Lake. Until our lame ass boss fired us."

The guys mumbled their regrets.

"Lily, you already know my brother. These are his friends, Milo and Scott." Scott with the dark hair had the biggest build out of the three, and sported a goatee. All of them were pretty cute, and she had to admit she kind of liked their rugged appearance. It was much more appealing than her metrosexual ex-fiancé and his friends.

The tequila arrived, and Hannah downed it and ordered another before the waitress could walk away.

"Take it easy, Hannah," her brother warned.

"If you're going to be my mother, Tyler, I'll go sit somewhere else."

He rolled his eyes and turned to Lily. "Anything else for you?"

She was about to say no, when Luke walked through the door, looking more than sexy in a cowboy hat and a button-down plaid shirt that outlined his chest and clung to his biceps. She ducked her head slightly. "I'll have a beer." She was already feeling the effects of the tequila, but she had a suspicion she'd need a little more sustenance to get through this night.

"Dance with me, Milo." Hannah stood and tugged him to his feet.

"Okay, okay." He placed a hand on the small of her back as she led the way to the dance floor. She threw her arms around his neck and plastered herself against him as they swayed to the sounds of Styx.

"What's gotten into her?" Tyler directed the question at Lily.

"You tell me. She's been antsy since we arrived. Worse after we ran into Luke Winchester, and she was awful to your mom when we got to the house."

Tyler grimaced. "Always the same old shit. She and mom didn't say more than two words to each other at dinner."

Lily hadn't realized they'd been that chilly to each other. Tyler and Hannah's dad had distracted her, plying her with a million questions about her life. She was about to state just that when Tyler lifted his gaze over her head and the other two guys followed suit.

"Speak of the devil."

The hairs on her arms stiffened as a shiver rolled over her shoulders.

"Got any extra room for me?"

"Sure, man," Scott answered and scooted closer to Lily, creating space for Luke between him and Tyler. "We haven't seen you here in a long time." Scott relaxed against his chair and casually rested an arm across the back of Lily's seat. She almost laughed out loud at his none-too-subtle marking of territory.

"Yeah. Been busy." Luke noticed Scott's move, too, and didn't seem very happy about it. That was exactly why she let Scott leave his arm where it was. After what Hannah had told her, Lily didn't want to give that bad boy any encouragement.

"So you know my sister's in town?" Tyler said to Luke.

He nodded. "I know. I saw her earlier." His gaze flicked to Lily as though he was waiting for her to say something.

She did her best to give him a vacant, uninterested look and turned away.

Their next round of drinks arrived, and Scott picked up the tab for Lily's beer and Hannah's shot. Hannah must have had her tequila radar turned on, because she and Milo arrived back at the table shortly after the waitress left.

She scowled when she noticed Luke. "Ugh. Who let you in?"

"Be nice," Tyler warned.

"You're going to have to forgive me sometime, Hannah," Luke said. "It's been eight years."

She flashed him a brilliant smile. "Never." She downed the contents of her glass, slammed it on the table and latched on to Scott's hand. "Your turn."

Scott flicked a quick glance between Lily and Luke, and Lily knew without a doubt, he was worried Luke would move in on what he thought was his turf. Too funny.

"Yeah." Lily nudged Scott's arm with a finger, coming into contact with some serious muscle. "Go dance with her now, and then I get the next one."

"Deal." He visibly relaxed, and Hannah snagged someone's bottle of beer as they walked away to the dance floor.

Luke immediately moved into Scott's vacant chair. "Can I interest you in this dance?"

"Uh...I don't think so." She shook her head, earning herself a wounded look from Luke.

"Ah," Tyler exclaimed, palming his chest. "The poor guy is shot down."

"Sorry, bud," Milo chimed in. "That really sucks." He turned to Lily. "But she's already promised this dance to me, right?"

"I did." Lily exhaled and stood, grateful for the save. She needed to keep as much distance between her and Luke as she could.

"Oh, come on," Luke called after them. "I don't believe that for a second."

She snuck a glance backward, her lips twisting into a grin at Luke's mock disappointment.

"I think he likes you," Milo said, as he put a hand on her waist and took her hand with his other. The music was more fast than slow, and back in L.A. or Salt Lake, they would have been much farther apart.

"Don't say that." She dared another glance at Luke, and sure enough he was staring directly at her. She turned away. The man's gaze was more than a little disconcerting, and she was having a seriously hard time ignoring the sizzle he sparked inside her. Not good. It must be that whole forbidden-fruit theory.

"Why not? He's an all-right guy."

"That's not what Hannah says."

Milo laughed. "That's because Hannah can carry a lifetime grudge."

"She said he's something of a womanizer."

He nodded. "Yeah, I guess he did sport a wild reputation a few years ago, but he seems decent now. Maybe he's changed."

That was the problem. She wasn't interested in a "maybe".

Milo stopped dancing, and Lily collided smack into him. "Girl, I don't know what kind of dance moves you think you're doing, but here in Aspen, the men usually lead."

Lily widened her eyes in surprise and laughed. "What?" She knew her moves hadn't synced well with Milo's, but she hadn't known it was *her* fault. "I thought it was you."

He grinned. "Let me show ya." He took her hand again and made very deliberate moves. "You go one-two, one-two-three. One-two, one-two-three. It's called the two-step."

She followed his moves, letting him lead her around the dance floor. "Okay." She laughed. "I think I've got it."

She had to admit, his more formal style of couple dancing was fun, and Milo was such a good sport for pretending not to notice when she missed a few steps. The other couples were pros, moving as one over the sawdust-covered wooden floor. Even Hannah, swigging a beer and draped over Scott's arm could keep up with the rhythm of the music. Lily refused to meet anyone's eyes, not wanting to know if they were laughing at her or not. It didn't matter, as long as she and Milo were having fun.

She wondered why this style of dancing had given way to modern moves in most of the dance clubs. She enjoyed the intimacy of it, like they were talking with their bodies as well as with their voices. It was a G-rated version of sex.

She continued counting off the steps in her head, enjoying the feel of a man leading her around the floor.

Then Milo turned them, and she found herself looking across the room, straight into Luke's captivating eyes again. She knew she should turn away, but something glued her in place. Maybe she felt some sort of protection, being in Milo's arms. Either way, she was playing with fire, but she couldn't make herself look away this time. Fascinated, she watched as Luke turned his sensuous lips into a smile. Shit.

This wasn't good. Her thoughts tangled and her feet followed suit. She stepped hard on Milo's boot again.

He half-laughed and half-groaned, the sound of it dragging her back to the present moment. "Oh, honey." He shook his head.

She covered her mouth with her hands, trying to hold back her laughter. "I'm sorry. I really suck at this."

"No. You just need another drink to loosen you up, and then we'll try again."

She could live with that. "Okay." She let him lead her back to the table, a giggle hovering on her lips. She was making a fool of herself, but enjoying every minute of it.

"Warning for ya, fellows," Milo announced. "This girl cannot dance."

"What?" Lily laughed, enjoying Hannah's friends. "I can dance, just not"—she twirled her finger in the air—"this kind of dancing." Luke stood and slid a chair out for her. His chivalry sucked away some of her merriment and replaced it with an intense awareness of him. "Thank you," she said as she sat.

"My pleasure," he said close to her ear and sat back in Scott's seat.

"I stand by my statement." Milo picked up his beer and held it out for a toast. "Here's to pretty women who can't dance."

All three men clinked glasses and drank.

"You guys are ridiculous. I can dance. Ask Hannah." She looked around for her friend, but couldn't see her or Scott anywhere on the dance floor or otherwise. It had only been a few minutes since she'd seen them dancing.

"Tyler. Where's Hannah?"

The rest of their party glanced about the room. "Maybe they went outside for some air?" Milo offered. "Hannah is hitting it pretty hard tonight."

Too hard, if anyone asked Lily.

"I'll check." Tyler stood and headed for the door, leaving her with Milo and Luke.

"I hope she's okay." Lily had been more than a little worried about her friend all evening. She'd seen Hannah over-indulge a time or two, but she'd never paired it with anger or irritation or whatever it was she had burning beneath the surface tonight.

Tyler returned a few minutes later. "She's puking…in the parking lot."

"Oh, my God." Lily stood, and Luke followed suit.

Tyler held up a hand. "Don't go out there. She's mortified enough. Apparently, she let loose all over Scott's boots and pants. So, he's headed home, too."

"I should go." Lily stepped away from her chair.

"Nope." Tyler shook his head. "She asked me to take her home. She wants everyone else to stay and have a good time." He narrowed his gaze at Lily. "Especially you. She didn't want to ruin your first evening on the town, as she put it."

"But—"

"You should stay, Lily," Luke said.

"Yes, you absolutely should stay." Milo banged his fist like a gavel on the table, declaring it so. "I don't want to be left alone with this guy." He indicated Luke with a jerk of his head. "He's a worse dancer than you."

It made her happy to know she wasn't alone in her humiliation. "Okay, fine. I'll stay."

"One more thing. Can I take your car?" Tyler raised his brows at Lily. "I rode in with Scott, and I hate to make him drive us all the way home wearing my sister's puke. I'll come back for you after I get her settled."

Luke held up a hand. "Don't worry about it. I'll make sure Lily gets home safe."

Tyler sent her a questioning look, asking if that was okay.

"Sure." She dug her keys out of her purse and handed them to Tyler. She'd sort of been teasing earlier when she'd refused to dance with Luke, but saying no now would be flat out rude. It was obvious Hannah had a real problem with Luke, and he was still very much on the avoid list. But the rest of the guys seemed to like him okay, and she didn't want to come across as a bitch. "I'll check on her when I get home, too."

Tyler left, and now they were down to an awkward threesome. Lily took a sip of beer as the song switched to a country ballad. Just as she set her glass down, a curly redhead appeared at their table.

"How about a dance, Milo?" The girl had a sweet, yet sultry look about her, and Milo's eyes immediately lit up.

"Absolutely." He turned to Lily and half-whispered. "Me and Sierra are going to go do our thing, but I'm leaving you in good hands." He winked and walked away.

Then there were two.

CHAPTER FOUR

L uke leaned back in his chair, studying her from beneath his cowboy hat. The sight of him, relaxed, his gaze smoldering, took away her breath.

She quickly glanced away. This was not good. She was in over her head, and she knew it. She didn't want to like him. Didn't want to appreciate how hot he was. She sure as hell didn't want to be attracted to him, but every time she looked into his eyes, her insides thumped with excitement. He was a heartbreaker, she reminded herself. Those tempting lips were one of his weapons.

"Dance with me." His mesmerizing gaze invited her to wander down an unexplored path that promised pleasure. The country singer crooning in the background enhanced his invitation.

She exhaled a nervous breath, wanting to say yes, but also knowing she should say no. "You don't want to dance with me. I'm pretty sure you saw how horrible I was." She lifted her beer and took a drink of the cool liquid.

"You just need the right partner," he said with all seriousness.

She took another drink, her mouth still dry. "Milo says you can't dance either."

He laughed at that. "Trust me. I can dance." Her breath hitched. She was pretty sure he could do more than dance.

He stood and held out a hand to her. "It's a slow song. You won't mess up."

There was no way she could reasonably say no. Or maybe, deep down, she didn't want to. She'd been getting conflicting messages concerning Luke since she'd arrived in town, and maybe she wanted to make up her own mind about him. "Okay." She stood and took his hand.

As she followed him to the dance floor with him holding her hand, she couldn't help but notice how tall he was. She stood at five-foot-nine without heels, and he still towered over her. She like that. Liked that he seemed big and capable and strong.

And wrong, according to Hannah. Completely wrong for her.

He pulled her into his arms, and she suddenly wished she'd worn something more substantial than an almost sheer blouse and short skirt. It didn't seem like enough protection from this man who assaulted all of her senses.

He splayed his warm hand on the small of her back, and her fingertips burned where she touched his shoulder. He started to move, and she found it easier than she'd thought to match his steps. He held her gaze, as a sexy, yet somehow dangerous energy coursed between them.

She wanted to look him in the eye, face her attraction and control it, but the longer she stared, the more intense their connection grew. Shit. She dropped her gaze to his lips to avoid his eyes. He owned the word desire. Maybe delicious, too. Like his mouth, the way his lips almost begged for a kiss. She knew without a doubt he'd taste sinfully good.

She blinked, derailing her traitorous thoughts.

Wow. She *really* couldn't go there. Not with this guy. She wanted to get to know him a little better, but she wasn't sure she could do that and still maintain a healthy distance. She turned her head away, trying to ignore his tantalizing smell of sunshine and leather, and how good it felt to be held by him. Each second that ticked by made it harder and harder to remind herself that Hannah said he was not a nice person.

"I think we're doing pretty good, don't you?" he said, his mouth close to her ear.

She lifted her gaze, realizing she hadn't had one misstep. That surprised her because she'd lost herself completely in her thoughts about him instead of concentrating on dancing. "I guess we're not as bad as Milo said after all."

"Maybe Milo's the one who doesn't know what he's doing. Fool that he is, he left you alone with me."

With any other guy, Lily would have been able to come back with a witty response, but Luke had this crazy way of stealing all her rational thoughts.

"I'm going to twirl you now."

"What?" Before she could panic, he leaned away and turned her in a circle before pulling her back into his arms. She'd made the move flawlessly.

Their bodies were closer than before, and he let go of her hand, wrapping both of his arms around her waist. She had no choice but to rest her hands on his shoulders. He pulled her to him, leaning his head next to hers in an intimate gesture. "I'm sorry if I'm being too forward. You just smell *so* good."

Her nose was close to his neck, and she couldn't help but inhale. "So do you." Too good.

He leaned back, capturing her gaze. "Yeah?" He arched a brow. "I'm glad you like it." He pulled her close again, and she allowed herself a moment to appreciate their dance. He was a good-looking man holding her in his strong arms, making her heart beat just a little faster. Most would consider her lucky. Plus, this might be the only moment they had in time, and it felt good. Damn good.

Shit. He was screwed.

Luke adjusted his hat as he followed Lily back to their table, which was now occupied by Milo and Sierra. He'd known he'd be exposing himself to a potentially volatile situation if he decided to show up at Swallow's in search of Lily, but he hadn't been able to stay away. After their interesting meeting earlier in the day, he couldn't forget the soft blond curls that he ached to touch, or the compelling smile she'd left him with as she'd walked away.

Showing interest in *any* of Hannah's friends was asking for another attack on his reputation. But then, he'd never been one to back down from a challenge. Still, he knew getting Lily to give him a second look was going to be one hell of a fight. By the way Lily had avoided looking at him when he'd joined their group, he knew Hannah had already buried her barbs in Lily's thoughts. So be it. He'd backed down all those years ago, but he was done with that. Right now, he was prepared to do battle.

He wasn't quite sure how Lily had done it, but she'd twisted her way inside his mind, and he couldn't seem to get enough of her. He didn't know if it was her looks or the way her gorgeous dark eyes seemed to see past what everyone else saw. Or at least he hoped she could see beyond the bullshit he knew Hannah had said about him.

He'd been willing to leave the past in the past. Why couldn't Hannah? What had happened between them had been eight long years ago. They were both far different people. At least he hoped so.

Lily glanced at her watch, surprised to find that two hours had passed since Hannah had left her alone at the bar. She'd really enjoyed Milo and Sierra. They were very cute together, both with a fun sense of humor, and she liked getting to know some of the townsfolk, liked feeling as though she might fit in even though she came from a very different background. People here were not as backward as Hannah would have her believe.

Then there was Luke.

Lord help her. She'd enjoyed being with him, too. More than she probably should have. He was a great dancer and an interesting conversationalist. She wished she could say she didn't care for his company, but that would be a lie.

Milo and Sierra didn't seem to have any problems with Luke. There had to be more to the story between him and Hannah. If he was such a bad person, why did so many people seem to like him? Sierra was a woman, which made her a prime target of Luke's according to Hannah, but she didn't seem to harbor any ill feelings toward him. Something was off.

Either way, Lily needed to head home before Luke got the wrong idea about her friendliness. Even if he wasn't as bad as Hannah had said, Lily owed her loyalty to her friend, which meant she needed to keep Luke at arm's length. "I should probably go," she announced to the small group at their table.

"So soon?" Milo asked.

"I'd better check on Hannah, make sure she's still among the living after her little binge." She really wished she could stay and enjoy these fun people, but duty called.

Luke stood and slid her chair out for her. Always the gentleman, and seriously a puzzle.

They said their goodbyes, and Lily was a little shocked that Sierra hugged her and made her promise to stop in at the coffee shop where she worked.

"Nice people," she said to Luke as they walked away.

"You'll find a lot of that in this town." He held open the door for her as they exited and steered her toward his truck that he'd parked on the opposite side of the street. She had to admit that she'd never considered trucks beautiful before and would have thought she'd prefer a Porsche, but his big black beast of a machine shined in the light from a streetlamp, looking like a sleek predator with the strength of a giant simmering beneath. It was like a sports car on steroids, and it shrieked testosterone and power.

She liked it.

He opened the passenger side for her, and she realized she'd have to climb up to get into it. "I feel like I should ask for a boost," she said with a laugh.

"I'll lift you, if you like." A mischievous glint lit his eyes.

"I'll just bet you would. But I think I'll try it on my own first." However, the thought of him touching her again tempted her.

"Grab that handle up there, put your pretty little foot on the bar, and give it a shot."

The height of the truck forced her short skirt higher, but she pulled herself up until she reached the soft leather seat. The crisp sent of a pine air freshener greeted her, emulating the clean interior. She looked down at him, enjoying the feel of being in his lair. He was rough, tough and masculine, and sitting in his truck made her feel that much more feminine. "Looks like I managed, after all."

He nodded, his engaging grin sending shivers bolting through her. "Looks like." He watched her for a few seconds before he slid a long, slow gaze down the length of her legs. "Those shoes sure look good on you."

The moisture in her mouth evaporated. "Thanks." She swallowed and turned away, needing to distance herself from his captivating eyes.

He shut the door, and a few short seconds later, he climbed in the driver's side. The engine turned over seamlessly, and she had to admit she liked the feel of the power rumbling beneath her. "Nice truck."

"Thanks. I like it." He cranked the vehicle around on the small two-lane and headed toward Hannah's place. Make that her place, too.

An awkward silence filled the space between them now that they didn't have Milo and Sierra to keep up the chatter.

She tried to steer her thoughts away from his intoxicating presence and come up with some small talk. "Have you always lived in Aspen?"

"Yep." He kept his eyes on the darkened road ahead of them. "Growing up, I dreamed of leaving. I did live in Salt Lake while I went to college, but I've since realized this type of lifestyle really appeals to me." He glanced at her. "I'm not much for the fast-paced world. I prefer something with a little more depth."

"Oh."

"You don't know what I mean."

"Yes, I do." She stammered. "Well, kind of."

"Have you ever spent much time in a small town?"

She shook her head, feeling like she'd missed an important part of life's education. "No, not really. Just today."

He nodded. "If you stick around for a while, you'll see what I mean."

"Don't you miss the excitement?"

"What excitement?"

"The energy of a city, the people, the convenience of having everything nearby."

"I've got everything I need right here."

He stopped his truck, and Lily realized they had already reached her little house. Wow. It seemed like it had been a much longer drive when she'd arrived earlier in the day. The house was dark. Only one light came from the big house up the hill.

"Let me get your door for you," he said, and then exited before she could agree or argue.

He opened her door, and as she swiveled and prepared to jump down, he grasped her around the waist. "Wouldn't want you to mess up those sexy shoes."

She more or less slid down his body until her feet hit the ground, the whole encounter a lesson in exhilarating sensations. He held her for a second longer than was necessary before he stepped back. Tugging her out of the way, he shut the door, cloaking them in virtual darkness. "Come here. I want to show you something."

She accepted his hand, afraid that she'd step somewhere she shouldn't. "I can't see a thing."

His soft laugh cascaded over the warm summer air. "It's okay. I've got you."

That's what she was afraid of.

He stopped near the front door, still holding her hand, and she was very aware of the strong male presence next to her.

"Look up."

She tilted her head back, not sure what she was supposed to be looking at. Then she saw them. She exhaled an excited breath. "Oh. Wow." Tens of thousands of twinkling stars sparkled in the midnight sky. Maybe even millions. She'd never seen so many. The longer she looked, the more they seemed to illuminate. "Where did they all come from?"

He let out a real laugh. "They've always been there, but you can't see them in the cities. Too much light. Too much pollution." His voice grew closer to her face, and she could tell he was focused on her now. "You miss all this in a fast-paced world."

He had a point, she thought as she gazed at the beautiful night sky. "You're right. It's just amazing."

Warm fingers found her cheek, and she froze. He traced along her jaw line. She tried to breathe as the pads of his roughened fingertips cruised over her lips. For a second, she considered resisting, but she couldn't deny she'd imagined this since the moment he'd walked into her life.

When his mouth found hers, a rush of hot sensation burst through her. She sighed as though she'd tasted the most sinfully decadent dessert. She shouldn't be kissing this man, but...

The air in her lungs evaporated as his arms snaked around her and he hauled her to him. Heat flared, pulsating between them as he tilted her head, giving him better access to her mouth.

She raised a hand to stop him, but it took her several moments before she put her fingers next to his mouth and gently pushed him away. He released her, but kept her hand, pressing a deliciously hot kiss on the inside of her wrist. A frisson of shivers left her unsteady.

Before she had a chance to react, he placed another soft kiss on her lips. "Thanks for dancing with me tonight. I hope I get to see you again."

His tactics effectively stole her words. She touched her fingertips to her lips, remembering the tantalizing feel of him. It was as if he'd permanently branded her. "Uh..." Shit. He was on that damned avoid list. "I'm sure I'll see you."

"I'd hoped to spend a little more time with you." The timbre of his voice seduced her to the point of almost breaking. "Can I call you?"

Avoid. Avoid. Avoid. "I don't know if that's a good idea."

"Because of Hannah."

Every fiber of her being rejected the idea of turning him away, but she had to remain loyal to her friend. "Yes."

"So even after all this time, she's still determined to ruin what's left of my good name." He sighed. "I'd hoped you were the kind of person who made up her own mind."

"I am." Lily was certain she'd heard disappointment in his voice. "It's not that I believe everything. It's just...she's my friend."

"I understand." He remained quiet for a moment. "Maybe after some time has passed, you'll see things in a different light."

He touched his lips against hers in a whisper soft kiss that made her want to beg for more. "Good night, beautiful Lily. Sweet dreams."

He left her at her front door, and she watched as he moved through the dark, his shadow a little blacker than the night. She missed him the moment he walked away. The interior lights from his truck provided a little illumination, but she couldn't see his face as he climbed inside.

He started the engine, his headlights glaring into the night. Gravel crunched as he turned his truck around. When he reached the main road, his tires squealed as they gripped the pavement, and he sped off into the night leaving her in utter darkness and silence.

She released the breath she'd been holding. Oh, wow. That hadn't gone at all as planned. She closed her eyes, touching her lips again, trying to picture him still there. Damn. She couldn't help it. He just didn't seem to be the jerk that Hannah had painted him to be. She liked Luke, like the sparks that flared between them.

His kiss would remain seared in her memory for a long time.

CHAPTER FIVE

The next afternoon Lily traveled back down the graveled drive and drove the few short miles into town. Things already seemed familiar, which was good. Traffic had picked up since the previous day. She actually had to wait for a car to pass before she could turn into the grocery store parking lot.

Lily's gaze immediately flicked to where the big black truck had been parked the day before. It was gone. Of course it would be.

She straightened her blouse, grabbed the envelope that held her resume, and headed into the real estate office.

Betty Johnson was a hardened older woman with silver cropped hair and a wiry build. "You must be Lily," she said as she rose from behind a wooden desk.

"I am, Mrs. Johnson." Lily extended her hand, and Betty shook it with a firm grip. "I came to apply for your part-time position."

"Yes, Sondra told me. Sit down." She indicated a wooden chair with a faded blue cushion that rested on the opposite side of the desk. "What are your qualifications?"

Lily slipped her resume from a manila envelope and handed it to the woman. Betty studied it for all of a half-second before she looked up. "Can you answer a phone and take down correct information?"

"Uh...sure. Absolutely." She supposed it was a pertinent question, but couldn't most people handle those duties?

"How are you on reliability? The last gal I hired never showed up on time on Saturdays because she stayed out too late partying the night before."

"I'll be here unless I'm on my deathbed."

The older woman laughed. "I don't know if you need to go that far."

"I really need this job, Mrs. Johnson. I promise I won't disappoint you."

"Then it's yours. Can you start now? Today is my anniversary, and my husband's taking me to dinner tonight in Roosevelt. I'd like to get a head start if I could."

"Sure." Lily tried to hide her surprise as the woman gathered her purse.

She slipped a key off her ring and handed it to Lily. "You can lock up at five. Until I can train you a little better, all I want you to do is answer the phone and take a message."

Then Mrs. Johnson was gone.

The small office was eerily quiet. Lily walked to the front of the building and peered out at the parking lot. It held exactly five vehicles, and she couldn't see many people. Quiet was an understatement.

It appeared the hardest part of this job would be finding a way to occupy her time. With a sigh, she opened up the browser on the computer and started searching for jobs. Sitting still and doing nothing was not in her nature.

Lily spent the past week settling in and unpacking. She'd steered clear of hanging out in town unless she was working, hoping to avoid an encounter with the sexy cowboy she'd been unable to forget. It wasn't that she didn't want to see Luke. Quite the opposite. But she'd lived long enough to recognize trouble when she saw it, and that man was a mountain-sized, testosterone-fueled bucket of trouble.

With today's workday behind her, Lily closed up the shop and headed across the parking lot to the grocery store. There was a new recipe she'd found for a tomato basil soup that sounded interesting, and she needed a few ingredients in order to create it. It would be soup for one, though. Hannah was in Roosevelt with friends. Her trips there had become a regular occurrence.

Lily didn't mind Hannah taking off, though. Her friend hadn't been the same since she'd returned home. Besides, Lily was quite fine being alone, enjoyed it actually. She could make dinner, and afterwards, go for a run. The quiet road in front of her house made the perfect jogging path. Very little traffic passed and being in the fresh open air lifted her spirits, reminding her that life was full of possibilities, and the little bump she'd experienced recently would soon be a faded memory.

She pushed through the doors of the market, still amazed at how tiny a country store could be. It carried the essentials and pretty much one brand of everything. It lacked the polished gleam of the superstores she'd visited in L.A. and Salt Lake, but she didn't miss the crowds.

"Hey, Lily." The friendly blond cashier greeted her with a wave.

"Hi, Ashley." Lily loved that people knew her name even though she'd only been in town a short time. She enjoyed feeling like she was part of a small, caring community. The residents always asked after her and Hannah's family, and they seemed genuinely interested in her response.

Lily removed her shopping list from her purse and headed down the first aisle, snagging a canister of oatmeal that would provide breakfast for the next couple of weeks. Next was basil. She'd probably have to use dried instead of fresh, but that was okay.

As she reached the end of the aisle, the sound of a little child squealing with laughter caught her by surprise. She looked up as a small brown-haired girl barreled around the corner from the opposite direction and plowed directly into her legs.

The collision knocked Lily back. Luckily, she righted herself before she tipped over. The little girl didn't fare so well. She crashed backward into a display of cereal boxes, the colorful tower tumbling down on top of her.

The little girl with a mass of wild curls had to be close to three, she guessed. She looked up at Lily, her big brown eyes wide. "Uh-oh."

Her mother rounded the corner. "Emma? What have you done?" The woman hugged a newborn baby to her as she quickly surveyed the disaster. She glanced at Lily. "I'm so sorry." Then turned to Emma. "You are in big trouble, young lady. You clean up this cereal right now."

Emma scrambled to her feet and started picking up boxes.

"It's okay." Lily smiled at the dark-haired mom sporting a ponytail and very little makeup. "I can help her."

"She's such a handful sometimes. Thanks for helping. I'm Caroline, by the way."

Lily introduced herself before kneeling down next to Emma. The little girl gave her a conspiratorial look that melted her heart.

They'd managed to stack two levels of boxes when a pair of cowboy boots stepped into Lily's peripheral vision. She glanced up to find Luke hovering. She swore he was checking out her rear end. He flicked his attention to Caroline.

"Need some help?"

Lily prayed interest and excitement didn't show on her face. He was sweet temptation all wrapped up in ripped jeans, a blue cotton shirt and a khaki ballcap. She had to withhold a sigh of appreciation.

"Luke!" Emma squealed and abandoned her boxes in order to throw her arms around his legs.

He laughed and scooped her up. "What have you done now, squirt?"

Caroline groaned as her daughter laughed and hugged Luke. "Don't ask."

Luke tucked a wild curl behind the girl's ear, reminding Lily of the day they'd met and he'd done a similar thing for her. "Emma, you've gotta quit giving your momma such a hard time. She needs you to be a big girl and help her now."

Emma put her chubby little hands on the sides of his face. "Okay. I will 'cause you asked nice," she answered with all seriousness. "Can I have a sucker?"

He laughed and set her down. "If you do a good job cleaning up these boxes and if your momma says so, I'll buy you a sucker."

Her cheeks pushed out as she grinned. "Okay." She started gathering the cereal boxes with renewed fervor, and Lily had a hard time keeping them straight.

Luke knelt down and relieved the stress of her trying to keep up with the haphazard stacking of a little three-year-old. "Hey Lily." He nodded.

She tried to force a normal breath and pretend he hadn't been her fantasy every night since she'd met him, but she caught the scent of leather and spice, and her resistance slipped a notch. "Hi Luke. How have you been?"

"I'm good." He shifted his gaze to Emma's mom. "You doing okay, Caroline? I stopped by to check on you earlier, but you weren't home."

"Oh, sure." The mom shifted her baby to her shoulder. "You know it's been a little crazy without Richard, but I've had a lot of help, and he'll be home tomorrow."

"I'm happy to hear that." Luke stacked the final box and stood, holding out a hand for Lily. She placed her fingers in his, unable to resist noting how warm and strong he felt. She caught his gaze, his green eyes probing hers. Interest? Desire? She wasn't quite sure what she'd found smoldering there, but he broke the connection as soon as she was on her feet.

"You let me know if you need anything else, okay?" He directed his conversation at Caroline.

"Thanks, Luke. You know you've been a lifesaver."

"No problem. Come on, Emma. Let's go get that sucker." He took hold of little Emma's hand and walked away without another word, leaving an uncertain and unfulfilled void inside Lily.

She wanted to call foul, but she had been the one who'd turned him away the other night. Somehow, though, she'd expected him to come after her like the relentless predator Hannah had made him out to be. Not only expected it from him, but maybe wanted it, too.

"He seems like a nice guy," she said to Caroline, trying to pretend she hadn't noticed that he hadn't said goodbye to her.

"He's a treasure. My husband's been gone for a couple of weeks, training with the military reserve. Luke has taken turns with some of the guys in town, and one of them has come by every day to help with chores. They've really watched out for me."

"Wow, that's so nice." How was she supposed to keep hating on this guy? He really did seem like a treasure.

"Whoever marries him will be a lucky girl." Caroline turned a curious eye to Lily. "I noticed him checking *you* out. I don't suppose you're single."

She'd noticed? Lily's cheeks heated from Caroline's comment, but her heart took flight to know that he hadn't been able to ignore her. "Actually, I am."

An interested look played across the mom's features. "If I were a single gal, I'd definitely be looking in his direction." She smiled. "Just sayin'." She stuck out a hand for her to shake. "It was nice to meet you, Lily. I'm sure I'll see you soon."

With that, Caroline was gone. By the time Lily gathered the rest of her ingredients and headed to the register, there was no sign of Luke, Caroline, or little Emma.

"Did Caroline already leave?" Lily asked the cashier. Really, she wanted to know if Luke had, but she didn't want to voice her interest.

"Sure did. Walked out with her cute little girl and Luke Winchester about two minutes ago."

"Oh." She'd hoped to have another opportunity to talk to Luke. Not that she had any idea what she would have said to him.

"Not sure why Caroline would keep his company, though. Especially with her husband out of town." Ashley took Lily's money and started counting change.

"Why is that?" Finally, someone who might give her some information.

"That Luke is a wild man. Rumor is he can sweet talk a lady out of her boots in no time flat. Then he moves on to the next without even a thank-you-ma'am. Definitely one to steer clear of if you have any brains. He's a walking heartbreak. Probably has STDs."

"I see." She nodded her understanding as she tucked her wallet away. That was not what she wanted to hear. "Good information to know. Who told you this?"

Ashley grinned. "Your friend, Hannah. She's told like *everyone*. Girls gotta watch out for each other, you know?"

Lily walked with her bag of groceries to the car feeling more than a little torn...and definitely frustrated. She'd heard two sides of the story while shopping and didn't know what to believe. Luke didn't seem like a bad guy to her, but maybe that was because she didn't want him to be. Hannah hated him. The guys liked him. Caroline and Emma adored him. She wanted to believe him and like him, too.

Of course, maybe that was how he played the game. Maybe the rest of the women had felt exactly like she had. Hannah had mentioned she'd thought she'd be the one to tame him, and now here she was experiencing similar feelings.

To make matters worse, she missed the hot and sexy Luke. This tempered version of him left her wanting more. She wanted the easy friendship he had with Caroline. Wished he'd hug her like he'd hugged Emma. She ached to see his face light up when he looked at her, too.

If she were smart, she'd forget him that instant. She needed to use her brain like Ashley said and accept the fact that Luke Winchester would never be a part of her life. It didn't matter if it was because he had a reputation or because she intended to be loyal to her friend.

Hannah was right. This town and the people living here did have a way of messing with a person's mind.

Tomorrow, she'd expand her job search. Denver may be her next destination. As much as she didn't like it, she wondered if her parents' gypsy blood also ran through her veins, and she would never be destined to settle down.

Lily stood in the doorway of the real estate office, taking in the afternoon sun. Several more days had passed in the quiet little town, and Lily hadn't caught one glimpse of Luke or his truck. Not that she wanted to. But she'd decided it would be a good idea to keep him on the radar so she could avoid him.

She returned to her desk and printed the marketing proposal she'd written for Betty. She'd completed it late that afternoon, and she couldn't wait to show it to her boss when she returned.

The door to the office opened, and Lily looked up, expecting to see Betty. Luke widened his eyes, seeming as surprised to see her sitting there as she was to see him. Day-old scruff and a tan cowboy hat left him looking dangerous, in an untamed, restless kind of way.

He gave the office a quick glance. "Is Betty around?"

Lily stood, shaking her head, her heartbeat kicking up a notch. She feasted on the sight of him. She didn't want to admit it, but five days had been too long to go without a glimpse of her forbidden eye candy and the addictive way his compelling gaze renewed her interest in life. "She's out with a client."

He nodded. "I didn't know you worked for Betty."

"I've only been here a couple of weeks."

"I see." His gaze flicked across the desk. "She didn't happen to leave a set of keys for me, did she?"

"No. I'm sorry." Betty hadn't mentioned him at all. If she had, Lily certainly would have checked her hair and slicked on some lip gloss. Not that she wanted to attract him, just that she wanted to look her best when he was around. There was a difference.

"Okay." He adjusted his hat and turned for the door. "Will you tell Betty to call me when she gets in? Maybe I can meet up with her later."

No. She didn't want him to go so soon. "I will."

He paused in the doorway, studying her with a serious gaze before settling on her lips. "Just so you know, I still think about that kiss. I can't get the taste of you out of my head."

A whip of desire tore through her, tripping her heart and flooding her with sensation.

Then he was gone.

Lily stared at the empty doorway, stunned, breathless. She fell back into her chair.

What the hell was she supposed to do with that?

She still sat there twenty minutes later when Betty flew through the door, tossing her briefcase on the desk in front of Lily. The sight of her boss looking rushed and haggard dragged Lily from the multitude of what-if scenarios she'd had running through her head.

"Busy day?"

"You could say." She flipped open her briefcase and started rummaging through the papers.

"Luke Winchester was just here, looking for you."

Betty groaned and closed her eyes. "Shoot. I forgot he would be dropping by." She glanced at the clock. "He needs keys for one of his rental properties. He misplaced his set and needs to make a duplicate." She glanced at Lily, looking completely frazzled. "I don't have time to run them by before Miranda and Bob come in to sign papers."

"I could take them." She shouldn't be looking for an excuse to see Luke again, not after what he'd just told her...but she was. She didn't know what she'd do or what she'd say when she saw him, but she didn't like the awkwardness between them. She didn't have to date him, but she didn't have to hate him, either. He hadn't done anything to her.

Relief relaxed Betty's features. "Are you sure you don't mind? You won't be able to get there and back before quitting time."

She shrugged, pretending it was no big deal. "It's not like I have a hot date waiting for me." Besides, Hannah was spending a few days in Roosevelt again, and she was pretty sure she wouldn't see her until tomorrow. If Lily could keep her resolve intact, she should be able to make amends with Luke and not cause any further damage.

"That would be so perfect, Lily." Her boss removed keys from a packet inside the filing cabinet and handed them to her. "I'll draw you a map so you don't get lost."

CHAPTER SIX

B right sunshine cast a cheerful glow to the afternoon, and Lily rolled down her windows in response. She was so far from anywhere that the radio only picked up a country station, but the singer belted out something about chillin' on a dirt road and drinking beer. It seemed appropriate, so she cranked it up.

Lily was certain she'd missed a turn somewhere as she continued down the narrow road, but she wasn't sure she minded. The warm air blowing in her window, tousling her hair and teasing her skin energized her spirit.

Where the hell was she, she wondered and then laughed. The Japanese would freak if they knew how much open space was sitting unused.

The road quickly turned from pavement to dirt, and she slowed her speed to accommodate, watching plumes of dust swirl up behind her. To the right and left of her, deep ditches shouldered the road. Beyond them, beautiful horses grazed in the fields.

Her good mood remained as she traveled the rest of the way until the dirt road led her to a paved circular drive that wound around a pond filled with ducks and led to the front of a massive wooden cabin. House? Structure? It was definitely not what she had pictured when Betty had said "cabin".

She parked near the front double doors, not seeing another vehicle or person in sight. Betty had said she'd let Luke know she was coming. Maybe he *really* didn't want to see her. But then why had he said what he'd said about their kiss? Thoughts of that man really messed with her head.

She turned and headed for the large wooden building and knocked. No one answered. She twisted the handle, not surprised to find it unlocked.

Inside, the splendor of the furnishings took away her breath. A huge, great room opened up before her. Large wooden columns drew her gaze upward to a second level of rooms that surrounded the perimeter. It was opulent, luxuriant, and not at all what she would have expected to find in this little country town. Perhaps it was one of those properties Betty rented to outside vacationers.

The wall of windows at the back of the house and the deck beyond called to her. She headed outside, warm sunshine greeting her. She leaned against the log railing. The cabin sat on a hill, so what appeared to be the main level of the house on the front side, ended up being the second level on the backside. A panorama of rolling hills and luscious trees spread out before her. Nothing but beautiful, fresh nature.

She closed her eyes and tilted her head upward, letting the sun's warmth hit her full on. She inhaled a breath and released it. It wouldn't be hard to get used to this lifestyle.

"Lily."

She opened her eyes to find Luke sitting atop a gorgeous black horse on the grass below the deck, a quizzical expression on his face. "What are you doing?"

She shrugged, embarrassed at being caught. "Enjoying the slower pace of life, like you taught me."

A smile crept across his lips, and he nodded. "Good." The muscles in his back and biceps worked as he dismounted his horse and headed toward the stairs that led from the lower level to the deck. Lily's pulse increased with each step he took, until he stood before her. Without her high heels on, he towered above her even more.

"You brought the keys?"

She dug in the pocket of her jeans and pulled them out. She was very aware of her close proximity to Luke as she laid them in the palm of his hand. "I didn't see your truck outside," she stammered. "I didn't think anyone was here."

"I was riding when you came through the gate, so I continued on over here."

"Is the horse yours?"

"One of many."

"They're all your horses? They're gorgeous."

"Some are mine. Some belong to my family. Others are being stabled here." He regarded her with a simmering gaze, like he wanted to reach out to her, but wasn't quite sure how she'd react.

She regretted that she'd put that hesitancy there, but what choice had she had? There had to be some middle ground where she could be friendly to him without causing problems between her and Hannah. She shifted her weight to one foot, not knowing where to begin.

He raised his brows in question.

This was awkward. "I wanted to apologize for the other night, or at least explain."

"Which is it?"

He wasn't going to make this easy, was he? She rolled her eyes and bit her lip to keep from smiling. "Look, I'm a pretty good judge of people. I've also heard rumors. I know Hannah has some hidden issues with this town, things that somehow involve you, but I think they may not be what she's portraying them to be."

His expression said she'd hit pretty close to the mark. "They? Them?"

"Okay, mostly you." Although Hannah did seem to have some issues with her mom, too.

He tilted his head, allowing her to see his eyes better. "What exactly are you saying?"

She fidgeted, afraid if she said what she intended to say and watched his expression, she'd be lost. "I'll admit there's some chemistry between us." Serious chemistry if anyone asked her. She snuck a glance at him.

His expression remained cautious. "I'm sensing a 'but' though."

She sighed. This was the hard part—the part she didn't want to say. "There is. You seem like a nice guy, but I don't want to put myself in the middle of whatever is between you and Hannah. I owe Hannah too much."

He leaned against the wooden rail. "You're taking her side without even giving me a chance."

"I'm not taking anyone's side." She blew out a tense breath. "I came to see you to hopefully fix things between us. I like you. I like to see you, to talk to you. And this is such a small town. You know we're going to run into each other, like today at Betty's. Can't we be friends?"

His tempting eyes shot off a dark, sensual look. "What if I don't want to be just friends?"

A shiver rushed through her. That was exactly what she shouldn't want to hear. She'd give anything if they could pick up where they'd left off that night under the stars, but they couldn't. It wouldn't be right. And she knew too well what it felt like to be on the painful end of someone's wrong choices.

She reinforced her determination. "The only thing I can offer is friendship, Luke. My stay here is temporary, and I don't want to create more drama between everyone."

"This isn't fair, Lily. Some days I'd like to damn her for what she's done."

"What did she do?"

He started to speak, and then stopped. "No. That would only give you two sides of the story and no real answers. Like you said, I'm not going to put you in the middle of this. She needs to come clean. To me. To you. To this whole damn town. She's the only one who can fix this."

"What if she doesn't? What if she just leaves again?"

"Not much I can do about it, then. At least things are better when she's not here. People forget, forgive."

Lily turned her gaze to the rolling green hills in front of her. What a mess. "Then I guess we're back to friends."

He shut his eyes for a brief second and then focused on her. "Yeah. Sure. Friends."

She nudged him with her elbow, trying to defuse the tension. "If we dated, you probably wouldn't like the real me, anyway."

Another tense moment passed before his frown lifted, and her mood followed. "You're probably right."

"Are you going to show me your horse?"

His body relaxed, and she felt like she could breathe again. "If you'd like." He held out a hand, indicating that she should proceed down the stairs first.

"Ever ridden?" he asked as they reached the bottom.

She widened her eyes and gave a nervous laugh. "No." Though the thought intrigued her. "I've seen some horses in a parade before, but never one up close and personal."

As they drew closer to the glossy black horse, Lily inhaled a sharp breath of appreciation. It was magnificent, with contrasting white feet and a white star between its eyes. The horse looked up. Lily slowed her steps as the animal studied her with intelligent brown eyes.

"Come on." He grabbed her hand, tugging her forward. "Don't be afraid. He's not going to hurt you."

"He's so big." Her chin barely crested his back. "And so beautiful. What's his name?"

"Hades." Luke nudged her closer. "Hold out your hand and let him sniff you."

Lily hesitated. "He won't bite?"

"Nah." Luke held out his palm and the horse nuzzled it. "See?"

Lily followed suit, the horse's whiskers tickling her hand. She reached up with tentative fingers and petted his neck. He swung his head, and she jumped back.

Luke laughed and stepped forward. He ran a hand down the horse's neck and patted him. "Want to ride him?"

"What? No way." The thought of climbing up on the majestic stallion both terrified and excited her. "I'm sure he'd buck me right off."

"He won't." Luke sounded pretty positive, and she really wanted to try. He took her arm and pulled her close to him and the horse. Excitement sparked inside her like crazy. "Put your foot in the stirrup, grab the saddle horn and haul yourself up."

"This is crazy." She couldn't have erased the stupid grin on her face if she'd tried. She held on to his arm, appreciating the tightly-corded muscles as she tucked her Nike into the stirrup. She gripped what she assumed was the saddle horn and pulled. Halfway up, Luke placed a strong hand on her butt and gave her an extra boost. She swung a leg over the other side of the saddle.

She was up and nervous as hell.

The horse shifted his stance. She gripped the saddle horn, afraid she'd be right back on the ground face first if she made any sudden moves. His horse was big, but she hadn't expected to feel so far off the ground. Giving control over to Hades would take some getting used to.

"Relax." Luke petted the horse's neck. "He can tell if you're tense."

"Great. Now you tell me this." She tried to loosen her muscles, but too much adrenaline squirted through her blood.

Luke removed her foot from the stirrup and adjusted it. He walked to the other side of the horse and did the same. He untied the reins from the deck and handed them to her. "How does it feel?"

"Wild." The horse had to weigh a thousand pounds, and she was completely dependent upon him exhibiting good behavior. "At the risk of sounding crude, it's a little unnerving to have so much power between my legs."

He laughed out loud. "That's an interesting way to put it."

She shook her head and grinned, loving this new experience.

"Take him for a turn around the house. Keep the reins taut and give him a little nudge in his ribs to get him to go. When you want to turn, tug the reins the opposite way. If you want to stop, pull back on both reins, but not hard."

"Oh, God. I have to make him move?"

"That's the point of riding."

She exhaled a huge breath. "Okay." She tapped her heels against the horse's side, and he started to walk. An embarrassing squeal escaped her lips, and she gripped the reins tight. She wanted to glance back at Luke, but she didn't dare take her eyes off the ground in front of her. Which was silly because watching the ground didn't give her any semblance of control.

The horse sauntered around the edge of the house, and she panicked slightly when she left Luke's sight. The horse's hooves clipped on the short amount of pavement right in front of the cabin, and then she was on the grass again, going down the slight incline and into the backyard.

She forced herself to relax. Wow. She, Lily Chandler, was riding a horse. Who would have thought?

Before she knew it, she and Hades had gone full circle. Luke stood, his thumbs tucked into his pockets, watching her with a smile on his face. A sharp twinge of longing shot through her, and she reminded herself again that he was on the bad boy list.

"You look good up there. A natural."

He looked better down there with his dark hair curling from beneath his hat and his silver earrings glinting in the sunshine, giving him a dangerous, sexy appeal. Something about a man in a hat made her salivate.

"Ha. I doubt that." Every muscle inside her was stiff and rigid, and she had to look like a total novice. Not that she cared. This was great.

"No, you do." He walked toward her and grabbed the horse's bridle, bringing Hades to a stop. He placed his other hand on the horse's side, next to her knee. Tilting his head, he looked up at her from beneath his cowboy hat, once again stealing her breath.

"How do you feel about extending your ride? I have another horse that could really use some exercise, and there's a cool place I'd love to show you that you can only get to by horseback."

She hesitated. She really wanted to but….

"Just going as friends," he said, reading her mind. "I promise I won't ravish you out in the backwoods."

She laughed at that. Of course, he wouldn't. Hannah might have her issues with him, but he seemed to be a decent guy, even if he went through women like there was no tomorrow.

Friends she could do. Besides, she had a whole evening full of nothing spread out before her. "Okay. I'd love to." She really wanted to take advantage of this opportunity to see a different side of life that she'd never experienced. Who knew if she'd ever get the chance again?

"Make room for me, then. We'll ride down to the barn together, and I've got a gentle little mare who would love to be ridden." He slipped her foot from the stirrup and replaced it with his own. In one smooth move, he gripped the saddle horn and hauled himself up behind her. He bumped her leg as he removed his from the stirrup, and all she could think about was how they were sitting pretty much ass-to-crotch, and all the erotic feelings that position stirred inside her.

She stiffened as he wrapped his arms around her waist, not expecting him to hug her. "You gotta relax, girl." His voice was so close to her ear.

"I know." She exhaled, trying to ease some of the tension inside her. "I will." Her voice was embarrassingly breathless. "I am. I'm good."

CHAPTER SEVEN

L ily gave the horse a gentle nudge, and Hades started moving. "Am I going to those buildings out across the field?"

"Yep," Luke answered. "That's the main barn at the ranch. This cabin is my mother's attempt at generating extra income by offering higher quality lodging than people can find in town for the rich, out-of-towners who come looking for a world-class fly fishing experience. I handle most of the details for her, along with Betty's help."

"Where's the river?"

"You'll see soon enough. In fact, why don't you give me the reins, and we can get there a little quicker?" He took the leather straps and tightened his arms around her. "Hang on tight to that saddle horn."

He kicked the horse into a gallop that stole her breath as he masterfully guided Hades over the lumpy grass terrain, racing toward the structures in the distance.

～

Luke brought the horse to an abrupt stop in front of his barn. The large wooden structure had been standing for as long as he could remember. The yearly coat of whitewash helped to keep it in good repair. He slid from the horse and held his arms up for Lily. A blush graced her cheeks from their brisk ride and excitement beamed in her eyes. She wrapped her arms around his neck, and he swung her down from the horse.

He stepped away before he was tempted to hold her longer than he should. But not before he caught another whiff of the honeysuckle scent of her hair. Damn, she smelled good. He pictured himself lying next to her, his face buried in her glorious blond curls.

What the hell had he been thinking, climbing up behind her on a horse? The dash across the fields had been his desperate attempt to save his sanity. She'd said "friends" so why the hell was he torturing himself this way?

"Wow," she said, still breathless. "That was wild."

An ache pierced him, and he wished he'd never heard the name Hannah Morgan. "I thought you might enjoy it."

"Your horse has so much power...and speed. That was...awesome." Her words burst from her in bubbles of excitement. "You just can't see the land-scape the same way from a car."

"You're starting to understand my point of view, aren't you?" Which didn't help matters one bit.

"I believe I am. A week ago, I might have argued the point, but not now. Maybe I'm really a country girl at heart."

He could totally imagine her staying in town. He'd eventually win her over. Then it would be him and Lily lying in a field of grass, a soft breeze rustling through the nearby trees, while the sun warmed their naked bodies. There would be no Hannah, no nasty, destructive rumors.

Just—no, he couldn't let his mind go there. He needed to figure out a way to redirect his blood back to his brain and think of a logical way to get beyond this mess Hannah had created. The more he thought about it, the more he believed Lily might be right. Hannah would probably leave before she'd ever admit what she'd done. Lily would leave, too, and if he didn't stop his attraction to her right now, she'd leave *him* with a broken heart.

He'd considered moving to the south part of the county many times over the years in an effort to escape the rumors. Instead, he'd dug in, not wanting to appear a coward. He wasn't about to be run out of town by Hannah's lies. Maybe that was just dumb thinking. He could easily move farther south and take over his family's oil rig operations in that area. Wayne was close to retirement anyway. It was enough distance that he might escape the damned rumors that seemed destined to haunt him until he died.

It was funny. He could forgive Hannah for starting the vicious gossip in the first place. Why couldn't she forgive him for something he hadn't even done and let them both move on with their lives? Why did she feel compelled to keep the damned lies going?

His mistake had been not denying what she'd said in the first place, and now it was too late to change everyone's mind. He'd originally taken the brunt of the gossip to allow her to save face in their small town.

Damn, that one had bitten him in the ass, hadn't it? If he let things continue, it would gnaw him until there was nothing left.

Maybe it *was* time to move on.

It didn't take Luke long to saddle a horse for Lily. He'd picked Charlee, his favorite chestnut-colored mare, and soon they were on their way again. He led the way down a small bluff. Lily caught up to him in a grassy field, a wide grin on her face. "Can this horse run?"

Luke nodded. "She can, but I think you need a little more experience before you go off galloping on your own."

"Okay." Lily smiled, but he could tell she was disappointed, and the thought that he'd caused it didn't sit well with him. But he couldn't very well let her get hurt.

"What happened to the tentative girl who climbed onto a horse for the first time thirty minutes ago?"

She shrugged. "She's gone. Been replaced by the girl who wants to try new things and see a side of life she's never seen before."

He liked the sound of that. He only wished he could be one of the new things she'd try. "Sounds like a good plan. No sense being afraid of life." Something he needed to remember.

"Exactly." She sent him an exaggerated pout. "Now, if we could only gallop again."

He laughed and shook his head. "You keep riding, and it won't be long."

Lily pulled back on the reins as they reached the edge of a wide, gently moving river. The horse slowed, but continued forward. She tugged harder, afraid Charlee would go right into the water.

"She just wants a drink." Luke let his horse step close to hers. The beautiful black stallion dipped his head.

Lily loosened the reins and let Charlee move forward. Late afternoon sunlight fractured on the gently moving river, making the water seem as though it was made of diamonds and mirrors. Rounded rocks and pebbles lay discarded along the edges. Larger rocks still hunkered here and there in the middle of the stream, causing the water to cascade over or around them, creating small patches of white water. The river twisted and turned until it disappeared around a bend and into the trees.

She studied the handsome cowboy, wishing she could steal his hat, place it on her head and give him a sweet kiss. "Thanks for bringing me here." It meant a lot that he'd taken the time to show her his special place. "It's amazing, just like you said."

He shifted in his saddle as he grinned. "You are more than welcome, but this isn't all we're going to see. This is just a rest stop."

She raised her brows, and he kneed his horse, giving Hades the signal to move forward. "Come on." His horse plodded through the water to the other side.

She sucked in a breath and gripped the saddle horn. It appeared her adventures were not over yet. The water splashed as her horse made her way across, but it was the incline on the other side that gave her the next adrenaline rush. She held on tight, but Charlee made it up the steep bank with no problem whatsoever.

A silly, stupid grin curved her lips. What a rush. Horses could do some pretty amazing maneuvering.

She followed Luke as he led them on a worn dirt trail through the trees, her gaze traveling over the contours of his strong back. He belonged on a horse. Hades seemed to be a natural extension of Luke's body, and together, they were a powerful combination.

The afternoon sun warmed her back as she followed him up a trail that led deeper into thicker trees. She liked these trees with their white bark and heart shaped leaves that shimmered when the soft breeze blew through them.

Luke finally halted Hades in the middle of a dense grove. "We'll need to leave the horses here."

"Here?" Lily looked around. They were like, nowhere.

He slid off his horse and helped her off Charlee, tying both animals to nearby branches. "Come on. You'll want to see this."

She followed him as he pushed his way through the thick trees. As she walked, the muscles in her legs cried out from being stretched across the horse's back, but it was a good kind of soreness.

The ground was uneven and several branches tugged at her hair as they moved forward, but when they came out on the other side a few minutes later, she inhaled a surprised breath.

"I didn't realize we'd climbed this high." She could follow the twists and turns of the river by following the winding line of trees. Beyond that lay the sweet, grassy fields, and in the far distance, she was sure she could see Luke's ranch.

"This is where I like to come to think. It kind of puts everything in perspective, you know?"

She could definitely see that.

Luke walked out on a large flat rock that over shot the edge. In a fluid move, he sat on the outcropping, his boots scraping the rock as he swung his long legs over the edge. "I especially love to watch thunderstorms roll in over the horizon. Unfortunately, I usually get soaked, but it's worth it."

A need to experience the complete picture enticed Lily forward. Below her tumbled a rocky ravine that would do some serious damage if a person were to fall over. She kicked a pebble and watched it cascade into sheer nothingness and drop a hundred feet to the floor below. Good thing she wasn't afraid of heights.

She stood at the edge of the rock, glancing across the horizon, wishing a thunderstorm would blow in while she was there so she could live the vision Luke had painted. Too bad there wasn't a cloud in the sky.

Lily ignored her sore muscles as she sat down next to him, very much aware of the energy sparking between them. It might have been a mistake to join him on this ride, but she couldn't regret it at the moment. He was handsome and charming, and it wasn't like she would take this any further.

"Worth the ride?" he asked, staring out at the setting sun.

"So worth it." She could easily admit she'd never seen anything quite this striking. Except, of course, the man sitting next to her.

They sat in silence for several minutes, but it didn't feel awkward. It was as though the splendid scenery before them deserved their reverence.

A warm energy flowed from Luke's direction, and she basked in the happiness she found in that moment. "I didn't know this kind of quiet existed."

Luke acknowledged her statement with a soft chuckle. "I've sorted out all kinds of life's problems from up here."

She wished she had a similar place where she could find solace. Her gaze wandered from the luscious beauty to the man sitting next to her. She eyed him from the corner of her eye, taking in his strong hands, following the dusting of hair up his arms to the attractive contours of his biceps peeking from beneath his t-shirt. She was pretty sure he'd earned his muscles through hard work and not a gym, and his tattoo only added to his appeal. There was something totally alpha about him, and she couldn't deny she found him extraordinarily attractive. He was a man. A real man. And the woman in her responded to him.

It was probably a natural, instinctual attraction, something passed down from her ancestors, back when a woman needed a good, strong man to protect and provide for her. Still, she couldn't deny what she felt.

"How long have you been coming here?"

He tilted his cowboy hat back farther on his head, giving Lily a perfect view of his stunning green eyes. A swish of butterflies tickled her emotions.

"My grandpa brought me here when I was little. It was our special place. He passed a few years back, so now I come here alone."

"That's such a happy, yet sad memory." Two of her grandparents had died tragically young, and she regretted that she hadn't really known them. "It must have been nice, though, to have him so close. Family wasn't really a priority with my parents. We were scattered across the country, and no one made much of an attempt to see anyone else. I have one set of grandparents living in South Carolina, but I haven't seen or talked to them since I was little."

"I can't imagine. Most of my family is within fifty miles of here."

She widened her eyes, trying to keep a sad smile from registering on her face. She sighed. "The only close relatives I have—had," she corrected, "was my sister. We had a serious falling out a while back, so I pretty much count Hannah as my only family."

"What happened between you?"

She had hoped he wouldn't zero in on that comment, but knew he would. Maybe that's why she'd mentioned her sister. Maybe she wanted to share her heartbreak with someone who seemed compassionate. Besides, there was no sense in hiding what had happened, she supposed.

"She slept with my fiancé." Even now, the image of finding Ethan bending her sister over Lily's kitchen table sent a sharp spear through her heart. Katrina had claimed it meant nothing, that it was just a quick and dirty, but it had left her with a broken heart.

Luke narrowed his eyes and winced. "Ouch. That's not very sisterly."

"Yeah." She forced a laugh. "Better to have found out *before* the wedding, though."

He studied her, his scrutiny making her uncomfortable. "You seem to be taking it pretty well."

"I've had some time to recover, and it wasn't as though I'd been given a choice in the matter." She swallowed the lump in her throat. She was so over them, both of them. They might as well like each other, because she didn't want either of them anymore.

The feeling of Luke's strong hand covering hers startled her. "You know what I think? I think you do a damn good job of burying your emotions."

That he noticed what she wasn't saying brought quick tears to her eyes. She blinked them away. She didn't want him to be *that* nice to her.

She'd rejected becoming bitter about the whole thing, refusing to give up the dream of true love, but she had to be careful with her heart. She dabbed the stray moisture from her eyes.

"What about you? Have you ever been engaged or married?"

He ducked his head. "Nope."

She straightened. "Nope? There's obviously more to the story than your one-word answer."

He raked the back of his hand over the scruff on his chin before he eyed her again. "Hannah pretty much made sure no one in this town would give me a chance, but there was a girl back in college." He chucked a rock over the ledge. "Things didn't work out." He leaned back and looked out over the valley. "She wouldn't have been happy here, anyway."

Lily furrowed her brows. "Why not? This place is gorgeous."

He gave her a sideways glance and grinned. Her breath quickened. "Let's talk about something else. The past is the past, right?" She inhaled pure oxygen and blew it out, hoping it would settle her out-of-control heartbeat. "What's the latest gossip? Aren't small towns supposed to be infamous for their gossip?"

He laughed then, and the intensity of their discussion blew away with the breeze. "I believe *you* are the talk of the town these days."

CINDY STARK

"Me?" The idea surprised her. Besides being in the bar that first night, she hadn't made much of an appearance. "How do they know who I am? I've only met a few people."

"You're the pretty gal with the sexy pink shoes. I believe Mrs. Parker called them hooker heels."

She dropped her jaw. "I don't even know Mrs. Parker." But she'd known Hannah's idea of going out on the town dressed as they had been would cause a stir.

"Don't worry. I'll spread the word that you were seen sporting a pair of Nikes and riding a horse. Not quite the same as cowboy boots, but people will stop referring to you as Miss Hollywood."

"Maybe you shouldn't say anything." She might be stuck with the Miss Hollywood title, but she'd have to suffer the consequences.

He drew his brows into a quizzical frown. "Why not?"

She twined her fingers together, wondering how would be the best way to phrase it. She groaned. "Why do people have to know we were together?" She clenched her fists and waited for the fallout.

The attractive energy cycling between them shut off like a turned valve. He'd closed her out, leaving her with an empty, cold feeling.

A look of disappointment settled on his face. "So what, I'm your dirty little secret?"

"Luke." This time she put her hand on his. "You don't understand. I'm not worried about what people think, but Hannah's been good to me, and I don't want to throw that in her face."

"Really? Hannah again?" He rolled his eyes. "Fine. I guess. I don't want to come between your friendship."

There he was being all gallant again. Each minute she spent in his company made it hard to continue to believe Hannah's version of events and easier to see Caroline's point of view.

This outing had turned out to be much more emotional than the fun horseback ride she'd expected. "Do you think we should go? The sun is starting to set." She hadn't paid attention to how long it had taken them to reach the top of the hill, but she was pretty sure horses didn't come equipped with headlights.

"Yeah. I suppose our time is up." He stood and held out a hand to her.

If her heart could have, it would have reached out and tugged him to her. Despite what Hannah claimed, she could tell he was a good man. Maybe he'd gone through some stupid adolescent period where he treated girls like toys, but she doubted he was still the same man today.

He started to say something and then stopped. He turned toward the direction of their horses, but quickly turned back again. "Lily? If I ask you a question, will you promise to answer it honestly?"

Luke's request took her by surprise. She couldn't imagine what it could be. "Sure."

"If I'd met you some other place, some other time where Hannah didn't exist, would you have given me a chance?"

An emotional wrench torqued her heart. There was no doubt. "You know I would." She tried to smile, but a sudden sadness overwhelmed her. This whole situation sucked.

He nodded, looking as unhappy as she felt. They walked in silence toward their horses. When they reached them, Luke untied her reins and handed them to her, before walking away.

"Wait," she called to him, and he turned back. She took a step forward, tilting her head and gazing into his intense eyes. She took his hand, knowing she was treading into dangerous territory, but also knowing she couldn't leave things like they were.

"Thank you for bringing me here. I'm sure this place will linger in my memory for a long time."

He studied her for an endless moment, and she wondered what he was searching for. "You're welcome."

When he started to pull away, she tightened her grip. Before she could change her mind, she lifted on her tiptoes and kissed him on the cheek.

He stood, frozen, as though he didn't know how to react. His haunted gaze pierced her, pulled her forward. Wariness shadowed his features.

She narrowed her eyes in concern and touched his cheek. He still did not move, did not make a play for her like a player would. The stubble along his jaw tickled the tips of her fingers. She stood on tiptoe again, locking her gaze with his and brushed her lips against his. She hadn't been able to erase his kiss from her lips, either.

He tasted of sweetness mixed with potent desire.

Heat licked at her, begging her to sample him again. She shouldn't do it. She should get on her horse and ride away while they were still just friends.

Or was it too late already? She'd never forget the way he'd made her feel when he'd held her, when he'd kissed her.

Luke released a weighted breath and took a step back, obviously being the one to keep his head about him. But Lily was thirsty for something, and right now, that something was still within her grasp.

"No. This isn't right." She dropped her horse's reins and grabbed Luke's shirt, stopping him in his tracks.

He warned her with a heated look, but she ignored it. She locked her arms around his neck and pulled his head toward hers. His lips were warm and intoxicating. She moved hers against him as though she were a match teasing dry timber. When he responded, she thought she might die from pleasure.

He wrapped an arm around her waist and pulled her to him, and she knew her kiss had unleashed something he'd kept tethered inside. Her heart thundered as his body heat mingled with hers. She loved the intense emotional draw she experienced when she was close to him. It was unlike anything she'd experienced.

He ended the kiss and cursed. She filled her lungs, immediately missing him, refusing to move beyond his grasp. He pinned her with a burning gaze, his lips mere inches from hers. "Don't play with me, Lily."

She tried to breathe. "I'm not."

"Then what the hell was that? One second you tell me you need to be loyal to Hannah, and the next you're kissing me."

"I don't know." Her heart warred with her brain. She wanted this man so badly and knew she'd regret it if she let him walk away without figuring out what was between them. But Hannah's issues with him left her with a serious dilemma.

She stepped back this time, ashamed that she'd taken advantage of his desire for her. "I'm sorry. It was wrong of me to kiss you. I'm truly sorry."

He rolled his eyes in obvious frustration. "Damn it, Lily. I'm so tired of Hannah and her lies. She's given me enough misery to last ten lifetimes. I'm fine with her hating me, but she's turned half the town against me. Just when people seemed to have forgotten, she shows up and everyone's whispering again."

"I'm going to talk to her, Luke, when we get back. Maybe I can get her to confess."

He picked up her horse's reins and handed them to her again. "Don't hold your breath." He untied and mounted his horse.

Lily climbed on Charlee and scrambled to keep up with Luke as he headed down the hillside.

Luke made it quite a distance back toward his property before Lily was able to get close enough to talk to him. She'd had to gallop her horse to make that happen.

"Luke?" she called out when he nudged Hades to go faster. "Stop."

The worry in her voice must have reached out to him because he slowed his horse and then stopped to face her. The last sliver of sun dipped behind the horizon, and it was hard to read his expression in the waning light.

"Luke? Please tell me what happened between the two of you." She moved her horse in close to his.

"I'm not going there, Lily." His voice vibrated with dark emotion. "I've already told you, she started the lie and she'll have to be the one to fix it. I can't. No one will believe me now."

"I'd believe you," she said quietly into the night.

"No, you wouldn't. You've already made it perfectly clear your loyalties lie with Hannah." He urged Hades to start walking again, and Lily followed.

"Why won't you try?" She didn't understand. "If Hannah lied all those years ago, why don't you just tell the truth?"

"Because me telling you won't change things. Hannah has to speak up. She has to clear the air, and she refuses." He glanced at her with a pointed look.

"That doesn't mean—"

An eerie screech stole her words, and she froze. "What was that?" she whispered.

"I don't know," Luke answered, also speaking softly. He shifted in his saddle and then pointed west, in the direction of town. "Look? Do you see those lights angling into the sky?"

Lily turned. "What are they?"

"I'm not sure, but I think something's wrong." The worry in his voice raised the goosebumps on her arms. "There aren't any lights out that way. If it was just headlights from a car on the road, they wouldn't be angled like that and they'd be moving." He dismounted his horse, holding his arms up for her. "Come on. You need to ride with me. I'm going to ride hard, and I don't want to worry about you getting hurt. I'll tether Charlee to Hades."

A moment later, she was in front of Luke again, his arms around her. Her stomach turned as he took off, and her heart thundered along with the horses' hooves. She wasn't quite sure what they'd find, but from all indications, it wouldn't be good.

CHAPTER EIGHT

M other of God.

Luke kicked his horse to a faster speed when he realized the lights he saw were the headlights of a car angled skyward, and it looked like a small fire burned in the grass. Someone had rolled a vehicle off the highway. As he drew closer, he could see that the upside down vehicle was a truck, and there was also another SUV off the opposite side of the road in a ditch. He didn't recognize the truck, but the red Bronco belonged to Caroline Delaney.

He galloped to Caroline's vehicle and jumped off his horse before Hades had come to a complete stop. Lily followed him down.

The whole ghastly scene unnerved him. The lights on the vehicles were still blazing, but other than that, it was deathly quiet. Hades whinnied his nervousness.

The scent of gasoline permeated the air, and even an idiot would realize this bad situation could get much worse if that grass fire met the leaking gasoline.

A dog barked from inside Caroline's SUV as he approached. He jerked open the door and found her slumped to the side, her seatbelt the only thing holding her in the driver's seat. The front windshield had been shattered, and she had a stream of blood trailing from a gash on her forehead, over her eye, and down her cheek.

In the backseat was little Emma still buckled in her car seat, staring at him with tear-stained, shocked eyes. Their black Border Collie stood watch next to her, growling at Luke. "It's okay, boy," Luke said to the dog.

"Good God," Lily said as she leaned over his shoulder. "Not Caroline and Emma. Where's the baby?"

Emma's bottom lip started to quiver and fresh tears pooled in her eyes.

"It's okay, sweetie," he said to Emma. "I'll get you out of there." He opened the back door and released the latch on her toddler seat.

"She didn't have the baby with her," he said to Lily as he shoved the frightened little girl into her arms. "Take Emma and call for help. Come on, Boo." The dog jumped from the vehicle. "There's fire and gasoline, and I need to get Caroline to safety."

"What about the driver of the truck?" Lily asked, her words echoing the fear that screamed in his head.

"I don't want you going near that fire. Take Emma, Boo and the horses and walk down to the bend in the road. Sit in the grass by the ditch. I'll get Caroline and then check on the other driver."

He swallowed his panic as he hurried to remove Caroline from her car. Getting her lifeless weight from the vehicle wasn't easy, but adrenaline gave him extra strength. He had no idea how bad she was hurt, but his priority at the moment was getting everyone a safe distance from the fire. He hoped he didn't hurt her worse by moving her, but the whole scene could blow at any moment.

When he reached Lily, he laid Caroline softly in the grass. "She's breathing. See if you can stop her bleeding."

"Luke."

He met Lily's frightened gaze and leaned down to give her a quick kiss on the head. "It's going to be okay." He kissed Emma, too. "I'll be right back."

Fear pumped through him as he hurried back to the truck. The scent of gasoline was much stronger on this side of the road, and Luke eyed the fire that burned a short distance away. It must have started when the vehicle rolled.

Luke dropped to his knees next to the driver's side of the truck. No one was inside. The roof had caved in, and pebbles of glass covered the area. He stood and quickly looked around. A lifeless mass lay ahead on the road. "Fuck."

He rushed over to the body, finding a bloody, gory mess. No sense checking for a pulse. There was no help for that poor soul now.

The scene around him grew suddenly brighter, and the hairs on his arms stiffened in response. The flames had found the gasoline.

He turned and ran like hell.

The sound of Lily screaming his name disappeared into a loud explosion. The percussion of it knocked him to the ground. He skidded across the pavement, the rough asphalt shredding his knees and palms until he rolled.

Then it was quiet.

He struggled to get air into his lungs. Wasn't sure he could move. But he was alive.

Then Lily was there, holding his face in her hands and kissing him. "Oh, thank God." She kissed him again. "Are you okay? Can you sit up?"

Another explosion rocked the ground before he could answer, and Lily screamed in surprise. He pulled her to him, instinctively covering her for protection. A chunk of red metal landed not six feet from them.

Emma's cries blended with the crackling of the fire. None of them were through the crisis yet. There was still the grassfire to worry about. Luckily, they'd had a wet spring and they were upwind from the fire, but the sooner help arrived, the better. He rolled off Lily. "We need to move." His breath came easier now. He helped Lily to a sitting position. The world spun a bit, but not so much that he couldn't stay upright. "You okay?"

"I think so," she answered, her eyes wide. "You?"

"Yeah." He got to his knees, and together, he and Lily stood. He took a couple of steps, pain radiating through his body from the hard landing. Lily picked up his hat, and he pushed it back onto his head.

With Lily's help, they made their way to Emma and her mother. The horses seemed to be tied to a fence post, and Luke was grateful Lily had had the forethought to have done that, or he'd have another worry on his mind.

He dropped to the ground, needing a moment to catch his breath. Lily had removed her outer shirt, and Emma now held it to the gash on her mother's head.

"Good job, Emma." Lily took over as the little girl jumped into Luke's embrace, her outright crying now turning to soft sobs. "She's lost a lot of blood, but her pulse seems strong."

"It's okay, honey. Everything is going to be okay." Luke removed his shirt and handed it to Lily. "Put this over Caroline's torso to help keep her warm. I'm sure her body is in shock."

"I called 9-1-1. What is taking so long?"

Luke snorted. "A drawback to living in the country. The EMTs will have to come from Roosevelt. That's a good fifteen to twenty minutes."

"No." Fear echoed in her tone. "She could—that could be a really bad thing."

"I know." The only thing they could do was pray Caroline held on that long and that the brushfire didn't rage out of control before then.

It seemed an eternity before Lily could hear sirens in the distance. Luke had called Caroline's husband shortly after the explosion, and he had shown up five minutes later with blankets, flashlights and some medical supplies. She was amazed at the calmness he'd shown while he and Luke had applied a gauze compress to her wound instead of Lily's shirt and had covered Caroline and Emma with warm blankets. Luke had put his t-shirt back on, but Lily couldn't bring herself to don her blood-soaked cotton shirt again.

Caroline's husband took his daughter and held her while he sat next to his wife, his face a mask of worry and anguish waiting for help to arrive.

When the ambulance drew closer, Luke stood, waving to them so they would know where to locate the injured person amongst the scene of devastation. Two fire trucks and a sheriff's SUV followed directly behind, filling the surrounding area with flashing red and blue lights.

Two young EMTs, one male and one female, hurried from the ambulance. Luke and Lily stepped back as the two began to work efficiently checking Caroline's injuries. The illuminated surroundings dimmed as the firefighters fought to extinguish the fires.

"Luke. What the hell happened?"

Lily looked up, surprised to find Milo approaching them outfitted in a deputy sheriff's uniform, his brows knitted together with concern.

Luke stepped across the highway toward him as the EMTs loaded Caroline into the ambulance. "I don't know, Milo. We found Caroline's vehicle in the ditch and the other one overturned. We were able to get Caroline and Emma safely away before they blew. Unfortunately, the other driver...well, there wasn't hope for him." He glanced at Lily and motioned her forward. When she was within reach, he pulled her to his side, wrapping a strong arm around her. She didn't resist the comfort.

She exchanged solemn greetings with Milo as the ambulance pulled away. Caroline's husband and Emma followed in his truck. Luke had insisted on taking care of Boo who now sat panting at Lily's feet.

"They said Caroline's stable." Lily leaned into the safety Luke offered as the emergency vehicle faded into the distance.

"Glad to hear that." Milo removed a small notepad from his pocket. "I couldn't believe it when the call came through. That whole family has been through a lot lately."

"Yeah." Luke sounded hollow, tired. "Let's hope she doesn't have internal injuries. Thank God, Emma didn't get hurt."

"I know." Lily wondered if the little girl would ever recover from the horrific experience. "I'm worried about Caroline." She couldn't believe this was all for real. Lily put a hand over her mouth as a violent tremble started deep inside her and radiated outward. She inhaled a shaky breath as the magnitude of what they'd just been through overtook her.

Luke finished giving Milo the rest of the details from their encounter. When he finished, a hush filled the void.

"She would have died if you hadn't gotten her out, Luke." Lily's voice hitched on the last word. "You almost died saving her."

Luke folded her in his arms and held her tightly against him. She buried her face in his chest. He was strong and solid and exactly what she needed at that moment.

"Man, you're a mess." Milo's flashlight flickered across them. "I think you might need medical attention yourself, Luke. You're bleeding."

Lily let go, trying to assess Luke's injuries, but he shooed her away. "I'm fine. I just need to get home and clean up."

Another violent shiver rolled through her.

"You're cold," Luke said, and pulled her to him. "I need to get her home, Milo."

"Sure. I think I have what I need from you for now. I'll call if I require anything else. Why don't you let me take their dog, too? You have enough to deal with, and he likes me."

Luke agreed, and Milo headed back toward his vehicle with the black dog following along behind.

Luke hugged her. "If you'd like, I can ask Milo if he'll give you a lift back to the cabin. It's chilly out, and you've been through an ordeal tonight."

"No." She shook her head. "I want to ride back with you. I need the time to collect myself."

"Okay, but you're on Hades with me. I'm sure the horses are super-spooked right now, and I'm not going to take a chance that Charlee might try to throw you."

That was more than fine with Lily. Being tucked safely against Luke was exactly what she wanted at that moment. She let him help her onto Hades's back and sighed when he climbed up behind her. She leaned into him as he spurred the horse forward, Charlee following along a few paces behind.

They rode the distance in silence, Lily lost in her reflections of the tragic night. When they arrived back at the barn, Luke insisted Lily wait in his truck with the engine running so she could get warm while he took care of the horses.

Lily curled into herself and huddled against the leather seat while she waited. She'd seen both sides of life tonight. The fragile side, where one mistake could force a soul from this earth whether a person was ready to go or not. And the strong side, where a man would risk his life for a neighbor and where a mother would fight the odds to stick around for her family.

Life was precious. She didn't know how many days she had left on earth, and look how much time she'd wasted being angry with Ethan and her sister. She was done with that. Done with them. This was her life, and she wasn't wasting it on worthless people any longer.

The driver's side door opened, startling her from her thoughts.

"You okay?" Luke asked as he climbed inside.

"Yeah. You?" This had been a much more traumatic experience for him.

He scrubbed his face and nodded. "Hell of a night. If you'd like, I can drive you straight home, and my dad and I will get your car to you tomorrow."

She shook her head. "I'm okay to drive."

It took them less than three minutes to travel the distance between the barn and the cabin where her car was still parked. Life had turned in a whole different direction since the time she'd exited her car earlier that day. It seemed like weeks had passed.

They arrived, and he shut off the truck, sending their world back into darkness. Like the true gentleman he was, he insisted on opening the door for her. She stepped down to the pavement below.

The world was entirely peaceful as he walked her to her car. She hesitated next to the driver's side, not wanting to dig the keys out of her pocket. "Are you headed home, too?"

He held up his hands. "I'm going to clean up first, and maybe chill here for the night. I don't really feel like a drive across town at the moment." He paused, as though waiting for her to speak. "Would you like to come in?"

"Could I?" She heaved a sigh of relief. "I don't feel like being alone at the moment. Hannah's gone for the night, and I could use someone to talk to."

"Absolutely. I'd love the company, too." He wrapped an arm around her and led her to the house.

CHAPTER NINE

Luke flipped on the lights as they walked inside the cabin. A golden glow fell from the rustic chandelier and bounced off the warm log walls. Lily was greeted again by the smell of a freshly-cleaned home, and the interior beamed with old-fashioned comfort and cheerfulness. Luke held up his hands, giving Lily her first glimpse of the damage he'd sustained from the blast. "I should probably clean these."

"Luke. Oh, my God." She took his hands and inspected them. "Why didn't you say something?"

He tried to steal them back. "I'm okay."

"No, you're not." The fleshy part of both palms was raw and red. Bits of dirt and tiny pieces of gravel were imbedded in them. She narrowed her eyes. "You do need medical attention."

"I'm fine." He pulled away and headed into an adjoining room. Lily followed him into the large, state-of-the-art kitchen. He walked to the sink and turned on the faucet, jerking his hand back as the water touched raw skin. "Son of a bitch."

Lily grasped his arm, putting her weight behind her grip to hold him in place. "You have to wash them clean, or they'll get infected. I know it stings. Give me your hand and don't look."

He eyed her. "I don't need you to wash my hands for me. I'm a big boy."

She shifted her weight onto one hip. "It's not going to kill you to let me help you. Besides, I could really use something to do right now."

One side of his mouth turned up in a grin, and she knew she'd won. "I'm gonna curse."

"Doesn't bother me."

She adjusted the temperature until it felt neutral to her wrist before she lifted his palm and ran it under the water. Sure enough, he let go a string of curses. She squirted a dab of soap in her hand and gently rubbed it over his raw flesh. Rough bits of rock broke free, and she rinsed it again beneath the faucet.

She frowned when she spied a larger piece of gravel imbedded at the base of his palm. "This might hurt."

He inspected his hand. "Damn." He nodded. "Do your worst."

"I'm sorry." She apologized in advance before she squeezed his flesh together and then slipped her nail along the edge of the tiny rock and scraped. The invader popped free, and the vacant hole filled with blood. "It's out, but I think I should make it bleed a little more to clean it out good." She squeezed until a large bead of blood overflowed the hole. Then she rinsed it again.

She grabbed a paper towel and patted his hand dry. "Next?"

He switched hands, and she was happy to see this palm was not as bad as the first, with only a few minor abrasions. She was able to quickly wash and dry it. "Better?" she asked and glanced up.

"Thank you." He stared at her for an endless moment. Jolts of energy snapped between them, but he didn't move. She wanted to reach out and erase a smudge of dirt from his cheek, but she didn't dare.

"Do you have a band-aid?"

"I don't need a bandage. I need a beer." He turned and walked around the other side of the island counter to the fridge, putting emotional and physical distance between them. "Want one?"

"Sure." She sighed. "I could use a drink after this day."

He popped off two caps and carried their bottles into a corner of the great room. He flicked a couple of switches, turning down the lights in the house and turning on a massive gas fireplace.

She took a beer and sank down on the rug in front of the fire, letting the heat from the dancing flames warm her. "What? No real logs?"

He dropped onto a comfy-looking sage-green couch near her, setting his hat on the table next to him. She longed to touch his face, to ease his weariness, but that would lead to some serious complications that she wasn't sure she was prepared to deal with.

"I prefer a real fire, but with guests in and out, this is safer and cleaner." He took a long swallow and sank farther down on the couch, stretching his legs out in front of him. "Still cold?"

"A little. I probably should have kept my shirt, but it had so much blood on it."

He nodded. "I still can't believe what happened. I sure as hell hope Caroline is okay. She's got a husband and two little kids counting on her."

"I know." She took a drink, the cool liquid soothing her tight throat. She hadn't realized she'd been so thirsty.

"I could come down there and warm you up, but that might not be such a good idea. Would you like me to get you a blanket?"

Her blood heated at his suggestion. "I'm okay. The fire feels good." She shivered under his scrutiny, her nipples tingling as they tightened. The sexual tension in the room increased tenfold, messing with her resolution to keep things friendly between them. She dropped her gaze from his, looking at the carpet, his boots, his jeans.

She sat up straight. "Luke? Your pants are shredded at the knees."

"I know. I was there when it happened."

She set her beer down and crawled over to him. Kneeling before him, she inspected the damage. There was nothing but strings of material crossing his knees. "It's impossible to tell how bad you're hurt with all of the caked blood and dirt. You need to clean this."

"It's on my list."

"But—"

He put two fingers on her lips. "Shh." He set his beer on the table next to his hat and leaned forward, sliding his fingers behind her ears, holding her head. "I hope you can forgive me." He crushed his lips against hers.

One taste of him and all thoughts of why she shouldn't be doing this evaporated. She leaned closer, angling her head, allowing him to deepen the kiss. Flutters of excitement built beneath her breast, leaving an ache that wouldn't be ignored. His tongue tangled with hers in a desperate dance, as though each of them was trying to take what they could before it was too late.

He pulled away, studied her eyes before giving her two more small lingering kisses. He sat back, leaving her breathless.

"I know I shouldn't have done that." He licked his bottom lip as though searching for a taste of her. Desire darkened his eyes and boiled inside her. He stood and helped her to her feet. When she was next to him, he cradled her face again, giving her another heated kiss. If he didn't stop, she was sure he'd have to hold her up.

But he did stop. "I'm sorry. Shouldn't have done that, either, but after everything that's happened today, I'm having a hard time remembering why I should consider Hannah's feelings." He stroked a thumb down her cheek. "But I will consider yours." He kissed her again. "I'm sorry. I keep doing that. I just don't know if I'll ever get another chance."

He stepped away. "I'm going to go shower and clean off the rest of this blood and grime. You can stay if you like, but I can't promise to behave tonight if you do." He came back for one more intense kiss and then headed for the stairs near the front of the house.

Lily watched as he appeared on the second level. He sent her a long, searching look before he disappeared into one of the bedrooms.

She stayed where she was, staring at the closed bedroom door for several long minutes. She desperately wanted who lay behind it. Luke could be hers if she'd reach out and take him. But could she betray Hannah like that?

Lily could rationalize her actions by saying Hannah had lied about Luke. At this point, that fact was pretty obvious, even though she didn't yet know all the details. Question was, did Hannah deserve her loyalty despite the fact?

Yes.

Lily headed toward the front door. Hannah had been nothing but good to her, despite what she might have done to others.

But did she and Luke have to suffer for that loyalty?

That didn't seem right, either.

She stopped near the stairs. Suddenly, the world was no longer black and white like she'd always believed it to be. Shades of gray crowded in, dulling the sharp edges of her memories and judgments.

Up until now, she'd judged everything in terms of right and wrong. But perhaps life wasn't always so clear cut. Maybe people did bad things for good reasons. Maybe the judgment of something being bad was really in the eye of the beholder.

Could she even go so far as to forgive Ethan and her sister for what they'd done? Obviously, there had been issues between her and her fiancé, or he would have never slept with her sister. Had she been blind to those issues? Could she be partially to blame? Not for the cheating, but for the breakdown in their relationship?

Possibly.

She stepped onto the first stair and looked upward. She could be making one of the biggest mistakes of her life, trusting a man with a flawed reputation who very well might break her heart. She'd certainly be risking her friendship with Hannah. Then again, she could also be making one of the best decisions ever, putting her faith in a man who treated her like a treasure and was willing to risk his life for others.

She had to go with her instincts.

She hurried up the rest of the stairs, not bothering to look back. She'd made up her mind, and she would see this through, repercussions be damned.

With a certain hand, she opened the bedroom door and heard the shower running in the attached bathroom. Her clothes seemed to fight her as she hurried to strip. Now that she'd made up her mind, she didn't want to wait another second to touch him, to show him that she cared and trusted him. Steamy air filled the bathroom, fogging the mirrors, making her lungs heavy.

The shower did not have a door, but instead sported two tiled walls placed to allow entrance, but also to keep the water inside. She stepped past one wall and peeked around the corner of the other. Luke stood with his eyes shut, his head back under the water, running his fingers through his hair.

She allowed herself a moment to appreciate every muscled, naked inch of his glorious body from his well-defined chest, down his abs, to his corded thighs. His poor knees were red and roughed up. He'd really taken a beating from the explosions. Of course, there were others out there who'd suffered far worse damage, but she couldn't think about them now.

His shaft, still thick with need, stole her attention. He wanted her, too.

That thought was enough to propel her forward onto the wet tiles.

⌒

Luke startled when someone touched his chest, and he jerked open his eyes.

"Lily," he whispered, not quite sure he wasn't hallucinating. He swallowed the hard lump in his throat as he soaked up the sight of her body. Breathe, he reminded himself.

He'd known she was beautiful, but...dear God.

He cleared his throat. "I thought you'd left." He wiped water from his eyes to make sure she wasn't an illusion.

She shook her head. "Do you want me to go?"

"Hell, no." He pulled her to him, his wet skin slippery against hers.

She seriously could be the woman of his dreams. A few hours ago, he was certain he'd never get the opportunity to show her how good he could be to her, and now here she was, naked in his arms. He couldn't quite believe it. "Are you sure about this?"

She splayed her fingers and slowly ran them up the contours of his pecs and across his shoulders, sensation after sensation exploding across his skin. Then she smiled up at him, and he was positive he had to be dreaming. Maybe he'd died in the explosion, and this was heaven.

"This is where I want to be." She slipped her fingers into his wet hair and tugged his head forward.

He was a goner. The second her lips touched his, he knew he couldn't turn back. He kissed her hard, demanding that *something* that had been missing in his life for so long.

He turned, moving them under the spray of warm water, cupping her bottom and hauling her against him. She fit him perfectly. Streams of hot water rushed over her shoulders and breasts and pelted his hands where he held her to him.

She tilted her head back into the stream and lifted her hands, pushing her wet hair out of her face. Luke ran his hands down her sides to her waist and then up her stomach. He hadn't thought he could get harder than he was, but the feel of her soft, slippery skin beneath his fingers left him with an aching, burning need to bury himself inside her.

He cupped her breasts, holding the weight of them in his palms, running his thumbs across her nipples. She arched her back, inviting him closer.

He dipped his head, sucking a sweet nipple into his mouth, and reveled in the shiver that enveloped her. She dug her fingers into his wet hair and held him there. He'd be happy if she never let him go.

He'd wanted this girl from the moment he'd first met her. He'd wanted to touch her and hold her. Now, he was, and it was more exquisite than anything he'd pictured.

He lifted his head, finding her staring at him with eyes the color of midnight. She parted her lips, her breasts heaving. "Luke," she whispered.

Damn. He'd never hear his name again without thinking of her.

He traced a water drop down her cheek. She turned her face, catching his finger with her teeth, drawing him inside her mouth and sucking. Shit. If he got any harder, he'd blow here and now.

He removed his finger and kissed her, unable to stop her slow teasing from taking the sharp turn into hot and explosive.

She closed her fingers around his shaft, smiling at his sharp intake of breath. Her eyes, drunk with seduction, darkened as she caressed him. Hot, pulsating need consumed him. He groaned, pressing himself into her hand, taking a moment to enjoy the sweet ache her touch created.

He reached between them, removing her hand. Turning her, cradling her back against his chest, he held the backs of her hands, leaving her palms free.

With their fingers entwined, he placed hers on her abdomen and slowly slid them upward over her slippery skin as steamy water pelted them. He helped her cup her own breasts, testing them and massaging them. She leaned her head back against his shoulder, her eyes closed, her mouth parted on a sigh.

"See how good you feel?" He took her pointer fingers and circled her nipples, and then flicked the crested buds with his thumbs. "You're so beautiful, Lily. So beautiful."

She shivered and tried to turn in his arms.

"Uh-uh. Not done yet." He trailed their linked hands down her sides and over her hips. With deliberate slowness, he dragged her closer to the place he wanted to touch the most.

She tried to hurry their descent. "Touch me, Luke," she whispered. "I'm going to die if you don't."

"Trust me honey, I'm going down in flames with you." He moved their hands to the sensitive place between her thighs, running her finger between her folds.

She bucked against him. "Oh, Luke."

He held her trembling finger as he retraced their path, this time delving deeper into her hot core. Even from his place on the outskirts, her slick juices covered him. "Lily. You're so hot." He sucked her earlobe into his mouth as he made her touch herself again.

Then he released her, searching for and finding her sensitive bud, totally turned on by the fact her hand remained as she continued to arouse herself.

She jerked again, went rigid, before she melted against him.

Damn.

He turned her, her lust-glazed expression drawing him deeper into her sensual world. "I need you, Lily."

She slipped a hand around his neck, bringing her face to his and giving him a kiss that scorched his lips. "So take me."

"Do we need a condom?"

"No," she whispered against his mouth.

He dug rough fingers into the soft flesh of her bottom as he lifted her. She wrapped her arms around his neck, and he anchored her back against the wall. He met her gaze and held it. Slowly he tested her resistance and then drove himself deep inside her.

She gasped as he relentlessly plundered the addictive pleasure she offered. He couldn't think beyond the space she occupied in his world. He needed her…desperately.

In the back of his mind, he registered the feel of her nails raking his back, but the sensation only added to the feral quality of the moment.

He thrust into her again and again as water rained down on them. Steam filled the air. Lily gasped and clung to him as he pushed them both toward ecstasy.

He couldn't stop. Not until he thoroughly satisfied her. Not until he appeased the deep ache inside him.

"Luke." Lily pulled his head toward hers, stealing his soul with a passionate kiss. She cried out as she tightened around his shaft.

He increased his momentum, giving in this time to the hunger that consumed him.

Pent-up pleasure crested, and his body vibrated with sweet release.

He took a moment to catch his breath, studying her eyes, amazed that he could feel so much for one person. "That was…wow." He kissed her until he couldn't breathe.

She gave a small chuckle. "Liked that, huh?"

"More than liked." Loved? It wasn't just lust or the afterglow of sex. Somehow, during the few short weeks she'd been in Aspen, she'd managed to ensnare his heart. The best part was, he didn't care that she'd imprisoned him. He wanted to tell her exactly how much he felt for her, but it was too soon. If he spouted the "L" word, she'd run, and he didn't intend on losing her. Ever.

He scooped her up before he said something he'd regret and carried her to the bed, depositing her wet, sleek body on the downy comforter.

She welcomed him with open arms, and then snuggled against his chest.

"Don't get too comfortable." He grinned. "You and I aren't finished yet."

CHAPTER TEN

A frantic pounding woke Luke from a deep slumber. He sat up, nearly toppling Lily as she apparently tried to do the same. "What the hell was that?" His heart thumped wildly from the abrupt awakening.

"Someone's at the door," Lily whispered, sounding breathless and scared.

Several more rounds of banging echoed through the house, confirming Lily's answer. Luke cursed. "Stay here."

Who the hell even knew he was there? He dragged on his boxers as he stumbled through the darkness and out of the room.

He flicked on a light switch and headed down. Whoever it was pounded again causing him to almost miss a stair. He grabbed wildly for the hand-rail to catch himself. "Hang on a damn minute," he hollered as he descended the rest of the steps.

He swung the door open wide, ready to kick someone's ass.

"Bastard," Hannah hissed as she shoved past him. Black mascara hung in half-moons beneath her eyes, giving her the appearance of a zombie. "Where is she?"

Luke made the mistake of glancing up the stairs, and Hannah didn't miss it. He tried to grab her before she hit the first step, but she was primed for battle and escaped his grasp.

He chased her, but couldn't catch her before she entered the bedroom. Hannah flipped on the light switch just as he reached her.

Lily stood at the side of the bed tucking the woven throw from the chair around her, her eyes wide pools of shock. "Hannah, what are you doing here?"

"I can't believe I was worried about you."

Anger emanated off Hannah in violent waves, and Luke stepped forward to put a protective hand on Lily's back. He wouldn't tolerate Hannah's emotionally abusive ways any longer. When he touched Lily, she shrugged him off. He took a step back, stunned and a little hurt.

"Slow down, Hannah. Why were you worried?"

"My mom heard about the accident and went to the house to check on you. When you didn't show up for a couple of hours, she got worried and called me. I hurried back from Roosevelt, and we've been looking for you for hours. I didn't know if you'd been hurt, too, or what."

Lily took a step toward her friend. "You can't get mad at me for that. I didn't know you'd come look for me. You weren't even supposed to be home tonight."

Hannah let loose a semi-hysterical laugh, and Luke wondered if she'd gone completely off the deep end this time. "That's right. You waited until I left town and then jumped at the first opportunity to trick Luke into bed."

Luke couldn't let this continue. "That's not what happened, Hannah."

"Stay out of it, jackass. It's pretty damn obvious you fucked her. The only question is, did you rape her like you did me, or did she use you for a good fuck like she said she was going to before she dumped you on your ass?"

"Whoa." Luke took the emotional blow, but didn't back down.

Lily slapped Hannah's face, the sound echoing through the room. "How dare you?"

"Bitch." Hannah raised her hand, but Luke caught it before she made contact with Lily and threw it back at her.

Adrenaline screamed through his veins, but he retained control. "I did not rape you. I did not sleep with you. I did not touch you. Take back what you said, Hannah. This has gone on far too long."

Hannah seemed momentarily stunned by the anger in his voice, but it didn't take her long to recover. "You're just lucky I never called the cops."

"Get out." His voice shook with every bit of anger and resentment he'd held toward her. Hannah opened her mouth, but he cut her off. "Now."

Tears flooded Hannah's eyes. "This isn't over. It isn't over by a long shot." She turned and stormed out of the room.

He met Lily's gaze and held it. She cringed when Hannah slammed the door.

He inhaled what he hoped was a sustaining breath. "I didn't rape her. I never even had sex with her."

"I know," she whispered.

"When is this fucking nightmare going to end?" He kicked a stool near him, sending it toppling over. Lily flinched again, but remained silent. He'd had all he could take. The years of lies, of people whispering behind his back, the way they looked at him like he was less than. Now she'd label him a rapist. He was done with it.

There was just one thing.

He pinned Lily with a look, needing to see her face when he questioned her, needing to know if there was one person in this God-forsaken town that he could love and trust. He swallowed the burning bile in his throat, knowing deep down how this would end, but praying it wouldn't. "Was Hannah lying about what you said, too?"

Lily's eyes watered over before she dropped her gaze. "Not exactly," she whispered.

"What the hell does that mean?" His heart might as well have been ripped from his chest. It couldn't have hurt any worse.

"I didn't mean it when I said it. It was before I knew you."

"So you routinely make suggestive comments that you don't mean?" He knew his bottled emotions had taken control of his words, but he didn't care. He had to get the hell out while he still had a shred of his soul. "Never mind." He grabbed his jeans, his keys jingling in the pocket. "Don't answer. I've stayed in this fucking town too damn long as it is."

She grabbed his hand, the gesture tugging at his shattered heart. "Luke, you have to understand. That was before I got to know you. I'd only heard Hannah's side of the story."

He shook her off. He wanted to believe her. He really did. But he was so damn tired of games and lies and trying to figure out who wouldn't ultimately break his heart. "Doesn't matter. I'm done. I don't need this shit. I don't need to wonder if you're really the type of girl who would do that. I don't need to wonder if you can get past something I never did." He looked her in the eye, wanting her to know how damn serious he was. "I'm done."

He ignored the heart-wrenching look on her face and left the room. Who the hell knew if he could even trust her expression?

He was over this town and these people. Fuck, he was an idiot for sticking around for so long.

Lily placed a hand on her chest, trying to breathe. This was wrong. So wrong.

She couldn't let Luke leave, not without having a real chance to explain what had happened, not without making him understand. If things didn't work out between them because they weren't well-matched, then so be it, but she didn't want him leaving because of the vicious words Hannah had spewed.

Lily hitched the blanket higher so she could move unfettered and hurried down the stairs. She had to stop him.

She'd made it halfway to the bottom when the blanket slipped from her nervous fingers, tangling around her legs and onto her feet. She panicked, trying to gather it again. Part of the blanket landed between her heel and the wooden stairs, creating a slippery surface that sent her tumbling down. Her ankle twisted as she tried to catch herself, and her elbow smacked hard against an edge.

She landed with a thud at the base of the stairs, her cheek smacking against the hardwood floor. She laid there for a moment, naked amidst a tangle of blanket, trying to assess what damage she might have taken. Air slowly eased back into her lungs.

"Shit." This wasn't how her magical evening was supposed to end. She rolled over, but before she could sit up, she heard the sound of a truck screeching away into the early dawn.

"No," she cried, hot tears flooding the corners of her eyes as pain radiated up her ankle.

Luke. Her insides squeezed in on each other, leaving her with a sick feeling. With everything that had happened to him in the past, he probably believed that she was as heartless as Hannah. This was another arrow to his heart, and of course, he would be hurting like hell. She had to find him.

She needed to talk to Hannah, too. She couldn't believe her friend had snapped like she had. What happened to the fun and carefree roommate she'd known in Salt Lake? Could a person really hide from her past like that? No doubt, Hannah had some serious issues she needed to deal with, but she was beyond Lily's reach now. Luke had to come first.

She got to her knees, wincing as she moved her left wrist. She rotated it an inch before a sharp pain made her cry out. She must have sprained it, and her elbow hurt like a bugger. So did her cheek where it had made contact with the wood flooring.

She had to admit, though, her heart hurt worse than any of her physical pains. She'd gone from lying in Luke's strong arms one minute to being laid out naked on the floor in the next.

Life could be cruel.

But she wasn't going down this time without a fight. She wouldn't give up and walk away like she'd done before. So what if life wasn't black and white, right or wrong? Maybe it was in the gray areas where all the happiness was found anyway. In time, she and Hannah might find a way to forgive each other, but she'd never forgive herself if she let Luke get away without telling him how much he meant to her.

The morning sun was well over the mountains as Lily pulled in front of the little house she shared with Hannah. She'd driven through the small town of Aspen and some of the surrounding areas searching for Luke's truck, but she had no idea where he lived, and the possibilities were just too vast. So, she'd gone home.

Battered and bruised, inside and out, Lily exited her car with care, prepared for another round of abuse. Inside, she found Hannah in her bedroom shoving a pair of Lily's jeans haphazardly into a suitcase. The closet door stood open along with all of Lily's drawers. Clothing trailed from the closet, across the floor, to a jumbled pile in the center of her bed.

Lily exhaled a huge breath, wanting to knock over her roommate, but knowing she had to pick her fights.

Hannah tossed a black pump and a pink bra on top of the jeans. She was obviously still operating under the influence of her wild emotions.

Lily stepped inside the room. "We need to talk."

Hannah stayed focused on her task. "I don't have anything to say to a traitorous, lying bitch." In went a white cotton shirt and a brown sandal.

Lily cringed, but said nothing about her friend's blatant violation. "Come on, Hannah. That's a little overkill."

Hannah whipped her gaze toward Lily, her brows arched with attitude. "So you say." She narrowed her eyes. "What the hell happened to you? Looks like he beat the shit out of your face."

Lily touched her cheek, the spot tender and swollen. Luke was not that kind of man. As messed up as things were, that was one thing she was sure of. "I fell."

"*Really?*"

Lily frowned. "Yes, really. I slipped and tumbled down the wooden stairs at his lodge after you lied to him, and he left."

Hannah smirked and continued to shove things into the suitcase. "Good." Lily had the sinking feeling that Hannah would have been even happier if Lily *had* accused Luke of physically harming her.

Emotion slammed her pulse against her throat, and she waited until she'd inhaled and then slowly exhaled before she spoke again. "I'm not sorry I've spent time with Luke, but I am sorry that it's hurting our friendship. That was never my intention."

She paused long enough to glare at her. "Whatever."

"Seriously, can we talk about this?"

Her friend turned to her and placed her hands on her hips. She opened her mouth to speak, but bit down on her lip instead. Fresh tears pooled in her eyes, twisting the knot of guilt Lily wanted to ignore.

Hannah tried again. "Out of all the people I know, I would think you would be the one person who would know what it's like to be betrayed." Her voice cracked with raw emotion. "I thought you'd have my back. That's the only reason I returned to this hellhole. Because you were coming with me.

Otherwise, I would have been happier living on the streets."

"Hannah—"

"I never should have listened to you about coming back." She wiped her nose with the back of her hand. "But it's all worked out real well for you, hasn't it? You have a job, the hottest guy in town. Even my parents love you more than me. You've succeeded where I never could. This whole town hates my guts...including my own family."

"No, Hannah. God." Lily twined her fingers, trying to figure out how to make this all better. "How can you say that? Your parents obviously worship the ground you walk on. So does your brother. I'd give anything to have what you have."

"Take them, they're yours. Oh, wait. You already have." Hannah laughed, the sound smacking of the deranged.

"That's not fair. I'm not trying to take anything from you. I'm truly grateful that you've given me a place to live."

"And look how you show your thanks."

"Come on. When you offered me a place to stay, you didn't mention the extent of the issues you had with this town or the fact that you expected me to hate everyone and everything while I'm here. I got a job to carry my own weight, and I've been as nice as I can be to your parents because I'm grateful to them for taking me in. I haven't done anything wrong."

Hannah directed a sharp, piercing gaze at Lily. "You slept with Luke. The one person I hate the most. I could take you showing me up to my parents and to the rest of the town, but not taking Luke's side. Not after what he did."

Here they were, back to what Luke had supposedly done to Hannah. "He said you lied about what
happened, and I think he's still paying the price for
that lie."

Hannah stared at her, venom shooting from her
eyes, and for a second, Lily wondered if she should
have come armed in case she needed to defend
herself. "Stop making him out to be a prince. Stop
taking his side. This is exactly what happened eight
years ago. Everyone took his side. He's a lying,
cheating—"

"Hannah." Lily spoke in a raised voice. "You're
better than this. The Hannah I know doesn't need
to disparage another to build herself up. She's kind
and loving, and not this person I'm seeing right
now. If you lied about what happened between you
and Luke, you need to come clean. It will help both
of you."

"It's this town. It messes with me." She inhaled a
hysterical breath. "No, Luke lied. He lied. He should
have taken me with him. He made me feel worthless
for…" She shook her head. "He deserves everything
he gets."

"Are you sure, Hannah? Eight years is a long
time to pay a price, especially if he didn't do anything to you."

"Oh, he did. He *humiliated* me." She stopped,
her eyes going wide as though she'd said something
she hadn't meant to. Lily knew she'd been just a few
words away from confessing.

"If he didn't hurt you, you need to clear his
name."

"He *did* hurt me." She put a shaking hand over
her mouth.

Lily raised a brow in question.

Hannah exhaled, her expression growing cold, less animated, and Lily knew she wasn't going to divulge any further information. "Doesn't matter now. I'm finished with this place, with Luke, with the whole fucking town. Consider our friendship over." Her mouth quivered. "You need to leave."

That was it then. Maybe things between them *had* gone too far down the dark alley of despair to ever find their way back. A spear of regret sliced through her. The price of sleeping with Luke would be her friendship with Hannah. Deep down, she'd known it, and there was no going back now. "You're right. I am sorry this has hurt us. It shouldn't take me long to pack."

CHAPTER ELEVEN

Despite her painful wrist and ankle, Lily had everything in boxes or suitcases by the time early evening rolled around. Although her car was packed, it didn't seem like much—most of her possessions were in the storage unit in Salt Lake. For all Lily knew, that unit might be her home until she could secure a job. At least she'd earned a little money and would have food to eat.

Hannah had left shortly after Lily had started packing, which was probably for the best. The less contact they had at this point, the better. Some things could not be repaired.

Lily stacked her last box in her little Honda and shut the back door, glancing at the cute house that had been her home for such a short period of time. Maybe this town did mess with people's heads. It seemed to tease everyone with what they wanted but couldn't have.

It had driven Hannah to insanity, had made Luke think he could move beyond his reputation, and it made Lily crave a slower pace in life, a life that might have been shared with a warm-hearted, sexy cowboy.

Hannah's mom had been kind enough to give her Luke's father's phone number. Lily could only hope his father would give Luke the message she'd left for him and that Luke would try to contact her. It was the best she could do, but his dad hadn't given her much hope. He'd said Luke had left town and didn't know when he'd be back.

Maybe he just needed time.

Lily climbed into her car and started the engine. Although it was getting late, Betty had agreed to meet her in town in just a few minutes to give up her key to the office. Her boss hadn't been happy she was leaving, but what choice did Lily have? This wasn't her town. She couldn't stay, especially not after what had happened with her and Luke, and with Hannah. Her small-town fairytale was at an end.

Betty stood in the parking lot outside her office, frowning as Lily approached. When she was within arm's reach, she pulled her into a big bear hug. "You poor thing."

Lily wanted to cry, but restrained. She couldn't dump her tears and fears on the woman who'd been so kind to her. "I'm sorry. I've really enjoyed working for you, and I hope I'm not leaving you in the lurch."

"Shh…" Betty shook her head, her expression full of concern. "Don't even start worrying about me."

"I really wanted to get that marketing plan launched for you. I know it's going to be fabulous."

"It will. I'm sure it'll do amazing things for my business." Betty nodded, tears welling in her eyes. "Are you sure you don't want to stay at my house?"

"I can't." Lily could no longer keep her own tears at bay. She'd fallen madly in love with this little town, and she was going to miss it desperately. "Promise you'll call and let me know how it goes?"

"Of course, I will." Betty grabbed her hands. "This is such a terrible tragedy. All these years I truly believed Luke was a good guy and that Hannah had lied, but look at you." She shook her head. "You should reconsider pressing charges. I hate to see anything bad happen to him, but a person needs to pay for his crimes."

Lily's brain spun, trying to make sense of Betty's words. "What?" She took a step back, dropping Betty's hands. "Why would I want to press charges against Luke?"

Pity reflected in the older woman's eyes. She gently touched Lily's cheek. "Oh, honey. I know women like to protect the men they love, but this just ain't right."

"No," Lily gritted out through clenched teeth. "No. Luke did *not* do this to me. Who told you that?" She didn't need an answer though. Hannah had done it. Hannah with her vicious lies.

"Everyone in town is talking about it. His parents are mortified. He's apparently left Aspen to avoid prosecution."

Lily blew out a heated breath. "This is *so* messed up." The temperature of her blood increased with each beat. "Look at me, Betty." She waited until Betty's gaze was solidly fixed on her. "Luke did not hit me."

Betty shook her head as though to disagree.

"This is another of Hannah's lies. Luke didn't hit me. I slipped and tumbled down some stairs. I had a blanket and it got caught beneath my feet and tripped me." She circled in the air near her cheek. "This is one-hundred percent me, okay?"

Betty nodded, and Lily started to believe she might be getting through to the woman. "Hannah did not like me seeing Luke, and she made up this lie after she saw my bruise this morning at our house. Luke left because he lost faith in me, in his town." Her voice grew more emotional with each word. "He left because of what *I* did, not the other way around."

"Okay, honey." She wiped a tear from Lily's cheek. "I believe you."

Lily hadn't even realized she was still crying. She swiped the rest of the tears away. Hannah was not going to get away with this again. "I have to stop her, Betty. This will kill Luke. He's such a good person, and no matter how things are between us, he doesn't deserve this."

Betty shifted her stance, glancing down the street. "Hannah's truck is still at Sparrows."

"She's here?" Lily followed Betty's gaze, and sure enough, Hannah's blue truck was parked on the corner near the bar.

"Lord help her," Betty said, as Lily marched down the street, scarlet anger coloring her world.

Lily pushed through the front door of the bar like an old west cowboy might in search of a showdown.

It looked like the bar had sprung for a live band that weekend, but they played the same eighties music. Lily recognized a few people from the first night she'd gone there. From her perspective, it contained a fair amount of Aspen citizens, which was exactly what she wanted.

Hannah sat at the bar, a shot glass and a full beer mug in front of her, flanked by Scott and Milo.

Lily walked up to her and shoved her shoulder. "You bitch." She yelled loud enough to be heard over the music. Her reputation would never recover from this, she was sure, but what did she care? She wouldn't be there for long. "Just who the hell do you think you are messing with people's lives like this?"

Hannah turned, shock darkening her features. She wobbled on her stool and then placed a hand on the bar to steady herself. It was obvious she was well on her way to drunk, if she hadn't passed it already. "Don't you call me a bitch, you whore."

The band stopped playing, apparently more interested in what was happening near the bar than they were in their music.

"Whoa, ladies." Milo held up a hand. "Calm the language."

Lily pointed a finger at Hannah. "She's a liar. The worst kind of liar."

Scott and Milo both raised brows. Hannah glared at her.

"She's ruining people's lives, spreading lies and deceit. Enough is enough."

Hannah lunged for her, knocking the wind out of her as they crashed to the sawdust-covered floor.

Luke hit the city limits of Aspen and slowed his truck. It almost killed him to reduce his speed. He needed to talk to Lily.

He'd spent a good part of the day in the south end of the county talking to Wayne before the reality of his situation had smacked him upside the head. For years, he'd tried to rebuild his life after everyone had listened to the lies and judged him guilty. The problem was, he *was* slightly guilty. He had liked Hannah, just not as much as she'd liked him. But he hadn't told her right away. He'd enjoyed having the cute little sophomore chase after him. He'd known she'd wanted to take things to the next level, but he was ready to head off to college and wasn't interested in anything serious. What he hadn't known was that she'd be so vindictive when he refused to sleep with her or take her with him.

He left for college, and by the time he returned on break, her lies had spread like a wildfire. But he hadn't wanted to call her a liar, hadn't wanted to hurt her any worse, so he'd let it go, thinking the drama would fade.

It hadn't, and people had judged him when they didn't know all the facts.

He was now guilty of doing the same to Lily. She'd tried to talk to him, to explain, but he hadn't listened.

Time and a little distance from town had improved his perception. He'd never be able to forgive her or forget her if he didn't give her a chance to explain. What she said to him may or may not change things, but he had to give her what the townspeople had never given him.

He cruised past Sparrows, and then the little shopping area, noticing Betty standing near the sidewalk with three other women. He nodded as he passed them. All four of them widened their eyes at him, but none returned the nod. Strange.

A sharp whistle pierced the evening air, and Luke glanced in his rearview mirror to see Betty standing in the middle of the road motioning for him to come back.

What the hell?

He turned his truck around and pulled to the side of the road.

A flushed-looking Betty popped her head in his lowered window. "You need to get to Sparrows, now."

"What's going on?"

"It's Lily and Hannah, and Lily's out for blood."

"Shit." He left his truck parked where it was and sprinted down the street.

Lily tried to catch her breath and keep Hannah from tearing out her hair at the same time. Whistles and shouts came from the crowd, and she really wanted to punch out all of them. This wasn't a display for their entertainment.

She and Hannah rolled a few times, but luckily for Lily, Hannah was pretty drunk, and it only took Lily a few quick moves to pin her to the floor. Lily sat on her stomach, holding Hannah's hands tight to her chest, ignoring the throb in her wrist. Hannah squirmed, but she couldn't throw her.

Lily glanced at the crowd around them. Scott's brows had climbed closer to his hairline in surprise, while Milo watched with an amused expression. Sierra's mouth stood slack.

"Hey, keeper of the peace, shouldn't you do something?" Scott nudged his buddy.

"Let's see how this plays out. I won't let anyone get hurt." Milo nodded at Lily as though he approved.

Good, 'cause she had something to say.

"See this bruise on my cheek?" She waited until she'd received several acknowledgements before she continued. "I'm sure most of you are calling Luke Winchester a son of a bitch for doing this to me. Well, I'm here to tell you he didn't. He's not like that, and I think most, if not all of you in town would agree that he's a good man if you stop to think about it." A few nodded.

"Hannah made up that lie to hurt him and me."

Hannah made a big push that almost unseated Lily, but she quickly regained her dominance. "Tell them Hannah. Tell them how you lied."

"Bitch," she yelled at her.

"While you're at it, tell them how you also lied about Luke all those years ago."

Hannah narrowed her eyes, shooting a steady stream of visual daggers.

"I know you did." Lily shook Hannah. "Tell them. He deserves to be free from your lies. Everyone knows you lied about the bruise on my face. They're not going to believe anything you say any longer, so you might as well tell them."

"Never," Hannah shrieked and tried to buck her off.

"Lily." A deep voice called to her from behind, and she shifted her gaze to find the crowd parting.

Luke emerged.

Her heart flopped with a sickening thud. How much had he seen? How much had he heard? She froze, not sure how to react.

"Let her go," he said in a calm voice.

"No." She shook her head, frustration forcing her emotions to the surface. "She needs to fix this."

Luke held out a hand to her. "It doesn't matter anymore. She doesn't matter. As long as you believe in me, that's all I need."

Hannah shoved again, and this time Lily grasped Luke's hand, setting Hannah free. Hannah made a swipe at Lily's legs, but Milo caught her, hauling her to her feet.

"Come on, Hannah. Show's over. Let me give you a ride home."

Hannah struggled for a minute, and then crumbled in Milo's arms, crying. He led her out the back door as the volume of the crowd's whispers increased.

Luke wrapped an arm around Lily. "Let's get out of here."

Lily nodded, grateful to have him to lean on. The rush of adrenaline that had spiked during her brawl with Hannah evaporated, leaving her drained. Betty, who had found her way into the bar, grabbed Lily's hand as they passed, giving it a squeeze. Lily smiled. At least she had one friend in this town.

Darkness dominated the sky by the time they emerged. Quiet replaced the noisy atmosphere, and it was a relief to be away from everyone.

"I didn't mean for that to happen."

"It's okay." Luke took her hand and led her up the sidewalk toward her car. His truck was parked in a haphazard fashion alongside the road next to the parking lot.

"I wanted to confront her, but I didn't expect her to go after me like that."

Luke laughed then. "Hannah's been known for her temper, but it looked to me like you were holding your own."

Lily half laughed-half sighed. "I guess I was." She looked up at him, her heart full of emotion. "I didn't know I had it in me."

"Guess you have a little redneck in you, after all."

"Guess so," she said as she reached her Honda, the overhead parking lot light illuminating the grit on her white paint.

"What's this?" He traced a gentle finger over the bruise on her cheek.

She felt like an idiot. "I fell down the stairs, trying to chase after you this morning."

He widened his eyes. "No."

She nodded. "Call me Grace."

"I'm sorry. I didn't handle things all that well this morning."

"Me, either."

Luke glanced over her car and then frowned. "Where do you think you're going? Looks like you've packed up everything."

"There's nothing left for me here." She twined her fingers to keep from reaching out for him. Things seemed better now, but she wasn't sure to what extent.

"What about me?"

She tried not to get her hopes up. "You left town before I did."

He pulled her into an embrace, his eyes full of emotion. "I did. I'm sorry about that, too."

Her reserve melted. She touched his face, running her thumb over his raspy jaw line. She had her man back in her arms, and she intended to keep him there. "You had every right to leave. I hurt you with what I said, but I really want you to know that I didn't mean it. I was kidding around, trying to offer support to Hannah, but I hope you'll believe that I'm not the type of person to use people like that."

"I know." He hugged her. "Me, either, Lily. There was a short period of time when I liked Hannah, but I never slept with her, and I never meant to hurt her."

Lily put her fingertips on his lips. "Shh. I don't want to talk about her anymore, okay? She has issues she'll need to deal with, but they're not ours any longer."

"Agreed." He lowered his head, touching her lips with a tender kiss that quickly heated, leaving her breathless when he pulled away. "Where are you headed now?"

She shrugged. That was her biggest problem. "I don't know. I can't stay here."

He tightened his grip on her waist. "Why not?"

"First, I no longer have a home, and second, how would I ever live down the scene I caused tonight?"

He kissed her again, leaving his lips lingering on hers. "Stay with me," he whispered against her mouth. "I don't want you to go."

"What about all the rumors, all the gossip?" She couldn't get enough of the taste of his kiss and helped herself to more.

"Who cares? Let them talk." He took her face in his hands, running his roughened thumbs over her cheeks. He searched her eyes, gave her a quick kiss on the lips. "Seriously, Lily, I've found the woman I want. Please give me a chance to love you. Living here might have its difficulties from time to time, but I'll stay if you'll stay."

Her heart fluttered in her chest, stealing her breath. "You love me?"

"I know it's hard to believe since we haven't known each other all that long, but I don't need more time to know what I know."

"Wow." She searched his face, unable to stop a grin from spreading across her lips. "I'm pretty sure I don't need more time, either." She didn't. Standing there in his arms was where she belonged, and she couldn't picture herself anyplace else. "I'll stay."

"Yes," he yelled toward the heavens and lifted her off her feet, turning her in a circle before setting her down again.

She laughed, not remembering if or when she'd ever felt so happy. "I love you, Luke, and if you let me, I'll stay forever."

Forever in their town. Forever in his arms. Forever in love.

The End

LAWLESS

(Aspen Series #2)

CHAPTER ONE

Deputy Sheriff Milo Sykes's police radio crackled to life. "All units respond to a reported 10-71 at Mt. Uintah Medical Center. Suspect is at large and considered armed with possible multiple weapons. Four wounded. Suspect is wearing a camouflage t-shirt and brown pants."

Milo's pulse paused as his brain digested the information. "Shit." He grabbed his radio. "2A12 responding to 10-71."

With a quick swipe, he gathered the driver's license and registration sitting on the clipboard on his lap and exited his SUV. He sprinted to the older model Mustang he'd pulled over for speeding and dumped the identification on the driver's lap. "Drive safe, ma'am."

Within a couple of seconds, Milo was back in his vehicle, lights blazing and sirens blaring as he headed the three miles back to Pinewood.

When he arrived on scene, the late-afternoon August sun bore down on two identical Chevy Tahoes that blockaded the entrance to the small two-story medical center that serviced the entire county. Another pair of SUVs blocked the staff entrance. There was no other way out. He scanned the area, not seeing anyone except the two officers in front of him squatting on the ground, peering through the sights on their shotguns.

Milo pulled up behind them and cut his sirens. He scanned the area, following the direction of the other officers' weapons. His heart pounded as he ducked out of his car and crept toward his two comrades. "What the hell is going on? We have a sniper?" The rural county hadn't experienced anything that dangerous in decades...if ever.

Charlie Adams kept his eye glued to the scope on his rifle. "We've got a gunman hunkered down behind the sand pile on the south side of the parking lot. Witnesses say he's shot one EMT and wounded three other civilians. Sheriff Williams is in contact via cell phone with one of the vics. Reports are the EMT is unconscious and bleeding severely. The others are wounded, but conscious and stable."

Deputy Eric Larsen removed his sights from his gun long enough to eye Milo. "Karen Jensen is the wounded EMT."

Milo jerked as though Eric's punch had been physical. "Not Karen." He and his cousin Karen had grown up together. They'd made mud pies as kids, gotten sick off a stolen cigarette when they'd been ten, and nearly burned down their town with illegal fireworks as teenagers. She couldn't die. She had two kids of her own that she'd only half raised. "What's the plan?"

"Sheriff Williams should be here any moment. We're keeping the gunman contained until he arrives."

"While Karen bleeds out?" Sheriff Williams was an exceptional peace officer, but that was a dumb ass plan.

"It's not like we have a SWAT team and air patrol," Charlie answered.

Milo peeked over the hood of the vehicle. A shot pinged not five inches from his head. "Son of a *bitch.*"

"Keep your head down," Eric responded. "The guy is an expert marksman. Must have some military training or something."

Yeah? He wasn't the only one. "Anyone else on scene, yet?"

"Nope." Charlie cracked his neck before refocusing on the sniper.

Enough time had been wasted. "I'm going to try to draw his fire away from the victims. Maybe that will distract him enough someone can help Karen. If I get a shot, I'm taking the asshole down."

"Kick some ass, bro," Charlie said as Milo slipped around the edge of the vehicle.

More shots exploded around him as he made his way along the row of cars. He had to wonder if he was the idiot, not Williams. But Karen's life was the prize, and with Milo's Army training, he was the most qualified out of all of Williams' men to take out the perp.

Milo reached the last vehicle on the row. Nothing between him and the ruthless marksman but 100 yards and a yellow VW bug. A bullet ricocheted off the metal next to him. The bastard was good. He'd give him that.

He followed the ritual he'd perfected in Afghanistan and took a second to clear his thoughts. Pinewood's summer-long heat wave had expanded into fall, and the glaring sun cooked his shoulders. A trickle of sweat ran down the back of his neck, but a cool composure blanketed his emotions. Years of training with the military and then the U.S. Marshals had forged him into a cool piece of machinery. Many accused him of wasting his talents on a rural county sheriff's department, but this was where he wanted to be.

The brilliant sun was good though. He'd taken up this position instead of moving around to the back of the hospital because, although he was more exposed, the bright glare would handicap his opponent.

He checked his weapon. Ready.

Milo changed his stance, lifting slightly. A bullet shattered the VW's front windshield and rear passenger window. Perfect. Having no glass would make his shot easier.

He positioned his rifle, ignoring the pinging of bullets around him as he sighted his subject through his high-powered scope. The man, somewhere in his late thirties, sported a head of unkempt bushy brown hair and a full beard. "Sheriff's Department. Drop your weapon and come out with your hands up. If you don't, I will use deadly force," Milo yelled across the distance.

"Fuck you, pig." Another shower of bullets danced off the metal around him.

Couldn't the guy come up with something a little more original than "pig"? "Last chance," Milo answered. He'd barely gotten his words out when a red hot piece of lead burrowed into the flesh above his left elbow. "Awe, shit," he cursed under his breath. The last bullet he'd taken had cost him a night's stay in the hospital.

With renewed determination, he ignored the fire in his arm, sighted in the prick, and squeezed the trigger. The rifle kicked against his right armpit, barely registering in his consciousness.

The perpetrator jerked before dropping from sight.

Milo lowered his weapon and stealthily made his way back between the row of vehicles getting as close to the shooter as he could without giving up his cover. A limp hand extended beyond the edge of the small sand hill, but Milo kept his weapon ready. Adrenalized blood thrummed through his veins as he peeked around the corner. The sniper's body lay prone, his weapon a good eight inches from his body, a neat bullet hole just left of center in his forehead.

He pushed the button on his shoulder radio. "Target neutralized."

Milo slumped at a stool in Sparrow's Bar and Grill, doing his best to ignore the rocking country anthem playing over the sound system. At the moment, he couldn't care less about partying all night long. He'd already stuffed in two pieces of apple pie, compliments of the grateful citizens of Aspen for saving their quiet little county from the big, bad sniper. Other than that, his life had come to a screeching halt. Not a good thing for someone with a restless spirit.

"Dude, you should be celebrating. You're the hometown hero." Scott lifted his mug of beer in a toast.

Milo drew a finger through the condensation on his glass of soda. "I know, but it's hard to get excited about two weeks off work when I can't do anything but sit around." He needed his job, needed to be busy. He was a live-hard, play-hard kind of guy. The shooting had cost him a minimum of two weeks of administrative leave while internal affairs conducted an official investigation. The bullet hole in his arm along with the consequential drugs from said shooting, left him with very little to do. No mountain biking, no dancing, and certainly no drinking, at least for a few days. "I can't even enjoy a damn beer." He'd been on leave exactly 18 hours and was already bored out of his ever-loving mind.

He should be happy. The shot to his arm was barely more than a surface wound as far as he was concerned and had only cost him a couple of stitches. No blood transfusions. No days in the hospital. Sheriff Williams had given him quite the dressing down privately for not following protocol, but publicly he'd proclaimed him as a quick-thinking hero who'd saved many lives. Karen, along with the three other victims, was still in the hospital, but all were expected to make a full recovery.

"That's tough." Scott swiveled on his bar stool to watch the few couples who'd come out to dance on a Thursday night. "You can still fish, though, right?"

He did have that. "Doc said no activity, but I'm pretty sure fishing doesn't count." The river that ran through his property provided some of the best fly fishing in the region and had afforded him solace on many occasions.

"When are you going to show me that honey-hole you keep talking about?"

"Never." Milo laughed. "A man does not share his honey-hole."

Scott gave him a sideways glare. "I think you're making it up anyway."

The vibrating phone in Milo's pocket saved Scott from his smart-ass remark. He pulled it out, surprised to see the name Quinn Crawford on the screen. Although they'd been close during their years together in the Army and the U.S. Marshal's Service, he'd only talked to his friend a handful of times since he'd left the service three years ago.

Milo pressed the answer button. "Quinn?"

"Milo, buddy. How have you been?"

He could barely hear his friend over the music. "Hang on a second." He looked at Scott. "Be right back."

He stepped out the door and into the early evening light, grateful for the quiet Aspen streets. He put the phone back to his ear. "I'm good, man." Except for the annoying bandage on his arm. "How are you?"

"Great. Sounds like you're a celebrity now."

The side of the brick building scraped his shirt as he leaned against it. "Heard about that, did ya?" Milo knew a couple of national networks had run a brief report on the standoff during the early morning news shows, but he'd expected the story to fade after twenty-four hours without much notice.

"I did, and I have to say it couldn't have come at a better time."

He drew his brows together. "How so?"

Quinn chuckled. "I'm about to make your loss my gain. I need a favor. I need to place a witness under your protection."

"A witness?" The proposal surprised him. "You know I'm no longer a marshal, Quinn."

"Exactly why I need you. This particular witness has been compromised four times already, and I'm starting to suspect our organization has somehow been infiltrated. She's a high profile witness in the

Trasatti trial, and I need to keep her safe for another four weeks."

"John Trasatti, the mobster?" He'd guess that pretty much anyone who'd turned on a TV during the past year had heard about the arrests of several members of the infamous crime family. It had been a sweet coup for the Chicago Police Department. "You think they have someone on the inside? That's hard to believe." The Marshal's Service prided itself on its flawless protection record.

"They want her pretty bad."

"Her?"

Another long silence crawled across the phone line. "The witness is Trasatti's daughter."

Milo whistled. "She's turned on her family? Wow. That had to take guts. She may never be able to show her face in public again."

"Yeah. She definitely has...uh...tenacity. Not to mention, her testimony is vital to bringing down several key players. Chicago PD has the granddaddy by the balls, but, with what she's giving them, the DA will be able to cripple the organization so badly, they'll never stand again."

Milo wondered if the girl knew exactly what she was getting herself into. She'd grown up with the mob, so she had to know they'd use whatever means necessary to seek her out and destroy her. The Trasatti organization was worth millions of dollars. Even if the grandfather sat rotting in jail, the rest would never go down without a fight.

"Okay, let's say I'll consider helping you. I still have a day job." Even though he was currently cooling his heels. "Also, the higher-ups are not going to be too keen on you using someone they now consider an outsider."

"Milo." Quinn used a cajoling tone. "These aren't things you need to worry about. You know me. I've already spoken with Sheriff Williams. He said you'll be down at least two weeks healing and waiting to be cleared for work again. Good ol' Bill also said he'd be more than happy to extend your time off if needed."

"Good ol' Bill? Since when have you been on first-name terms with my boss?"

Quinn chuckled. "Like I said, you know me, Milo. I need someone extremely discreet that could shoot the balls off a chipmunk from two hundred yards away, and you're that man."

It was Milo's turn to laugh. "Damn, you make me sound good."

"You are good, and I need you. What do you say? Can you meet me in Salt Lake to take custody of her?"

He sighed. "Why the hell not."

Back inside, he dropped a five on the bar for a tip. "I'm outta here," he told Scott. "Looks like I've found me some entertainment for a few days."

"Must have been a good phone call. What's up?"

"I'm headed to Vegas. An old friend is getting hitched, and he just invited me to attend." At least the old friend part was true, and if Scott and his other buddies expected him to be out of town, it would give him a chance to get this woman hidden before anyone started nosing around. "It sounded like a good excuse for a wild weekend, and it's not like I'm doing anything else." He glanced at his bandage. "Well, semi-wild weekend."

Milo woke with a start and automatically reached for the Glock he kept on the nightstand. He had his hand wrapped around the butt of the sidearm before he remembered he was in a hotel room on the outskirts of Salt Lake, and the noises that had woken him were from other guests. He'd honed his knee-jerk reaction from his days in the military, and sometimes when he wasn't quite coherent, his old training automatically kicked in.

He flopped back on the bed, hot and sweaty. The temperature had registered 95 degrees when he'd driven into town late yesterday afternoon, and it hadn't cooled one bit.

He glanced at the clock. Five minutes to six. Quinn and the woman would be touching down in another hour. If he got up now, he'd have time to gas up, grab some snacks for the way home, and eat a decent breakfast before he was supposed to meet them.

As he showered and dressed, he couldn't shake the strong feeling that agreeing to help had been a mistake. Sure, he and Quinn were friends, but he'd left the Marshal's Service because he didn't want that kind of stress and pressure in his life. Now here he was, right back in the thick of things. Maybe, deep down, he really hadn't shaken that underlying need to make up for what had happened three years ago.

Sixty minutes later, Milo pulled into a secluded neighborhood park in a suburb of Salt Lake, not surprised to find it deserted except for a man and a woman. He recognized Quinn immediately. Brown hair, muscular build. He sat on a shady bench facing away from Milo. Next to him was a woman wearing a white ball cap, her dark ponytail sticking out the hole in the back of her hat.

Milo exited his truck, a hot wind blowing in his face. Quinn caught his eye before he had taken two steps toward them. Always the alert one. That's part of what made his friend so good at his job.

As Milo drew closer, he could hear the woman speaking.

"...ridiculous. I don't understand why I can't stay here close to the city. This place is out of the way. No one will find me here. And it's not so far from civilization that I feel like I might suffocate."

"You know the mob is everywhere, Ariana. Your family might not have direct connections with anyone here, but word gets out."

Milo paused a few feet from their bench to allow them to finish their conversation before he interrupted.

Ariana slumped her shoulders. "I'm so tired of this game. Why can't I testify now, give a deposition or something and be done with it? If I'd have known what this entailed and how drawn out it would be, I might have made a different decision."

If first impressions were correct, it appeared Milo might have a spoiled diva on his hands. If so, he'd be giving Quinn hell later for not mentioning that part of the deal.

"You made the right choice. You only have to tough it out for one more month."

"This isn't right. It seems I'm being incarcerated along with my father. When this is over, I expect you to send me somewhere warm and tropical. Hawaii. San Juan. Somewhere far away that has a pulse, with perhaps a library and a university nearby. These nowhere towns are stifling."

Milo took a step forward, but stopped when she continued speaking.

"I don't understand why you think this small town cop can protect me better than anyone else has. You haven't been able to keep me off the radar so far. How is some backwoods deputy going to be a match against the Trasatti men?"

Quinn cleared his throat and looked over his shoulder at Milo. "Ariana Trasatti, I'd like you to meet Milo Sykes. Milo, this is Miss Trasatti."

The smart-ass remark Milo had poised on the tip of his tongue evaporated when the woman turned. The unusual color of her eyes fell somewhere between green and blue and completely captivated him. She blinked a couple of times, her long lashes fluttering as her mouth turned downward into a frown. She tossed a nasty look at Quinn. "You knew he was behind me, didn't you?"

CHAPTER TWO

Quinn had been a constant thorn in Ariana's side from the moment he'd been assigned to her case. Of course she was grateful he'd done his best to keep her safe, and yes, she wasn't the easiest person to protect, but it was the snarky little things he did like letting her make an ass out of herself in front of Deputy Sykes that got under her skin. He obviously enjoyed one-upping her every chance he got. That was fine. Anything that challenged her these days was a godsend.

The small-town deputy certainly was not what she'd expected. She'd pictured him older, maybe overweight, with definitely a lazy expression on his face, not this blond Viking god with eyes the color of the Mediterranean Sea. If he wasn't wearing cowboy boots, she'd wonder if he was a mirage she'd conjured from spending too much time in the heat.

Ariana stood, tilting her head upward to meet his gaze as she extended her hand. "Deputy Sykes."

He smiled and grasped her hand, his eyes twinkling. Confidence radiated from his self-assured stance, and he didn't seem insulted at all by her unflattering remark. In fact, he seemed somewhat entertained by it.

"Miss Trasatti." The firmness of his grip along with the intelligence in his startlingly blue eyes set her on edge.

Quinn stood and shook Milo's hand as well. "Good to see you, buddy. You're looking fit. Except that little band-aid on your arm."

Indeed, he was. Ariana took advantage of their focus on each other to give the deputy a closer inspection. She wondered about the white bandage circling his arm, but said nothing.

The curve of Milo's grin showed obvious affection for his friend. "I could say the same. Life seems to be treating you well. Settled down yet?"

The dark-haired marshal shook his head, giving his friend a half-cocked smile. "Never. I've managed to elude that distraction this long. I think I'm safe."

Milo's brows shot upward. "Yeah, but you're so afraid of falling in love that you avoid the ladies. Think of all the fun you're missing." His gaze slid to Ariana's. They connected for the briefest of seconds, but it had been long enough to stir her blood and send her mind wandering.

She wanted to ask him if his look had been a warning or an invitation. Perhaps the look had been an unconscious view into his thoughts. Or maybe it had been nothing more than a coincidence that he'd glanced at her the moment he'd uttered those words.

It was also possible that utter boredom might have short-circuited her brain, causing her to imagine sexual encounters with the handsome deputy.

"How about you, Milo? I don't see a ring on your finger." Quinn threw the challenge back in his friend's face.

"Too busy having fun." Again, he looked at her.

"What?" She couldn't let the glance go unanswered this time. "Why do you keep looking at me?"

Milo kept his face expressionless as he studied her. Not a lifted brow, smile or frown to give away what he was thinking. "I'm just wondering how much trouble you're going to cause me with the ladies if I take you home...to keep you hidden, that is."

Again with the sexual innuendos. Both he and Quinn regarded her with interested looks. "I'll try to stay out of your way. Wouldn't want to damage that ladies' man reputation you seem so fond of."

Both of the men had the sense to appear chastised.

The smile dropped from Milo's face. "I apologize, Miss Trasatti. That remark was out of line. This is a business meeting. I'll try to remember that."

Quinn agreed. "I'm sorry, too. I've been around you enough I guess I got too comfortable, and I shouldn't have." He nodded at Milo. "And this guy has the tendency to bring out the worst in me." They exchanged quick grins.

Their apologies took her by surprise. She hadn't had her feelings recognized or valued by a man her entire life. The men in her family received respect. The women were there solely to serve and to please... at least while the men were around.

Since her first boyfriend, Danny, had been murdered eight years ago just after her sixteenth birthday, she'd spent very little of her social time around men. Her separation from boys during the first couple of years had been forced. Her father would not tolerate anyone of the male species touching his daughter again. After that, she'd avoided male relationships, partly out of fear of her father, and partly because she couldn't bear to lose someone else she loved.

She blinked, trying to process her emotions in a rational way. "No harm done." She took hold of her suitcase that rested next to the park bench. The nondescript black fabric bag contained everything she could now claim in her life. "Which way is your car?" The sooner this month ended, the better.

"Would you like me to get that for you?" Quinn asked.

"I can manage."

Milo took the suitcase from her hand, giving her a second surprise that morning. "Sorry, but my momma taught me how to treat a lady." He headed off toward the parking lot, acting as though her suitcase weighed nothing.

Ariana glanced at Quinn. He smiled and shrugged. "Milo will take good care of you. I promise. I feel safer leaving you with him than with anyone else in the world. He's a good man. Don't forget to keep your head down. Remember the rules."

She wanted to give him a snarky "yes, sir", but she knew he had her best interests at heart. "I will."

"One month, okay? You can do this."

For a quick moment, she wanted to cry. She wasn't sure what had brought on that unwanted emotion, but she didn't like it. She'd been taught from day one weakness would not be tolerated. Not from a Trasatti.

She pulled her sunglasses from her purse and slipped them on, using the opportunity to also don her mask of indifference. "You know me, Quinn. I'll survive."

"I know you will." He gave her hand a squeeze as they walked toward Milo's truck.

Milo opened the passenger door as she approached, and her nerves clutched her stomach, leaving her feeling sick.

"Your carriage, milady." Milo offered a gallant gesture indicating she should enter. She climbed into the vehicle that would whisk her away to the next unknown segment of her life.

"I won't be in constant contact like I've been before." Quinn told her. "I want it to appear as if you've vanished. This may be the only way to keep you safe." He tucked a small cell phone into her hand. "This can't be traced to either of us. Use it only in an emergency." His usual confident expression gave way to worry as he leaned in and hugged her.

"Okay." She worked to keep her voice steady. "Thanks for everything, Quinn. I appreciate it." Guilt soaked into her thoughts, making her wish she hadn't made his life harder than it had to be. He really had done his best protecting her.

He softly punched her arm. "See you in a month. Until then, I'll start working on that permanent exotic locale you've been requesting."

She blew out a breath weighted with anxiety. "Deal."

If only she could call her best friend and vent about her messed up life. One tiny call. Five minutes speaking with Kenzie could possibly save her sanity. Too many disturbing scenarios continually flooded her brain, and she couldn't help wondering about what had transpired back home after she'd agreed to work with the police. If she could just get a little news from Kenzie, she'd be able to relax. But phone calls, contact of any kind was strictly forbidden. Quinn had drilled that mantra into her head a thousand times over.

Searing acid burned Manny Mincione's stomach as he made his way into the visiting room of the Cook County Jail. The air in the old building smelled like petrified urine, like it was never circulated. Like it was doing time with the rest of the inmates.

The feel of the whole building gave him the creeps. It was cursed. From what he'd heard, there weren't many guys who'd entered that left as whole as the day they'd came in. It wasn't like the juvie hall or local holding cells where he'd burned a fair amount of time. Hell, those had given him some valuable networking opportunities. Not this place. This place was purgatory as far as he was concerned.

John Trasatti had now spent eleven months residing in said hell. This was the first time his boss had summoned him. Half of Manny was insulted the mob boss didn't ask for him sooner. But the other half, the smart half, knew what would happen if he couldn't get the job done.

With his heart sloshing in sickening thumps, Manny slid into the visitor's chair. A few minutes later, the devil planted himself on the other side of the filthy glass. The prison garb that replaced Mr. Trasatti's fancy, fine suits only made him look more ruthless.

Manny picked up the phone. "Hey boss." He tried to sound cheerful as though they were meeting in a park on a Sunday afternoon to talk football or something.

Trasatti's face remained stone cold. Still as a dead man's. His glittering black eyes bored into Manny's as though he could rip out his soul through his sockets. "Words cannot express how disappointed I am, Manny."

Manny glanced at his hands, clasping his scar-encrusted fingers together to keep him from shaking. "I know, boss."

"Were my expectations unclear?"

"No, boss." Poor Sal and Johnnie Boy had known what was at stake.

"You're different, though. Right, Manny? I've treated you like family. Let you close to my own family."

"I know, Mr. Trasatti, sir. I appreciate the opportunities you've given me." It was true. He'd been counted as a family member on more than one occasion. Practically grew up with Paulie and had reported on Ariana through the years until she turned traitor. She'd never seemed that dense, but she had to know she couldn't be allowed to live. Not after what she'd done. Rules were the only things that kept their world operating in a civilized manner.

He dared a glance into the death-filled eyes. "I'm going to fix this for you, boss. I am."

"You are aware of the consequences."

Manny swallowed and nodded. From this point forward, it was him or Ariana, and as pretty as Miss Trasatti was, she didn't deserve life more than he did. "I'll handle things, boss. Don't you worry."

⌒

Milo didn't quite know what to make of his charge. As they entered another pine-filled canyon on their way to Aspen, he glanced at Ariana. She'd checked out over two hours ago, her head resting against the seat, her mouth slightly parted. It appeared she preferred to sleep than to converse with him in the confined vehicle.

The next four weeks should prove interesting. The Trasatti organization's case had intrigued him from the moment the story had broken. Long-lost evidence had surfaced after many years. Evidence that took out the head of the family. That had been the first chink in the Trasatti's armor. It couldn't be as painful as this crack, though. For many mobsters, family was everything. To have one turn traitor was an unforgivable sin. It was no wonder they'd relentlessly tried to track her.

Ariana muttered in her sleep, followed by an almost pained whimper. She jerked and then sat upright. He twisted his gaze to the windshield before she could catch him watching her. After a moment, he glanced back as though it was the first time he'd looked at her. "I'd say good morning, but it's closer to afternoon. We should hit town in about fifteen minutes."

She removed her sunglasses and fussed with her eyes. "I shouldn't sleep with my contacts in."

"Everything okay?"

She looked at him with a startled glance. "Yes. Why?"

He shrugged. He wasn't about to ask about her bad dream if she didn't want to discuss it. "No reason." He pressed on the accelerator, gaining speed to pass a slower moving vehicle. "We need to talk about your identity before we get to Aspen."

"What do you mean?"

"We need to figure out what name you're going to use. Give you some kind of a background in case you come in contact with the locals, even though I don't expect that to happen. We want you deep undercover."

She frowned. "The program is supposed to provide that. Name, identity, the whole thing."

"Didn't Quinn tell you? You're not exactly in the program at the moment."

She stared at him, then blinked. "What do you mean?" Her eyes flicked from window to window as though she were now seeing things through a different perspective.

Milo cursed. "I can't believe Quinn didn't fill you in. I used to be a U.S. Marshal, but I left three years ago. He called in a personal favor, asking me to keep you safe, but not within the confines of the program."

"But that's how I stay safe. I've read about the program. They've never lost a person who's followed the rules. Quinn pounded that into my head every single time I spoke with him. Now he's the one deviating?"

"After the number of times your identity has been compromised, he's concerned there might be a marshal who's gone rogue. He can't prove anything yet, but he's afraid to keep you in the system."

She widened her eyes and slumped in her seat. "You're kidding me."

"He's really going out on a limb for you. This is completely against protocol. If anyone finds out what he's done, he could lose his job. He plans on reporting you as AWOL."

"Then I'm not guaranteed safety."

"That's what I'm here for, darlin'." He smiled for her benefit, but he could clearly see the image of the last woman he'd protected. She really had broken the rules, and it had cost her dearly. The moment he'd lifted the sheet to identify the body remained etched in his mind forever. "Don't worry. I'll protect you with my life. Along with my previous marshal training, I served in a combat unit in Afghanistan, and as you know, I'm currently a deputy."

"Of a small town." Uncertainty colored her words.

"I don't want to brag, but you'd be hard-pressed to find a better shot than me." He didn't like having to defend his expertise.

"But you are bragging."

He sighed and glanced at her. "Because you're questioning my abilities."

"I want you to teach me to shoot like you do. I want to be able to protect myself."

He snorted. "I can teach you to shoot, but you're going to need years of practice if you want to come close to being the marksman I am."

She folded her arms. "Bragging again."

"I'm just telling it like it is."

She rolled her eyes and sighed. He knew his statement would get a reaction out of her. That's why he'd said it. He couldn't deny he'd like the chance to run his fingers along her skin and sample her soft lips, but she was a diva through and through. "Your perfume smells nice."

Confusion settled between her brows. "Thank you."

He loved turning the conversation on a dime. A tactic he'd found that kept people slightly off balance and left them more pliant. He sensed he'd need all his tools in order to survive the month.

"I think we'll call you Anna if necessary, although I'm not anticipating you coming into contact with anyone. It's a common name, but close enough to yours in case I screw up."

She shrugged. "What do I care? It's not like I'll have the opportunity to make friends here."

⌒⟶

Ariana watched out the window as the small strip of businesses in Aspen came into view and then disappeared just as quickly. She blinked, wondering what happened to the rest of the town. She'd seen flashes of potted chrysanthemums, the city hall, and a tiny huddle of stores. "Is that it?"

He laughed. "That's it. Now you can see why no one will find you here. Most don't know this town exists."

Oh God. This was worse than the last four places combined. She'd hoped she'd be assigned somewhere habitable, but this...this was a punishment. Perhaps one she deserved.

How would she ever survive?

It was another ten minutes until Milo turned off the main highway, and then a couple more minutes down a bumpy, unpaved road. Plumes of dust kicked up behind them, leaving the sights in her rearview mirror nothing but a brown, hazy cloud.

The little square house sat at the end of the road like a disappointment. Shade from a huge honey locust tree speckled the white-washed building and the surrounding lawn. A rickety wooden fence separated his home from green pastures. Out in the field, several cows grazed.

Milo pulled his truck right up to the front of the house, next to a marked sheriff's SUV. No driveway.

No sparkling fountain surrounded by flowers and manicured lawns.

She tried to breathe through her frustration as he exited the vehicle. How had this happened? She was an educated, intelligent person, but her choices had backed her into corner that she hadn't seen coming.

Lord help her. She quite possibly had traded one version of hell for another.

Milo opened her door, and she turned her gaze in his direction, wishing she could plead for help. But she'd created this mess, and she had no choice but to see it through.

He narrowed his eyes. "Everything okay?"

"Of course." She wouldn't admit otherwise.

"You're pretty pale. Did the long drive get to you?"

"That must be it." The gravel driveway crunched when her heels hit the ground. She'd definitely be packing these shoes away for the duration and searching out something more durable. Fancy and fashionable would be eaten alive in this place.

She filled her lungs with air so fresh it stung as she took in her surroundings. There wasn't a house or car to be seen. "You're really isolated out here."

He looked around and smiled. "I like it this way."

"Don't you ever feel like you're going to be swallowed by the nothingness?"

"I don't know what you mean by nothingness. I look around and see everything good in the world. Blue sky, green grass, beauty as far as the eye can see. No smog. No noise pollution. How could anyone really miss those things?"

She looked skyward and let her gaze trickle down, trying to see the world through his eyes. She liked to have her space. Just not this much space. "I guess you're right." She faked a smile. She assumed he took her gesture as genuine because he nodded and led the way into his house as though they were checking into the Four Seasons.

The sight of a gorgeous brown leather couch, complete with turquoise throw pillows and a creamy white throw folded on the edge stopped her in her tracks. An exquisite woven rug covered a gleaming wood floor and provided a backdrop for a beautifully handcrafted wooden table.

"Wow." He had oil paintings and candles, even floral arrangements. "I was expecting more of a bachelor pad." The room was a little smaller, but his furnishings could rival her family's.

He stopped his descent down the hallway with her suitcase and grinned. "Didn't you know? What you see isn't always what you get."

"You did all this?" Deputy Sykes puzzled her.

His lips turned to a sheepish grin, and he shrugged. "Okay, I confess. My last girlfriend was an interior decorator who liked spending my money."

The reminder of his all-important girlfriends, past and previous, stoked her unhappiness. She narrowed her gaze. "That makes much more sense."

He seemed offended. "Hey, I paid for it and let her do it. I should get some credit."

"Of course." She strode toward him. "Take all the credit you wish," she said as she stopped directly in front of him. "Makes no difference to me." She glanced between what appeared to be two bedrooms at the end of the hall. "Which room is mine?"

CHAPTER THREE

Ariana spent the next hour in her room unpacking and changing into a tank top and jeans that seemed more apropos for this little country town. Her room was also fashionably furnished. A warm green comforter accented the contemporary walnut headboard and dresser. She fell in love with it at first sight. Whoever this girl was that had stolen Milo's heart had impeccable taste.

Which was just fine with her. Deputy Sykes could have all the girlfriends he wanted. She didn't care. In fact, she should be more concerned that she'd been so preoccupied with this unknown woman. It had to be the stress of relocating again and, of course, the impending trial. She sighed. The thought of facing her father in a court of law sickened her. She couldn't let her thoughts go there. Not right now.

She glanced at the cell phone she'd placed on the dresser. It beckoned her. Quinn had given it to her for emergencies. Would he consider the loss of her sanity an emergency? It was a simple, little pay-as-you-go phone. There was no way the mob would be able to trace it. She climbed off her bed and picked it up. Her fingers danced over Kenzie's number. It would be so simple. If she kept the call short, what could it hurt?

She groaned in frustration as she opened a dresser drawer and tossed the temptation inside.

She needed to leave her room and face Milo. As it was, she'd already tempted fate too many times. The sexy deputy could distract her before she made another mistake.

Ariana found him asleep on the couch. He looked peaceful as he lay there, his crossed arms lifting with each breath he took. She missed the animated sparks that now hid behind his closed lids. An urge surfaced, and she resisted smoothing a lock of rumpled blond hair from his forehead. She wished she could know that kind of tranquility in her life. It didn't seem to matter if she was awake or asleep, her past continually haunted her. She prayed that would change when they locked her father behind iron bars.

She made as much noise as she could as she plopped down in an adjacent beige wingback chair. Milo didn't budge. His chest rose and fell as though he was in a deep, relaxed state. A tendril of fear wound through her stomach and chest. The hit men her father employed had surely been sent to find her. The Feds had a pretty good case against him without her testimony, but she would be the one to put the irremovable nail in his coffin.

The threat against her life was a certainty, and although she doubted they'd find her in Aspen, the man sleeping on the couch was her only protection. At the moment, he wasn't inspiring her confidence. She shifted in her seat and emitted a loud sigh.

Still no movement. What kind of protection was this?

Maybe she needed to go into hiding on her own. If only she had a way to obtain some kind of identification and money. Of course, she knew people who could procure things like that, but they were all associated with her family. Family and friends from a past she could no longer claim.

She was well and truly on her own. Not to mention vulnerable.

She lifted a travel book about Scotland from the coffee table and set it back down with a thud. Nothing.

"Something you need?"

His voice startled her, and she squeaked. She eyed him, surprised that he still appeared to be in a deep slumber. "I thought you were asleep."

He lifted a lid, exposing one ice blue eye. "I already mentioned, appearances aren't always what they seem."

She adopted a nonchalant attitude, hoping he wouldn't notice her pulse slamming against her throat. "I suppose they're not."

"You forget, I spent time in the army. Sometimes the only sleep we got was ten minutes at a time on the side of the road in the middle of the day. I learned how to make the most of it."

She nodded, feeling the idiot. "I can't imagine what that must have been like. Thank you for your service to our country."

He regarded her with a studious gaze as though sizing her up and then nodded.

She glanced about the room, not comfortable with him watching her. "I'm wondering what there is to do around here."

He sat up and stretched his arms above his head. She watched, fascinated as his triceps bulged outward. The white bandage that circled his left arm expanded with his movements.

"What happened to your arm?"

He glanced at it and snorted. "By-product of the job."

"How do you mean? What happened?"

"Got shot during a standoff. The guy had already wounded several people."

She widened her eyes. He spoke of it like being shot was nothing. "I thought you were this expert marksman."

"I said I was good, not perfect." He eyed her with a serious look. "However, if you're concerned about my abilities, don't ask him."

"Why not?"

"He's dead."

She sucked in a breath, trying to shake off an impending shiver. "Do you always take killing this lightly?" She didn't want his attitude about murder to be the same as her father's.

A pained look shot across his expression before he transformed it into a blank mask. "Of course not. The men I killed while I was in the army haunted me for months. The man I shot the other day was the first person I had to take out while serving in this capacity." His voice cracked on the last syllable. He cleared his throat. "No one ever goes into those situations wanting to take a life. But he wouldn't surrender peacefully, and I couldn't allow him to hurt another citizen that I've sworn to protect. The situation is under investigation as we speak, but Sheriff Williams is telling me they think he wanted to die. Suicide by cop."

She nodded. She'd spent several hours hiding in a dark warehouse in Chicago, consoling Danny because his uncle had done something similar. He'd double crossed her father and death-by-cop had been a more humane way to die than what her father would do to him. "I'm sorry. That was unfair of me to suggest you took it lightly." She couldn't keep comparing every man she met to the thugs who had pervaded her younger years.

Milo stood. "Speaking of shooting, I'm pretty sure I still have some old coffee cans in the shed that would be perfect targets. We can work on your shooting skills if you'd like." He seemed to have reburied the distress she'd brought up.

Her spirits lightened as well. "Okay." If she was ever going to feel safe in this life, she'd need to know how to protect herself, and she'd always been intrigued by the different weapons her father's men had carried. The one time she'd handled a revolver her father had stashed in his desk, she'd been backhanded so hard she'd tumbled across the floor, horrified to find blood dripping from her lip. But that world was no longer her world, and in her new life, she could shoot if she pleased.

Milo made them both a couple of roast beef sandwiches before they headed outside. They were heavy on the meat and light on veggies, but hers tasted surprisingly good. He was definitely right on the fact that appearances weren't what they seemed. So far, he'd proved to be quite enigmatic and interesting.

When he retrieved his gun holster and strapped it around his waist, a silent thrill rushed through her. He looked damn good sporting a pistol. She watched with fascination as he checked his weapon.

Under the circumstances she'd had growing up, she should hate weapons, but she was smart enough to recognize it wasn't the gun that killed people. It was the person standing behind it. She also couldn't deny that guns meant power. That was something she'd inherited from her family whether she liked it or not—she enjoyed power. Not that she was proud of that fact.

With a jerk of his head, he indicated she should follow him out the kitchen door.

The sun had crept to the west side of the house by the time they headed outside, leaving the sprawling backyard shaded. A sweet-scented breeze tickled her skin. She folded her arms and waited near a swing on the back porch while he crossed the yard and entered a small wooden building. The sound of metal banging and things being shuffled around drifted from inside the structure.

She glanced about his yard. No signs of a woman's touch out here. It had an untamed or old-fashioned feel to it. No landscaping. The grass was mowed, but wild pink roses grew up and over the surrounding wood fence while tall grass clung to the posts. An old hammock strung between two tall shade trees beckoned to her. The tool shed commandeered one corner and a large pine sat squat in the other. To the far left, a vegetable garden overflowed with ripe tomatoes and peppers. She couldn't really picture Milo spending his time gardening, but then again, there were many things about him that didn't fit with the descriptive labels she'd given him.

He emerged from the shed, a cocky grin curving his lips, a stack of old coffee cans in his hands. "Got 'em."

Good Lord. The image of him standing with his gun slung low on his hips, his t-shirt outlining every glorious curve of his chest, and his blue eyes lit with excitement would remain seared on her retinas for a long time to come. A shiver of attraction rolled through her as she stepped off the porch and walked toward him. "Great." She had no idea what to do with the pistol or with the unwanted attraction that had sprung up like the wildflowers growing up the fence.

Milo balanced all five cans on separate posts of the fence and then stood in the middle of his yard. "Come here."

She moistened her lips, swallowing an intense thread of excitement as she joined him. When she stopped, he moved closer, removing the remaining space between them. He slid his gun out of the holster and displayed it in front of her. "I'm sure I don't need to tell you that handling a weapon is serious business."

A wicked bit of heat rushed to her cheeks. He was not talking about *that* weapon, though handling it *would* be serious business, indeed. She cleared her throat. Sex had been off her radar for a long time. It shouldn't be popping up now. "Yes, I know guns can kill."

He blinked, then nodded. "Of course you do. Have you ever fired a weapon?"

She shook her head.

"This is a 9mm handgun. It holds 15 rounds in each magazine." He wiggled a black clip before shoving it up inside the handle until it clicked.

"Okay."

He held out the weapon to her, and she took it. The pistol was lighter than she'd imagined. She wrapped her fingers around the butt of it, the gun fitting nicely in her hand. Her nerves stretched taut. She released a breathy smile. "What do I do?"

"Aim it at that first can."

She held the gun out from her, her hand shaking from anticipation. "Do I just shoot?"

"Squeeze the trigger."

She relaxed her stance, embarrassed that she was such a novice. She fired. The gun went off, kicking back against her hand. Not one of the cans moved as the bullet sailed into the green pasture.

Milo laughed and approached her from behind. "Let me give you a few tips." He moved in close, energy radiating off his chest into her back. "Hold out the gun." He lifted her right arm, the weapon aimed toward the cans. "Now take your left hand and support your right hand along the wrist." He covered the outside of her hand and moved it toward the gun as he leaned over her shoulder. "See how that keeps you steadier?"

"Uh-huh." She was pretty sure she was anything but steady at the moment. If he were to back away, she would fall to the ground. She tried to inhale a calming breath, but that only forced her closer to him. The crisp, woodsy scent of his cologne teased her senses, increasing her attraction to him.

He let go of her wrist and trailed his fingers across the back of her neck, tugging her hair out of his way. She froze as shiver after shiver radiated down her body.

"Your hair smells nice." His nose bumped her head as he took another long whiff and exhaled an appreciative sigh.

"Thanks."

He lifted her arms, reminding her that she'd let them droop. "Many people choose to turn their head to the side and close one eye to help them sight in their target. You probably have one side that is more dominant over the other, so try practicing with different eyes shut and see how you do."

As she adjusted her aim using only one eye, he released her hands, dropping his to her waist as though to hold her steady, still watching over her shoulder. Her gaze blurred, and she blinked. She couldn't think, let alone shoot with him that close.

She focused again, letting out a slow breath. The can sat dead center in her gaze. Just as she pulled the trigger Milo's breath caressed her ear. Her shot went wide, sending splinters flying from the side of the small wooden building. "Shit."

He laughed. "I think you just killed my shed."

"It's your fault." She turned, and he tipped the point of the gun downward, making her feel even worse.

"How's it my fault?" Merriment danced in his eyes.

"I can't keep my concentration with you that close."

Interested brows rose over his blue eyes. "Oh, really?"

She clamped her lips shut, not happy that she'd given herself away. But she couldn't keep them closed. She needed to give him a piece of her mind. "You did that on purpose."

"I don't know what you're talking about."

She studied him for a moment, staring deep into his so-called innocent expression. After a few seconds, a hint of a smile tugged at his lips, and she knew she'd won. "You are so busted. You blew in my ear on purpose, trying to distract me."

He held his hands up in mock surrender. "Okay. I'll admit it. You're just too cute not to tease."

Her heart jolted at his admission. He liked the way she looked. Shouldn't matter to her, but it did. She grinned. "You should take a step back, mister, and don't forget who's holding the gun here. Wouldn't want to distract me too much."

He moved backward a few steps, his face alight with amusement. "Absolutely, darlin'. You're in control now."

She snorted. The man was a master of sexual innuendos.

She turned, sighted in the first can one more time and fired. The coffee can flew in the air and landed on the other side of the fence. "Woo!" She turned with an excited smile, and again he tipped the gun toward the ground. "Sorry." She tried to look chastised, but she'd actually hit her target.

Her grin resurfaced as she focused on the second can. She fired. "Crap," she mumbled under her breath. She fired again, and the rusty can sailed high over the fence. Yes. The next two also took her a couple of times, but she hit the fifth one with her first attempt.

"Ha," she said as she glanced over her shoulder. "I can shoot."

He approached wearing a contagious grin. "You sure can." He took the gun from her and holstered it, before he continued toward the fence. He hopped it, his moves sure and strong. She knew he'd done it to impress her...and it had. He replaced the coffee cans and jumped the fence again, walking toward her, his gaze holding hers, with a smile that said he knew she couldn't help but watch.

He handed the gun to her, giving her a sexy, sideways glance. "Go again, hot shot."

She fired off several more rounds. Hitting some and missing more than she'd like. Each time she finished, he hopped the fence and then swaggered back to her with a sexy grin. Each time, increasing the heat building inside her. She wasn't quite sure what was going on between them, but she was definitely more entertained than she'd been in the previous places Quinn had placed her.

By the time she finished her tenth round, he called it quits. "I'm tired of playing fetch for you, darlin'. Let's call it a day."

"Really?" She frowned. "I was just getting good at it."

"You definitely have a shooter's eye."

"I don't need you to set up the cans. I can do that." She shrugged. It was no big deal. She'd just enjoyed watching his muscles flex as he jumped the fence. Having a man around to do her bidding had been rather pleasant, but she could do this for herself.

He walked closer, stopping just feet from her, tilting his head so he faced her dead on. Her pulse paused and then sprinted. He held her gaze as he reached between them. She shifted a nervous glance downward to see him working the buckle on his holster. She looked up, the happiness inside her flipping into a smile.

He removed his holster. He broke eye contact with her as he slid the leather strap around her waist, his fingers grazing the skin near her belly button. She was suddenly glad she hadn't changed out of her tank top like she'd planned. It was an innocent touch, but she liked the sizzle he left on her skin.

She'd done an excellent job in the years since Danny's death keeping men at arm's length. She'd convinced herself she didn't want or need a man's touch to be happy. She certainly didn't want to risk someone's life by falling in love. But this attraction and playfulness was kind of fun, and if her father knew, it would really piss him off.

She wasn't sure why flirting with Milo held such appeal for her. Deputy Sykes had something about him that had snuck over or around her protective emotional walls, and she wasn't certain she cared. She'd only known him a few hours, but he'd charmed her to the point she couldn't stop flirting with him.

She glanced at his face as he tightened the buckle around her. Light brown stubble scattered along his jawline, giving him a rugged, sexy look. A small scar dipped into one side of his top lip. Lips that were full and tempting, and really only inches from hers.

She sighed and moved her gaze to his eyes, surprised to find him watching her.

"Is this okay?"

More than okay. "The belt?"

"The tightness." He tugged on the leather around her waist. "It doesn't feel like it's going to fall off, does it?"

She gratefully escaped his vivid stare for a moment while she gave the belt a tug. "Feels great— fine," she stammered. "It's not going to fall off."

She glanced back, his intriguing orbs a point of distribution for the awareness that coursed through her body. He held her gaze as though he, too, knew they were communicating on more than one level. "Have at it then."

She stood frozen for a moment, really, really wanting to ask him if he meant what she thought he meant...but she couldn't. She turned, sensing his full gaze on her as she walked to the fence and climbed over. When she reached the other side, sure enough he still stood where she'd left him, his intense gaze watching her every move, a satisfied grin twisting his lips.

Lord help her.

CHAPTER FOUR

G ood God. He leaned back in the porch swing, trying to remind himself he was currently on duty and not entertaining a potential lover. He should be shot for his behavior around Ariana. She was *not* one of the local gals he loved to turn around the dance floor. She was a witness in a major organized crime trial. He was a sworn officer of the law, and even though he was no longer a part of the U.S. Marshals, he'd promised Quinn he'd protect her.

Not flirt with her. Not tease her until she smiled. And definitely not undress her with his eyes. He watched with utter interest as she climbed the wooden fence again, admiring the way her tight jeans showcased the curve of her ass as she straddled the fence. "Mmm-mmm." Then there was always the hope that she'd have her ass toward him as she bent to pick up a coffee can.

She turned to him, and he tried to keep his face as passive as possible. "Did you say something?" she called across the distance.

"No. About done?"

"I want to do a few more, if that's okay."

"Knock yourself out." And knock some sense into him, too. He would have her under his protection for the next month until she was scheduled to testify against her murdering mobster of a father. It would show a complete lack of professionalism if he was to start a personal relationship with her. If he was still with the Marshals, he could be fired for it.

Ariana bent over, giving him the perfect view. Damn. She stood and looked at him over her shoulder as though she'd known he was watching. He quickly glanced away, but he was more than a little certain she'd busted him.

Oh hell. Someone save him. Why couldn't she have been a fat old man?

He let her go another round, unable to look away while she seemingly taunted him. Then, he'd had enough. He waited until she retrieved the five cans, trying to ignore the fact she either gave him a nice view of her ass, or faced him, giving him a peek-a-boo glimpse of her cleavage as she bent over. If she looked, she'd find a bulge of heated desire in his pants.

She sauntered toward him, his gun swinging from her hips. She gave him a smile full of mischief.

Enough torture for one day. He'd reached his breaking point and needed to cool down.

He approached her and pulled his weapon from the holster, earning a surprised look from her. "Want me to show you how it's really done?" He turned and fired in rapid succession, sending all five cans popping from their posts in less than two seconds. He raised his brows, giving her a cocky grin as he re-holstered his gun before he turned and headed for the house.

"Show off," she called after him.

Okay, so she'd been teasing Milo. He deserved it. She had to do something to get even for the way he watched her. Ariana stopped on the porch, grinning as she took Milo's seat on the porch swing. The cushion was soft against her back, and the swing creaked and groaned as she rocked it.

The guy had been tossing sexual barbs at her from the moment they'd met. It was more than fair that she'd caused him to be just as heated as she was by the time he called the game. She wasn't a little schoolgirl who could be swept off her feet by a good-looking guy, even if she'd always dreamed about a hot cop who'd ride in and save her from her family. No. She would be the one who would extricate herself from her pathetic family. But if he wanted to engage in a war of wits while she passed her days, she was up for it. To her, there was nothing sexier than a challenge of the minds.

He might have out shot her that day, but only physically. She leaned forward and unbuckled the leather holster, slipping it from her waist. She held it in her lap, caressing the worn belt that had looked so good on him. It was obvious the soft piece of leather had spent many hours riding his hips. She found that infinitely sexy and nothing like the vile holsters her father's men wore.

She took a few moments to appreciate the quiet outdoors and then stood. Everything fun and interesting in her life now waited inside the door, and the flirting games had just begun.

Ariana woke with a start like she had every morning since she'd gone into hiding. She'd woken in far too many different beds during the last eleven months, and she wondered if she'd ever have a home again.

The previous night had been a disappointment. She rolled out of bed and straightened the bedding. After she'd returned inside, Milo had buried himself inside a ridiculously large book, something about honorable men. He hadn't surfaced until sometime after she'd given up thinking he might entertain her, and she'd gone to bed.

She glanced at her closet. She should probably toss on something to cover the skimpy pink tank top and short shorts she wore as pajamas, but there hadn't been room for a robe in her suitcase. The irritating sting of being annoyed the previous evening hadn't purged from her system yet, and she decided if her attire caused him some discomfort, the more the better.

She emerged from her bedroom to be seduced by the blessed smell of fresh brewed coffee. Her eyes drifted shut as she took a moment to inhale the lovely aroma. Having someone to look forward to seeing in the morning, someone to share a meal with…it was nice.

Living alone in different safe houses for the past few months had been difficult. It wasn't the same as a person who lived by themselves. They saw others during the day. She'd been *totally* isolated. She'd had no one to call, no one to talk to except Quinn, and he couldn't be available twenty-four seven. It was no wonder she'd had her weak moments.

She walked the rest of the way down the hall and into the small kitchen. She stopped, the smile slipping from her face.

Milo stood at the counter whisking ingredients in a silver bowl. Something in the room looked extremely good, and it wasn't the food he prepared. He wore no shirt, exposing a massive amount of tanned, muscled chest. The white bandage stood out on his tanned arm. His blue flannel pants rode low on his hips, and his blond locks stood out, as though he'd done nothing but run his fingers through his hair that morning.

She had to wonder if he'd had a similar plan to try and exact some vengeance for her relentless teasing the previous evening while they'd been shooting targets. If so, he scored some serious points.

Milo chose that moment to look up, the whisk slowing and then stopping as his gaze inched down her body. A point for her? Or two points for him, she wondered as her body reacted to his searing look. Perhaps she'd made a mistake offering up so much bare skin in an attempt to tease him.

"Morning," he said as their eyes met again. He gave a slight shake of his head and focused on the bowl in front of him.

"Morning." She approached, achingly aware of her attraction to him. "Can I help?"

He looked at her from the corner of his eye. "Sure. You can wash and cut up the strawberries in the fridge."

She padded to the other side of the sink, stealing several glances at him while his back was to her. A rogue thought snuck under her radar, daring her to run a finger across the firm skin of his back. She resisted, but it was no easy feat.

The potency of her thoughts surprised her. She'd never had a hard time steering clear of men. But one look at this small-town deputy, and she couldn't stop thinking about what it would be like to find herself in his arms.

It seemed her sanity would be the price of her time in isolation.

She couldn't help her thoughts, though. The man had a multitude of attractive qualities. It seemed he could cook a decent meal. He was funny as well as charming and wielded a pistol like a deadly extension of his body. And the twinkle in his blue eyes was enough to melt the coldest woman's heart. Yet, he was still single.

"Why aren't you married?" The words slipped out before she'd realized the implications of her question.

He glanced her over as though sizing her up. "I don't know. I guess I'm waiting for the right one to come along."

A quick flash of energy zipped through her. "Of course. I didn't mean to pry." She shouldn't have asked in the first place. She busied herself removing the package of strawberries from the fridge.

"Colander?" she asked as she stepped to the sink.

"In the cupboard above the stove." He bent over and removed a waffle iron from a cabinet.

She glanced between his rear end and the over-head cupboard as she opened it and stood on tip-toes, reaching for the silver strainer that was stacked on top of various mixing bowls. He had such an attractive build. For someone of Milo's stature, the colander would be a breeze to reach, but it was just out of her grasp. She slid the whole stack of bowls toward her, intending to remove them all to reach the colander, but he distracted her as he stood, and the stack tipped.

His bare arm brushed against hers as he made a quick move and caught the dishes before they tumbled down on her. He slid the bowls back in, removing the colander and holding it out to her.

He was so close, and all her attention centered on the spot where their bodies had touched. She tried to inhale, wondering if he'd somehow stolen the oxygen in the room. "Thank you," she whispered. She turned on the water, using the strawberries as a distraction.

They worked in silence for several minutes, him cooking the waffles and her slicing juicy red berries. When everything was complete, they carried their offerings to the table. Ariana poured two cups of coffee and sat. Milo joined her with a can of whipped cream in his hand.

She eyed the can and then him as he sat opposite her. "Whipped cream for breakfast?" she asked, unable to resist the tease.

"I like it." He raised a challenging brow.

She smiled as she lowered her gaze to the stack of golden brown waffles in front of her and slid one on to her plate. She topped it with strawberries. Flirting with him might be a dangerous pastime, but she couldn't resist the flush of adrenaline that flooded her veins every time they bantered.

"How come *you're* not married?" he asked.

The return volley of her question took her by surprise. The haunting memory of Danny's murder flared along with the too-familiar anguish that owned her heart. Eight years had passed, and she could still hear his voice crack as he begged her father for mercy. She forced herself to chew and swallow the bite of waffle she had in her mouth. She couldn't meet Milo's gaze. "Umm…I guess I haven't met the right person, either." She pushed a strawberry around her plate, wishing she could find a way to conquer her past so it wouldn't have the power to sneak up on her and send her straight back into her tortured hell.

"Hey." Milo reached across the table and covered her hand. "Are you okay?"

She tried to mask her emotions before she returned his gaze. "Of course. Why do you ask?"

"I don't know. You just seem off."

He studied her as though deciding whether or not to believe her, and she prayed he wouldn't see through her. The horrific pain of Danny's death was something she'd never shared with anyone, and she never intended to. She hadn't been able to save her sweetheart, but she'd never forget him and what he meant to her.

He was the first person who'd ever loved her.

She slid her hand from beneath Milo's and lifted her coffee cup. The hot liquid scalded her tongue and was a welcome relief from other pains.

A few uncomfortable minutes passed. She took several small bites, using the time to shove the powerful memories back to the bottom of her heart and compose her emotions.

"I hope the food is okay."

She smiled and immediately appreciated the fact her gesture had come easier than she'd thought. Being around Milo with his quick grin and flashing eyes helped. "It's wonderful."

"I'm going to head into town tomorrow. If there's anything you want, let me know."

Her gaze jumped to his. "Can I go?"

"No." He didn't hesitate one tiny second before he answered.

Her spirits plummeted again. "Why not?"

He softened his features. "You are in deep hiding, darlin'. No one should know you're here. After the last four times of having your cover compromised, I don't think we can be too careful."

She silently cursed herself. She'd dug this hole, and now she'd pay the price. "This is the smallest town I've ever been in. The last time anyone besides Quinn saw me, my hair was blond. I'm sure no one will notice or recognize me."

He studied her until the silence grew awkward.

"What?" she finally asked.

"Well, first of all, it's pretty hard to go unnoticed in a town where everyone knows everyone else and..." He paused for another moment and then smiled. "I'm trying to picture you blond and can't quite do it. Dark hair looks good on you."

She blew out a breath. "You're trying to change the subject before we're finished discussing it."

"Nope." He stood and picked up his plate. "There is no discussion. You're not going."

She gathered her dishes and followed him to the sink. She'd barely touched her food, but her appetite had vanished. "I'm going to go crazy if I can't leave this house."

He looked at her plate. "You didn't eat much."

She pushed past him and put her dishes in the sink before turning to him. "Please? Spending all this time being isolated is driving me insane."

He glanced down at their bodies as a grin tilted his lips, enhancing the outline of his scar. Ariana followed the direction of his gaze. Barely two inches separated them. Desperation had led her actions, and she'd gotten right up in his face without realizing it. If she completely filled her lungs, her breasts might touch his chest. She took a step back, conceding space.

He stepped toward her, and she knew in that moment she shouldn't have showed weakness. But she hadn't been able to help it. Being so close to him had a way of blurring her thoughts, and she needed a clear head right now. She wanted to take another step back, but she held her ground. "Maybe I could just ride along and stay in the car?"

He lifted his hand, and she froze as his fingers grazed the skin below her collarbone. He picked up a strand of hair, twining it around his finger. "I don't think so. No chances."

She snatched her hair away. "This is messed up. I shouldn't be the one being punished. I'm trying to do the right thing. My father and his men are the ones who deserve to be locked away until they go crazy, not me." When she stopped her rant long enough to take a breath, she realized she sounded a bit juvenile. "I'm sorry." She took several steps away from him now. "This has dragged on forever. I just need the trial to be over so I can have a life again."

He gave her a look full of compassion. "I know. I'm sorry. I can't imagine how difficult this must be for you."

She turned, not wanting him to see the tears that threatened to escape. "I'll be fine. It's almost over. I guess I needed to blow off some steam. I didn't mean to take it out on you."

He came up behind her and touched her bare arm. When she looked up at him, he removed his hand. "I thought maybe I'd take you fishing."

CHAPTER FIVE

Never in her life had Ariana done anything as outdoorsy as fish, and quite frankly, she couldn't understand the attraction of it at all. But, considering her circumstances, she wasn't going to forego an opportunity to escape her current prison.

Milo had sent her in to change into jeans. She came out to find him in the kitchen looking pretty damn hot in a ripped pair of faded jeans and a tight-fitting gray t-shirt sporting a wicked looking cross. A ball cap covered his blond hair. Two fishing poles waited by the back door while Milo stared intently at the small television resting on the counter.

As she stepped into the room, the screen flashed a picture of her father followed by another image of her with straight blond hair and large, dark sunglasses. The reporter told his audience the daughter of infamous mob boss John Trasatti had gone missing and the most recent reports indicate she might be a victim of foul play. "Oh my God."

Milo jerked his gaze toward Ariana and turned off the TV.

"Wait." She rushed forward. "I want to hear that."

Milo shook his head. "Don't let it concern you. Quinn said this would happen. In fact, he's kind of been hoping it would. If your family thinks you're dead, they might back off searching for you."

She laughed at that. "I've betrayed my family, Milo. The ultimate sin." A thousand times worse than what she'd done with Danny. "My father will not rest until he has firsthand proof of my death." And if it was up to him, her murder would be a thousand times more painful than Danny's.

Milo gave her a brief nod of acknowledgement. "But you're safe here, and you can't think about that now. Worrying is not going to help you any."

That might be true, but how was she supposed to ignore it? "What if others besides my family also believe it? I have a friend from school…"

"A guy?"

She frowned. "No." Kenzie had befriended her the day she'd arrived at the private all-girls school her father had enrolled her in. They'd continued to stay as close as sisters throughout college. She wouldn't be quite so worried about her friend—she'd warned her that she'd be off the grid for a while—but Kenzie's mom had died from cancer not long ago, and her friend had to be an emotional wreck. The last thing Ariana wanted to do was add to her worries. "Why does it matter if it's a man or woman?"

He shrugged as he zipped shut a stuffed backpack and buckled on his holster. "I don't know. It was just an innocent question."

But it wasn't.

"Ready?" he said before she could respond.

"Do you think taking your gun is necessary?"

"I'm comfortable you'll be safe, but there's nothing wrong with being careful."

He held out a folded lightweight blanket to her. "Hope you don't mind carrying this."

"I don't mind." Milo was manipulating the situation, but maybe it was for a good reason. She'd trusted him with her life, so she also needed to trust that he'd make the best decisions regarding her safety. At least for now. She allowed her thoughts to return to the current moment. Kenzie would be okay. If worse came to worse, she could have Quinn call her friend and reassure her. For now, she'd pretend that world didn't exist, and she'd allow Milo to distract her.

She wanted to laugh at the insane idea of her fishing. Instead, she rolled her eyes and smiled. "I hope you know what you're getting yourself into. I do not have clue one when it comes to tossing a line in the water."

"Are you afraid to learn?" He arched a brow.

She wanted to growl at him. He'd obviously figured out she hated to back down from a challenge. "Of course not."

"Then let's go." He slung the backpack over his shoulder and grabbed the poles.

Instead of going out the front toward his truck, Milo led the way out the back door and across his yard. The overworked muscles in her thighs and butt cried out in protest as she climbed the back fence once again. She hadn't realized she'd given them such a workout the day before.

The sun warmed her bare shoulders as she followed Milo on the narrow dirt trail that led through a grass-filled pasture. "Are we trespassing?"

"Nope. This is all my family's land."

All? She scanned the vast open space. "Do you come here often?" She really didn't need to ask. By the looks of the foot path, someone had traveled this particular stretch of land many times.

He looked over his shoulder at her, and the sight gave her a small thrill. "As a matter of fact, I do."

Cows grazed in the distance, but other than them and a few buzzing insects, she and Milo were alone in their own little corner of the world. She couldn't explain quite why, but that filled her with a peace and an unexpected happiness she hadn't experienced in a long time.

It might be because she was out of the house and doing something different that would challenge her. Or perhaps it was because this little town allowed her to pretend she wasn't really a Trasatti. She was no one special. Just another soul on the face of the earth breathing air and trying not to hurt her fellow companions. That's all she'd ever wanted out of life. Yes, she'd enjoyed her father's money, and as she'd grown older, she'd carried tremendous guilt over that, knowing the money that had paid for her clothes and education may have cost someone else his life. She hadn't done anything about her guilt for a long time. She could only hope her testimony now would relieve some of her burden.

She put extra bounce in her steps just because she could. Milo wouldn't see her, and for all that it mattered, there wasn't another person in the world who *could* see her at the moment.

However, the longer they walked over the hilly land, the more Ariana found herself watching Milo and not the serene surroundings. He had a self-assured, confident gait, and she enjoyed watching the muscles in his back and thighs stretch and contract with each step. His broad shoulders tapered to a fit waist. In another life, she might have had the opportunity to win him over. She might have wanted to. The best she could hope for now was a bit of fun flirting, and someone to occupy her thoughts during the day and keep her from getting lonely.

Fifteen minutes into their walk, they approached a line of trees thicker than the occasional tree they'd passed on the way. Between the sentry of aspens and pines, she caught sight of a beautiful flowing river. She'd seen plenty of rivers growing up, but those massive flows of water were nothing like this. They were dark and deep enough to float a barge. People joked about giving someone cement shoes and tossing them in, but she happened to know for a fact that Hector Malone had encountered such a fate. Some of her father's men had thought it would be funny to reenact the urban legend.

She'd grown up in a sick, sick world. Danny's death might have been the most painful thing she'd encountered in life, but her getting caught with him had ultimately saved her life. Her father casting her out had seemed beyond cruel at the time, but now she could see leaving the heart of her family had saved her soul. She wished she could have taken Danny with her.

But that was the past, and this was now. All she could do was move forward.

The softly burbling water in front of her was more of a stream than a river. She might be able to float a paper boat on this water, but not much else. Maybe a canoe. As they approached, she could see the depth was at best guess about three feet, possibly four in some of the shadowy areas beneath the trees. The river twisted and turned lazily through the grassland, and the water seemed impossibly clear. Sunlight reflected off it, occasionally blinding her, but she didn't mind. The sound of water caressing the rocky shores was like a sweet lullaby from the heavens.

"What do you think? Will it tame your restless spirit for a while?" Milo watched her with a satisfied expression on his face.

"It's beautiful. Very different than the rivers in Chicago."

He snorted. "You are correct in that."

"Have you been there?"

"I have actually. I spent some time there several years ago while I was still with the Marshals. It's a very beautiful city, but while the energy there is flickering with vitality, the energy here has a way of healing a person."

She couldn't have said it any better.

"Let's set our stuff here."

Ariana spread out the soft blanket, and Milo proceeded to unload his backpack. She was surprised to see he'd packed a small collapsible cooler as well as a box full of different-colored lures that looked like miniature plastic fish.

It only took Milo a few minutes to get a pole ready, and he headed down to the water. "If we had more time, I'd teach you to fly fish," he said as he stepped on a large, flat rock at the edge of the stream and motioned for her to join him. She followed, very aware of where she put her feet so she wouldn't fall in. He gave her quick instructions on how to work the reel before he handed the rod to her. "Go ahead and toss it out." She flipped her bright yellow lure out into the water. "Now just sit there. If you feel a tugging on the line, start cranking your reel."

He'd no sooner taken a few steps away from her, heading back toward the blanket for his pole, when her rod dipped and the line tugged.

"Oh my God," she muttered and started turning the little handle on the pole. The fish tugged harder. "Milo?"

"Give me a second."

She reeled harder. "I think I have something."

He hurried back to her, laughing as the silver body of a fish flashed into view. "I'll be damned. It's a nice one, too." He let her reel the fish before he grasped the end of her pole, and reached down into the water to retrieve the fish. He pulled pliers from his back pocket and used them to disengage the hook from the fish. "Looks like we'll be eating fresh trout tonight." He glanced at her. "I cook a mean trout."

Happiness bubbled from within. "I can't believe I caught a fish my very first time trying, and I love trout."

"Ah, darlin', if this is your first time fishing, you've really led a shallow life."

She swallowed past the hurt that tried to surface. She was not going to let thoughts of her father and her childhood ruin this moment. "Yeah? Well, I'd say you'd better get busy and catch yourself a fish. You don't want to be upstaged by a novice fisherwoman."

He put her fish in the cooler and checked the lure on the end of her line. "You're ready to go again. If you catch another before I get my line in the water, I'm going to seriously doubt you're a novice."

She grinned. "It must be beginner's luck."

"Must be."

Unfortunately, she didn't hook another one before he headed back to her. She really would have liked to show him up her first time out, but the odds were against it. That was okay. She could be happy and feel accomplished catching only one fish.

"You'd better hope the cops don't show and ask to see your license."

The thought of being in trouble set off her instincts, and she glanced over her shoulder to make sure they were still alone. She'd never gotten over being busted by her father and the ensuing nightmare. "I thought you were one of the officers around here."

"That's right." He walked out onto the outcropping next to her. "I could have you arrested for fishing without a license."

She dropped her jaw, knowing that he teased her, but that she was also probably being illegal. "Why didn't you tell me I needed a license?"

"What difference does it make? I could have purchased one before we left the house, but what ID would you use? You're a wanted woman."

"Thanks for reminding me." She elbowed him in the side, and he shifted his balance to avoid falling off the rock and in the water. It would serve him right. "Yet, you're standing there and encouraging me to break the law. What does that tell me about you?"

A wide grin split his lips. "I guess I'm one of the cops who prefers to follow the spirit of the law as opposed to being a hard ass about everything. We won't catch more than the limit for one person, okay?"

"Okay."

They stood side by side tossing out their lines and reeling in nothing. She didn't care. Just being there with Milo was enough for her.

"You mentioned college." He tossed his line again. "What did you get your degree in?"

"I have two bachelor degrees. One in education and one in mathematics."

He turned to her, a look of appreciation showing in his features. "Wow. I'm impressed. I didn't realize you were such a smarty-pants."

"Are you sure about that? I think you've been challenging me subtly since the moment we met." And turning her on and on with each passing second. "I get the impression you're a bit of a scholar yourself."

He shrugged. "Maybe. I do have a degree in criminal justice, but I think I've learned more being on the streets than I ever did in school."

She studied his face, the intelligence buried within his brilliant eyes. "I don't think it matters how one educates him or herself. Just that they do. Life is so much richer when a person takes the time to learn about the surrounding world."

"Agreed. But I have to say you're failing at one thing."

She drew her brows together, confused. "What?"

"The whole time you've been chatting, there's been a fish on your line."

She jerked her gaze away from Milo and toward her line. "No." She laughed and started cranking the handle. "I think this one is bigger than the last."

"I think you're right."

When she finished reeling it in, she held out the end of the pole to him, the fish wiggling in the air.

Instead of grabbing the end of the pole and removing the fish, he took the rod and held the end out to her. "If you're going to fish, you need to learn how to remove the hook, too."

She tried to hold back her grimace. "Does that mean I have to touch it?" Lord, she wasn't sure she could.

He nodded, and she was certain he took some kind of perverse pleasure in pushing her limits.

"Fine." She wasn't about to back down. She gripped close to the end of the pole to steady it and grasped the fish. Cool and firm in her hand, the silver fish actually had a pinkish band that traveled the length of it. Black dots careened over the green-tinted back. Must be why it had been given the name, "rainbow". She supposed if she'd refused to touch it, she'd never have gotten such an intimate look at the beautiful species.

"Use the pliers to take hold of the hook. Kind of twist gently to back the hook out the way it came in."

She wouldn't admit it, but removing the hook terrified her. With unsteady fingers, she used the pliers and gripped it. The fish arched and bent, its movements surprising her. In a swift, instinctive move she squealed and flung the fish. Her actions put her off balance, and she stepped back to steady herself. In a stalled second, she realized her mistake. Her foot hit a slippery rock. Just as she started to fall, Milo reached for her and missed. Her leg sunk to the bottom, and she flailed her arms as her other foot found the bottom of the riverbed. The water hit her crotch-high, but she managed to keep herself upright.

She stared at Milo, his eyes wide as she tried to register the fact she hadn't gone completely under. She started to laugh. "I can't believe I just did that."

Milo joined her laughter as he held out a hand and pulled her from the cold river. "Are you okay?"

"Yes…no. I can't decide if I'm mad I fell in or happy that only half of me is wet." She should be angry or embarrassed, but even though the bottom half of her was soaked, this day still ranked up there with one of the best times of her life.

She shifted on the rock to get a better footing, and Milo latched on to her waist as though he was afraid she might fall again. "If I'm supposed to be protecting you, I guess I'd better step up my game."

She smiled. It felt impossibly good to be standing there with him, having him care about what happened to her. Yes, it was his job, but it still stirred her emotions. "I'm going to dry off. You'd better see what you can do about earning your dinner."

"You're all wet. I think we should head back."

"No." She was not about to let a little water ruin her day. The thought of being trapped inside a building when she could be here was not acceptable. "You're not using that excuse as a way to justify me catching more fish than you."

He let out a genuine laugh, the sound filling their serene surroundings with beautiful noise. "I see how it is." He lifted her pole, the fish still on the hook. "Caught one. Now we're even."

She shook her head. "Nope. That one's mine, too. I earned it the hard way. The score stands at two-to-zero, zippo, none. I can't believe a big, bad cop like you is going to let himself get upstaged by a city girl."

He narrowed his eyes as laughter teased the corners of them. "Oh yeah? Then game on, darlin'. Prepare to lose."

A thrill rushed through her as she stepped off the rock. "Game on, deputy."

Her shoes squeaked with each step she took, water leaking out the sides. By the time she'd traveled the short distance to the blanket, it sunk in exactly how uncomfortable she would be to remain in her water-laden attire for very long.

She slipped out of her shoes and peeled off her socks, stepping onto the dry meadow grass. She wiggled her toes, the blades tickling her as she dried her feet. Why had she never taken the time to get this close to nature before? It fed her spirit like nothing else.

She glanced at Milo, who seemed more intent on watching her than fishing. "Don't you think you should be concentrating on what's on the other end of your line?"

"I am."

"Uh-huh. Turn around. I'm going to strip out of these wet jeans."

"You tell me this and then ask me to turn around?" He arched a seductive brow.

"Turn." She twirled a finger in the air. When he complied, she popped the button on her jeans and began to work her way out of the wet denim.

CHAPTER SIX

Good God almighty. Was he being punished for all of the times he'd flirted with women and then left them wanting? Knowing that the woman who'd haunted nearly every thought he'd had since he'd met her was half-naked within viewing distance was more than he could resist. He'd like to meet the man who could.

He managed to keep his eyes off Ariana for all of ten seconds before his gaze slid in her direction. He'd have to concede he was no gentleman, but the ding to his honor was worth the prize. He let his fishing pole go slack as he feasted on the sight of barely-there turquoise panties clinging to the nicely rounded pale flesh of her ass. She wiggled as she shimmied out of her wet jeans, and he grew instantly hard. He forced a swallow past the thick lump in his throat. Damn.

She bent over to slip her feet from her pants, and the pole slipped from his hand. The movement jerked him from his lusty thoughts, and he grabbed it before it slipped into the water.

When he glanced back at Ariana, she narrowed her eyes. "You peeked." She tucked in the edge of the blanket she'd wrapped around her waist.

He gave her his best innocent look and shook his head.

"Don't try to lie to me. It's written all over your face." She sauntered toward him, her long dark tresses caressing her bare shoulders, her blanket-covered hips swinging with each step. She stopped in front of him, her gaze penetrating his façade. "Admit it."

He searched her eyes, sparks flying between them, and he knew in that moment he was in deep shit. He wasn't admitting anything. To do so would only sink him further into the mire. Instead, he grinned and turned back to the river.

"Fine." She picked up her rod and stepped in close to him. "I hope you did look, and I hope you're eating your heart out right now."

He let out a slow, easy breath in an effort to release some of his pent-up tension as he reeled in his line and cast it again. She had no idea of the current state of agony she'd put him in.

One thing was clear. He'd have to keep up his guard, or she'd snag him faster than she had her first fish.

Their outing had ended much too soon for Ariana, even if she had spent a good portion of the afternoon without her pants. Storm clouds brewed on the horizon, prompting Milo to call it a day. It would be a while before she'd let him live down the fact she'd caught two trout compared to his one.

Dinner had been a feast. Milo had lived up to his promise of delivering a meal to die for, but now that they'd finished eating and cleaning up, her protector had dove back into the thick volume of nonsense he was reading, and she was left to her own devices once again.

She let the screen door slam as she stepped out onto the back porch and sank into the swing. Ominous clouds rolled across the darkening sky as an unseen pressure thickened the air. A soft breeze carried the delightful scent of rain although no moisture had hit the ground yet. It was the proverbial calm before the storm. The threatening sky mimicked her life. Right now, there were only stirrings of activity, but it wouldn't be long before all hell broke loose. She was safe from the approaching thunderstorm, and she could only hope she'd remain safe until she testified at her father's trial.

She kicked the ground, sending the swing into a rhythm of creaking and groaning that fit well with the pensive atmosphere. A streak of lightning split the sky in the distance, and she counted off the seconds to predict how long until the storm arrived.

Four seconds later thunder rumbled through the heavens.

She loved it.

She tucked her feet beneath her as a swirling wind gusted into the yard. Branches in the pines rustled against each other as though jockeying for the best position to ride out the storm. The coffee cans they'd used the previous night for shooting practice tipped and rolled off the porch, the wind tumbling them toward the fence. She thought of jumping up to go after them, but they were quickly plastered against the clumps of tall grass along the fence and wouldn't be able to escape.

Another flash of lightning lit the sky, followed by a huge, resounding boom that vibrated in her chest. This time, only two seconds separated them. Fat droplets of rain splattered against the covered porch, first one-by-one, but quickly the volume of singular sounds increased, turning into one constant drum roll.

She jumped as streaks of white light filled the sky, earth-shaking thunder hot on their tail. The pounding on the roof increased in intensity as raindrops morphed into small pebbles of hail and began to bounce on the grass. Her instincts warned her to seek shelter, but she couldn't take her gaze off the fascinating light show.

"You should come in."

She jumped at the sound of Milo's voice and put a hand to her chest. "I think you just took five years off my life."

He grasped her hand. "Come on. It's getting wild out here."

She let him lead her inside, missing his touch when he released her to shut the door. Just as he did, another thunderclap shook the house. "Damn. That's some serious weather pounding out there. It hasn't hit this hard for years."

"Don't you love it?"

"Yeah. Nothing like a good storm to liven things up." He smiled and walked out of the kitchen.

She followed him to the front of the house and found him back in his chair, his book propped on his lap. She could not spend the rest of the evening cooped up in the house watching him read. "We should do something."

He flicked a quick glance at her but went back to reading his book.

Getting his attention was a little like fishing. She needed some good bait. A box of poker chips on the bottom of a bookcase snagged her curiosity. "Any good at five-card stud?"

The book sagged in his hands as he met her gaze. "I've been known to lay down a winning hand or two." Just like a fish nibbling on her line. He sat straighter in his chair, and she knew she'd hooked him. "Another challenge?"

She arched a brow. "Only if your ego can handle losing."

"Oh, darlin', you don't know when to quit, do you?" He set his book aside and stood.

Excitement bubbled inside her. This was far better than landing a trout. "What are you talking about? I caught more fish than you did today."

He walked toward her, stopping just inches from her. If he was trying to throw her off by his close proximity, she couldn't deny it was a good tactic. Already, her heart rate had nearly doubled, but she wasn't about to let him get the upper hand. Besides, the throb rushing through her veins right now beat sitting in her room alone. She tilted her face upward. "Well?"

"If we play, I'm not going to show you any mercy."

She laughed. "Oh, wow. Pretty certain of yourself, huh?"

"You're the one who invited me to play. If you don't think you can handle it, better back out now."

She pulled the poker chip case from the shelf and pushed it to his chest. "Not a chance."

His eyes sparkled with excitement, and she loved that she'd brought about that reaction.

Milo set up the game at the kitchen table, and Ariana brought a bowl of leftover berries with her as she took the seat across from him.

She leaned forward on the table, watching his deft fingers flip the cards. "What should we play for?"

He shifted his gaze to her. "What are you prepared to lose?"

Her insides heated another notch. She loved this flirtatious side of him. "Funny."

"How about whoever loses cooks dinner for the week?"

She rolled her eyes. "Bor-ring." She gave him a wicked smile. "How about clothing?"

Both of his brows lifted in surprise. "Strip poker? You're not serious."

"Dead serious. Watching you cook my dinner might be fun, but I think I'd rather see you stripped down to your boxers...or briefs. Whichever it may be." Unless he wore neither.

"God, woman." A laugh burst from his chest. "What makes you think you won't be the one flashing all the skin?"

She smiled, knowing he was only seconds from agreeing. "I guess the cards will decide. The overall loser can cook dinner, too."

He opened his mouth and then narrowed his eyes at her. "You and me half-naked could be dangerous. One of us needs to protect the integrity of our relationship. Keep it professional."

"What makes you think our relationship will lose its integrity just because you have your clothes off?" She must be crazy egging him on like this, but she couldn't help it. "Are you insinuating that clothing is the only thing keeping us from having carnal knowledge of each other?"

"Are you insinuating it's not?"

She laughed, thoroughly enjoying herself. "You are pretty certain of yourself, Deputy Sykes. All you need to do is take off your clothes and women throw themselves at you, right?" If he said yes, she'd probably believe him. He'd be a hard man to turn down.

"You're the one who said it, not me."

"Wow, you're cocky." And far too attractive for her good. "Then let's add another bet on top of this one. I'll bet you can sit in front of me totally naked, and I can walk away. You can bet the same and protect your precious integrity. Care to wager?"

Mischief lit his sexy eyes as he held out his hand for her to shake. She placed her hand in his. Instead of shaking it, he tugged her toward him. She lifted out of her chair and met him halfway across the table. "You're going down," he whispered.

She laughed and pulled away. "Deal the cards, sucker." She plopped a strawberry in her mouth and let it melt against her tongue.

Milo shuffled the deck a few more times and positioned it in front of her to cut the cards. She did and slid the deck back to him. He placed his hand over hers on the deck, and she had to slide hers from beneath him, the experience a seductive play of sensations that she was sure he meant to happen.

That was okay. Two could play this game. Ultimately, she would not lose.

A brilliant flash of lightning lit the room as they anted up. Milo placed a card face down in front of her and then one for him. She smiled as he dealt her the jack of diamonds face up. Then he placed the eight of clubs in front of him. "Not looking too good for you," she taunted.

"It's only one card, darlin'. The game is far from over." He lifted the corner of his face-down card and smiled.

He was only goading her, trying to make her think he had something good. She was sure of it. Or almost sure of it. She peeked at her card. King of hearts.

A grin spread across her face as she looked at him.

"I'll start with two." He tossed a couple of chips in the middle of the table.

"I'll match your bet and raise you two." She slid four chips toward him. He arched a brow.

He matched her bet and then flipped their next cards. Another king for her. The five of spades for him. She kept her half-smile in place as she met his gaze.

"Your bet."

She slid two more chips into the pile, giving him a playful smile. "Ready to fold?"

"Hardly." He added four more poker chips to the center of the table and returned her grin.

She matched his bet, searching for a hint of emotion in his expression. He couldn't seriously think his hand beat hers. At this point, if she'd only held a five and an eight, she'd fold. What was he hiding?

He dealt two more cards, an eight for her and a three for him. She tossed down another bet, and once again he upped it.

"You're bluffing. You haven't got anything." She matched it and added another four.

He tossed in more chips. "You seem a little worried to me. Perhaps you should be."

"I don't think so."

The last round of cards gave him an eight and her a jack. Triumph flared inside her. There was no way he could win now. "You think you've beat me,"

Milo said, a touch of laughter in his voice. "I can see it in your eyes."

"Perhaps." Between their two hands, three eights lay on the table. The odds of him having another eight were off the charts. The best he could have would be two pair, and it would be hard to beat the two pair she held.

He snorted. "Did I mention I get to pick which piece of clothing you lose first?"

He looked so damn confident. He had to be an excellent bluffer. Had to be. She glanced at her cards again.

"Fifty." She tossed her chips on the pile. "If you want to see what I've got, you'll have to pay."

He studied her, his startling blue eyes leaving her anything but cool. He slid a pile of chips into the center. "Call."

She flipped her cards, pairing her kings and jacks, giving him a smug grin.

She was surprised when his smile not only stayed on his face, it grew larger. She lowered her gaze, widening her eyes as he turned over another eight. "No way."

"Way." He crooked his finger at her. "Come here, darlin'. So I can have a better look at what you're wearing before I decide what goes."

A shiver rushed through her. "I don't think so."

"Are you going to be a sore loser?"

"No, but there was no discussion beyond removing clothing. Nothing said about you inspecting me."

He called her again with a nod of his head.

"You know if you torture me now, it's going to come back to haunt you when you lose."

"Maybe. Maybe not. Now get over here." A loud roll of thunder accentuated his words.

She grudgingly stood and walked toward him. He watched with heavy-lidded eyes, obviously enjoying her approach. She stood in front of him and jutted one hip to the side in a show of attitude. "Do your worst."

"Oh, I intend to." He shifted in his chair, eyeing her up and down, his gaze leaving a smoking trail down her body. "I'd really like to see you out of those pants, but since I've already had that view, I think I'll go with the shirt first."

"What?" She gave his arm a friendly smack. "I told you not to look."

"But I didn't agree."

"You are not an upstanding officer of the law."

"Honey, I might be a lawman, but I'm still a man." He tugged on her shirt, looking up at her under raised brows. "Off."

She exhaled a sigh of frustration. He was good. Damn good. There was nothing she loved more than a worthy opponent. Well, except a worthy opponent with *his* shirt off.

The first button on her cotton shirt offered no resistance as she undid it. The second quickly followed.

"Wait. Slow down. I want to enjoy this."

She lifted a brow, her internal temperature shooting through the roof. He wanted a show, did he? Fine. She'd give him one that would make him regret his little professional relationship speech. She might have lost the first round of cards, but she'd be a fool to not take advantage of her current opportunity. "Whatever you say, deputy."

She stepped forward putting one of her thighs between his, bringing her breasts just above his eye level. She wasn't sure where the hell she was going with this, but right now she didn't care. She'd spent so many months hiding from her father and essentially from life. The sparks between her and Milo were intense, addictive, and she couldn't stop.

She trailed her fingers down the gaping vee of her shirt to the third button, his eyes widening with interest. She popped the button open, revealing a good expanse of her bra.

His smile grew bigger. "Mmm…purple. Sexy." He took hold of her hips as though he was afraid she'd bolt.

She removed his hands. "Touching was not part of the game."

His gaze jumped to hers and then narrowed. "Touché."

She finished unbuttoning her shirt with agonizing slowness, wondering if she was torturing him or her more. When she finished, she put her hands behind her back, tugging off her sleeves, and conveniently thrusting her breasts forward.

The feel of his warm breath on her skin and the dark desire burning in his eyes caused her to inhale sharply.

"Shit." He stood so fast his chair nearly toppled. He backed away from her, his face a mixture of passion and agony. "I concede. You win this round." He headed for the back door. "I need some air." The alluring smell of rain rushed in as he walked out.

Just like that she stood in his kitchen, shirtless and stunned. "What the hell?" she muttered as she pushed her hands through her sleeves and followed after him. He couldn't walk away like that.

CHAPTER SEVEN

Milo strode out the door, continued past the porch, stumbling to the center of the yard. He lifted his face toward the heavens, letting the blessed cool rain wash away some of the heat consuming his body. The back door slammed. He knew she'd come outside, but he wasn't ready to face her yet.

She shoved his arm, her anger evident as he turned to her. "What the hell was that?"

"Go away, Ariana." He owed her an explanation, but he wasn't sure he could explain the fiery ball of desire that had overwhelmed him while the storm raged. He'd thought their teasing might have been a fun way to spend the evening, even though he knew he'd ignored many policies the U.S. Marshals would have held him to. But he wasn't in the Marshals any longer, and they were both adults.

He'd been dead wrong. He'd thought he could handle himself with her? Big joke. Even now with her standing in the rain, her shirt still unbuttoned, all he could think about was how badly he wanted to pull her to the grass and make fierce love to her.

"No. You need to talk to me. One second we're flirting and having fun, and then you bail with no explanation. That's not okay."

He gave her a chilly, don't-mess-with-me look. He was such a dumb ass. How could he have forgotten what had happened the last time he didn't follow the rules? Yes, Ariana was the sexiest thing he'd come across...maybe ever, but she wasn't his for the taking. Intense chemistry between them made the situation extremely volatile. He had to remember she was only a client, not the smartest and sexiest woman he could remember meeting. His job was to protect her life. Her job was to stay alive to testify and then move on to a permanent new identity. He'd never see her again. But she'd be alive. "I've already explained to you about maintaining the integrity of our relationship."

"Yes, you did, but I thought we agreed we could handle it. You seemed so cocky, so self-assured inside. What happened?"

He'd never be able to explain how much his feelings for her terrified him. He glanced down at her chest where her blouse still remained open. "You need to button that."

She frowned, clearly unhappy with the direction their evening was headed. "Not until you talk to me." She pushed away the wet strands of hair that had plastered to her cheeks.

He worked the muscles in his jaw, trying to maintain some semblance of control. "Why can't you do what I ask?"

"I'm going to be stuck in this house with you for the next month, so I need answers. If there's a problem, let's talk like adults. If that's not an option, I'll pack and find somewhere else to stay."

An angular flash of lightning cracked the sky as his heart jolted. "Do not leave my protection." God, the last time that had happened...he couldn't think about it.

He grabbed her hand and more or less dragged her to the porch, out of the rain. "If you want to stay alive, you need to listen to me when I tell you to do something." A drop of water cascaded down her neck, capturing his attention as it ran over the curve of one breast and under her purple bra. "You need to do up those buttons, or better yet, go inside and dry off."

She folded her arms under her breasts, lifting them higher, and he cursed under his breath. "Talk to me."

The fact that he couldn't control her heightened his frustration. Emotion warred beneath his surface. He had to make her see reason. He pushed her backward, trapping her against the door. She widened her eyes, but it wasn't fear on her face. The smoldering look she gave him sent a sharp, pointed tremble straight through him, undoing everything the rain had cooled.

He leaned down so his face was inches from hers. "You really want to know? Fine. I'm attracted to you. Extremely attracted. But I've been charged with your protection. I should have refrained from flirting with you. Rule number one—don't get personally involved with your clients. It's not ethical, and it's not smart."

And it could cost a client her life.

He gave her the most intense look he could conjure, hoping she'd get the point. It was the only way they'd survive the month intact. If he was still in the Marshals, he could ask to have her reassigned. Not now. He was her last hope.

She searched his eyes, and he was almost certain he'd gotten through to her. "I don't care."

Before he could question her further, she snaked her arms around his neck and pulled him to her, pressing her lips against his in a possessive kiss.

Her warm lips tasted like the berries she'd nibbled, and he couldn't deny himself any longer. Need exploded inside him. He shoved her against the door, framing her face with his hands, losing himself in the exquisite feel of her.

Her tongue danced against his, her hands slipping under his wet t-shirt and finding bare skin. Unbelievable sensations sent his blood shooting through him, making him rock hard. He kissed her until he couldn't breathe. When he came up for air, reality gave him the bitch-slap he deserved. He stumbled back.

"Damn it." He raked shaking hands through his hair, drinking in the sight of her standing in the yellow glow of the porch light, her eyes wide with surprise, her breasts heaving from their heated interaction. He took a step back, her surprise turning to confusion. "That can't happen again. That can never happen again."

She watched him for several long seconds, and then without a word, she went into the house shutting the door behind her. He would have preferred it if she'd slammed the door. Her anger he could understand and, therefore, could handle. If she'd even left the door open signaling there might be some sort of reconciliation after they'd cooled, that would have been better.

Instead, a frighteningly cool shield had slipped over her expression, like what they'd done, what she might have experienced meant nothing to her. Was that truly how she felt? 'Cause it meant a lot more than nothing to him.

He'd really fucked up this time. He scrubbed his hands through his soaked hair again and went inside the house to face the aftermath.

Ariana stayed in bed much longer than she should have. She'd awoken with a startle as usual, but she hadn't been able to make herself get out of bed. Instead, she'd tossed for more than an hour, trying to fall back asleep. Facing Milo required more courage than she had at the moment.

She'd made a complete, unadulterated ass of herself the previous evening. She'd pushed Milo into a corner, forcing him to choose between playing strip poker or seeming like a prude. When he'd gotten caught up in the moment, she'd seduced him, and when he'd tried to cool things, she'd kissed him like there was no tomorrow.

Maybe that's because there might not be a tomorrow for her. Or maybe because too many of her yesterdays were tortured, lonely, or just plain unhappy days. What a disaster her life had become. She'd hoped testifying would be the first step toward improvement, but the trial was taking too damn long to arrive. The more she was left waiting, the worse choices she made.

She'd done too many irresponsible things, enough that Quinn had pulled her from the Marshal's protection and placed her with Milo. Then she'd turned around and created chaos here as well, and she'd only been living with him for two days. Good Lord, somebody stop her.

The sound of a door closing and an engine starting brought her upright in bed. She jumped up and raced to her window to see Milo's truck driving away.

He'd left her alone.

A driving spear of sadness sank deep within her. She shouldn't feel bad. She was perfectly safe. Not a soul other than Quinn knew her whereabouts, and Milo had mentioned going to the store. It's just that she'd really wanted to go. Even if it was only to sit in the car. She'd been forced into seclusion for far too long.

She wallowed in her misery long enough to pour herself a glass of orange juice, and then she gave herself a mental kick in the butt. She had less than a month. The worst was nearly over. A couple more weeks and then she'd be able to move forward. She could do this. She had to.

Milo had left a note on the table letting her know he'd headed to town for groceries and to check on his mother, and he'd be back soon.

Soon. But not soon enough.

She took her juice out and sat on the porch swing. The evening's storm had moved on, leaving only trace remnants of twigs and leaves scattered across the lawn. Morning sun heated the porch. She tucked her legs beneath her, letting the bright light warm her.

Being in the peaceful fresh air helped lift her spirits. With the exception of the little issue she'd created with Milo the previous night, perhaps Quinn sending her to the middle of nowhere had been his best idea yet. She might be isolated, but she wasn't trapped inside a building. Here, she could wander and explore without worry of being found.

No one said she couldn't entertain herself while Milo was gone.

She quickly dressed and strapped on his pistol. The likelihood of her father's men finding her was slim, but she wasn't fool enough to think it was non-existent.

Soon, she was following the same footpath Milo had taken her along the day before. It would do her good to get some exercise. She could walk to the river and be back long before Milo returned.

As predicted, it didn't take her long to reach their spot. The quiet river from the previous day had swelled from the massive amounts of rain they'd received, partially burying the rock she and Milo had fished from. She smiled, remembering her ridiculous dive into the river. It had been a good day. A really good day...until she'd messed it up.

She slipped off her shoes, not wanting a repeat experience of walking home in squishy Nikes. She removed Milo's pistol for the same reason and placed it on her shoes. The river rushed by as she sat on the edge of the rock, the coolness of the stone filtering through her jeans. The water was faster today, more powerful. Leaves and small branches cruised along the surface, apparent victims of the storm. Still, it carried the same appealing sound, the same ability to wash away her stress.

Maybe she'd been wrong about small towns all along. During her previous relocations, the obscure places where she'd been forced to live had stifled her. There'd been nothing to do, nothing but boredom to suck the life out of her. She'd craved going to the theatre with Kenzie or dining at a fine restaurant, the things her father's tainted money could purchase. She'd been torn, wanting to rid herself of that lifestyle, but missing it all the same.

This time was different. Instead of viewing her temporary surroundings from behind a plate of glass, she was actively interacting with nature.

Feeling the grass beneath her feet, listening to the rush of the river, and smelling the sweet air.

She dipped a toe into the cold water. This *was* a place she could heal. Once the trial was over, she'd have vindication for Danny's death. She wouldn't be coming back here, but maybe she could go somewhere similar, somewhere she could finally put the first part of her life behind her and look forward to building a new future, a future she could proudly claim. All she had to do was hold out for a month, and then she'd have a new chance at life.

She never should have kissed Milo. As amazing as he'd been, kissing him had only provided a temporary distraction and had definitely muddied the waters between them. Not fair to either of them. If she messed things up with her protector, she'd have nowhere to go. Quinn would kill her figuratively, and if she came out of deep cover, her father might kill her literally.

The sound of approaching male voices jerked her from her reverie. She slid Milo's gun from the holster and tucked it in her waistband, covering the weapon with the hem of her shirt.

"I can't do this, Quinn." Milo sat in his truck along the side of the road, just a mile from his house. He'd been to the grocery store, but had forgone stopping at his mom's house. She'd know in a second something was wrong, and she wouldn't stop until she had the truth. "I can't remain objective and focused where Ariana is concerned. I don't think I'm the one who should protect her. It's not fair to her."

A laugh came through the speaker on his phone.

"This isn't funny."

"I know she can be a bit of a firecracker."

"Quinn, I'm trying to have a serious conversation with you. This is her life we're talking about."

His friend cleared his throat. "You want a serious conversation. Then here you go. You are her last chance. I thought I made this clear before. There are *no* other options. She's been compromised too many times to be put back into the system. Her father has long-reaching arms, and somehow, he's infiltrated the Marshals. My most recent reports state he's trying to get the trial postponed again in an effort to give him more time to find her. He wants her, Milo. He wants her dead."

"I understand this, but having Ariana in my home is more difficult than I thought it would be. Before long, they'll call me back to work. Maybe she could stay with you for the next couple of weeks."

"Your work situation has been handled. There's been a glitch in the investigation, and it will take a couple more weeks to get back on track. And no, Milo, she can't stay with me. I'm being watched. Why do you think I sent her to you in the first place?"

Milo sighed. "She's a beautiful woman, Quinn."

"I'm well aware."

"Did she flirt with you? Tempt you and tease you like this is all a big game?"

A silent pause came across the phone. "No. Is she flirting with you?"

"She took her shirt off last night during strip poker. Picture her, man. Popping buttons open, inches from your body, flirting with you like crazy." He couldn't bear to talk about the sizzling kiss they'd shared. "How am I supposed to remain professional?"

"Explain to me why you were playing strip poker in the first place."

Milo scrubbed a hand down his face. "I don't know. There was a big storm. She was bored. It was supposed to be regular poker, but she somehow convinced me to play."

"Seriously? *She* was bored? *She* convinced you? Do you realize how moronic that sounds?"

Ah…shit. He did. "You don't understand. She's very…distracting." He knew the moment he'd muttered the words they wouldn't help his case.

"What happened to the cold-blooded soldier I knew in Afghanistan? The guy who could stay completely focused on a target despite the chaos raining down around him?"

He drew his brows together, now wondering the same thing. He wasn't some weak-ass kid out of high school. He had skills. He had training. Why the hell wasn't he using them? "You're right. I let her mess with my head." She'd slipped under his radar when he hadn't been paying attention, but he had her in his sights now. He'd figured out her MO, and he could deal with this.

"So you're good then? I'm counting on you, man. If not you, I've got nothing."

"I'm good. I can handle her." Hell, she was just a woman. He'd been up against insurgents and rebels. People who wouldn't give a second thought before killing him.

He'd manage Ariana.

"Thanks for setting me straight."

"Any time. Don't let her get to you, Milo. She needs you to be strong. She may not show it, but she's under a tremendous amount of emotional stress right now. This has dragged on for many months. I think she can sense the end is in sight, and she's starting to fray a little at the edges."

He was an idiot. He should have been able to figure this out for himself. He'd allowed her to get under his skin, and he'd reacted instead of anticipating and planning ahead. That wasn't like him at all. "You're right. Sorry for the call. I'll take good care of her, Quinn."

He shut off his phone, disappointed in himself. When had he ever had a job he couldn't complete? Never. That's all protecting Ariana was. A job.

Keeping that reminder at the forefront of his thoughts was all the armor he'd need.

She was a job.

Ariana could barely breathe as the male voices drew near. She'd run, but she couldn't be certain where the men were, and she'd likely end up running right into them. The other side of the river was banked by a fairly steep bluff, and she couldn't see anyone up there. She glanced across the grassy fields behind her and couldn't see anyone there either. But the voices were coming closer.

She snatched her shoes, but before she could get them on, two fishermen appeared at the bend in the river. They walked along the edge of the riverbank, poles resting on their shoulders. She stuffed her feet in, prepared to run if necessary.

Both were tall with dark hair peeking from beneath baseball hats, one sporting a goatee. They continued to chat, still unaware of her presence. She wished desperately she could sink into the river and go unnoticed, but they were too close.

"We should have driven here, Luke," the goateed one said. "I'm sure Milo's still in Las Vegas. He'd never know we were checking out his honey hole."

"Yeah, I don't know. Lily swore she saw his truck pass through town a couple days ago."

"Must have been someone else with a similar vehicle. Milo would have called—"

The man with the goatee stopped mid-sentence when he caught sight of her. His brows shot upward. "Good morning."

His friend who had been studying the river as they walked swiveled his gaze toward her, a similar expression on his face.

"Morning," she replied, wondering if she should pull out the gun or wait.

The two men exchanged glances and then searched the surrounding area.

"Are you out here alone?" the one named Luke asked.

Wariness crept through her veins. "Is there a problem if I am?"

"Well, no."

"You're scaring her, Scott," Luke replied. "Sorry, miss. We're not used to running into people we don't know in this area. It's kind of hard to get to without crossing private property."

Trespassing like they were, she wanted to remind them. "I have permission to be here." Sort of.

"You know Milo?" Scott narrowed his eyes as though if he looked hard enough, he might recognize her.

She stood, brushing the dirt from her backside, praying the gun didn't show through her shirt. "I do. Do you?"

Luke laughed. "Apparently not as well as we thought." He extended a hand. "Luke Winchester. This fool is Scott Beckstead."

Scott shook her hand as well, the friendliness in both men's expressions putting her a little more at ease. "We've known Milo since we were kids."

"I'm Anna." Ariana smiled. "Must be nice growing up in a small town."

"Can be," Luke answered. "I can't quite place your accent."

She swallowed, not sure how to answer. "Midwest." A vague reply was good. "But I've moved around a bit, so there's some intermingling going on." This was bad. Milo was going to kill her.

Both men nodded.

Scott glanced around again. "So, Milo left you all alone out here? I can't quite picture him doing that."

"He went into town for groceries and then to stop and see his mother."

Luke cocked his head. "I guess I was thinking you might have been on a date with him, and he went back to his house for something. But he's at his mother's? Interesting."

Good Lord, she was digging a deeper hole by the second. Perhaps the truth would set her free. "We're actually living together." Or incarcerate her, if she could judge by the expressions on the guys' faces. "And I put in a load of laundry that's probably ready for me. It was very nice meeting you, Scott and Luke, but I should go." She snatched the holster from the ground without explanation and kept walking.

She rolled her eyes in disgust at herself as she turned and headed back toward Milo's house. It took a tremendous amount of willpower to keep her gait at an even pace instead of sprinting, although running would not save her now. She'd given the men a questionable story, told them both where she was staying, and now Milo would hear about it for certain. She never should have ventured from the house.

As soon as they were out of sight, she strapped on the pistol and started running. From what or to what, she didn't exactly know, but suddenly, she wanted to be back inside, out of the glaring sunshine that rained down on her like a spotlight, exposing her to the world. She wished she'd never backed Milo into a corner the previous night, and she was starting to wish she'd never turned in her father to the police. Her life had been a series of nightmares ever since.

CHAPTER EIGHT

Milo pulled into his drive feeling like a new man. His little talk with Quinn had straightened out his head, gotten him back on track. He wasn't sure why he'd allowed Ariana to have such an effect on him in the first place.

He retrieved the groceries and glanced about his yard as he walked to the house. It was a gorgeous day after the rainstorm. The air carried a fresh smell, and the warm sun coaxed an earthy scent from the ground. He'd have to get out later and clean up the branches the storm had knocked down, but it was a good day to do it. If the grass dried out, he'd mow the lawn, too.

He unlocked and opened the front door, ready to greet Ariana with his new arsenal. "I'm back," he called into the quiet.

Barbed tendrils of tension snaked through him when he didn't get a reply. "Ariana?"

He dropped the groceries on the kitchen table and hurried down the hall toward her bedroom. He doubted she'd still be asleep this late in the morning, but he didn't really know her that well.

He knocked and then opened the door, finding her bed made and her gone. It took him less than a minute to rush through the rest of the house. She was not there.

Back in her bedroom, he threw open her closet. Her clothes were still there, so she hadn't left like she'd threatened the previous night. But where the hell was she? Had someone gotten to her? Could her father's men have found her, and she was dead already?

A cold sweat enveloped him. Flashbacks from his previous failure to protect threatened his composure.

He checked the front and back doors, but no signs of forced entry. The front entrance had been locked, but the door to the kitchen hadn't. He glanced at the porch swing and the rest of the backyard. No sign of her.

"Shit," he hollered into the empty house as he hurried to retrieve his weapon from the hook in the pantry.

When he found the gun missing from the hook on the pantry door, certain fear gripped his insides with icy fingers. Beyond target practice, there was no other reason for her to take the gun.

"Damn it!" He slammed the pantry door shut. Where the hell was she?

He had to force himself to take a calming breath so he could think rationally.

He needed a weapon. He hurried to his bedroom and dug his father's service handgun out of the closet and checked it for rounds.

"Don't panic," he reminded himself. Ariana was a decent enough shot she might be able to protect herself. Fuck, he was an idiot. He'd done nothing but screw up since he'd taken on her case.

If the mob had found her, there would be some sign of a struggle. Maybe they'd come upon her outside. He hurried to the back door, wishing he could find a clue, but praying he wouldn't find anything bad.

⁓

Ariana topped the last little bluff, grateful to see Milo's quaint house not too far in the distance. She increased her speed, wanting to be inside and lock the doors. Her pulse kicked up another notch when Milo emerged out the back door.

"No," she whispered under her breath. Now that she'd met Luke and Scott, it was unlikely Milo wouldn't learn about her excursion, but she'd hoped to put off the lecture until later. Still, Milo couldn't get too mad at her for going to a place he'd considered safe the day before, even if he had taken his gun. Her throat tightened, though, when he started running toward her. There was something about his posture, his gait, something that radiated tension and set her on edge.

As she neared, she realized he had a gun in his hand, scanning the horizon with his weapon pointed to the side. Terrified, she glanced behind her, sure someone chased her. She couldn't see anyone and wouldn't know where to point her gun if she removed it from the holster. Had Luke and Scott been more dangerous than she'd thought? She faced Milo, his features etched with concern, sending her internal alarm through the roof.

"Get down," Milo yelled.

She dropped to the ground, dust sailing up around her.

It took him only seconds to reach her. He crushed her in his big, strong arms, as he rolled on top of her. His body covered hers stomach-to-stomach, both of their chests expanding in rapid succession as they lay on the dirt path between the tall grasses.

"Where are they? I couldn't see them."

His question confused her. "Wait? Who? *You* were searching for someone. I saw you scan the horizon."

He pulled back a little, scrutinizing her. "Whoever you were running from."

"I wasn't running from anyone. I was running home."

"No." Irritation sparked in his eyes. "I came home and couldn't find you. When I walked out the back door, you were running, looking behind you, like the devil himself chased you."

She pushed him off her, both of them moving to a sitting position. "No. I was running home, as in exercising. You came out waving a gun and scared *me* to death."

"There's no one chasing you?" He said it with such disgust that she flinched.

"I never said there was," she volleyed back at him.

"Shit." He stood, dusting off his jeans before tugging her to her feet. "You can't keep playing these games, Ariana. I know you're bored, but we're dealing with some serious circumstances here."

She jerked her hand from his. "I don't know what the hell you're talking about, Milo. I'm not playing games beyond the poker *you* walked away from last night."

He opened his mouth to say something and then stopped. She was sure he was thinking about their heated kiss. The muscles in his jaw flexed as sparks snapped from his icy eyes.

Her gut told her it wouldn't be wise to push things, but she was just angry enough to not care. "Say it. I can see you're holding back. Don't let me stop you."

His nostrils flared as his chest expanded. "Let's go back to the house." He took her by the elbow and started walking.

She pulled away, her emotions still raw. "I'm quite capable of walking by myself." How dare he insinuate she played games when she'd only been trying to survive each day? Yes, she'd teased with him the previous night, but they'd both participated in that play. Now, he made it sound as though she'd done something backhanded or dirty. That was how her father operated, not her.

She increased her pace, trying to lengthen the distance between them. His legs were longer than hers making her task difficult. By the time they reached his back fence, she only had a little lead time, but it was enough to enter through the screen door and allow it to slam in his face.

God almighty, Ariana would be the death of him. Every morning for the past ten days since they'd had their misunderstanding in the field, Milo had found her in the kitchen, standing in her skimpy tank top pajamas cooking breakfast, clearly wearing no bra. He'd done his best to ply her with books and movies, even allowing her to shoot every night. They'd cooked and worked in his garden. Anything to keep her safely entertained.

He couldn't be sure, but he suspected she was still trying to get even with him for accusing her of playing games. So much for having his head on straight. One look at her, and he was right back in the confusing mire of lust. Trying to remain civil yet pleasant to the woman who made his blood boil had been a constant battle and had worn his self-control down to the nub. Reminding himself that she was just a job worked great until they were in the same room. Then all he could think about was the moment he'd pressed her up against the door and let his basal instincts take over. She'd tasted so damn good. When this was over, how would he ever forget her?

For unknown reasons, the fates had thrown his Achilles heel right in his face. Maybe it was a test from the heavens. Maybe it was God's way of laughing at him and his attempt to be half the man his father was.

Whatever it was, trying to keep a professional distance from the woman who tempted him at every turn was his version of a living hell.

This morning, she stood near the counter watching television, bright sun coming through the window. The warm light added hints of honey to her already sun-kissed brown hair and silhouetted her figure from the side. Her full breasts beckoned him like lush fruit, and he ached to walk up behind her, kiss the curve of her neck while he slipped his hands beneath her top and indulged in her bare flesh.

He imagined her turning to him with a smile on her face and a kiss on her lips that would send them barreling head first into a fiery haze of passion.

A man's voice on the TV mentioned her name and yanked his attention back to the present. She had the station turned to the damn news channel again. He draped his shirt over a chair. "I wish you wouldn't watch that. It only makes things more difficult for you." He strode forward, intending to turn it off. As he reached to take the remote, she put her hand on his, stopping him.

"Wait." Her hand remained on his as though to control him.

The spark of desire he'd ignited a moment ago with his thoughts jumped back to life at her touch. The smell of spring lilacs drifted from her hair or maybe her shoulders, and he leaned in closer to try to decipher the inciting location. He feasted on the sight of her while the reporter kept her distracted.

"Quinn," she murmured, and he glanced at the annoying screen.

The blond woman reporter interviewed an unknown man dressed in a suit, but in the background Milo caught a glimpse of his good buddy.

"No, this is not a case of the U.S. Marshals failing to do their job. Miss Trasatti left protection of her own accord. We have never failed a client who followed procedures. Regardless of what happens to Miss Trasatti, the U.S. Marshals have done their job well."

"What about the reports of a woman being pulled from her car at the Chicago Airport and forced into a black sedan? Eyewitness accounts indicate it may be Ms. Trasatti."

Ariana inhaled sharply. "Kenzie will see this."

The Marshal's public information officer shook his head. "I've received no information on that incident. That would be a question for the Chicago Police Department."

"The prosecution is still saying they can produce her. How can they do that if she's dead?"

The PIO's eyes shifted to the side in an awkward movement giving Milo the impression he was uncomfortable answering the question. "I think it's best we let the Chicago PD fully investigate this crime before we start speculating. At this time, we have no further information to add."

"Thank you for your comments, Mr. Carlson." The reporter turned to the camera. "As you've heard—"

Milo clicked off the TV.

Ariana turned to him, anxiety creasing her brow. "My friend will be so worried."

He knew exactly the road her thoughts had traveled. "Try not to think about it. Your friend will be fine."

"You don't understand. She's already mourning the death of her mother. If she thinks she's lost me, too, it will devastate her."

"I'm sure she's smart enough to not believe everything she hears on TV. Television stations love to sensationalize stories, and that story had no substance. It's going to be okay."

"It's not okay," she whispered. "None of this is okay."

He took her by the shoulders. "Look at me." When she finally focused on him, he mirrored her serious gaze. "Things will work out. Sometimes doing the right thing can be tough, but you are doing what you need to."

She didn't respond other than the tears welling in her eyes. She bit down on her bottom lip, but he caught the tremble before she fully sank her teeth into the soft flesh. Every ounce of his reserve crumbled like the rock barriers he'd encountered while fighting halfway across the world.

"Ah, hell." He pulled her against his bare chest, folding her in a protective embrace. She laid her head against him, a shuddering sigh escaping her. She slid her hands around his waist and clung to him in a way that tugged at his heart. It was imperative he keep a level head.

He tried to pull back, but she tightened her grip. "Please, can you hold me for just a minute longer?"

How could he refuse? "Of course." His words came out raspy with emotion. She really was messed up by this whole thing. Who wouldn't be? He leaned his chin on her head and stroked her soft strands. "I'm sorry I've made this more difficult for you than it had to be. I should never have let things between us get out of control. I never should have kissed you."

She lifted away from his chest, meeting his gaze. "Do you regret it?"

Her blue-green eyes burrowed into his soul. He wanted to tell her yes. If he did, it would be a great first step to getting them back to the protector-client relationship. "No."

Her mouth softened, leaving a hint of a smile, and he yearned to claim another kiss.

He drew his index finger across her bottom lip even though his common sense screeched a continuous warning to him. "It can't happen again, Ariana." He removed her hands from his waist and held them between their bodies. "No matter how much I want to, it would be grossly unfair to you."

"What if I want it, too?" She searched his face, her eyes begging him to agree.

It killed him to shake his head. "You're in no condition to start anything. Your current predicament has put you in a vulnerable position, and I won't take advantage of it." She started to speak, but he cut her off. "Not only that, but if I'm constantly thinking about...us..." Damn, he couldn't even go there in thought without getting hot and bothered. "Any distractions could be detrimental to you. I need to be focused on my job."

Her smile slipped, but she nodded. "I understand." She pulled her hands from his and crossed them in front of her. "I admire that you're dedicated to your job."

He raised his brows, not certain of her sincerity.

"No, really, I do. I've spent plenty of time around men with no scruples. Your answer might not be the one I want, but I respect it."

He relaxed. They should have had this talk the first day she arrived. "Thank you." Already the tension between them had eased. "Now that we're both off the hook, maybe we can work together to keep you safe and find ways to enjoy the time until your court appearance. Nothing says we have to be miserable while you're here."

"I'd like that."

The sound of Milo's doorbell ruined their contented moment. He hadn't heard anyone pull into the drive. He grabbed his handgun from the pantry door and tucked it into the back of his pants. "Stay in here, out of sight. If anything were to happen, run like you did before, back to the river and then head south. It'll take you directly to my friend Luke's ranch. He could offer assistance."

Fear darkened her gaze, and it ate at him that he'd put it there.

"Don't worry. That's a last resort. No one knows you're here, and I'm quite capable of handling things."

She didn't look at all reassured as he headed out of the kitchen, toward the front door.

Ariana put her fingers over her mouth, listening as Milo greeted his friend, Scott. This was bad. Really, really bad. She blew out a guilty breath. She'd tried to find a good time to tell Milo about her excursion and meeting his friends, but they'd been at such odds, and she didn't want to add to the tense atmosphere that had pervaded the house. Another choice she now regretted.

When would she learn? She was making decisions based on her upbringing, but the people she dealt with now were thankfully nothing like her family. She needed to make openness and honesty her first reactions instead of relying on hiding and secrets to protect her.

"Where's the honey you've been hiding?" Scott asked in a jovial tone.

"Excuse me?"

Ariana eyed the back door.

"The woman I met at the river the other day. The hot little brunette who told me and Luke she was living with you. I gave you some time, thinking you'd call and want to introduce her, but I haven't heard shit from you since you got back. What's up with that, man? I thought we were tight."

A long pause followed Scott's tirade, and Ariana could only imagine what must be going through Milo's head.

"You're right, Scott. I've been a selfish jerk. Hang on a sec."

Ariana bit her bottom lip so hard she tasted blood.

Milo appeared in the kitchen doorway, anger sparking in his glacier blue eyes. "Could you come here for a second, darlin'?" His honeyed voice was a complete contradiction to his murderous gaze. "There's someone I'd like you to meet."

"I'm sorry," she mouthed.

He glared and then jerked his head, indicating she needed to go with him. She snagged his shirt as she passed the table and shrugged into it, needing something to shield her from Scott's gaze and Milo's wrath.

Milo gripped her hand in a crushing embrace just before they entered the living room. "Follow my lead."

Scott glanced up, an attractive grin curving his full lips. She could see where his dark hair and goatee might give him a dangerous appeal if he held a serious expression. Tack on the bulging biceps peeking from beneath his Harley t-shirt, and he appeared to be one serious bad-ass.

"Hello again." His dark eyes flashed with amusement.

"Hi." She pulled Milo's shirt closed.

Milo glanced down at her with a smile that didn't reach his eyes. "Scott, I'd like to officially introduce Anna."

Thank God she'd used the fake name Milo had given her.

"Honey, this is Scott Beckstead, one of my long-time friends." He tugged her toward him, wrapping an iron arm around her waist. "She didn't mention she'd run into you at the river. Otherwise, I would have called sooner."

"So?" Scott looked at Milo with expectant eyes.

"What?"

"God, man, you're dense." He shifted his gaze to Ariana. "You sure you want to be connected to him?" He glanced back. "I'll tell you what worries me. Here's my best friend neck deep in a new relationship. No details? Last I checked, you were a confirmed bachelor headed to Vegas. What the hell?" He looked at her. "No offense."

She couldn't imagine how Milo would explain her.

Milo shrugged. "What can I say? We met in Vegas."

Scott raised his brows, as if asking for more to the story. "I thought what happened there stayed in there." Doubt flashed in his eyes.

She had to help. "It was unexpected. We met at the poker table and just kind of connected."

"Connected?" He looked back to Milo. "Dude, I've seen you *connect* with hundreds of women, but you've never brought any of them home." Back to Ariana. "Again, no offense."

Milo shifted, his fingers digging into her side. "I guess when you meet the right one, there's no point in waiting. We got married."

Silence encompassed the room as though it waited for everyone to take a collective breath.

"*What?*" she and Scott asked in unison.

Milo squeezed her waist. "I'm sorry, honey. I know we were going to wait a bit before we told everyone, but Scott's my best friend."

"What the hell, man? Were you drunk?"

She ignored Scott's slander, still reeling from Milo's announcement.

Milo removed his hand and stepped forward as though to protect her from any potential verbal attacks. "What exactly are you insinuating, Scott? That I made a mistake? That I would never have married my beautiful wife if I wasn't drunk? That because I made a quick decision, it's wrong?" He folded his arms in a menacing manner.

Scott blinked several times before he glanced at her. She was sure the surprise on his face mirrored hers. "Uh...no. No, I wouldn't insult you like that." He looked back and forth between them, and then released a short bark of a laugh. "Damn, man. I just...never would have expected it of you. But you seem like you're of sound mind, and she doesn't seem like she could pull the wool over your eyes." He held out his hand to Milo. "I guess I'll be the first to offer my congratulations."

When Milo reached forward to shake it, Scott tugged him into an embrace and clapped him on the back. He released Milo and approached her. "I apologize, Anna, if I offended you."

"None taken." Milo watched her closely, and she wanted to reassure him she wouldn't blow her cover. But *married?* Seriously?

Scott gave her a quick squeeze. "Welcome to the family."

"Thank you." His comment brought tears to the surface, as though he truly was welcoming her into the fold. A rapid succession of blinks took care of the moisture. She hadn't belonged anywhere since she'd turned sixteen. She missed it. "I promise I have no evil plots to use and abuse him."

Both men laughed, and she released a sigh of relief. Tense situation diffused.

Scott stepped back and looked at them both. "Wow. Just wow. Wait until Luke hears about this."

Milo cursed under his breath, but he seemed genuinely happy as he leaned against the back of the couch. "I'll never hear the end of it."

"Very true. However, your shocking announcement does segue very nicely into the other reason I stopped by. A couple of the guys, uh, obtained a certain amount of alcohol, and they're planning a barbeque for Saturday night out at the pond just past old man Jackson's farm." He grinned at his friend, and Milo responded with a chuckle.

"You know I know the place well. Are you telling me there's going to be a wild-ass party going on? You do recognize I'm a sworn officer of the law."

"Exactly why I put it so delicately. But don't worry, Kim's agreed to be the designated driver for anyone who needs to be home before sun up, and, unlike a few years ago, we're all of legal age now. Come on. It's most of the old gang, and we can celebrate your recent nuptials."

Milo slipped Ariana an uneasy glance. "We'd love to, but—"

She couldn't be seen in public.

"If you don't show, everyone will be talking about you. I can only imagine what they'll say." Scott wiggled his brows, promising a juicy story.

Milo leaned away from the couch, standing straight. "Not if you don't tell them anything." His previous tension returned two-fold.

His friend didn't catch on to his change in temperament. "I can try, but there's no telling what might come out of my mouth once I have a few beers in me."

Ariana closed her eyes. This was why she shouldn't have let herself be seen by anyone. It had been a critical mistake.

"We'll be there."

She met Milo's gaze with surprise.

"Great." Scott beamed. "I knew I could convince you. If you could round up some firewood, that would be great. Party starts at seven."

Each second that passed until Scott said good-bye tied another knot in Ariana's nerves. By the time Milo closed the door behind him, she was a tangled mess. She watched him with a wary gaze as he turned toward her.

He stared at her, not a trace left of the friendliness he'd shared with Scott.

"Married?" she whispered, afraid to say more.

He released a long, slow breath as though he needed the time to gain control over his words. "It was the only thing I could think of, being blindsided like I was. Trust me. I'll pay more than you ever will for making that up."

"I'm sorry, Milo. I only went to the river like we'd done the day before. I thought it was safe."

He raised his brows. "Why do I still feel like this is all a game to you? Do you not understand how vitally important it is to keep your identity hidden?"

She breathed past the large dose of regret that threatened to choke her and met his hard gaze. "I understand better than anyone how lethal my father's men are. That's why I'm testifying." She didn't need that lecture. "I'm sorry I didn't mention meeting Scott and Luke. That was the day I'd run home, and you'd thought someone was after me. Then everything went to hell between us and…" She dropped her gaze to her hands, holding her palms up. She intertwined her fingers and clasped her hands to keep them from shaking. Never in a millions years had she dreamed her life would become so difficult. She looked up. "I apologize. I know you're only trying to do your job, and I'm complicating things. It's not my intention."

He released a drawn out breath, shaking his head. "Damn. It's hard to stay mad at you."

"Should I call Quinn?"

He scrunched his brows together. "What for?"

"To come get me? To tell him I'm leaving? If he could get me some money, I think I could lose myself in the outskirts of Salt Lake for a couple of weeks without drawing attention."

Milo stepped closer to her, his bare chest and intense eyes spiking her pulse. "Number one, since you've officially left the program, there are no funds Quinn can access on your behalf. That is no longer a viable option. Number two, there's no way in hell I'm letting you walk out of here alone. Did that once, and it ended badly."

Ariana widened her eyes. She'd really backed herself into a dark corner this time. "Then what are we going to do? My cover has been blown." She'd allowed her self-pity to rule her emotions and decisions far too often lately, and now she'd destroyed her best opportunity to stay alive. "I can't stay here."

"Your cover might be compromised, but it hasn't been blown."

He couldn't be right. "What about Scott? You know he's going to tell Luke at the very least. Then Luke will tell someone. It's only a matter of time before everyone knows." Cold fingers of despair wrapped around her.

"Think about it, Ariana. What exactly does Scott know?" He took her hand and held it. She soaked up the comfort. "I know you're worried, and you damn well should be. Ultimately, being seen could be a costly mistake, but right now, the town is talking about their favorite deputy sheriff and the shooting at the hospital. As soon as Scott starts talking, the gossip will be about me bringing home some stranger I married in Vegas. They're talking about long, dark-haired Anna, not blond-haired Ariana Trasatti. Finding a person of notoriety in their midst is the last thing on their minds. They'll be wondering if you've cast some evil spell and now control me. They probably think you're after my money, not that you're running from the mob. Why do you think I came up with that outlandish story?"

"I didn't consider that. Smart thinking." She certainly wasn't going to suggest he'd voiced a fantasy of spending their lives getting to know each other, even if she'd toyed with those thoughts. She knew two people couldn't know enough about each other after this length of time to commit to anything, but waking up in the quiet solitude of Aspen every morning with a man like Milo greatly appealed to her at the moment. "What do we do about the party? They're expecting us."

"We go."

She pulled her hand from his and took a step back, shaking her head. "I can't go. That's more exposure."

"We don't have much choice at this point. Not showing will cause more speculation. The best thing we can do right now is act natural. If you hide, they'll start searching the web for info on you. If you go, they'll take one look at you and understand why I was smitten."

Smitten? Did he mean that or was he acting the part? "That makes sense."

"It's all we have to work with right now. I'm going to shower. Do what you need to get ready." He walked past her and down the hall. "Our next move will be to introduce you to your new mother-in-law." He stopped at the bathroom door. "She'll kill me if she hears this from someone else first."

Ariana let her head fall backward as she released a quiet groan.

CHAPTER NINE

Milo parked in front of a small, maroon-brick house and killed the engine on his Dodge. Silence infused the vehicle. Ariana couldn't bring herself to open the door and get out, and Milo didn't seem to be in any hurry, either.

"She's a nice lady. I think you'll like her."

Ariana expelled a restrained breath. "I'm sure I will." Why did this feel so much like the real thing? She'd taken extra care with her hair and makeup that morning, needing to impress the woman who'd raised the remarkable man sitting next to her. When Milo still didn't make an attempt to exit the vehicle, she shifted her gaze toward him.

A smile played with the corners of his mouth, but he seemed more nervous than happy. "I have something for you." He dug in his pocket. "Give me your hand."

She held out her fingers.

"Other hand."

A rush of energy flooded her chest, crowding her lungs, making it harder to breathe. Was he doing what she thought he was doing? She raised a brow, a frisson of shivers radiating through her body as she switched hands.

He grasped her fingertips, singling out her ring finger. He slid on a gorgeous diamond ring. He didn't release her, but studied the ring instead, cradling her in his tanned, rough hand. The silver setting held a large, round diamond surrounded by tiny, crusted diamonds and intricate detailing. "My grandmother left this for me to give to the woman who steals my heart."

Ariana couldn't speak.

He released her hand, and she ached to reach out to him.

"Of course, it's just for show."

"Of course," she forced through tightened vocal cords.

"But my mother will know something's up if you're not wearing it."

"Of course," she repeated, unable to locate any other words.

He exhaled. "Let's do this."

She admired his strong, sure gait as he walked around the front of the truck to open her door. As they started down the short cement walk to the front porch, he folded a strong hand around hers and didn't let go.

Damned if this didn't feel like the real thing. Damned if she didn't want it to be.

He released her hand long enough to open the door and let her enter, but then quickly claimed her again. It was almost as if he needed her support as much as she needed his. How could she not admire a man so dedicated to protecting her that he'd lie to his mother? And look how she'd treated him.

No longer.

She'd behave herself if it killed her. She wouldn't flirt or tease him. She certainly wouldn't leave the house without him again.

Ariana glanced around the homey living room, loving the overstuffed tan couch complete with varying shades of rusty red pillows. Photos featuring Milo at every stage of life crowded a sofa table sitting against the wall.

"Mom?" Milo called out.

A scuffling of pans echoed from the kitchen, followed by the appearance of a slender, fiftyish woman with long blond hair cut in a fashionable style. "Milo." Her voice radiated the same affection that shone on her face. Her gaze quickly jumped from her son, to Ariana, to their connected hands. "Looks like you brought company."

"I did." He tugged her forward until they were firmly ensconced in his mother's personal space. "Mom, I'd like you to meet Anna. Anna, this is my mother, Nancy Sykes."

"Mrs. Sykes." Ariana extended her hand, and Milo's mom shook it with a surprisingly firm grip.

"It's nice to meet you, Anna. Please, call me Nancy."

The warm energy emanating off the older woman flooded Ariana's nerves, relaxing her and coaxing a smile. "Thank you. It's very nice to meet you, too."

"Mom, I have something to tell you." He squeezed Ariana's hand so hard, she wondered if she'd loose circulation. "You might want to sit down."

The woman glanced at Ariana, a touch of wariness now in her eyes, before turning her gaze to her son. "I prefer to stand," she said with a fake smile.

He blew out a deep breath. "I met Anna in Vegas, and we got married."

The color drained from his mother's face. She didn't say a word, only stared intently at her son as though they somehow had the capability to communicate through silence.

Tension rolled off Milo, clinging to Ariana, making her stomach churn. She couldn't let him put his mother through this kind of drama. "This is my fault."

Milo tightened the vice grip around her hand. "No—"

"Don't make excuses for my son." Gone was the friendly, small-town warmth.

Ariana swallowed her next words, sensing it was better to remain silent for the moment.

Nancy seemed appeased with Ariana's reaction and turned her attention to Milo. "I want to know why you *ever* thought it would be okay to exclude me from your wedding. My God. I saw your grandmother's ring on her hand and thought you'd gotten engaged, which was bad enough since you've never brought her around before. But you went and married this pretty young thing? You are my only child, my only chance to see my child wed. How could you take that from me?"

Several long seconds of silence roared through the small living room.

Agony etched stress lines across Milo's features. "I'm sorry, Mom. I didn't consider that."

"Of course you didn't." She threw the words at him. "You're just as dense as your father was."

Although Milo had great intentions, this was wrong. She would not allow her mistakes to drive a wedge between these people who obviously cared a great deal about each other. "I can't do this."

Milo and his mother both turned to her with incredulous looks on their faces.

"I don't care how messed up my life is. I'm not going to let it ruin yours, too." She switched her glance from Milo to Nancy. "We're not really married."

"Shit." Milo folded his arms and glared at her.

His mother blinked a few times before dropping to the couch. She took a deep breath. "Someone better start explaining."

"Damn it, Ariana. How the hell are we going to make this work if you can't follow orders?"

"Ariana?" His mom looked at Milo. "Orders?" She turned to Ariana.

"I don't care, Milo. I'm not going to make it work if it's going to hurt people like this. My father has already done enough damage to far too many lives." Ariana took a seat at the opposite end of the couch.

The older woman shifted a wary gaze toward her.

"I apologize for the upset, Mrs. Sykes. Milo has been guarding me until I testify at my father's trial. I was supposed to stay out of sight, but a couple of Milo's friends saw me. Milo came up with this story as a cover. But I can see now, it's never going to work."

"It would work just fine if you'd do what I ask," Milo threw back at her.

His mother turned a questioning brow to her son. "I thought you'd left the Marshals Service. Is there something else you need to tell me? And since when is it okay to lie to your mother?"

"Her life is in danger, Mom. I have to do whatever it takes." He sat in a chair opposite them. "Quinn was out of options where Ariana is concerned and asked me to help out."

His mom nodded as though she was finally connecting the pieces. "Ariana...would that be Ariana Trasatti?"

Milo cursed. "See Ariana? Now two people in Aspen know your identity. Soon it will be four, then eight."

"Excuse me, young man. I take offense to that. I am quite capable of keeping a secret."

"Yeah? What about Sue? You tell her everything. Do you really think she's going to keep quiet?"

So much for helping the two of them reconcile.

"You know for a fact I don't tell her everything. I didn't say anything about—" She stopped, flicking a glance at Ariana. "I can keep things to myself. Don't you dare insinuate that I can't."

Milo rested his elbows on his knees and dropped his face into his upturned palms. A half-growl, half-groan rumbled from deep in his chest. He sat up, giving Ariana a pointed look. "Short of burying you in an underground cave, Aspen is still our safest bet. We're going to continue with this charade, and you *will not* tell another soul. Do you understand? I don't care how bad you feel for them. These are *my* relationships to worry about, not yours."

The whip of his words stung, reminding her she was the outsider here, no matter how much she'd warmed to the small town.

He eyed his mother with the same severe expression. "You are sworn to secrecy as well. If you talk, she could *die.* Do you understand?"

Nancy tossed a challenging glare at him.

"If neither of you say anything, we can still pull this off. It's less than three weeks. Twenty days. Do we have an agreement?"

His mother's annoyed glare remained firmly in place. He returned the expression before shifting to Ariana. "Well?"

"I promise."

The look in his eyes demanded compliance. "I *will* hold you to it."

"Enough of your browbeating, Milo. We both agreed." His mother stood. "I hope you're planning to stay for dinner."

"Nah, we gotta go."

"I haven't seen you in over two weeks, and you're refusing dinner?"

Milo rolled his eyes. "Ariana should stay out of sight as much as possible."

"I think being inside my house is just as much out of sight as your house is. Come on, daughter." She held a hand out to Ariana. "We can make some sweet tea while Milo works off his frustrations that we women seem to cause him." She turned to her son. "I can barely open that damn gate."

His gaze flickered between the two of them. "Fine." The twinkle in his eye reappeared, and it warmed her like sunshine after a week's worth of rain. "But no conspiring while I'm gone."

Ariana grasped Nancy's hand and stood, grateful the woman's overall pleasant attitude had returned.

Milo's mother fibbed about making tea. She already had a pitcher chilling in the fridge. She piled two glasses with ice and poured the refreshing liquid over the cubes, making them crackle and pop. "It's such a nice day. Let's sit on the back porch."

Nancy's kitchen door led to a beautiful garden haven. The edges of the raised redwood patio segued into an old-fashioned garden. Pink and rose hollyhocks danced on the other side of the railing, poking their heads in to say hello. A gorgeous white rose crept up a trellis nailed to the side of the house.

Off to the side, two teakwood rockers and a small bistro table awaited them. Nancy relaxed into one, and Ariana followed suit.

Before either of them could start the conversation, Milo came around the side of the house, carrying a large red toolbox. The muscles in his bicep strained from the weight of the container. He stopped at the stairs to the patio and set down the tools. "I forgot to mention, I checked on Karen. She's out of the hospital and doing much better."

"I know," his mom responded with a playful, yet sassy reply. "Who do you think drives her to therapy?"

"You, of course." He flicked a glance back and forth between the two of them, narrowing his eyes. "My gut still tells me it's a mistake to leave you alone."

"There's not much you can do about it now, is there?" His mom winked at Ariana, and the camaraderie between them lit a dark place inside her.

"I hate to say it, but no, it doesn't appear there is." He grasped the bottom of his shirt and tugged it over his head, tossing the piece of clothing to his mom. His muscled chest gleamed under the midday sun, and Ariana traced each curve of his glorious skin with her eyes.

"For heaven's sake, put your shirt back on, Milo." His mother threw it back to him. "This woman is not your love interest as you pointed out, and you don't need to be strutting around half-naked, making her uncomfortable."

Milo hung his shirt over the railing instead. "This is one of my good shirts. I'm not about to get it dirty. You asked me to fix your gate, and I am. You don't like seeing me half-naked? Don't look." He picked up the toolbox again, his muscles flexing to accommodate the weight, and he headed toward a little gate that separated the backyard from a chicken pen. The chickens clucked and scurried around as he approached.

"I'm sorry, dear. He really was brought up with better manners than that."

"It's fine." It was more than fine. She tore her gaze from Milo to find his mom watching her with a discerning look. "I had a brother who always ran around with no shirt, so I'm used to shirtless men." Goodness. That sounded bad. She took a drink of sweet tea, hoping to cool her heated blood before Nancy figured out she had daily fantasies about her son.

"*Had?*"

She fought to get her brain on track. "Well, technically I still have my brother, but I doubt I'll ever see him again. When I turned against my father, I more-or-less kissed my whole family goodbye."

"I see." His mom rocked in her chair. "That must be very difficult for you."

The sound of a power drill snagged Ariana's attention, and she turned to find Milo crouched down by the small gate. She took another sip, watching him over the rim of her frosty glass. A man who could work with his hands was a very attractive thing.

He leaned and put something on the ground before using the drill again.

"Ariana?" His mother interrupted her appreciation of the spectacular view.

She focused on her pretend mother-in-law, praying her cheeks weren't as red as they were warm. "I'm sorry. What did you say?"

The corners of her mouth twitched, and Ariana was sure she'd been busted. "I said it must be very difficult for you to leave all your family behind."

"It's been very challenging. I've had a strained relationship with my father for years, and my mother died when I was young." Quite possibly at the hands of her father. "So, I don't miss them so much. But my brother and my cousins, I do. And I continually worry about my best friend. She knows I'm in protective custody, but there has been so much speculation on the news about me. I wish I could speak to her, just for a second, to reassure her. She's been the one truly positive person in my life."

Kindness and understanding radiated from his mother's blue eyes. "But no contact, correct?"

She nodded. "No contact whatsoever. Especially now that I'm in deep cover."

"Milo and I can appreciate your loss. His dad was killed a few years back. It can be tough learning to live without people you love."

"What happened to him, if you don't mind me asking?"

"He was a deputy sheriff, just like Milo is now, which has been a sore point of contention between us. At the time, Milo was stationed overseas in the Army. It was an ordinary day, much like today. My husband pulled a car over for speeding. They were drug dealers traveling en route from Los Angeles who couldn't afford to get busted for the third time. They chose to shoot Milo's father instead. In the end, they still went to prison, and we suffered for nothing."

Ariana stopped rocking, sick with heartache for them. "I'm so sorry. I can't imagine how horrible that had to be."

"For me, yes, but especially for Milo. He slapped on a coat of guilt faster than you can blink an eye. He says he should have been here. Like that would have made a difference. He's always had this desire to protect people, you know. I guess it bothered him that he wasn't able to save his father from harm. After that, he followed an army buddy, and they joined the Marshals. That was all good until that girl got killed."

"What girl?"

His mom finished her tea, the ice cubes clinking when she straightened her glass. "That's something Milo will have to tell you. I promised to stay quiet on the matter, and you know he's already accused me of being a blabber mouth."

The drill whizzed again and then thumped.

Ariana glanced back to Milo. He stood and lifted the gate to the side before turning toward them. He sauntered across the lawn, his ripped jeans hugging his hips, his gaze trained on her. She watched with fascination. He reminded her of a wildcat approaching its prey. If he took her right now, she wouldn't care. Well, except his mother was there.

He climbed the steps to the patio, looked down at her and smiled. "Enjoying your afternoon?"

"It's a little warm out here." She licked her bottom lip, trying to add moisture, but her tongue was just as dry.

"Really? I thought it was perfect." He held her gaze for a second longer than a person would in a platonic relationship, and she started to wonder if he referred to her instead of the weather. Then just as quick, he looked away. "Where did you put the new hinges, Mom?"

"They're on top of the fridge."

Milo left to retrieve the hardware, and the conversation stalled until he returned. He said nothing when he reappeared, but headed straight back to the gate.

She withheld the hum of appreciation that hovered on her lips as he crossed the yard.

"Honey?"

Not again. She jerked her gaze back to his mother, releasing an embarrassed laugh. "I'm sorry. I'm a little distracted today."

"I can see why. Milo's a handsome man."

Full-blown heat erupted on her face this time. "No, I mean—"

"It's okay, Ariana. You're not the first woman to trip over my son." She heaved a deep sigh. "I'm just waiting for the day he falls for a good girl. I'd like to have grandbabies before I'm too old to enjoy them."

"He had a serious girlfriend at one point, didn't he?" The woman had redecorated his whole house. "What happened to her?"

"Dena? She was a two-bit, white-trash…" She stopped. "You get my drift. She wanted Milo's money, but she couldn't keep her legs together long enough to get it."

That had to be an interesting story. She was sure it must have been painful for Milo, but she couldn't bring herself to feel sorry that they'd broken up. "That's terrible."

"It was. Everyone knew about her and kept warning Milo, but he's a loyal sort of guy. He didn't want to believe she'd lied to him. When he finally learned the truth, it broke his heart, and he's done nothing but play with women since then." She shook her head. "Don't get me wrong. He doesn't hurt them the way Dena hurt him, but he does have a way with the ladies."

Ariana wished he'd show more of that side to her. They'd had their one flirtatious evening along with one hell of a sexy kiss, but then he'd shut down like an illegal firearms dealer busted by the feds, and she hadn't been able to get anything out of him since. And she wasn't going to try, she reminded herself.

At least she understood Milo better now. Danny's brutal murder had closed off a vital part of her heart as well. "I guess sometimes things happen that cause a lot of damage. Damage that deep takes time to heal."

His mother widened her eyes. "Sounds like you have some experience with this as well."

She nodded. "More than I would like."

"All done," Milo announced as he approached the house, carrying the toolbox. From the look on his face, it was obvious he was enjoying the moment. She didn't know if his happiness stemmed from being at his childhood home, or the beautiful sunny day, but she liked seeing him relaxed and unguarded. And sure enough, there was a dark smudge across his impressive abs.

"Looks like you're a dirty boy," Ariana teased, wanting to reach out and wipe the mark from his stomach.

"Yeah?" He set down the tool box and stepped toward her. "Want a hug?"

"No." She laughed and shrank back in her chair.

A wide grin split Nancy's face as she glanced between her and Milo. "Milo, why don't you get cleaned up and join us?"

The rest of the afternoon and evening rushed by in a haze of laughter and great food. Milo's mother was a wonderful woman, and spending time with her magnified the hole left by her own mother.

"We have to get going, Mom." Milo stood and extended a hand to help Ariana out of her chair.

Nancy glanced toward the sky. "Always in a hurry."

"We've been here five hours." Milo leaned in and kissed her on the cheek. "We'll come again soon if that's all right with you and Ariana."

Warmth rushed through her. "Are you kidding? I'd love it. I haven't had a conversation with a woman in a long time. Thank you, Nancy, for welcoming me into your home." Ariana leaned in to hug her pretend mother-in-law.

"Let me stand up and hug you proper." Nancy rose and pulled Ariana in for a tight embrace. "I like this girl," she said to Milo. "You'd better bring her back before she has to leave."

The thought of leaving Aspen left a bittersweet mark on Ariana's full heart.

"And don't you be saying anything if I show up at your place. After all, she's supposedly my new daughter-in-law. It's only natural I'd be visiting her."

The next day, Ariana waited until the dust from Milo's truck had settled on the road before she hurried into the kitchen and turned on the TV to the national news channel. Milo had advised her to not watch, but trying to contain her curiosity about what was happening in the outside world was like trying to keep a bee away from its hive.

She filled the kitchen sink with sudsy water and slipped in their bowls and mugs from breakfast.

She'd barely washed a cup when the familiar image of her popped up on the screen. Funny, but she couldn't remember anyone taking that photo of her.

As usual, the reporter recounted the basics of the case, the same information she'd heard before, including reports of her death. She would think most people would be tired of hearing this story by now.

"In an effort to aid the investigation into the disappearance of lead witness, Ariana Trasatti," the news anchor continued, "a woman claiming to be her closest friend stepped forward and offered to identify a body that was pulled from the Chicago River yesterday. The police declined MacKenzie Harmon's request to be of assistance, stating they had sufficient evidence to identify the body, but they were holding off on the official announcement. Ms. Harmon, a college roommate of Ms. Trasatti's, spoke to our own Kent Davis and had this to say."

A heavy lump of despair choked Ariana as a visibly upset Kenzie appeared on screen. Her normally gorgeous auburn hair had been pulled back into a lanky ponytail and obviously hadn't been washed for days. She'd forgone makeup, leaving noticeably dark moons hovering beneath her eyes.

"I don't know why they won't let me see her. I could save them a lot of time and taxpayer dollars spent trying to identify her."

"You and Ms. Trasatti were close then?"

"She was the only sister I've ever had." Kenzie's voice quivered as she spoke, and Ariana knew without a doubt, she was clinging to her last thread of sanity. "I know that bastard murdered her." Desperation grew with each of her words. "I just want to see her.

I want to hold her hand one last time. I don't care what shape her body is in."

"When you say 'sister', do you mean biological sister?"

"She's my sister in every way that counts, and I love her. Why won't they let me see her?"

Ariana tried to swallow past her own tears now coursing down her cheeks.

The camera abandoned the pitiful picture of Kenzie and cut back to the anchor. "As you can see, there are many who are waiting and wondering about the identity of this young woman. Authorities are saying the information is forthcoming, but they refuse to give an exact date or time."

Ariana watched blindly for another minute before shutting off the TV. The haunting sound of an empty house echoed around her. She wiped her tears with the back of her hand and then sought out a tissue.

Shutting her eyes, she willed the image of Kenzie to fade, but the thought of her poor, tormented friend slashed at her with razor-sharp claws. She couldn't let Kenzie suffer on her behalf.

She padded down the hall to her bedroom, knowing what she had to do. The phone Quinn had given her lay in the drawer where she'd stashed it the first day she'd arrived. She pulled it out, her insides nauseated by distress. She dialed Quinn's number and waited. After five rings, it went to voicemail.

She hung up, frustrated. Where the hell was he? What good did it do to give her a phone if he wasn't going to answer? She closed her eyes, willing the rational side of her to emerge. She'd call his office. He'd said not to call in case it could be traced, but she knew better than anyone that it was unlikely the Marshals had been infiltrated.

An office assistant answered, but was unable to give her information beyond the standard 'he's out of the office', and she didn't know when he'd return.

A sick haze washed over her. Each second that ticked caused her friend great anguish. It could be hours before Quinn got back to her, and she couldn't wait.

She dialed Kenzie's cell number and let her finger hover over the call button. It would be nearly impossible to trace her call. First, the pay-as-you-go number was an unknown. Second, she'd only stay on the phone for a minute. Just long enough to let Kenzie know she was okay. The odds were highly in her favor. And really, wasn't it her call to make if she wanted to take that chance?

There was no point thinking through the consequences of her intended actions any further. She needed to spare Kenzie additional pain. That's what sisters did for each other.

She pressed call.

CHAPTER TEN

"**H**ello?" Kenzie's voice came across the line, uncertain and weary.

Ariana couldn't hold back her sob. "It's me, Kenzie." She hadn't heard her friend's voice in so long, and the sound of it nearly undid her.

"Oh my God."

Tears streamed from Ariana's eyes. "I had to call. I had to let you know I'm okay." She grabbed the discarded tissue from the top of her dresser and wiped her nose.

"Where are you?"

"I can't say."

"But you're okay?"

"Yes, I'm good. I'm safe." Another sob escaped her. "Are you okay? I found your mom's obituary online."

"It's been tough." There was no denying the grief in her friend's voice. "I'm better now that I've heard from you."

Seconds ticked in her mind like a bomb ready to explode. "I need to go, Kenzie. I'll be back in Chicago for the trial in a few weeks. I can see you then. Please don't tell anyone we talked. No one."

"Okay. Stay safe little sister."

"I will. I love you."

"Love you, too."

Ariana hung up and then waited for the world to crash in on her.

After a few moments of breathless anticipation, she convinced herself everything would be fine. She'd spared Kenzie, and that was worth the risk.

She finished washing the breakfast dishes and dressed before she heard the high-pitched ringtone coming from her bedroom. She raced to answer it, knowing the ringing would not be a good thing.

She clicked the answer button and immediately Quinn's voice jumped across the line. "Ariana? What's wrong?"

She tried not to accept too much of the guilt his frantic voice created. She'd done the right thing. "Nothing. I'm fine."

Several seconds of silence passed. "Then why did you call? This phone is for emergencies."

"I'm so sorry. I didn't mean to make you worry. It was just...I had a moment of panic. I saw Kenzie on the news. She looked awful, Quinn. On the verge of a nervous breakdown."

"Did you call her, Ariana?"

She bit her tongue to keep from telling him. If he knew the truth, it would only complicate matters. Quinn would be forced to try to figure out another scenario for her, and she was out of options. "No." She had to be the worst person ever for lying to him. It sickened her that she'd discarded so easily her promise to herself to be honest. But telling the truth would create unnecessary trouble for everyone. "I wanted you to let her know I'm okay."

He blew out a frustrated breath. "Fine. I'll give her a call. You're going to have to destroy that phone now, I hope you know. Milo will need to replace it."

"I'm sorry, Quinn. I know I've made things difficult for you. I just couldn't let her suffer."

"I know. It's okay. Let Milo know what he needs to do and have him send me the number of your new phone. I'm sorry I wasn't available when you called the first time. I'll make sure that doesn't happen again."

"Thank you, Quinn."

⌒

"You can call me a mother-fucker, but don't call me dumb." Manny set down his phone and threw a wadded, hamburger wrapper at Tony. It hit his nephew in the chest and then bounced to the floor of the dank apartment he'd called home for the past four years.

"You're a slob." Tony lifted his laptop long enough to scratch his balls. It was a shame how much he looked like his mother with dark hair and a big honking nose.

"I'll clean it up later along with the rest of this place. Right now, I got a bitch to catch, and I got a hell of a lead. An out of state number just called Kenzie Harmon's cell phone. I'm betting it's our little honey."

Tony widened his eyes. "You got a trace on her friend's phone? How the hell did you manage that?"

Pride rushed through his veins, warm and powerful. "What? You don't think I got connections?" He feigned outrage. "This is why the boss picked me. He knew I could get the job done."

"Then let's go get her." Tony closed his computer and stood.

"Can't yet. I need her to make one more call, could be to anyone, and I'll have her exact location." Manny slurped a long drink of soda and then belched. "But we can get our asses to Utah, so we'll be in the area for when she calls again."

"You don't know it's the girl. It could be anyone."

"Don't question me, dumb shit. It's her, and she's mine."

Manny wondered if she knew her time had almost expired.

⟨⟩

Four days passed and the world continued to revolve, much to Ariana's relief. She'd put the whole Kenzie phone call incident out of her mind. She wasn't going to ask Milo to buy her a new phone. She had two weeks left. Her father's men weren't going to find her there if they hadn't already.

She didn't want Milo to know she'd talked to Quinn or Kenzie. He'd overreact and worry without cause for her safety. Better that she let things alone. She was safe, and her home life had settled into a comfortable existence with Milo. It seemed they'd found their middle ground, a place where they could enjoy each other's company while keeping enough distance between them to discourage any action caused by their attraction. They'd both vowed to keep things professional which disappointed Ariana, but also made things less strained. It was for the best.

Saturday night arrived, and she was once again harassed by the nerve-wracking thoughts of meeting Milo's friends. Acting like a new bride while trying to conceal her identity would be a challenge. One she wasn't sure she was up to. But, despite her pleas, Milo insisted they go. Not showing up at the party would only raise more questions. He helped her pick clothes that wouldn't stand out from the crowd, and they'd rehearsed their story several times until they were both comfortable with it.

Conversation was almost non-existent as she and Milo headed toward Scott's party. She couldn't bring herself to act like she didn't have a care in the world. Milo appeared preoccupied as he drove them straight toward the waning afternoon sun, the bright light harsh in her eyes. A few hills and turns later, he swung into the drive of a dilapidated, old farm house. The years had worn away any paint that might have covered the barn along with most of the whitewash on the house. Remnants of broken glass remained in a few of the windows while tall weeds owned the surrounding property and grew through what was left of the wooden porch.

"Nice place you've brought me to," she said, hoping the tease would relieve some of their tension.

"Like it, do you? Now that we're married, I've been thinking we should get a home of our own. Should we make an offer on it?"

"Oh, definitely." Even though her situation was temporary, she was determined to be grateful for the moments she had.

Ariana twisted his grandmother's ring that graced her finger and allowed herself a moment to dream. What if this was all real instead of pretend? What if they really loved each other and had run away to Vegas to get married? What if Nancy was her new mom, and Ariana gave her the grandchildren she longed for? Ariana could teach school part-time and help Milo with his garden, and they could make sweet love every night if they wanted to. It would be heaven compared to the hell she'd grown up with. Her children would never know the palm of their father's hand. They'd have a loving grandmother, and they'd only know a gun as a means to protect, not as a vicious weapon of destruction.

"Hey." Milo's voice brought her back to the present. "Where did you go? One second, you're laughing, and now…" The truck bumped as they left the smooth drive and followed the dirt road that led along the edge of the old farm toward a tangle of trees on a small hillside.

She shook her head, clearing out the emotional thoughts, and focused on the sexy man sitting next to her. "Sorry. I got sucked into old memories, but I'm good. Today is a good day."

"I agree." He reached across the console to give her hand a quick squeeze. "Let's enjoy it."

He put his hand back on the steering wheel, and she wished he would have left it longer.

The deep rutted road tossed them about in the front of the vehicle, leaving a dust trail behind. Milo shouldered the sides of the biggest ruts to steady their travel, but it didn't help much. She bounced and grinned as they crossed a small dry river bed. This world was a far cry from her father's house in Chicago. She knew it was an exaggeration, but it seemed this place had claimed everything wonderful and good, while her father's world had been coated with death and darkness. There was no doubt which she preferred.

As they crested the hill, they reached a line of trees. Milo maneuvered his truck along the narrow path that cut through the aspens and pines. "Not many know this road is here. We cleared it back when we were teenagers."

"So you could sneak out here and party?"

He grinned. "More or less."

The sight waiting on the opposite side of the trees captured her heart. A pristine mountain pond took center stage with the sentry of pines and aspens as its captive audience. The late-summer sun cast a golden glow over the whole production, giving it a surreal quality. "I can't believe how beautiful it is here. I mean, I've seen similar settings in movies, but they pale in comparison to actually experiencing a place like this first hand."

Milo chuckled as he parked his vehicle a good hundred feet from two other nearly identical big trucks. The only difference she could see between them was one was as black as an inky river, and the other gleamed red like a stop light. A silver SUV and a smaller pickup rested a short distance away.

Not far from the vehicles, several people had set up a day-camp of sorts. Their little group was completely isolated, and all of the members currently stared with interested gazes, making her more than a little nervous. She was sure Scott had spread the rumor by now, and of course, they'd be curious about the woman who'd married their friend on a whim in Vegas.

Really, what kind of sane people did that?

Milo opened his door and climbed down, walking around to get her door for her. "I hope you don't mind helping me carry some stuff."

"Of course not."

At some point, he'd filled the back of his truck with the necessary party items and covered them with a tarp. He pulled out two camp chairs and slung one over each of her arms. "This okay?"

She nodded, capturing his smile.

Next came two old quilts which he pushed toward her chest. She wrapped her arms around them. "I'm not overloading you, am I?"

"Do I look like a wimp?"

He paused to give her a once over. "Wimp isn't exactly the word that comes to mind." He held her gaze for a half second longer before turning away. She wasn't sure what had resuscitated his flirting, but knowing they weren't at odds while his friends were around was a comfort to her.

He slid out an ice chest, sitting it on the ground while he closed the tailgate. He held up his keys, jingling them in front of her. "Keys are going in the pocket." He slipped them into his jeans.

"Okay," she said with a questioning laugh.

"It's important to note. There has been an occasion or two where they've gone missing."

"Would this occasion be another time when you were out here drinking?"

"Quite possibly. But just know, that's all the information you'll get out of me concerning this subject. All you need to know is that the keys are in my pocket, and no one will be driving drunk."

She tried to contain the happiness that resulted from their friendly bantering. As they neared camp, the warm energy rushing through her chilled, the tension in her nerves tightening like the line on her fishing pole when she'd snagged her first fish.

Coolers and camp chairs surrounded the large, roaring fire pit. Someone had carted in a small table which now held a variety of chips, hot dog buns and marshmallows.

But the crackling fire and food held no interest for the occupants of the camp. All eyes were on her. She recognized Luke and Scott and was supremely grateful they both had smiles on their faces. The rest wore pleasant, almost amused expressions, except one girl with long mahogany hair who'd pressed her lips into an unfriendly line.

Milo dropped his cooler and relieved Ariana of her items before taking her hand, tugging her forward. "Everyone, I'd like you to meet Anna." He wrapped a protective arm around her, making her feel a little better. "Honey, I'd like you to meet Lily, Luke's new wife."

A beautiful, blond woman in cutoff jeans and a black tank top stepped forward along with Luke. She hugged Milo, and then surprisingly extended the same greeting to Ariana. "So happy to meet the woman who finally captured Milo's heart. I have to say, I'm impressed. He's kind of like a tiger. Cute, but always on the prowl."

"Hey," Milo and Luke both said at the same time.

"Don't call him cute." Lily's husband tugged his wife's long hair, earning him a narrow-eyed warning.

"Yeah. I'm not a tiger. I was nice to you when you first came to town, remember?"

Lily winked at Milo. "Didn't say you weren't nice. Just said you're always on the prowl. Don't deny it."

He glanced at Ariana as though he'd been caught cheating. "I don't prowl."

"Not anymore." She squeezed his hand and smiled into his eyes, playing the part of a newlywed, but she knew once she left town, he'd be back to his old hunting ways.

"Anyway, congratulations. I'll call you in a few days, Anna. You'll need someone to show you the ropes in town."

"She's got me," Milo said, pulling her close to him again.

"A woman, Milo. She's going to need girlfriends. Someone to talk to when you piss her off."

"I'm not going to piss her off."

Both she and Lily raised their brows at him.

"You women are vicious when you get together." Milo laughed and shook his head.

"You'll have to call me on Milo's phone until I can get a new one. Lost it in Vegas." Ariana didn't know how else to explain her lack of a cell phone.

"Must have been a wild night." Lily laughed. "Lose a phone, gain a husband. I can't wait to hear all about it." She slid her hand into Luke's. "Right now, we're hogging your time. We'd better let the others have a chance to meet you."

As Luke and Lily walked away, another cute couple, both with midnight dark hair approached. The tall, lanky cowboy walked as though he'd spent most of his life on a horse, and his cute little wife carried a very round belly. Milo introduced them as Jerry and Kim.

"Looks like congratulations are in order for you, too," Ariana offered after they'd all shook hands.

Kim rested a hand on the top curve of her stomach. "Four weeks left. It feels like an eternity."

She could totally relate to the dragging time. "But then you'll have a beautiful baby. Do you know if it's a boy or girl?" An unexpected jealousy burrowed, leaving a void inside her. It was obvious the couple shared a deep love for each other, and soon, they'd be welcoming a precious soul into the world. She ached to feel that kind of love, that kind of belonging.

"It's a girl." Kim smiled. "I guess you and Milo will want to start a family before too long, too. I know he's always wanted kids."

Milo's gaze jumped to Ariana. She swallowed a sharp tug of regret. For a cruel second, she wanted to be the one who would give him that family. But she couldn't be. The choices her father had made, the choices she'd made would never allow that. "I'm sure we won't wait long. I've always wanted a family, too." Milo, of course, would think she was playing her part.

"Glad you guys could make it." Scott interrupted their conversation, and Ariana was relieved. A few more minutes down that vein, and she might not have been able to keep her feelings buried.

Milo and Scott shook hands, and Ariana received her second hug from Scott.

"You keep hugging my wife, and I'm going to start wondering about your intentions, dude." Milo punched him in the arm.

Scott laughed. "Yeah, right, man. Hey, I want you to meet Jen." He motioned to a voluptuous woman still sitting in a camp chair.

"Always a boob man," Milo whispered to Scott. Ariana elbowed him.

Jen was cute with her dark-haired pixie cut, and Ariana was certain none of the men minded her low-cut pink t-shirt that showcased her ample breasts. Her green eyes fired every time Scott teased her. After her, an auburn-haired man with intense brown eyes introduced himself as a life-long friend of Milo's.

"I guess Sierra's not talking to me?" Milo asked Tyler.

"Nope. She's pretty pissed."

Ariana slid her gaze toward the redhead with large brown eyes. She, too, watched them, and when her gaze connected with Ariana's, she turned away.

Sierra left her seat by the fire and walked to a blue cooler where she retrieved a bottle of beer. She twisted off the cap and chucked it toward the burning logs.

Milo winced. "I should go say something to her." He glanced at Ariana. "You okay for a minute?"

"Of course." Sierra was obviously one of Milo's girls who now suffered because of the story he had concocted to protect Ariana. The thought weighed heavily on her. If the romance between her and Milo was real, then that would be one thing, but Sierra's pain and suffering were for nothing. For all Ariana knew, Sierra and Milo would reconnect after she was out of the picture.

The whole situation was messed up. She turned and headed toward the pond, needing a moment to align her emotions. Her initial lust for Milo had morphed into something deeper each day she spent with him. He was willing to put his life on hold for her. But when the end of the month and the trial rolled around, her life and the lives of these caring, decent people would be tossed around again. Without a doubt, there would be another gaping hole in her heart. Not that Milo had meant to make her care. On the contrary. He could only be accused of being himself, a kind, funny, and far too sexy man.

A soft breeze skittered across her bare shoulders and sent ripples racing across the surface of the pond, wrinkling the reflection of the setting sun. The scent of burning wood mingled with a woman's laughter. Probably Jen. She seemed the most vivacious of the group.

"Hey." Milo had come up from behind and took her hand. "You okay?" The concerned look in his eye only increased her melancholy.

"Of course. I'm just playing the part of the new wife, jealous that you're talking to an old girlfriend."

He lifted one side of his mouth, giving her a crooked grin, but there was nothing genuine about it. "I didn't think about how that might appear to everyone."

"I'm sure they wonder if you still care for her, and as a new bride, I shouldn't be very happy about it." She winked, burying her sadness beneath a layer of teasing.

He widened his grin, becoming more sincere. "Great. I'm in the dog house. Now I'm going to have to spend the rest of the evening trying to win you back." He glanced at his friends, and she followed suit. No doubt, the newlywed couple was the talk of the evening. "Guess I'd better start now."

Before she could question his intentions, he pulled her toward him, wrapping his arms around her waist. Her hips bumped against his, and she inhaled a surprised breath as hot desire spiked her blood.

"What are you doing?" It was one thing to tell everyone they were married. It was quite another to act the part.

"Trying to make up with you." He lifted her hand to his lips and kissed her knuckles, as his bright blue eyes sparkled with mischief. "I'm so sorry for talking to my old girlfriend. I promise, you are the only one for me."

Her chest compressed against her heart. Her brain knew he was acting, but her heart questioned if there was a hopeful spark of truth in his words. The spot on her fingers where his soft lips had been moments before burned, and she was immediately transported back to their passionate kiss beneath the raging stormy sky. She couldn't speak even if she could find the words.

He lifted a hand and tucked a strand of hair behind her ear. "Please don't be angry with me."

She looked down, afraid her expression might give her away. "Okay. You're forgiven."

He chuckled. "I'm glad you're so easy to please. All wives should be like you."

She flashed him a warning look that made him laugh again. "If we were truly married, you wouldn't get off near as easy." He still held her, belly-to-belly. The caution bells firing in her head advised her to back away, but he wouldn't let her go.

"Yeah? Are you the jealous type? What would you do?"

She swallowed. This was all a little too real for her. "Who wouldn't be jealous? If we were in a committed relationship, I would expect you to respect me, to respect us. If you were flirting with your old girlfriends, I would have a problem with that. Don't tell me you wouldn't if I flirted with other guys."

His expression softened. "I wasn't flirting with her. I only felt I owed her an explanation, since we had been pretty friendly in the past."

Was he really apologizing to her? "It's okay. You can talk to her."

He ran a thumb down her cheek.

"This feels like more than acting." His action affected her as though it was real.

He traced a finger across her bottom lip, scaring her. "Does it?" He leaned in and brushed a soft kiss across her lips. "I must be doing a good job then."

She pulled away and headed along the edge of the pond, away from Milo, away from the others.

He caught up to her within a few seconds. "Okay. I admit it. That was a dumb move on my part. I thought it would look good for the others."

She kept walking. She needed distance. Distance from the man who protected her life, but endangered her heart.

He tugged her to a stop, but she refused to meet his gaze. "I apologize. I lost my head there for a minute. I thought it would make things look more authentic."

She jerked her gaze upward. "You promised. We promised we'd keep things professional, for both our sakes. That kiss was anything but professional."

He scrubbed a hand over his jawline, turning his gaze toward the pond. "You're right. I let myself get caught up in the fun, but that's not an excuse." He looked back at her. "I truly was trying to give them a good show, but I lost my head and took it too far. Maybe we should make our excuses and head home. They'd all think it was because we had a fight."

"No." She crossed her arms, trying to ward off a chill. With the sun so close to the horizon, the breeze rolling across the water had nothing to warm it. As difficult as it was pretending with Milo, she craved the company and the chance to be out of the house. "I'm sorry, too. I overreacted. It was just a kiss, right?" She needed to ground herself in reality and fast. "These are your friends, and I don't want to make things more difficult for you. You caught me off guard with that kiss, but I'm good now. I'd prefer it if we go back and try to have fun. I want to roast a hot dog and drink a beer and forget about the world for a while. Besides, I like your friends, and it beats sitting home."

⤙⤚

Ariana stood at the tailgate of Luke's truck, using the light from the full moon and Lily's cell phone to help her sort through the songs on her iPod, trying to create a playlist of music appropriate for their wild ass party as Lily called it.

"What do you think about Jason Aldean?" Lily tossed her long blond ponytail over her shoulder as she eyed Ariana.

"I don't think I know him."

Lily laughed. "Oh girl, you are missing out. When you get home, you'll have to look him up on the internet. He is one hot cowboy. Kind of reminds me of my Luke."

Ariana smiled. Luke could definitely hold his own in a room full of handsome men, but Milo had him beat hands-down. "I'll check him out tomorrow."

"Okay, but in the meantime, we're definitely putting *My Kinda Party* on the playlist, and don't feel bad. I didn't really know country music until I met Luke, either. I'd always listened to pop and rock, and I was surprised at how many songs I could relate to."

"Thanks for being kind to me, Lily."

"What are you talking about? Why wouldn't I be?"

"I'm a virtual stranger who stole one of Luke's best friends when no one was looking. I'd expect you all to be a little leery of me, maybe even a little hostile." Although it seemed Sierra had that area covered. She no longer shot Ariana visual poisoned arrows, but she'd steered clear of her the entire evening, clearly preferring to spend her time talking to Tyler and Kim.

"You're crazy, Anna. From the second Milo introduced you, I could see how much he loves you. It doesn't always take people eons to know they're meant for each other."

Love?

"And it's obvious you love him, too." She tilted her head, studying Ariana's face. "Don't you?"

"I do." She did...and that thought didn't sit well with her. None of the scenarios she'd imagined ended well for her or him if they fell in love.

"See? It's all good." She arrowed down on the iPod. "You might find yourself worrying about acclimating to a small town after being in a big city, because really what could be smaller than Aspen, but I think you'll find you love it. The people are just so wonderful."

Ariana smiled. "I love what I've seen so far."

"Do you work? I have a background in marketing, but I've made it work for me here, too. I've helped most of the local businesses, and I'm expanding into the surrounding areas. Plus, I've found a few clients online. With all of the tools at our disposal, we can do so much more from a remote location."

Ariana laughed. "You have this all figured out, don't you?"

"I do. When Luke asked me to stay, I knew I wouldn't be happy just sitting home, so yeah, I worked some things out." She grinned.

"I have degrees in education and mathematics, but I haven't really put them to use yet."

Lily raised interested brows. "Look at you go, girl. I'm impressed. I know they're searching for two new teachers at the high school to replace some retirees. Maybe you'd be interested in teaching there."

If only. "You know, I believe I would enjoy teaching high school. Some people find older kids to be difficult, but I think I'd like challenging their minds in fun and interesting ways." When she spoke to Quinn again, she'd add that to her list of possibilities for her new identity.

"Good. Talk to Milo. He's good friends with the principal there, and he could tell you how to apply and maybe put in a good word."

She nodded, a twinge of sadness pinging inside her. If she were lucky, she would be able to teach kids, but it would never be in this county.

Lily plugged the iPod into a set of speakers and suddenly the sounds of a rocking guitar filled the night air. A sexy country voice followed.

"Jason," Lily said with a smile as she moved her shoulders to the beat. "Mmm…"

"I love this song," Jen said as she joined them. She started dancing to the music, and Lily jumped off the tailgate and followed her lead.

Jen motioned to her. "C'mon, girl. Put that bottle down and get over here."

"Come on," Lily coaxed as she twirled in a circle.

What the hell. She would only live once, and no one knew for how long. She slid off the tailgate, and Lily grabbed her hand, pulling her into a dance.

CHAPTER ELEVEN

Milo took a hearty swallow of his third beer. The bitter liquid chilled his throat, and he hoped it would cool the rest of him. A slight buzz cruised through his veins, calming his mind and easing the tension that had been an inescapable part of his life since he'd met Ariana. Normally, he wouldn't drink while on the job, but Ariana was safe here, and his doctor had finally cleared him to consume alcohol again.

God knew he needed the temporary distraction and a chance to let off a little steam. Between the fire and Ariana moving her sexy body to the beat of the music, he'd overheated and fried his brain. He leaned back in his chair, eyeing her over the flickering flames. She laughed as Lily tried to teach her a dance step. He remembered when he'd taught Lily how to two-step back before she'd hooked up with Luke, and now she was teaching Ariana.

Small world.

It made him happy to know the two girls had hit it off. The sound of Ariana's laughter was a balm to his restless spirit. She'd been through a lot recently, and she needed this chance to unwind as well.

Luke turned a log in the fire before sinking into the chair Ariana had vacated a while ago. "I like her."

Milo snorted. "Glad you approve."

"Not that you care. I can't believe you went to Vegas and came home with a wife, and didn't tell any of us. That is not like you at all. Bet your mom is ticked." His beer hissed as he twisted off the cap and tossed it into the fire.

"Yeah. She wasn't too happy." He shook his head wondering why he'd ever thought it was a good idea to keep his mom out of the loop. He'd done it to protect Ariana, but man, had that backfired.

The sound of raucous feminine laughter stole his attention. Lily stood inches from Jen's body, shimming her way down and back up in a series of sexy moves. When she stood, all three women laughed again. No doubt the beer had loosened their inhibitions, but they were having a great time.

"You try it," Lily persuaded Ariana.

Ariana took a long draw on her beer before setting it on the tailgate. She moved in close to Lily. With slow, fluid movements, she gyrated her hips to the tempo. Twisting her hands in sensual moves, she alternated between caressing her own body, tugging her t-shirt up to expose her stomach, and drawing invisible patterns in the air. Good God almighty. He tried to swallow past the dry knot in his throat.

Ariana descended toward the ground and then rocked her way back up. She looked expectantly at her companions who seemed to pause in surprise before they all started laughing again.

"Woo, Anna! You've got some sweet moves." Jen held out her bottle, waiting for the other two to claim theirs and make a toast.

Luke jumped out of his chair. "I'll be damned if I'm going to sit here while my woman's making moves like that." His beer tipped over in the dirt as he walked away.

"Damn," Milo whispered under his breath. Scott apparently had the same thought as Luke and left his conversation with Jerry to dance with Jen.

Ariana leaned on the tailgate, laughing as the men joined in. Lily and Jen practiced their moves on the guys. Luke tried to mimic them, but fell on his ass, making the crowd laugh. Scott was apparently the smart one and didn't waste any time pulling Jen into his arms.

Milo glanced at the other couples still sitting on the sidelines, jerking his gaze back to Ariana when he realized Sierra had him in her sights. He couldn't have her thinking there was trouble in paradise. For the moment, all of his friends needed to fully believe he and Ariana were in love. He'd deal with how to explain the break-up later on.

Speaking of love, he'd better get his ass in gear because now he had Scott alternating between glancing at Ariana and giving him a what-the-fuck look.

If Scott was the intelligent one for claiming his woman, and Luke was the clumsy one who'd still get his wife, what did that make him? The jackass who left his girl sitting alone watching the others.

Yeah. Not good.

He stood, his movement attracting Ariana's attention. There was no mistaking the intense desire burning in her eyes as she watched him approach, and he couldn't deny that her expression made him ache to hold her. With her, it was one tricky situation after another. He held out a hand. "Care to dance?"

She raised a brow as though questioning his intentions before she slid her fingers across his palm. Damn if Quinn hadn't put them in an impossible spot. Of course, there was no way Quinn could have predicted this insane attraction between him and Ariana.

He pulled her into his embrace the way a good husband would, ignoring his senses that fired in rapid succession. It was hard to discount the satisfying way her body molded perfectly against him, so he'd have to find a way to disconnect his attraction from his actions.

If he were still with the marshals, protocol would require he be reassigned. Something he should have done three years ago. Not that he'd been physically attracted to Jane, at least not like he was with Ariana, but he'd come to really care for her, which had kept him from making unemotional decisions. Deep down, he knew it had been her choices which had ended her life, but that didn't erase his contributions to her death. If he had it to do over, she'd be alive today. Now, here he was in another compromised situation with absolutely no way out. He couldn't act on his feelings, but he couldn't leave her, either.

"You have some impressive moves there."

Amused laughter spilled from her as they slow-danced to the music. "My college roommate and I spent hours watching music videos, trying to learn the dancer's moves. That one is a little risqué, but I think Lily and Jen liked it."

He snorted. "Forget the girls. *I* liked it."

"I didn't realize you were paying that much attention." She pulled from him ever so slightly, the rocking of her hips and shoulders growing more pronounced as a flash of naughtiness lit her eyes. If they had been alone, he would have stopped her before she could take it further. But with all his unsuspecting friends around, he was helpless to do anything but watch.

Her gaze never left his as she danced her way down his body, her fingers sliding from his neck and trailing across his chest. When they dipped dangerously low, she smiled, and slowly made her way back up.

He leaned close to her ear, ignoring the enticing scent of her hair and the way the breeze tickled the soft strands against his skin. "Oh, darlin'. You like to test me."

"I do." She turned, leaning into him. He rested his hands on her hips as she gyrated against him in one sexy move after another.

He couldn't let her continue. He was already rock hard, and each move she made stole more blood from his brain.

In a minute, he wouldn't be thinking at all. In a desperate attempt to regain control of the situation, he twisted her in his arms.

"Sorry. I don't mean to keep encouraging you like that. Flirting is a bad habit of mine, made worse by beer and a pretty woman."

"Don't worry. I'm on to your seductive ways." She traced a finger along his jawline and over his bottom lip.

He swallowed hard. "Ariana," he whispered in a warning tone.

She tugged his head to her. "Anna," she whispered back. She met his gaze, and he knew he was in deep shit. Wanting and need burned as bright in her eyes as it did inside him. Her lips were inches from his, and it didn't take her long to close the distance. He should move. He should pull away, but he didn't.

Her slick, glossed-lips slid against his, and he was lost. He crushed her to him, her soft breasts pressing into his chest. A slight hint of cherry tickled his tongue as he slipped inside her mouth.

She matched the passion of his kiss. The feel of her fingers slipping beneath his shirt, her nails digging into the flesh of his back nearly drove him insane. He slid a hand along the curve of her ass and hauled her to him.

A hard punch to his right arm broke them apart.

"Get a room, ya horny bastard." Scott laughed. "I recognize you're newlyweds and all, but if you keep up that shit, you're going to get everyone all fired up, and we'll be having us an orgy around the fire."

Milo glanced at the group, astounded at how easily he'd lost sight of his goal to remain unaffected. Apparently, everyone had stopped dancing and talking to catch the Milo and Ariana show. Everyone but Sierra. He laughed to cover his embarrassment. "Sorry guys." He shrugged and glanced at Ariana who didn't seem sorry at all. She widened her eyes and bit her bottom lip. He could sense the laugh ready to burst from her lips. The beer she'd consumed had obviously loosened her inhibitions more than his.

He grabbed her hand. "We'll just take a walk," he told the group. "To cool off, you know?"

"Uh-huh," Scott replied. "You do that."

Ariana allowed Milo to pull her along as he made his way past the vehicles, closer to the pond, away from the flickering flames. There was no doubt everyone expected he'd take her somewhere private and have his way with her. He wouldn't of course, but she did wonder where they were going.

The chill in the air was more noticeable away from the fire. The breeze had grown stronger, but it barely tempered her heated skin. She'd known she and Milo had dipped their toes in dangerous waters, but at the moment, she was drunk enough she didn't care. Flirting and dancing with Milo was like nectar to her love-starved soul.

When there was nothing but silence and darkness surrounding them, he dropped her hand and rounded on her. "I'm sorry, Ariana. I'm totally messing this up. People are now aware of your existence, and you're being forced to live a lie, even if it is only temporary. I've created a disaster, and the more I try to fix my screw ups, the worse this gets." He leaned against an aspen, the moonlight shadowing the contours of his tortured expression. The depth of his concern surprised her.

"Milo." She stepped forward into his personal space, her footsteps the slightest bit wobbly.

He reached out to steady her. "We should keep our distance."

She laughed. "Are you afraid I'm going to attack you in the wilderness?" She took another step, and he put a hand up between them. She took it, pressing it between both of her hands before she wrapped her fingers around it and held it to her breast.

"Ariana," he warned.

"It's okay, Milo."

"It's not."

She opened his palm and pressed it against her wildly beating heart. "Can you feel that?"

"Ariana."

"It means I'm alive."

"It means you're drunk, and we're both going to regret anything that we let happen tonight."

"No," she said with plenty of conviction. "It means no matter what you do, there are no guarantees that either of us will have a tomorrow. Right now, we're alive, and this was turning into the perfect evening. When was the last time you relaxed and laughed like that?"

He pulled his hand away. "I don't relax. Ever. Not when someone's life is at stake."

"Seriously." She pushed against his chest. "You are wound so tight I'm surprised you haven't had a heart attack."

He stood his ground, his gaze boring into hers. She sensed he was on the verge of coming uncorked, and she was just drunk enough she didn't care.

"You've got your life all buttoned up perfectly." She walked her fingers up his abdomen. "You're the hometown hero, with nerves of steel. You tease the ladies, but you'll never commit to one of them. On the surface, you're Mr. Perfect, but deep down, you're the one that's truly messed up."

Several seconds ticked by with nothing but their breathing and the sound of crickets to fill the void. The intensity of his stare shot a frazzled shiver straight to her core. Still, he didn't break.

She heaved out a frustrated sigh and stepped back. "And I thought my life was a disaster." She turned to head back to camp.

"The last time I relaxed while protecting someone, she died, Ariana. Did you hear that? She *died*." His voice cracked as he said the last word.

She stopped and turned. If she'd thought he'd looked tortured before, his expression was ten times worse now. The pained look on his face broke her heart. "Milo…" He didn't stop her this time when she got close to him. She lifted a hand, resting it on his cheek. "I'm so sorry. Will you tell me about her?"

He shook his head as though gathering his emotions. "She walked. She'd been confined for a long period of time, just like you. She kept threatening to walk, insisting her life wasn't worth living if she couldn't be free."

His words hit home. "Just like me."

It was his turn to cup her cheek. "Just like you."

The sadness in his face made her want to cry. "That's why you were so angry with me the day you couldn't find me. It's why you were so worried."

He nodded.

"I'm sorry. I'm so sorry. You're doing this as a favor to a friend, and I'm making your life hell."

"No." He pulled her closer, brushing his lips across hers in a soft kiss. "Never hell."

"What happened to her?" She shouldn't ask. She was far too close to a similar situation, and it wouldn't do anyone any good if she was frightened of her own shadow.

"She's was a party girl. Pretty. Enough that she caught the attention of a high-powered drug dealer. He messed her up one night, and she thought turning him over to the cops would be a great way to get revenge. It worked out for the Feds. Not so much for her. She didn't have the fortitude to stay away. She snuck away one night and called her party friends." He dropped his gaze. "They found her two days later in a muddy ditch on the outskirts of New Jersey. If we didn't have her fingerprints on file, the authorities would have been hard pressed to identify her."

A stone-cold shiver skittered across her skin. She folded her arms. "That wasn't your fault, Milo. No one can make us follow the rules if we choose not to." She swallowed, thinking of her own infidelities. "She put her life in danger. Not you."

He took off his flannel shirt and draped it over her shoulders. "I could have done more. I should have seen the signs." He shook his head. "It weighs heavy on me."

"It would me, too." That was a huge burden to bear even if it wasn't his fault. "But she lived her life her way, Milo. I know you were trying to help her, but you can't take away her right to freedom. Part of me can understand why she walked." She tucked her arms inside his shirt, loving the way the soft cotton smelled of him, warming her inside and out.

He gripped her hand. "Don't ever do that to me, Ariana. Promise me you won't do anything that might bring harm to you."

"Okay." She tried to give him a reassuring smile, her guilt as heavy as a fifty-pound block of cement. "Don't worry about me. My days are almost up, and then I can have my life back."

Milo held her hand as they walked through the quiet moonlight. He hadn't said much after he'd given her a peek into his psyche, but she could appreciate how hard opening up had to be for him. Taking her on, doing this favor for Quinn, had cost him more than it would most people. This warmth that now surrounded them spawned from a different place than the sexual heat that forever blazed between them. She liked the comfort it brought her, and she could only hope it brought him the same kind of fortitude and solace.

Their path took them on another downward slope. It seemed they'd gone up and down several times. Tall brush grew just off their path, with pines and aspens giving them solitude. "How far are we from camp?" The full moon hovered high in the sky, and she had nothing to mark their heading. For all she knew, they were completely lost.

He stopped, taking her arms and turning her a quarter of a turn. Coming up behind her, he put a hand on one hip, and pointed past her with his other. "There's a hint of our fire, if you look right through those trees."

Ariana followed his direction until she spotted the glow. "I see it. It seems like we've been walking forever, but we're not that far away at all. For all I knew, we were walking in circles."

He laughed then, the first hint of amusement or happiness since they'd danced by the fire. "Busted. Not circles necessarily, but not a straight line, either. I wasn't ready to head back to the others yet, but we probably ought to now. It's getting colder."

She snuggled deeper into his flannel shirt, warmed by the thought that he'd purposely kept her out there in an effort to spend time alone. "That's okay. I just didn't want to get lost."

"No fear of that. I've been roaming these hills forever."

They kept the banter lighthearted as they made their way back, and Milo had taken her hand again. She liked it though she had to wonder if it was because he liked her, or because he thought she'd trip on the uneven, unfamiliar terrain.

When they walked into camp, their group of friends had become noticeably smaller.

"Where did everyone go?" Milo asked as he sat next to Scott. Ariana planted herself in the camp chair next to him.

"Kim wasn't feeling well," Scott replied. "Jerry took her home. Sierra didn't want to stay if Kim wasn't, so she and Tyler left, too." He twisted the top off another beer. "Looks like it's just the six of us."

Ariana swiveled toward Milo. "I thought Kim was our designated driver."

"Aren't you guys staying?" Luke adjusted his ball cap as he tossed the question to Milo. "You always stay."

Milo glanced from Ariana to the others. "Uh, actually, we'd planned on catching a ride with Jerry and Kim, and picking my truck up tomorrow."

Ariana nodded.

Scott laughed. "Looks like you're shit out of luck. I don't think any of us are in any shape to drive. Hope you brought sleeping bags."

Ariana's brows shot skyward. "Sleeping bags?" She glanced about the camp. "There's not even a tent."

"We sleep under the stars." Lily nudged her husband. "Like Luke, Milo and Scott did as boys, right? Except we pile in the backs of our trucks so we're not on the ground where the crawly things can get us."

"Crawly things?" Ariana's gaze slipped to the dirt.

Luke scoffed. "There are no crawly things to be worried about. We've been over this a hundred times, Lily."

"Don't tell me that," Lily threw back at him. "There are snakes. I've seen them."

"Snakes?" Ariana lifted her feet off the ground as she eyed Milo, feeling the slightest bit panicky. "You took me walking in the dark with snakes around? Are you crazy?"

"You're freaking her out, Lily." Milo took Ariana's hand. "There aren't any snakes that are going to get you. There are mostly rattlers out here, and they only come out during the day. Right now, they're curled up under rocks sleeping."

"Rattlesnakes are poisonous." She shook her head. "You're not helping."

"Honey, I've been coming out here for years. Roaming the hills, sleeping on the ground. I've never been bitten. No one else here has either."

"There was—"

"Scott." Milo cut him off. "There's nothing to be afraid of. I promise to keep you safe, okay?"

She let that thought settle in her slightly fuzzy brain. She'd trusted Milo with her life where her father's men were concerned. There was no reason to not trust him now. "Okay." She tentatively rested her shoes back on the ground.

"Don't worry, Anna," Jen joined in. "I don't like snakes, either, but we're not going to run into any tonight. They don't like the fire, and like Milo said, they'll be hiding under a rock somewhere. Not bugging us."

Ariana nodded. "Thanks. That makes me feel better." She appreciated how all of Milo's friends seemed concerned for her welfare.

"Now that that's settled, we're still screwed. I've got a couple of blankets, but I didn't bring sleeping bags." Milo looked at Ariana. "I hate to ask you, but hopefully you'll be okay crashing in the front of the truck for a couple of hours until I'm good to drive. Usually, I'm better prepared."

"We've got an extra bag and an extra quilt in case it gets too chilly," Lily offered. "Coupled with your blankets, do you think that will be enough?"

Ariana glanced at Milo with no idea what his reaction would be. Never in a million years could she have pictured herself sleeping next to a mountain pond in the bed of a truck under the stars. She couldn't get much farther away from downtown Chicago.

"Up to you, Anna. Are you feeling adventurous?"

All eyes in the party turned to her. If she said no, she'd disappoint them. She couldn't do that to these kind people who'd treated her as one of their own. She gave them a smile that was a hundred times more confident than she felt. "Okay. Why not?"

Luke twisted the cap off another beer and handed it to Milo. "Better keep her, man."

"I'm planning on it." Milo took the chilled bottle from his friend, but didn't laugh, didn't echo the teasing sentiment of his friend.

Ariana studied his profile. Her deputy certainly was a great actor. If she didn't know better, she'd believe he meant every word.

CHAPTER TWELVE

It was nearly two a.m. before the guys extinguished the fire. Scott complained he was tired, but from the way he hurried after Jen to his truck, Ariana was pretty sure he had other things in mind besides sleep.

Luke and Lily called it a night as well, which meant she and Milo needed to follow suit or appear suspicious. Lily carted over the extra bedding to Milo's truck, and Luke was kind enough to give Ariana his pillow.

Beneath the soft glow of the moon, Milo spread the quilts on the bed of his truck before laying the sleeping bag over them. He sighed. Then he picked everything up and put the sleeping bag bottom first this time. "I hope we don't freeze our asses off, but I think we'll be more comfortable this way."

She eyed the makeshift bed with trepidation. It wasn't a real bed. There would be others not far away. Unfortunately, there was maybe five feet from side to side, and that felt pretty damn intimate to her. How was she supposed to fall asleep next to the man who haunted her dreams?

Milo tossed the pillow to one side of the truck before walking to the tailgate. He extended a hand down to her. She grasped it, put one foot on the bumper, and he hauled her up.

He folded the quilts out of the way, and she stepped forward. "This is kind of awkward," she said in a low tone the others wouldn't hear. "Us sleeping together but not really sleeping together."

The low rumble of his laugh sparked shivers inside her. "Think we can behave?"

"We have to, don't we?"

"Yes." His reply was firm, but edgy, too. The sparks between them were undeniable. It was easier to ignore her attraction when they weren't in such close proximity, but that wasn't an option tonight.

She lay down next to him, leaving as much space between them as possible. He pulled the layers of quilts over them. "Warm enough?"

"I'm good." Between his shirt, the blankets, and being so close to him, lack of heat was not an issue. The uneven surface of the truck bed, however, wasn't exactly a comfy mattress, but she wouldn't complain. She fluffed the feather pillow and tucked it beneath her head.

Milo released a weighted breath. Darkness and silence crept in, making it seem like they were cocooned in their own little world. The stars above glimmered like they'd done for centuries, and suddenly, everything about her life growing up in Chicago seemed surreal. "It's funny how looking up at a sky full of stars can make you feel insignificant. Like all your problems are almost silly."

"Having a price on your head isn't insignificant."

"But it is. If I were to die, look at the millions of other souls here on earth that would fill in and take my place. I'm just a tiny drop in the world's bucket."

He shifted, tilting his head to face her. "Maybe to the world, but to those who know and care about you, your loss would be devastating."

"Maybe for my best friend, but I'm guessing that would be all."

Silence crept in for several beats. "It would devastate me."

His admission scratched at a long-held scar. "Only because it would mess with your confidence to protect the fine citizens of this county. Not because I would be gone. You don't know me well enough to miss me."

He rolled onto his side. "How can you say that? We've been together 24 hours a day for more than two weeks." He flattened out on the truck bed and huffed. "I know you better than you think."

It was her turn to lift up on her elbow. "Really? What is it you think you know so well?"

"You like your coffee black."

She snorted. "So does half the world."

"You enjoy a long bubble bath."

"How do you know that?"

"There's always bubbles left in the tub when you're finished, and they smell good, like you."

Her heart squeezed, leaving a too-familiar ache. "Still, that comes from spending time together, not really getting to know each other." She lay back down. He didn't know her at all.

Another minute of silence passed before he spoke again. "You're an extremely brave person who wants nothing more than to be loved." His quiet words were a dagger ripping into the dark corners of her heart. "Your family, who should have loved you, didn't. I'm not sure exactly what happened, but they, maybe your father, hurt you deeply. At first, I thought you were testifying to get some sort of revenge for being ignored, but now, I think it's something more."

The ache inside her swelled, closing her throat and forcing tears into her eyes. She steeled her jaw and focused on the vast dark sky, willing it to steal her away into the night.

"Am I close?"

He waited several moments, but she couldn't answer. With only a few words, he'd laid bare her soul. Throughout her life, she'd done an excellent job keeping people from breaching that barrier, but now that Milo had, she was clueless on how to protect herself.

"Ariana?" He rolled toward her, his fingers searching out her face, finding her damned tears. "Shit," he said under his breath. "I'm sorry. I didn't mean to make you cry."

He drew a rough thumb beneath each of her eyes, dragging her tears across her cheeks. She pushed him away, embarrassed that he'd seen through her carefully crafted mask so easily.

"I'm such an ass." He scooted closer beneath the blankets and pulled her against his chest. She wanted to resist, but having a soft place to fall was worth more than her pride. She curled against him, allowing her distress to eek away from her little by little.

She waited until she'd regained control of her emotions before she spoke. "My father is a ruthless man who dominates his world with a merciless and vile fist." Her first words were followed by a shuddering sigh, and she hesitated a moment to see what would follow.

Relief. The tiniest bit of relief soaked into her. Kenzie had a good idea what her family life had been like, but Ariana had never told her everything. Because of that, Ariana had never experienced the release that came with exposing her tragedies.

"I'm sorry," he whispered against her hair. "No person should have to grow up like that."

"Many do, though. I suppose I was lucky that at least I had money to spend. My father took great pride in the fact that we wore designer clothes, that my brother and I attended the finest schools."

"Don't justify his behavior, Ariana."

She blew out a deep breath. "I'm not. Those things he did for us, well at least for me, were like paying to have the landscape meticulously maintained. It was for show. No one would ever accuse him of not having the best of everything. His children were an extension of that." She rested a shaking hand on Milo's chest, his heart pounding against her palm, strong and sure. "My brother is a little different. He's being groomed to take over in the organization, but I'm not sure my father has shown him love, either. Maybe."

She lifted her head, needing to see the expression on Milo's face. "My testimony will likely harm my brother, too."

He gave her a consoling smile and hugged her to him. "And that bothers you."

"It does." Fresh tears pooled in her eyes. "He's never had a choice concerning his future, either. This was forced upon him."

"It's okay, Ariana. You're doing the right thing. I'm not going to say it's not going to cost your brother time in a cell, but in the long run, you may be saving him. He'll have the opportunity to reform, and depending upon what crimes he's committed, he may not serve that many years. Or maybe he'll turn state's evidence and be given a reprieve."

Another layer of worry fell away. "I hadn't thought of that."

He caressed the side of her cheek, tucking her hair behind her ear. "Think of the people you might be saving from dying at his hand. In effect, you'll be saving your brother's soul."

She nodded. "Thank you for saying this to me. I can't tell you how much it helps."

"Are you worried about sending your father to prison, too?"

"No." Her conviction echoed in her reply. "I hope he rots."

"I kind of figured that. Can you tell me about him?"

A fistful of pain lodged in her throat. It was several moments before she could swallow past it. He'd trusted her with his hurts. Maybe she could trust him, too. "I'm not sure I can," she managed.

He hugged her tighter. "It's okay. You don't have to."

She lay on his chest several moments, listening to the crickets chirp, letting the feel of him comfort her. "I was in love once. When I was sixteen."

"Yeah?" His voice was lighter, as though he believed she'd changed the subject. "Not since sixteen?"

She couldn't answer that question, couldn't comment on what she'd dealt with in the years since Danny's death. "His name was Danny. His father worked for mine. That's how we met." A painful smile trembled on her lips as she remembered how much she'd loved to spend time with him roaming the streets and hanging out in abandoned warehouses, tossing rocks into the river, and how she'd loved it when he'd kissed her. Back before her father paid much notice to her.

"Danny," Milo repeated. "I might be a little jealous of him." He chuckled.

"No." She shook her head. "My father caught us together one night." She paused, but Milo remained silent. "The night I lost my virginity."

"Ariana," Milo whispered, his voice no longer upbeat. "No."

She tried to inhale a calming breath, but her tight lungs only allowed air in tiny, ragged increments. "My father tortured him, forcing me to watch."

He put a hand against her cheek. "You don't have to do this."

"Before he killed him, he had someone cut off his..." The horrible memories fired in her brain with enough power to make her shudder.

Milo tightened his arms around her, crushing her against his chest. "It's...God, I don't even know what to say to that. Just know, he'll never do it again."

"I know. That's why I have to testify. Even if Kenzie begged me not to. I owe that to Danny and to all the people he still may hurt if I don't do what I can to stop him."

He kissed the top of her head, sending a scattering of peace over her. "You are an amazing woman, Ariana. Not many would dare go up against that kind of person."

"It was my fault he died, Milo. If Danny hadn't loved me, he'd still be alive."

"You don't know that, Ariana. He might have followed in his father's footsteps and found himself mixed up with the wrong people anyway. You have to let that guilt go."

"Maybe after I testify I'll be able to. It kind of feels like things have come full circle. Maybe gaining a new life and a new identity will help me to move on. I'd like to be able to do that."

"You should."

"In some ways, you and I are similar. We're both carrying around some serious baggage."

He inhaled a deep breath, his chest expanding against her cheek. "Yours is a little different than mine."

"How? We both feel responsible for another person's death."

"First, you were a kid. Second, it was my job to protect Jane."

"Still, maybe it's time to let go."

"I'd like to, Ariana, but it's not that easy. Sometimes I wonder if it will haunt me until the end of my days."

She lifted off his chest, gazing at his face in the moonlight. A good-hearted man hid beneath the exterior of her sexy deputy. "Thank you for listening. I've never been able to talk about this with anyone, but telling you feels like I've dropped a boulder of guilt. I just wish I could give you the same kind of peace."

⌒

Ariana woke with a start. She wasn't sure how many hours had passed since she and Milo had drifted off to sleep, but she was freezing, and her right hip hurt from pressing into the truck bed. She rolled onto her back and looked in Milo's direction. Clouds had covered the moon, leaving utter darkness to settle around them. If she hadn't been able to hear his deep breathing, she might wonder if he had deserted her. She slid a hand across the sleeping bag and came in contact with the hard muscles of his stomach.

She hated to admit it, but she found him more attractive now that he'd shared his vulnerable side. Plus, he had learned the worst about her and hadn't judged. Words couldn't express how grateful she was for that.

She fluffed her pillow and closed her eyes, trying to will herself back to sleep. They'd stayed up late, so it couldn't be too long before the sun rose over the hills. She could manage until then.

A restless few minutes passed and then she heard movement. Scuffling on the ground, a rustling of the bushes. Something was in their camp.

Her breathing grew shallow as she tried to discern which direction the sounds came from. It was close. For all she knew, it could be a bear or something. She really had no idea what kind of wild animals roamed the area, but something was out there. She swore it was getting closer.

Fear drove her to ply herself against Milo. She put her mouth to his ear. "Milo," she whispered. He moaned, but didn't wake. "Milo."

Before she could comprehend what was happening, Milo wrapped steel-banded arms around her middle and tossed her on her back, covering her in a dominant position. Thoughts of what was outside the truck bed took a secondary position to the hulking man on top of her.

"Milo," she squeaked. "Get off me."

He didn't move. She couldn't see his face to know if he was wide awake or tossing her in his dreams.

"There's something out there," she tried again.

"I hear it," he whispered back.

Relief flooded her. He was awake and coherent. "Could it be my father's men?" She hadn't been able to think those thoughts a moment before while Milo had been asleep.

"Shh…"

Her quick reprieve shifted back to worry.

"Not a person. Mountain lion, maybe," he whispered.

Adrenaline kicked in. "What?" she squeaked. She tried to move, but he had her pinned.

"I'm just kidding, darlin'." His deep chuckle vibrated through the darkness. "It's most likely a raccoon. Nothing big that's going to get you."

It took a few seconds for his words to register. "You…" She pushed against him, trying to decide if she was grateful their lives weren't in danger, or if she was mad at him for teasing her.

"Sorry, but that's what happens when you wake me from a hot-as-hell dream. I can't have you in real life, but damn…"

The adrenaline rushing through her veins took a sharp curve toward long-thwarted need. "You were dreaming about me?" Acute awareness of his muscled body pressed to hers flooded her brain. Her breasts pushed against him with each breath she took, and the evidence of his physical need for her wouldn't be ignored.

"Yeah." His admission came out as a breathless whisper. "I just, uh…I should move off you, but you feel so damn good, Ariana."

She loved the way he said her name, sounding a little sleepy, and more than a little turned on. "What were we doing in your dream?" She shouldn't have asked, but she wanted to share the fantasy.

"Mmm…" The sound rumbled in his chest. "It kind of started out like the night we played poker. You were doing this sexy kind of strip tease dance for me. You wore this lacy turquoise bra that played peek-a-boo with your nipples."

She swallowed, trying to wet her dry mouth. With just a few words, he'd sucked her into his heated dream. She wanted to do that dance for him. She wanted to turn him on. Wanted him to feel the aching need that she experienced over and over again every day they were together.

"You slipped off your jeans and your turquoise panties looked like the ones you had on at the river."

"I still haven't forgiven you for peeking," she said, breathless.

He rolled off her with a groan. "Oh God, Ariana. How could I not? You're the…sexiest thing that's ever stumbled into my life. From the moment I saw you, I wanted you. But you're like the sweetest piece of candy I can't have. The more I know you, the more I like you, but I can never have you. It's a sick game the fates are playing with my head. Forgive me for my moment of weakness."

His words stunned her. She'd known she'd caught his eye, but she had no idea he experienced the attraction to the degree she did. He might not agree they should have their moment in time, but she couldn't be sure she'd ever feel like this again, and she wasn't about to miss the opportunity.

She slid next to him, snuggling a leg between his and resting her head on his chest.

"What are you doing?"

"Shh…" It was her turn to silence him. She took his face in her hands, finding his lips with her thumbs. He didn't move as she slid her mouth across his. The warm, soft feel of him against her was all the encouragement she needed.

She paused, rubbing a thumb across his bottom lip, reveling in the moisture she'd left there. Still, he didn't move. Stubble tickled her fingers as she traced them along his jaw.

She kissed him again, adding pressure to his lips this time, sucking his bottom lip, and running her tongue along the crease of his mouth.

Soft streams of moonlight returned as he growled and rolled her over, once again pinning her down. He held her wrists on the pillow next to her head. "We can't do this."

"Why?" She wasn't going to take no for an answer this time.

"It's unethical."

"The hell it is. You're not working in an official capacity. You're doing a favor for a friend." She tried to wriggle free, but he was too strong. "This is right, Milo. Maybe not tomorrow. Maybe not ever again, but for tonight, it's meant to be."

"I'd be using you when you're vulnerable."

"Don't tell me that. I might be in a state of flux, but I'm far from broken. We deserve to be happy. Making love with you will make me happy." She tried to break loose again, but couldn't. "Are you saying you don't want me?"

He remained silent, and she could sense the war raging inside him.

"Let me go, Milo."

He released her wrists, but still hovered above her.

She ran her hands beneath his shirt and up his sides, his skin warm and taut beneath her fingers.

She hadn't touched anything quite so wonderful. "I want you," she whispered. "Please don't deny me."

She slid her arms around his neck and tugged on him until he surrendered. His lips met hers in a frantic kiss, as though now that he'd reconsidered, she'd somehow disappear. His tongue tangled with hers as he possessed her mouth, tasting, demanding. His kisses threatened to steal her soul.

"Milo," she whispered when he pulled away, afraid that by breathing, she'd broken the spell.

"I can't do this. It goes against everything I've believed."

Chapter Thirteen

Ariana climbed on top of Milo, straddling his waist. "It goes against what you *thought* was right, but maybe things aren't that way. Maybe this *is* right." She slipped his flannel shirt from her shoulders and the tank top over her head. Night air caressed her, cooling her heated skin.

He watched, an enthralled look on his face as she took his hand, cupping her breast. She sighed as he rubbed a thumb across the lace covering her nipple, sending an explosion of excited shivers through her. It didn't take much to break him.

He teased her bud until it strained against the black lace of her bra. "Oh," he said on a breath. "Ariana." He lifted his other hand, claiming both breasts. She leaned into his touch, allowing him to take the full weight of them as he molded her to his hands.

He slipped his fingers around her back and undid the clasp of her bra. Her unrestrained breasts fell forward, heavy and aching with desire. He captured a nipple, sucking her inside his hot mouth, making her muscles clench. A second later a breathtaking firebomb of desire erupted inside her.

She sucked in a ragged breath of fresh mountain air, trying to regain some semblance of control.

She'd never known a man's touch could be so powerful.

"Damn," he whispered.

Her brain spun in a million different directions, focusing on sensation and ignoring any sensible thoughts. The only thing she knew was she needed more of him touching her and tasting her.

Her slack bra fell off with a shrug, and she jerked at the button at her waist. It popped open, and she unzipped her pants.

"Whoa, darlin'." He stilled her hands. "There's no hurry. If we're going to do this, I intend to enjoy every second of it. We've got a couple of hours before the sun comes up."

The thought of making love to Milo for hours was more than she could have asked for.

"I just, I want you to touch me before I wake up and realize this is a dream."

"Trust me. This is so much better than a dream." He tugged her down with him, onto the sleeping bag. "Get under here with me. It's cold out there." He pulled the quilts up around them and then rolled partially on her, covering her thighs with his leg. "I can't believe I let you talk me into this."

"Touch me, Milo." The center of her ached for him like a sinner at heaven's gate craving forgiveness. This was nothing like the innocent attraction and awkward first time she'd had with Danny. The intensity was a thousand times as strong.

He drew a finger across the top elastic of her panties and slowly traced upward. She shivered as he neared her breasts, but instead of touching her there, he continued through the valley to her collarbone where he followed along its lines. "Is this good?"

"No, not even. Don't tease me, Milo."

He trailed down, caressing the sensitive flesh on the underside of her breast, and the ache rose to a new level. "How about this?"

"Better." She shifted and closed her eyes on a moan when he circled her nipple with his tongue. The open air reacted with her wet areola, tightening it, sending a ripple effect straight to her core.

He cupped her breast, massaging the mound upward and forcing her nipple out. He nipped her and another brilliant explosion tore through her.

"Milo," she whispered. "I need you now." She recognized the fact that she'd had very little experience with men, and that she probably came across as a novice, but the building sensation between her legs demanded a proper release. "I can't wait."

Milo chuckled. His warm lips covered hers, stealing her attention away from other areas, but not for long. Soon his hand slipped along the edge of her panties again, this time dipping beneath the silky fabric. She gasped against his mouth as she arched to give him better access. "Yes." He was so close.

"Ariana." He gazed into her face, but the moonlight behind him hid his expression.

Tiny sensations burst as he crossed her mound. She inhaled in anticipation as he slipped between her folds.

"Good God almighty. You're so wet."

"I know," she whispered in a shivered breath. Her body acted of its own accord. She whimpered as he drove a finger inside, making her arch, and increasing her hunger for him.

What he'd found there must have changed his mind about going slow. He nearly ripped her panties and jeans from her body and discarded his clothes just as quickly. He fussed for a minute with a condom before he pulled her against him, resting a naked thigh between hers. His rock hard penis pressed against her hip, tempting and taunting her.

"Oh, God, Ariana. This is just…" He claimed her mouth in a possessive, dominating kiss. She wrapped her arms around his neck, holding him to her. He was so close, and she wasn't going to let him go. Not until he gave her what she craved.

He cupped her, dipping another finger inside. "Shit." He rolled on top of her, spreading her thighs with his knees. "I can't wait, either."

She smiled as he positioned his penis at her apex and buried himself inside her. She cried out as he filled her, and she hurried to cover her mouth so she wouldn't wake the others.

"Damn, you're tight."

"Don't stop," she gasped as pain-tainted pleasure rushed through her.

He thrust again, stretching her to accommodate him.

She knew she would be taut. She'd only ever made love the one time.

With each stroke, her body softened and warmed. She loved the sensation of him filling her and then leaving a void, only to fill it again. The feel of him slipping into her was beyond compare. He was so large and hard, and it was as though each thrust claimed another piece of her, leaving her in awe of this powerful act.

She angled her hips to give him greater access, and she swore she could feel him hit rock bottom. Another shiver of desire raced through her at the thought. "More," she whispered.

He pulled from her and rolled her over as though she was nothing but a ragdoll. He lifted her bottom until she was on all fours. Grasping her hips, he filled her again, hitting different muscles, creating a mass of delicious sensations. She gripped the sleeping bag as he slammed into her, her breasts tingling as they rocked each time he drove inside.

When she could no longer contain the white, frenzied heat licking at her, her muscles contracted and went slack. She lost her balance and fell forward into the pillow. He rolled her again, penetrating her over and over until her mind was a blurry haze of sensation. She gasped and clenched again.

Milo swore and went rigid, not moving for a few long seconds, before he collapsed on top of her.

The quiet night settled around them again, cooling her overheated skin. It was several moments before anyone spoke.

"I don't know what to say, Ariana." His voice was hoarse, breathless.

"I do." She gave him a long, lingering kiss. "Thank you, Milo. I'll always treasure this."

"Shit," he whispered under his breath. He rolled, hauling her against him, cradling her with strong, protective arms.

The harsh morning light hit Milo square in the face, waking him from a beautiful slumber. He opened his eyes and blinked, his brain slow to process the devastating scene in front of him. Ariana lay next to him, wearing only his unbuttoned shirt, the lower half of his body having no trouble responding to her luscious breasts that peeked from beneath the flannel. Her hair had scattered in a tumbled mess on her half of the pillow they'd shared. Both of their jeans and a pair of silky black panties sat tangled in an accusing pile to the side of her.

He closed his eyes, wishing he was home in his bed and this had all been a sweet fantasy.

When he opened them, she still lay there in all her beautiful glory. Already, he craved her touch and the feel of her body giving in.

"Hell," he whispered. He'd really fucked up this time. Did he have no moral scruples at all? He'd had the best damn night of his life, but he'd tossed his self-respect out the window when he'd allowed the midnight magic and Ariana's sweet charms to convince him honor didn't matter. The reprehensible part was, he knew without a doubt, he'd turn around and do it again. His father would be ashamed of his behavior.

He found his shirt and boxers and slipped them on. With stealthy fingers, he slid the quilts up to cover her so he wouldn't be tempted to take her again. He reached across her and snatched his jeans, leaving her clothes to fare it alone. He maneuvered his feet into his pants and wrestled until they were over his hips and buttoned.

The gentle sounds of nature pervaded the area, giving Milo one last shot at peace before he woke Ariana and the fallout began. He visually caressed her face, the contours of her cheeks, the graceful curve of her lips. In a perfect world, he'd be able to lean over and kiss her, make fiery love to her once again in the early morning light before anyone else woke. Unfortunately, this was far from a perfect world.

"Fuck." He blew out a breath and leaned close to her ear, catching a hint of her lilac perfume. The provocative scent instantly took him back to the previous night and the third time they'd made love. She'd curtained them with her long tresses while she'd ridden him to paradise. That image of her would forever be etched in his mind.

This was going to be a hell of a hard mess to clean up.

"Ariana." He gently shook her shoulder. "Wake up."

She lifted her lids, peering at him with her unforgettable turquoise eyes and smiled. "Good morning," she said in a sleepy voice.

"Morning," he replied more gruffly than he should have. He climbed out the side of the truck. "I'm going to gather our chairs and cooler while you get dressed, and then we'll head home."

He caught the glimpse of hurt and confusion in her eyes before he turned away, but she had to recognize there would be consequences for their careless behavior the night before. Whether they wanted it or not, they had no future together.

With careful precision, Ariana sighted in one of the coffee cans and pulled the trigger. The bullet ripped through the late evening atmosphere and nailed the can. Hitting her target didn't make her feel any better. A week had passed. She and Milo had barely had a decent conversation. He'd provided her with everything she needed as far as food and a place to sleep, but he'd retreated inside a shell so far she couldn't reach. Days were spent with him working in the yard or fishing with his friends. She'd been allowed to tag along, but there had been no personal moments alone. If no one else was around and there were no chores left to do, he'd immersed himself in his precious book.

His message had been loud and clear. He regretted their night together and intended to stay as far away from her as possible.

She couldn't bring herself to feel the same way. Being with him, making love to him had been the best thing she'd ever done.

She aimed and pierced the tin of another can. Bored out of her mind, she'd spent a considerable amount of time shooting, and it was starting to show. More times than not, she'd hit the coffee can first shot. She'd even moved farther away from the targets and could still hit them a good portion of the time.

But enough was enough. She barely had a week left with Milo, and she was surprised to find she now spent more time worrying about leaving him instead of testifying. In fact, she almost looked forward to accusing her father face-to-face and watching him pay for his crimes. Now that she'd seen the possibilities life had to offer, she cursed her father for ruling over all the lives around him like a vicious dictator. He deserved to die for that if anyone asked her. Years in jail would not replace the precious time he'd stolen from those around him, whether it was out of fear for their lives or for the lives he'd carelessly taken.

No more wasting her life on fear. She'd own her time and live each day to the fullest. If that meant she died sooner, at least she'd perish while she was living. And this mess between her and Milo, this not talking to each other, was ridiculous, and she'd had enough. She slipped the gun into Milo's holster and headed inside.

She left the handgun hanging on the pantry door and moved to the entry of the living room. He sat on the brown leather couch, his eyes glued to the pages of his book. She knew he knew she was there. If he could sense her presence while he was asleep on the couch, he damn well could sense her now.

"We need to talk." She walked forward until she stood directly in front of him.

"No, we don't." He didn't spare her a glance.

"I say we do."

He looked at her beneath his brows. "Are you safe? Are you cared for? Then my job is complete."

If she didn't know his background, she'd be deeply hurt. "I'm sorry our night together had such a profoundly negative effect on you. For me, it was a night I'll cherish forever."

He slammed the book shut and shoved it to the side as he stood. His black t-shirt showcased the outline of his well-defined chest, and she had to refrain from reaching out to him.

"Damn it, Ariana. Don't make it sound like I'm some insensitive cad and that making love didn't mean as much to me as it did to you."

She much preferred the fiery side of him to being ignored. "If it meant so much, then why are you so cold to me?"

"Because staying away from you is the only way I can guarantee I won't make the same mistake again."

"So making love to me was a mistake?" Even though she understood what he meant, it still stung.

"Don't twist my words. Don't make me out to be a jerk. You know very well why we shouldn't have done what we did."

"That's just it, Milo. I really don't understand. You're not doing any less of a job because of it.

Nothing bad has happened. Nothing has changed except for the fact you now avoid me. Help me understand."

He drew his brows together, a pained looked echoing in his eyes. "Being close to you messes with my perception. It's hard to keep a clear head when all I can think of is us by the lake, and the sight of you laying there." He closed his eyes, and she wasn't sure if that helped him block her out or gave him a more vivid picture of them together.

She put a hand on his chest. "I want you like that now," she whispered.

He opened his eyes, agony and confusion reflecting from within.

"Deny it all you want, but I can tell you need me, too." She moved her fingers to his jawline, tension pulsing beneath her fingertips. "Why do we have to resist? Why can't this just be what it is?"

"Because." He heaved a sigh and took a step back. "Because you have a price on your head. Because I was charged with protecting you. Because not keeping a clear head could endanger you. The list goes on. Beyond all that, you're leaving in a week, and we won't see each other again, so what's the point of allowing myself to grow more attached to you? It will just be a bigger heartbreak in the end."

That hurt the most of all. She'd fallen for him, too, and it seemed like such a tragedy if they never had the chance to find out how deep their love could grow. They deserved that chance. "What if I come back? After the trial? What if I ask Quinn to make this my home?"

Emotions played across his face, and he didn't answer for a few moments. "Is that what you want?"

An excited, yet terrified tremble rolled through her. She'd never fully given herself the luxury of dreaming that staying with Milo might be a real possibility. She'd yearned for it, but never believed it had a chance of happening. "I know I don't want to lose you."

"Could you be happy here? When I first met you, you insisted to Quinn you wanted to be sent somewhere tropical."

"That was before I knew what existed here. I'll admit I'm surprised Aspen has stolen my heart, but I think I've fallen for this quaint little place and the people here."

He wrapped an arm around her, and she happily fell against him, her heart bursting with joy. He claimed her mouth in a desperate kiss, and she answered with equal hunger. The taste of his kisses was her own special paradise. He turned and laid her on the sofa, following her down until he covered her. She wrapped her arms around his neck as she sent him a glowing smile. "Who needs tropical when I have you to keep me warm?"

He laughed as he moved in for another kiss. "Who knows, with the two of us around, this place might turn tropical."

She wiggled beneath him, loving the weight of his warm and hard body pressing against her.

A rumbling sound interrupted their silliness, and Milo turned to give his vibrating cell phone a dirty look. The offending device continued to pulsate on the coffee table next to them.

"Whoever it is can call back later." Milo captured her mouth again, and the phone stopped.

CINDY STARK

He pushed her t-shirt up over her breast and tugged down her bra. "Mmm...turquoise. My new favorite color."

She gasped as he sucked a nipple into his mouth, knowing she'd never tire of the tiny explosions he set off inside her. "I have to admit, I was worried I did everything wrong the other night."

He stopped and looked up at her. "What do you mean?"

"I just...you know, don't have much experience with men."

"You weren't a virgin. You told me about Danny."

She smiled, loving the concerned look in his eyes. "Danny was the only person I've slept with besides you."

He paused as though digesting the information. "Shit, Ariana. I didn't hurt you, did I?"

"No." She trailed her fingers down his cheek. "It was amazing, and I'm glad it was you." She arched toward him, offering her breast again. "Make love to me, Milo."

He stared at her, and she was afraid she'd ruined the moment for them. Then he nodded. "Okay." His mouth closed over her, and she shivered with delight.

The phone vibrated again.

"No," he whispered as he moved to her other breast.

She slid her fingers through his hair, holding him to her, not caring if his touch made it hard to breathe. The hard proof of his desire pressed against her, and she moved, allowing him to settle more firmly in her apex. She knew from experience the other night, she needed to be patient and enjoy all the facets of lovemaking, but the anticipation of

302

having him slide into her, of him stretching her as he filled her sent a sharp quiver straight to her core.

The phone vibrated for a third time, and Milo stopped. "Damn it. Why the hell can't they leave us alone?"

He shifted and grabbed his impatient cell phone. His annoyed features chilled as he looked at the screen. "It's Quinn," he said, sending her a worried glance. "Hey," he said into the phone.

He listened intently, never taking his eyes off her. Something about his gaze left an uneasy mark on her intuition. "Uh, no. She didn't."

She tried to swallow past her building fear.

"No, she didn't tell me that, either." He frowned. "Okay. You could be right, and that would be a problem. Let me check."

He stood and headed into the hallway toward their bedrooms. Ariana jumped up and followed. She was pretty sure she knew what Quinn had told him and where he was headed.

CHAPTER FOURTEEN

Ariana entered her bedroom to find Milo glancing about the room, the phone still at his ear. "Where is it?" He directed the question to her.

She bit her lip to keep it from trembling as she stepped forward and removed the cell phone from her dresser drawer. He shook his head at her, a look of deep disappointment on his face. He turned on the device and pushed a couple of buttons. Her call log popped on the screen.

He wouldn't meet her gaze then, and she knew she'd broken something between them.

"There are three calls. One to your cell, one to what looks like your office, and one to someone with a seven-seven-three area code." He glanced at her then, his gaze harsh and demanding. "Who'd you call, Ariana?"

Shame swelled inside her. She'd thought she'd completely trusted Milo, but she hadn't. If she had, she would have told him. "Kenzie. My friend."

Milo relayed the information to Quinn, who spoke to Milo for another minute before their conversation ended.

He pocketed his phone, eyeing her with such distrust that it clawed at her soul. "How could you do that, Ariana? Worse yet, why didn't you tell me?"

"I don't know. I didn't think you'd understand. I knew you'd be mad, and I didn't want to cause any more problems." Her lip trembled as the first brick in her world crashed to the ground. Others would surely follow.

"How can I understand if you don't give me the opportunity? And cause problems? Really? Five minutes ago, we were planning a future together, and yet you couldn't trust me enough to tell me? I'd say that's a problem."

"I'm sorry." More than she could say. She swallowed, trying to get a grip on her breathing. "Kenzie was on TV, very upset. She thought I was dead. I couldn't let her believe that. Not after her mother just died."

"You should have told me. I could have helped." She couldn't bear the accusatory look in his eyes.

"I did call Quinn, but he didn't answer. I couldn't let her suffer, Milo."

"So you put your life in jeopardy. Not only yours, but mine." He shrugged. "This whole town, really. If these guys traced that call, they're going to come here looking for you, and who knows what will happen if someone gets in the way."

She covered her mouth with a shaking hand and blinked, forcing unshed tears down her cheeks. "I wouldn't do that."

"You did, probably without a second thought." He shook his head. "That's a pretty selfish way to live."

His blow sliced deep into her heart. Maybe she was more like her father than she realized. No. She folded her arms and tried to swallow. She'd reached the farthest edge of her corner, and there was no way out but to tell the truth. It would come at a hell of a steep price though. "No one is going to come after me here."

He snorted. "You don't think? Whoever your father has hired has some far reaching guns. They've tracked you down to four different locations, and Quinn is a master at disguising and protecting people. For all we know, they're on their way here right now. Where did you put my gun?" He turned toward the door.

"They're not coming, Milo," she nearly yelled. She covered her mouth as a whimper escaped. She couldn't be more ashamed of herself. "They haven't found me. They never did."

He stopped and turned toward her, eyeing her with a piercing look. "What do you mean?"

"I made it up." She sniffed, praying she could get her words out before her tears overtook her. "I told Quinn I'd been spotted so he'd move me. I was going crazy, being holed up in the same spot for months."

Milo's jaw went slack for several seconds before he closed his mouth. "You're kidding me. You let Quinn risk his job so you didn't have to be *bored*? Good God, woman."

"I'm sorry. I had no idea Quinn would do that," she whispered. She slumped on the mattress and wrapped her arms around her, afraid if she didn't, her soul would shatter into tiny pieces. She dropped her gaze to the carpet, no longer able to meet Milo's condemning look.

"Well, that's just great, isn't it?" He slammed a fist against the door, making her flinch. "Quinn will be here tomorrow to pick you up. I'm sure it will be a comfort to him to know your life isn't in danger."

The room went silent. Milo turned and left. A few seconds later he slammed his bedroom door.

Ariana got to her feet and quietly closed her own door before she curled into a ball on her bed.

"Got it, Tony." Manny turned to his nephew with a triumphant smile. He wouldn't admit it to anyone, but he'd started to question his ability. He'd expected Ariana to make another call that day or even that week. When that hadn't happened, his life had started to look like a very expensive bet gone wrong.

He could have lost it all.

Tony looked up from his own laptop sitting across from Manny's on the tiny round table in their cheap-ass hotel room in Salt Lake. "You serious, man?"

"I told you she'd call her friend, and I told you she'd turn on the phone again." He leaned back in his chair, pretty damn pleased with his brilliance. "Boss is gonna be real happy with me."

"With us," Tony corrected. "You're giving me some credit, right?"

"Yeah. That's what I meant." At least that's all Tony needed to know.

When Ariana woke the next morning, Milo was gone. It was barely past dawn, but his bed was made and only his sheriff's SUV sat in the drive. She tried to take a breath, her lungs still having difficulty accepting oxygen. She didn't need to look in a mirror to know her eyelids were swollen from crying.

She was grateful though, at some point during the night, she'd come to terms with the consequences of her bad decisions. She was *not* like her father. He made choices to purposefully hurt people. Yes, she'd been careless and was still to blame, but she'd never intentionally hurt someone.

No doubt she'd pay a price for her lies, though. In all likelihood, she'd destroyed whatever she'd built with Milo. With each of life's lessons, there was a cost. But being here with him had taught her many things about herself, and she couldn't regret that. The first of which was she was stronger than she'd thought. The second was there was still happiness to be found in the world. If she couldn't find it with Milo, she'd heal and search until she found it somewhere else. There may never be another man who could compare to her sexy deputy with the startling blue eyes, but she'd find a way to be happy.

In the kitchen, Milo had left a note stating he'd gone into town and that Quinn would arrive around noon. She wanted to call Milo a coward for not sticking around to see her off, but she wouldn't judge how hard this might have been on him, too. She'd known he'd cared. She slammed a fist against her heart as a wave of pain rippled through. God, she'd miss him and regret for the rest of her life the choices that had pushed him away.

It took her less than fifteen minutes to pack her belongings in a suitcase and tuck the cell phone in her pocket. No sense throwing away a good phone, and she'd already wasted enough of Quinn's and Milo's hard-earned money. Somehow, she'd find a way to pay them back for the kindness she'd taken for granted.

Now she was cursed with time, waiting for Quinn to show. Waiting for the trial that would begin in a few days. Waiting until she could start a new life. A life she would cherish and not mess up.

Milo's handgun fit well in her hand. Ariana shot off several rounds, sending cans rocketing into the air, enjoying the way the gun kicked as she fired. Power. She liked it, but she would not abuse it like others in her family had.

She climbed the fence and reset the cans. It would be at least another hour before Quinn arrived, and she could not sit around doing nothing. Empty time generated anxious thoughts in her head. Thoughts about Milo. Thoughts over what Quinn would say. He might forgive her even if Milo couldn't. At least she hoped so.

She scaled the fence again, surprised to hear an engine cruising down Milo's drive. She glanced at her watch. Was Quinn early? A thought popped into her brain, and her heart soared. Maybe Milo had come back to say goodbye.

She hurried around the side of the house, her hopeful heart prepared to meet whoever it was.

The violent sound of wood shattering stunned her. It sounded as though someone had kicked in the front door. From her stance, she could see a foreign black sedan parked in the drive. Illinois license plates caught her attention and nearly cut off her blood supply.

Her father's men had found her.

The irony of her situation didn't escape her. She'd become the little boy who'd cried wolf. Only she didn't intend to die.

If she ran down the road, they'd find her before she ever made it to someone's house. And then there was that possibility she'd put her rescuers in danger. She couldn't do that.

Especially not now.

Her best bet was to head to the river and hide out there. If they didn't see her leave, they might think she wasn't living there any longer. Without wasting another second, she dashed to the back fence, adrenaline allowing her to hop right over it. She'd call Quinn. Not Milo. He might be closer, but she couldn't put him through the angst he'd suffer from leaving her alone.

She made it several hundred yards when she heard a holler from behind. Whoever was after her had spotted her and hiding was no longer an option. She'd have to follow the advice Milo had given her weeks ago and head south to Luke's house.

The sound of a gun exploded behind her, but she didn't think the bullet had come close enough to reach her. She glanced back, spotting two men sprinting through the prairie grass, far enough away that she doubted even Milo could hit her if he were behind the gun.

She pulled the phone from her pocket and hit redial on Quinn's cell number. The second she heard his voice on the line, her words burst from her. "They're here, Quinn. Two men. They have guns." Her voice came out rough and choppy from running.

"Shit. Where are you?"

"Running. Toward the river behind Milo's house. I have a good start. I'll head south once I reach cover of the trees. Going toward Luke's house like Milo told me."

"Good girl. I need to hang up to call for back up, okay? But I'll call you back."

"I have Milo's gun." She was far from safety, but hearing Quinn's voice helped.

"Don't stop to shoot unless it's necessary. Don't let them get close. Just keep running, honey. I'm not far away."

She hung up and pocketed the phone, needing to focus on running. She took another glance back. The men seemed to be farther away than before.

She had a chance. And she had a weapon. She wasn't powerless like she'd been when she was sixteen. If she got a good shot, she could take down her assailants.

Milo spotted the black vehicle in his drive the same moment his phone rang. Quinn's name showed on the screen. "Hey." If his friend could have been patient a second longer, he could talk to him in person.

"Milo."

It only took one word for Milo to recognize the fear in his friend's voice.

"There's a situation at your house. Ariana is being chased by two armed men. She has your gun. She's headed toward the river, and then to Luke's house. I have aerial support on the way."

"Oh, Jesus. I just pulled up." He shoved his truck in park and tucked the phone in his pocket.

The closest weapon he had was the sniper rifle in his SUV. He grabbed it, not bothering to check his house for intruders and ran full out to the backyard and over the fence.

If Milo couldn't reach her in time, he prayed Quinn would.

There was no doubt. He would not survive Ariana's death.

Ariana's lungs burned like a wildfire in her chest. No matter how hard she tried, she couldn't get enough air. Focusing had become a difficult chore. She glanced behind her. She couldn't see her assailants, but she'd coursed up and down several small hills so it was possible they were just out of sight. The river lay not too far ahead, along with trees that would provide some cover. Once she reached the water, she'd slow down. She had to. Then she'd head south, and maybe if the fates were on her side, she could reach Luke's property before the gunmen caught up to her.

Excitement at reaching the sparkling river gave her an extra squirt of adrenaline, and she raced toward the rushing water. Without hesitation, she stepped into the thigh-high stream, careful to avoid the deep parts and to keep her phone and Milo's gun out of the water. Thank God she'd been outside shooting when the men had arrived. It had given her half a chance to survive if she could keep a clear head. If she'd still been asleep, she'd be dead for sure.

She made it to the other side with no problem. She had to pull herself out of the water using tree branches in order to make it up the steep slope, but this side of the bank had more trees and bushes. She could only hope the men wouldn't think she'd crossed.

Her wet shoes mixed with the dirt as she hurried across downed trees and rough terrain, slowing her progress. But the less-frantic pace allowed her to catch her breath a bit. She pulled the phone from her pocket, wondering why Quinn hadn't called her back yet.

She hit redial again, but the screen had gone blank. "No." Panic raced through her as she pushed the power button, hoping it had been turned off. Low battery registered on the screen before the phone shut down again.

She tossed the useless device aside, her head pounding with fear and lack of oxygen. She jogged along, jumping tree roots and small rocks. Was it even possible to make it to Luke's?

She'd just about convinced herself she could, when she misjudged the height of a root and tripped. Tendons in her ankle shrieked as she twisted and hit the ground. What little air she had whooshed out of her lungs on impact. Swift and violent pain radiated from her ankle, bringing tears to her eyes.

Desperation overtook her, knowing her running had come to an end. Ahead, lay a large rock that appeared to have tumbled and crashed into a grouping of thin aspen trees at some point in the past. She crawled and dropped behind it, gasping for air.

A long minute passed before the dizziness in her head cleared, and the pain started to ease. Maybe the men would never find her. She'd gotten a good head start on them, and the area was quite vast. Plus, she'd have the police out looking for her soon. She'd just need to hold her ground until help arrived. She wiped the dirty sweat from her brow. It wasn't the best possible situation to be in, but it wasn't impossible, either.

She tried to swallow, but her exertion had dried the saliva in her mouth and left her wishing for a cold drink of water. She wiped her crusted mouth and scooted closer to the rock, peering over the edge, using the trees for cover.

Nothing. She sucked in another breath and let it slide out. The endorphins released when she'd twisted her ankle were fading, leaving pain and swelling to build in her ankle. She could try to stand on it, but that would be foolish. She was safe where she was for the moment. Even if she could stand, the best she could do would be to hobble.

A movement from the corner of her eye rocketed her straight back into panic mode. She could only see one of the men, but he had crossed the river, too, and was headed in her direction.

She could no longer use her flight response, so fight would have to do. She scooted farther around the edge of the rock, hiding herself as best she could from his view. She slipped Milo's gun from his holster. There was no doubt in her mind, either she or the unknown man jogging toward her would not see the end of the day. She couldn't bear the fact she wouldn't have a chance to apologize to Milo and thank him for everything he'd done for her.

She had everything to live for, everything to lose, and she refused to die.

She rested the gun against the rock to steady her hand and waited.

Her pulse pounded in her head with each step the man took. He was close now. Had to be several years younger than her, and she was sure if he really looked he could spot her. She held still, grateful she had on a black shirt and not something eye-catching like red.

She narrowed him in her sights, aiming for his heart, and squeezed the trigger.

CHAPTER FIFTEEN

A shot rang out in the distance, and Milo's heart rolled with a nauseating thud.

Holy Mother of God. No.

No shots without him present. No shots until he was close enough to protect Ariana. Already, he swore he could feel her life blood slipping away, and the thought tormented him. He forced himself to breathe and run like no other. The river wasn't too far away. He prayed she'd found cover there.

Ariana waited with her gun trained on the spot where her would-be attacker had stood. She was pretty sure she'd hit him, but she'd closed her eyes at the last second and now wasn't taking any chances.

More movement across the river drew her attention. A heavier-set man made his way along the edge of the water, his weapon drawn, his gaze scanning the riverbank as he made his way north. "Tony," he called out, and she was certain she recognized the voice.

Manny? Her father had sent Manny to kill her? They'd played together as children, and now he would try to take her life. There really were no scruples in her father's world. She slid down farther from view.

"Tony," he called again.

"She's over here."

Her blood chilled at the sound of Tony's voice coming from her side of the river. She hadn't hit her target after all, and now they both knew her location.

Manny wasn't quiet as he splashed his way through the water and up the other side. It appeared the additional pounds he carried slowed his pace, but what difference did it make? He had a gun, and he was coming for her.

He stopped not far from where she'd shot her first bullet and ducked to the ground. She could hear their voices, but not what they said. Then Manny moved again.

"Come on, Ariana. Give yourself up. I'm not going to hurt you. Your father just wants to talk, a chance to convince you to see his side."

She didn't answer. The thought of killing someone sickened her, but they left her with no choice. She was sure Manny knew her general location, but she wasn't going to pinpoint it for him. She slowly lifted her weapon and trained it in his direction. He was good, keeping to the trees, using them for cover. But he couldn't stay hidden one hundred percent of the time.

She aimed for a spot ahead of him where the trees provided an opportunity and waited for him to step into it. When he did, she kept her eyes wide open and pulled the trigger. A queasy sickness shot through her as the bullet hit somewhere in his chest cavity, and he fell to the ground not a hundred feet from where she lay hidden.

Dear God. She'd just shot and quite likely killed a man. Another still hunted her.

She waited for what seemed like forever, her heavy breath loud in her ears. Nothing moved on her side of the riverbed, and the not knowing what had happened tortured her.

Then she saw him.

Milo.

He crept low along the riverbank, getting closer to her and to the gunmen.

Trepidation for his safety and relief that he was on scene battled inside her, making it hard to breathe.

"Milo," she cried out, unable to help herself. "I'm across the river." Just as she answered, the sound of helicopter blades cutting the air interrupted the false serenity of the area.

"There are two men over here with guns," she yelled out, hoping Milo could hear her over the noise. A splinter of wood shot from the edge of the tree near her head and landed in her lap. She flattened herself to the ground. One of the men was still shooting.

Another shot rang out, and she tried to discern which direction it had come from. Maybe from the other side of the river. Maybe not.

Then the sound of boots on the ground became clear. She raised her gun, ready to shoot if necessary.

She nearly pulled the trigger out of fright when Milo's face appeared above her. He dropped to the ground next to her, crushing her in his arms as a number of voices sounded from across the river.

"How many men are out here, Ariana?"

"Two." She swallowed. "I think I killed one." She pointed to the motionless body lying on the ground not far from her.

"I took out the other one." He stood and walked to Manny's body.

She knew she shouldn't look at him, but she needed to see what she'd done. She got to her feet and hobbled over just as Milo rolled him onto his back. Tatters of blue material surrounded the gushing hole in his chest. The pool of crimson blood beneath him grew larger.

He blinked, sending an eerie shudder through her. He wasn't dead. She fell on her knees next to him. "Manny. How could you? I thought we were friends."

"I'm sorry." His words came out as a gurgle. "Your father. Me or you."

"Does he know I'm here?" She couldn't stand the thought he would send others after her and endanger these new people she'd grown to love.

"No." His head lolled to the side, but his hazy eyes remained trained on her. "I bugged your friend's phone. Wanted to find you first."

She couldn't believe him. "Tell me the truth, Manny. No one can help you now, but you might be spared burning in hell if you tell me the truth."

"Promise. No one, Ari." He took a shuddering breath and closed his eyes.

A cold shiver raced across her as his spirit departed.

She and Milo both jerked around at the sound of heavy footsteps approaching. Quinn ran straight to her and pulled her into a strong embrace. "Thank God." He focused his strained gaze on Milo. "Thank God you got here in time."

Milo couldn't deny the overwhelming jealousy that blanketed him as Quinn cradled Ariana in his arms. She started to cry, an after-effect of their drama for sure, and Quinn handed a handkerchief to her. Milo didn't even have a tissue to offer.

Armed officers flocked the area. What was quiet a few minutes ago, was now a hive of activity.

"Let's get you the hell out of here," Quinn said to Ariana, taking a step.

She winced. "I twisted my ankle pretty badly."

"I'll help you. These men can deal with this mess. Milo? You'll give them a statement?"

He nodded.

"Good. They can get Ariana's later. The helicopter's waiting." Quinn scooped Ariana into his arms and started down the hillside, leaving a huge, gaping hole in Milo's soul.

At one point, she glanced over Quinn's shoulder and met Milo's gaze. He couldn't tell from the expression on her face what she might have been feeling. He sure as hell recognized the wretched heartbreak he'd been left with.

Her time was up. She'd testify in a few days, and then she'd be free to pursue her new life. A life without him.

Ah…God. "Miss me, darlin'."

Chapter Sixteen

Four months later…

Milo walked along the edge of the frosty river, his boots crunching the crusted snow. Dusk descended upon him at a rapid pace, and he wished time itself would cruise by as fast. Ominous clouds hovered overhead, promising a new layer of the white stuff by morning. The locals would be happy to have the water the melted snow would provide in the spring.

He couldn't care less at the moment.

The green leaves of summer were now a forgotten casualty of fall, leaving the twisted branches bare on the trees. It was colder than a witch's tit, as his dad used to tell him. Still, he walked this route every day.

It was a memorial ritual, he supposed. The last place he'd seen Ariana.

As far as his heart was concerned, she did die that day.

Gratitude filled the rest of him, though. He'd done his job, and she was still alive and breathing. Probably laughing as she soaked up some tropical sun. It made him happy to think of her that way. She deserved it.

She'd gotten her wish, and her old man currently rotted in jail. There were a few in the Trasatti organization that were trying to piece together their outfit, but the vultures were circling, and it wouldn't be long before someone else took over their territory.

Milo kicked a clump of snow into the river and turned toward home. Christmas would be a bitch this year. He'd lied to his friends, telling them Ariana had gone to take care of a sick father. At first, they'd commented on what a kind and thoughtful daughter she was. Now, months later, they no longer asked about her. Only his mother knew the truth.

If he could bypass that holiday and fast forward to spring when he could occupy himself by biking or fishing, things would surely be easier. He knew from experience time would heal, but he'd dug deep and had not been blessed with patience.

The scent of burning wood caught his attention as he stepped inside the kitchen door. A quick glance told him nothing in the kitchen was on fire. He rushed into the living room.

He froze when he saw her.

She sat on the couch, wearing a soft black sweater. She turned, her turquoise eyes flaring to life when she caught sight of him. She'd kept her dark hair, and an infectious smile tilted her lips. A bright fire roared in the fireplace.

"I let myself in. I hope you don't mind."

He said nothing as he crossed the room in three quick strides. She stood as he reached her, and he crushed her in his embrace, burying his nose in her soft hair.

He held her like that for a long time, afraid to open his eyes, afraid she wasn't real.

She released a soft chuckle as she leaned back and captured his gaze. "I'm glad you're happy to see me. I wasn't sure after everything that had happened."

He captured her lips in a kiss. Sometimes actions could speak louder than words. Her scent, the taste of her, the feel of her next to him scorched away the chill he'd held inside him for far too long. "Where have you been?"

A touch of weariness settled on her features. "The trial took a while. Then Quinn arranged for me to spend some time with Kenzie before I had to leave again." She sighed. "Plus, it took me some time to figure out where I wanted to go, what I wanted to be when I grow up." She smiled. "Quinn's amazing. He arranged for me to be a school teacher, just like I requested."

"I see. So why are you here? To say goodbye to me, too?" The thought kicked him in the gut like a wild mustang.

She placed a hand on his cheek, emotion watering in her eyes. "Goodbye? I'm here because I missed you. Isn't that what you said as I left? Miss me, darlin'?"

An incredulous hope rose inside him. "I didn't think you heard me."

She placed a soft kiss on his lips. "I did. Or I read your lips. Or something. Somehow, I heard what you said." She kissed him again, this time not so softly. "I've thought of that moment every day since. Prayed you wouldn't forget me before I could come home."

"Home? You're staying?"

"I hope this can be my home. Quinn is going to be really angry with me if I have to ask him to place me somewhere else." She lifted her left hand, and his grandmother's diamond winked at him. "I'm really hoping I can keep this."

It seemed impossible could be possible after all. "Are you asking me to marry you, darlin'?"

A brilliant smile lit her face. "I believe I am, Deputy Sykes."

The End

COWBOYS AND ANGELS
A Holiday Story

(Aspen Series #3)

CHAPTER ONE

Katy Rivers blinked, trying to keep her focus on the near white-out conditions flashing between her rapidly moving windshield wipers that fought to keep the view clear. The snowstorm had snuck in overnight, turning a light scattering of snow into a blinding mass of winter. If her monthly expense reports weren't already overdue, she would have stayed tucked in bed in her little two-bedroom house that she'd inherited from her grandmother. But bosses didn't care about things like life-threatening road conditions when money was concerned. Especially not in Pinecone, Utah, where serious snowstorms during December were an expected occurrence.

One at a time, she wiped her sweat-soaked palms on her skirt and then rolled her shoulders. Trying to keep her little Rio on the slippery road had been no easy feat. Another half mile and her normal twenty-minute-turned-one-hour commute would be at an end.

A pair of headlights emerged in her rearview mirror and bore down on her at a fast pace. She glanced between the snow-packed road ahead and the mirror, her pulse increasing as the space between the vehicles lessened. The driver had to be insane going so fast in icy conditions.

When the SUV appeared to be inches from her bumper, the driver switched to the oncoming lane and flew past her crawling little car in a haze of dark blue metal and swirling snow. Katy let off the gas to increase the distance between them.

Idiot. Just because a vehicle had four-wheel drive, didn't mean it couldn't slide off the road.

A few minutes later, grateful relief settled her anxiety as yellow lights from the medical center broke through the white haze. The two-story building had been erected at the northern edge of town on a large open space that would allow for growth over time. That had been twenty-five years ago, and her mother had been one of the first women to give birth at the new facility. Years had passed, and the time for the first upgrade to the medical center was currently underway, as evidenced by the dump truck in the oncoming lane, waiting for its turn to enter the parking lot.

Katy signaled to turn and pressed on her brakes, preparing to take a slow and easy entrance into the snow-covered lot. She turned the steering wheel. Instead of her car moving toward the right, the back end swung toward the parking lot, the front end now aiming at the massive yellow truck.

Panic flared. She pushed harder on the pedal, the sound of her anti-lock brakes echoing around her as she tried to steer her way out of the slide. Her car would have none of it.

She gripped the wheel and cringed as her car hit the truck with a thud and bounced off, her body mimicking the action.

Then it was over.

The roar of nerves inside her head stopped, and quiet descended around her like the fluffy snowflakes falling from the sky.

A man appeared at her window, his face dusted with brown and gray whiskers, his head covered by a greasy blue ball cap. "You okay?" he called through the glass.

She opened her car door, the sharp chill of winter kissing her face and sneaking beneath her wool coat as she stepped outside. Snowflakes flew at her from all directions, and she pulled her hood over her hair. She wished she'd worn a thick jacket and insulated work pants like the man had instead of her fashionable black skirt and knee-high boots, but when she'd dressed that morning, she'd only intended to be outdoors as long as it took to get from her car to the medical center. She took one step and slipped, the burly construction worker catching her before she fell. "Oh, my gosh. Thank you."

"Careful. It's slick out this morning."

The urge to remind him she was well aware of that fact disappeared when she caught sight of the battered front end of her car. Yellow paint mixed with the maroon color of her Rio, leaving a nice bruise on the dented and scratched front end. Remnants of glass from her car's headlight sparkled on the ground like the fresh-fallen snow.

"Doesn't look *too* bad, miss."

But it did. His vehicle seemed to have fared a little better with only a few smudges of maroon paint on the front bumper. "I am so sorry. I don't know what happened. One second, I had everything under control. The next..." She shrugged and sighed. "I have insurance to cover the damage."

"It's just a few scrapes. Happens all the time in the construction business."

"Still, I insist on paying to have it fixed." Her insurance man wouldn't be happy to hear about this. Her rates would go sky high, and it wasn't like she was a careless driver at all. But that's what her record would show.

"You'll have to talk to my boss about that."

"Fine. Let's exchange information, and I'll call him when I get inside to my desk."

"He's in your building, in a meeting. Probably shouldn't bug him right now. Give me your name and number, and I'll have him call you if he wants to fix it. Your car took the brunt of the damage anyway."

Her poor little baby. Her Rio had been the first new car she'd owned. She'd bought it straight off the lot after she'd received her first paycheck from the Mt. Uintah Medical Center. She'd been lucky to land herself a job so close to home right after finishing her accounting degree.

Katy dug through her purse and found a scrap of paper. Her hand shook as she tried to write her name and number. Apparently, she was more upset about the crash than she'd realized.

She gave her information to the worker. "Again, I'm so sorry. Please have your boss call me."

Luckily, the damage to her car was superficial, and she didn't have to have it towed. With nervous, careful movements, she drove her car from the middle of the road, into the parking lot. She'd call her insurance rep as soon as his office opened.

It appeared the maintenance men had been waylaid by the weather, too. A good foot of snow still covered the parking lot and sidewalks. Katy sloshed her way through, trying to keep her face away from the cold wind. From beneath her hood, she caught sight of the dark blue SUV that had flown past her earlier and gave a disgruntled huff. The truck sat without a scratch on it, its driver already safe inside her building.

The irony of the situation couldn't be ignored.

In this case, playing it safe hadn't paid *at all.*

If she stopped to think about it, she wasn't sure it had done her much good for most of her life, either. She'd faithfully followed her parent's guidance. She'd stayed out of trouble and finished college in record time, but she also had the distinct feeling she was missing out on far too many of life's experiences.

Inside, a blast of warm air instantly melted the snowflakes that had landed on her, leaving her coat with a damp film of moisture. She slid the hood off her hair, trying to fluff her flattened tresses.

She pushed through the second set of doors, her gaze snagging on a taller man who stood at the front desk, speaking to the receptionist. As she moved closer, his gaze connected with hers, recognition beaming inside her.

Scott Beckstead. The ultimate bad boy. At least as far as her little town was concerned. During high school, he'd been the one to sluff, had gotten caught with a beer in his locker, and he'd been accused of taking the principal's car for a joy ride, although she didn't think that last one had ever been proven.

It might have been several years since she'd seen Scott, but he looked as hot and dangerous as ever in his black leather jacket with rugged boots peeking from beneath well-fitting jeans. The sight of him thrilled her and frightened her, just like it had all those years ago. Short, dark hair. Sexy, sinful eyes. A neatly trimmed goatee that outlined a very kissable mouth. Her friends used to joke that five minutes was the longest a girl could be in his company and still keep her virginity. She wasn't sure she didn't still believe that today.

She tightened the sash on her coat and forced her gaze to a painting of a waterfall cascading through majestic pines that hung on the opposite wall.

But, she couldn't resist glancing in his direction one last time as she passed him.

He stared at her, one corner of his delicious mouth curving upward as he gave her a nod.

Her mouth betrayed her, smiling in return, before she jerked away her gaze as though she'd been caught doing something she shouldn't.

The temperature in the building suddenly felt unbearably hot, and she undid her coat as she headed toward the elevator. She pressed the up button and waited for the elevator car to arrive. The rise in temperature had nothing to do with her attraction to Scott Beckstead and was more likely caused by maintenance turning up the heat because of the blizzard outside.

"Heard about your news, Katy."

She cringed, every nerve inside her firing red, as the woman who'd made it her job to make Katy's days miserable joined her. Katy knew she shouldn't let Nina get to her, but she didn't know how to protect herself from the barbs her nemesis continually flung in her direction. Katy did a great job psyching herself up for Nina's attacks when she wasn't around, but the second she showed her flawless face, all of Katy's defenses jumped ship. Katy turned, facing Nina and her chic blond haircut, cunning gaze and designer blouse. The woman had her eye on the top of the corporate ladder and didn't hesitate to undercut anyone who got in her way.

"And what would that be, Nina?" The only "news" she had was that she'd broken up with Will. No one knew about that except Will and her mother.

The doors slid open, and she stepped into the elevator. Nina followed. The doors started to close, but a very masculine hand reached inside, stopping them. In the next second, the hottest guy in town joined her and Nina, increasing the tension in the small space. He nodded at Nina and took a place next to Katy. His musky cologne made her want to purr with appreciation.

"Hi." The smile he gave her warmed every inch of her that the first blast of warm air had missed.

"Morning," she offered, little jitters of excitement percolating inside her.

"I heard the news you crashed your poor little car this morning," Nina said with a gleeful tone. "Right into a big, ol' dump truck." Of course Nina would try to steal Scott's attention. If she could embarrass Katy in the process, all the better.

She fired a searing gaze at Nina, but refused to answer.

"What an awful way to start your morning," Nina continued. "Especially after the way Will dumped you last night."

Katy gasped as both she and Scott swiveled their heads toward Nina. This was not happening. "That's really none of your business, Nina."

Scott smiled, and she tried to shut off that tender part of her that was so easily wounded by ridicule. "Besides, he didn't dump me. I'm the one who called it quits."

"Well, if that's true, you're a fool." Nina batted her eyes at Scott before turning back to Katy. "At your age, chances of meeting a decent, single guy who'll want to marry you are slim."

Nina was an expert at throwing together words. Had she meant it was hard to find a man who wanted to get married? Or was it a personal attack, and she meant that *Katy* would have a hard time?

Either way, she was correct. Most of the girls in her little town were married by the time they'd hit twenty-three. Here she was ready to turn twenty-six, and she hadn't been able to find a good man to look in her direction. Okay, Will had been decent. But he bored her to tears. She'd thought she'd convinced herself that the initial attraction didn't matter. It would fade in the first few years, and it was better to have a stable man who would help provide for their family.

Then she'd come to the conclusion she'd wither if she stayed with him. Sometimes life threw a person a curveball, and she would be forced to endure a hardship, but it was downright asinine to throw one at herself.

Her mother had been horrified about what the town gossips would say. Or rather, were already saying.

Katy narrowed her gaze at Nina, unable to find the words to put her in her place. Embarrassed heat singed her cheeks. Of course, Nina would pick the most humiliating moment to throw her ugly opinion at Katy.

"I wouldn't be worrying yourself about that, miss."

The sound of Scott's voice surprised both women. Katy followed Nina's gaze to find Scott watching Nina with a sharp eye. Then he turned to her. "Right, sweetheart?" He slid a supportive hand around Katy's waist and tugged her to him.

Surprise warred with titillation as she stared into his midnight eyes. It would take nothing but a smile from him to seduce her, she realized. "Right." She hesitated only a second before she leaned into him for show. A little voice in the back of her mind asked her what the hell she was doing, but she couldn't let Nina win this round.

The warmth of his body reached out through his t-shirt and soaked into the silk of her blouse. Humor sparked in his eyes as she played along with his game, but she froze when he slanted his head and kissed her.

Soft, sensuous lips played over hers, warm and inviting. He tasted of cinnamon and something dangerously seductive that she couldn't name.

The sound of the elevator dinging penetrated her haze, and Nina exhaled a sigh of disgust. Katy couldn't pull herself from the most tantalizing kiss she'd ever encountered.

A man cleared his throat, and Scott pulled away. Katy blinked, trying to anchor herself back in the present. One of the pediatricians eyed her with annoyance.

Scott grinned at him and held her hand as he led her from the elevator. Several people, including Nina watched as they emerged. "I'll see you later. Have a good day."

"Okay," she managed to whisper.

CHAPTER TWO

Scott Beckstead had kissed her…right in front of Nina. Katy still couldn't wrap her mind around it.

She'd spent the past two hours working through a haze thicker than the snow storm that raged outside, trying to finish her expense reports. She hoped he'd only been messing with Nina, giving her a dose of her own nasty medicine. She couldn't imagine he'd actually kissed her because he'd been attracted to her. He hadn't given her anything more than cursory glances back in school. Or maybe he'd picked up on her attraction to him. If so, she needed to do a better job of hiding her feelings. The last thing she needed in her life was a bad boy playing with her.

A cute, young doctor with plenty of ambition was what her parents expected her to bring home. Not this kind of hot temptation.

"Winward wants to see you."

She glanced up to find her immediate boss's assistant, Teisha, standing at the door to her office. "Me?" She'd never been summoned by the head of the medical center before. "Why? Where's Janet?"

"I don't know," the older black woman said. "I'm a little worried. It's not like her to miss the Monday morning construction meetings. You can fill me in after your meeting with Winward."

Katy stood and smoothed her skirt, glad that she'd dressed up, despite the weather. She grabbed a pen and a pad of paper, not sure what one took to a meeting like this, and headed to the large corner office at the other end of the second floor.

James Winward had his head bent, appearing to study the paper in front of him as Katy approached his office. She tapped on the open door. "Excuse me. Teisha said you wanted to see me."

Mr. Winward lifted his gaze, peering at her over the wire-rimmed glasses that rested halfway down his nose. "Come in, Miss Rivers."

Katy swallowed and entered the lush chambers decorated with rich, mahogany furniture and gold accents. She perched on the edge of a chair opposite his desk and waited for him to speak.

"We have a little problem."

Her heart sank. "I'm sorry, Mr. Winward. I know my expense reports were due last Friday, but—"

"Janet has eloped."

His statement stalled her tongue as she tried to process the information.

"She got married? To who?" Katy hadn't known she'd been dating anyone seriously.

"Doesn't matter. What matters is that she's gone on an extended honeymoon and won't be back for three weeks. She's left me high and dry, right in the middle of several serious projects including finalizing budgets for the next year while trying to keep the construction costs within budget."

"Oh, no." That was kind of a selfish, irresponsible thing to do. "I'm sorry to hear that." Still, she wasn't quite sure what the whole situation had to do with her.

"Yes, I'm a little upset." He tapped a pen repeatedly on his desk. "When I asked her how she expected me to handle everything while she's off worshipping the sun with her blissfully wedded husband, she suggested I use *your* talents." Irritation left jagged edges on each word he spoke. She wasn't sure if he was more distressed that Janet had left or that she'd suggested Katy as a suitable replacement.

"Of course. I'd be happy to help." She'd worked with her boss on many projects including the budgets, but she'd never been the lead accountant on anything. It would be difficult, but there was no way she would turn down the opportunity.

"Good. I realize it's not much notice, but she gave you a glowing recommendation, so I'm expecting you to step up to the plate and perform. I'm sure her assistant will be of help to you."

"Yes, I'm sure she will." Katy only hoped Teisha had more of a clue about what was going on with these projects than she did.

"Fine. You can begin by bringing the latest construction costs to the meeting at two. We rescheduled it from this morning after Janet didn't show. Have Teisha pull the report from last week's meeting so you'll know what kind of figures I'm after." He tossed his pen down on the desk between them. "I'm counting on you, Miss Rivers. Don't disappoint me."

"I won't, Mr. Winward." Katy clasped her hands as she stood to keep them from shaking. "I'll get started right now."

He nodded, dismissing her.

She exited his office with hurried steps, nerves clashing with her excitement. This day was getting crazier by the minute.

⟨⟶

Katy's stomach snarled, and Teisha looked up from the opposite side of Janet's desk.

"Sorry." Katy covered her stomach. "I'd intended to run down to the café for lunch, but never found the time."

"If you're going to do a good job, you can't be skipping meals." Janet's assistant tossed her a disapproving look. "You're already two sizes too skinny. A man likes some meat on his woman's bones, if you know what I mean. Ain't nothing sexy about a toothpick."

Katy had learned a long time ago there was no arguing with Teisha. And why would she want to? The woman might be on the heavy side, but she'd been happily married to her husband for forty years. She was a woman who knew how to keep her man happy.

"You think I'm too skinny?" Katy glanced down at her clingy red angora sweater and black skirt.

Teisha narrowed her eyes, giving Katy a once over. "Nah, I'm teasing. You're fine, girl. I'm just saying, you don't want to be losing anything you got. And boobs are always the first to go, you know."

Katy folded her arms across her chest as though that would protect her from losing her breasts until she had a chance to grab something to eat. "Thanks, Teisha. I'll remember that." She glanced at the clock and then down at the papers spread across Janet's desk. Five minutes until the meeting. "This looks good, doesn't it?"

"You're the accountant, Katy." Teisha gave the pile an uncertain look. "All I can say is these are the reports Janet takes to her weekly meetings. It's up to you to say if the numbers are correct."

Katy released a sigh heavy with nerves. "I think they're good." She prayed they were. She gathered the papers, placing them in order and stood. "Wish me luck."

Teisha laughed. "You'll be needing it." At Katy's frown, she continued. "Don't worry. They're not gods or anything, even if their egos tell them they are."

Katy tried to accept the shot of confidence. "You're right. They're just people like you and me. I'm presenting them with information, not offerings." Although, at the moment, it felt like she was offering gifts in exchange for her life...or at least her job. "I'll see you in an hour or so." If she survived that long.

Out in the hall, it seemed as though everyone stared at her. Several whispered. Another accountant, a dark-haired woman named Lucy stood up from her cubicle as Katy passed. "You get a promotion or what?" she said a little too loudly.

"No." Katy shook her head. "Just filling in for Janet for a bit."

"Why?" another guy asked.

Katy had no idea how to answer. She certainly didn't want to light a fire under the rumor mill. "You'll have to ask Mr. Winward," she said as she hurried past.

"Like he'd tell us anything," Lucy called after her, followed by several other murmurs.

Katy cringed as she hurried to the other side of the floor, grateful when she'd passed the entrance to the administrative office where the atmosphere changed from noisy to quiet, and no one looked at her differently.

She turned a corner and nearly collided into the person coming in the other direction. Her surprised gaze landed on a slick, leather jacket and quickly traveled upward to find Scott grinning down at her.

"We meet again."

If there was a way to record his sexy voice and lock it tight in her brain so she could replay it over and over, she would have. "I'm so sorry. I wasn't watching where I was going."

"That's certainly not a problem for me." Flirtation twinkled in his eyes.

She tried to breathe. It was one thing to be close to him, even kiss him, with someone else around. She'd been goaded by Nina and fueled by derision when she'd kissed him. But they were alone now, all alone, in the hallway and that felt far more intimate...and dangerous.

She took a step back.

He advanced forward. "I was hoping I'd run into you again today."

She smiled, uncertain how to react. Every womanly thing inside her urged her to flirt with him, but her conscience warned her to be careful. Hot things could burn. "Me, too," she forced out. "I wanted to say thanks for the save in the elevator. Nina can be such a..."

"Go ahead. Say it." His look dared her.

Katy took a breath. "Bitch. She's a bitch, and I hate her." A spurt of soft laughter escaped her lips. "Wow, that sounded really grown up, didn't it?"

"Who cares? She is a bitch. Anyone can see that."

A genuine smile hit her lips. "Thanks for that, too, then. I'm sure it was your intention to make me feel better, and you've accomplished that. So thanks." She extended a hand of friendship toward him.

He took her gift, but instead of shaking her hand, he wrapped his around hers and tugged her forward. Surprise left an excited lump in her throat. She inhaled, the delicious scent of cinnamon combining with his musky cologne.

His warm brown eyes drilled through hers until he reached an unexplored place inside her. "Don't ever think I did that as a way for you to save face. I'm not that nice. I took advantage of a situation that was offered to me, and I kissed you because I wanted to."

She stared into his eyes, unable to move, unable to blink.

A smile split his lips, and the spell he'd cast evaporated. "But if you're wanting to thank me, let me take you to dinner."

"Dinner?" She couldn't picture herself sitting at a table for two with him.

"Yes, dinner. You do know what that is?"

"Of course." She gave herself a mental kick. It was beyond her to tell him no. "I'd love to."

"Great." He seemed genuinely pleased. "How about Friday night?"

Voices sounded at the end of the hall, and she took another step back as she looked to see who approached.

Mr. Winward and his assistant.

"Sure. Friday sounds good." She glanced down the hall again.

"Can I get your number?" He seemed completely unaffected by people interrupting their intimate party.

"Uh…" Her boss was almost within hearing distance though she didn't think he'd noticed her yet. "I'm late for a meeting. If you stop at the reception desk on your way out, she'll give you my work number. Work is probably the best place to reach me anyway." She stepped around him. "I've got to go."

She hurried down the remainder of the hall toward the meeting room, walking inside just after Mr. Winward and his assistant. There were only two remaining seats at the conference table, and she chose the one next to Kevin, the soft-spoken IT guy.

She placed her folder of papers in front of her on the table and glanced at the others who comprised the construction committee. In addition to Mr. Winward, his assistant, and Kevin, there were three doctors, a records clerk and a guy dressed in jeans and a flannel shirt that she suspected worked for the construction company. Katy released a quiet sigh and tried to reassure herself that she was well-prepared and things would be fine.

Mr. Winward glanced around the room. "It looks like almost everyone is here." Just as he finished his sentence, the door to the conference room opened. Katy widened her eyes in disbelief as Scott walked in, carrying a cup of coffee. She glanced at all the faces around the table, expecting to see surprise or questioning in their eyes, but they all remained passive or smiled at Scott.

"Good." Mr. Winward picked up his own coffee and took a sip. "Let's get started."

CHAPTER THREE

S cott sent Katy a private grin as he took the seat on
the opposite side of the table next to the other
outsider.

"Thank you all for adjusting your schedules so
we could meet this afternoon," Mr. Winward said.
"Again, I apologize for the glitch with our accounting department. Janet will be out of the office for
several weeks, so I've asked Katy Rivers to replace
her on this committee. Ms. Rivers has excellent cre-
dentials, and I'm certain she'll keep us all in line."

She dared a glance at Scott who smiled and nodded at her as though he had all the confidence in
the world for her.

"Katy, you know everyone here except for Scott
Beckstead, the head of BCI, our construction company. Next to him is Kirk Lawler, our architect."

Katy smiled a greeting at both men who recipro-
cated the gesture.

"Okay," Mr. Winward continued. "I'd like to
start by thanking everyone for staying on track with
our projected schedule. The holidays are only a few
weeks away, and I realize people will be taking days
off, but I'd like to maintain our current pace if possible. Scott, your men have done an excellent job
with the renovations in other areas of the building,

and to the rest of you, please thank your staff for being so cooperative and patient."

Several people nodded and murmured their agreement.

"Next on the agenda is our financial report. Ms. Rivers, if you please."

Katy opened her file and cleared her throat. How was she supposed to concentrate with the sexiest man alive sitting directly across from her, his dark, devilish gaze making her feel as though every inch of her was exposed to him.

She stared at the top report, trying to get her bearings. "First, I'd like to give a basic overview of the project's budget. I'm sure most, if not all, of you have already received this information, but I'd like to make sure we're on the same page." She passed around copies of the report Teisha and she had created which listed each line item.

Mr. Winward sent her an impatient look.

Katy heeded his silent warning. "Actually, in the interest of time and since this isn't new information, we'll skip the review in this meeting, and you all can look at it later at your discretion and let me know if there are inconsistencies."

Mr. Winward gave a slight nod of his head.

"This next report will show where the budget is as of the end of last Friday. It reflects last month's installment to BCI, but not the invoice for wiring that we received this morning. According to information received from your office, Mr. Winward, the project is twenty percent complete. The second column from the right edge of your document shows the amount we expected to have spent this far into the project, and the last column shows actual expenditures. Information received from the construction company shows the project stands at three percent under budget."

"Yes, we were able to negotiate a better price on flooring," Scott interrupted. "That accounts for the savings."

Mr. Winward nodded. "I'm sure the shareholders will be pleasantly surprised by that news."

Scott nodded to several people at the table, but when his gaze landed on Katy, she swore the IT people had somehow connected an electrical wire between her and Scott that left her smoldering. She could only hope the rest of the committee was oblivious to the current racing between them. "They will also be happy to hear, despite the snowy conditions outside, we've been able to move ahead with digging the hole for the new wing."

"I'm impressed, Scott. There were some on the board of directors who were hesitant to go with a contractor who'd been in business such a short time, but you've proven time and again you're doing a damn fine job."

"I appreciate your confidence, James."

James? Katy raised an eyebrow at Scott. There wasn't one person in the room besides Scott and perhaps the architect who addressed Mr. Winward by his first name.

"Okay, let's move on. Our pharmacist has suggested a couple of changes to the pharmacy that he feels will work better. Are we still okay to make changes to the interior designs?"

The architect grimaced. "Superficial changes, yes. Anything else will set back the project and be very costly."

Katy caught Scott's gaze again, and the other's voices faded into the background. His dark eyes flashed with amusement and seduction.

What was she thinking? She had no business flirting with a business associate. Rule number one: never date a guy you work with. If things went south, she'd either have to pretend they'd never known each other or find another job. The first was unacceptable, and the second was unthinkable. She'd never be able to replace her job without moving to another city, and she loved her quiet little country town.

She also had to consider the fact that he was far more experienced in life than she was. He would eat her alive. She crossed her legs, seductive thoughts sneaking in under her radar. Plus, how would she ever take a guy like him home to meet her mother?

That was too scary to even think about.

Sweet Mary, she had to squash this thing now.

"Katy?"

She jumped at the sound of her boss calling her name and caught a quick grin flash across Scott's lips as he looked down at the papers in front of him. "I'm sorry," she said. "What did you say, Mr. Winward?"

A frown creased his brow. "I asked what kind of numbers you have budgeted for new equipment in maternity."

Katy flipped through her notes and mentally blew a sigh of relief when she located the correct report. "I have it right here."

She gave her boss the information he requested.

"What about the amount we've received from our building grant?"

That she didn't have. Teisha hadn't mentioned it, and she hadn't seen a similar report in the stack of papers Mr. Winward's assistant had given her. "Uh, that one slipped through the cracks, Mr. Winward.

Her boss didn't seem too happy, but he waved it away. "Have your assistant email the info to me as soon as possible."

"Of course."

She refused to look at Scott again for the rest of the meeting for fear of being drawn into his intriguing world and the sensual thoughts that followed. At the conclusion of their conference, she was the first to head for the door. She needed air. She needed space. She needed to be away from the sizzling hunk of temptation who made her heart dance with excitement.

She made it as far as the end of the hall before Scott caught her elbow. "Hey. Hang on a second."

She turned, glancing past him to see if anyone else had entered the hall. So far, they were alone. "I'm sorry. I really need to go."

A puzzled look crossed his face. "I just wanted to apologize for distracting you in the meeting."

"It's okay, but I can't talk right now. I have a lot of things I need to complete before I head home this afternoon including that report for everyone." Her stomach gave another rumbling growl.

Scott raised his brows.

Katy put a hand over her noisy mid-section. "Didn't have time for lunch."

He nodded. "Why don't you give me your number, and I'll let you get back to work? Congratulations on the promotion, by the way."

"It's not really a promotion. I'm just stepping in while Janet is away." She glanced at the file she had clutched to her chest before facing him again. "About that date, I've had second thoughts."

"What kind of second thoughts?"

"I didn't realize you owned the construction company working on our building." She had to admit that part impressed her. "And now we're sitting on the same committee." She swallowed not wanting to say her next words, but knowing she had to. "I've made it a rule to never date anyone I work with."

"I guess I could argue that we don't technically work together, but if you don't want to go, I understand."

She forced her lips into an awkward smile. "Thank you."

He studied her for a moment. "Let me know if you change your mind." He turned and walked away, leaving her feeling like she'd just made the biggest mistake ever. She watched as he moved farther down the hall, admiring the way his jacket fit his wide shoulders and the way his jeans outlined his rear end.

She was such a coward...and a fraud. She continually wished her life was more exciting, telling her friend, Sienna, she'd give anything if she could find a heartbeat in their town. But when the opportunity presented itself, she failed.

At the end of the hall, Scott stopped and looked back. Her face warmed at being caught staring. He sent her a sexy smile that said she was welcome to look all she wanted before he nodded and left.

She sagged against the wall and put a hand over her wildly beating heart. That man could make even the stodgiest nun forget her vows.

Now that he'd disappeared from view, he didn't seem like such a threat to her...What had she been so afraid of? That he might decide he liked her? That she'd like him?

She straightened and headed for Janet's office.

She complained that her life was so boring. But she'd made it that way. She was too afraid to do anything slightly crazy. She'd never dare elope, and unfortunately, it appeared she was too scared to date a guy that heated her blood. If she wasn't careful, she'd end up a dying spinster like Nina had labeled her. Or worse, end up married to someone like Will.

She needed to start taking more chances, creating more opportunities for new experiences. That was living.

Today had been her wake-up call, beginning with the car wreck, the kiss from Scott, and the chance to impress her big boss. If she were a smart girl, it would have ended with her giving her number to Scott.

Could she wise up and be brave enough to let him know she'd changed her mind?

She let herself into Janet's office, closed the door, and dropped her head to the top of the desk. The day's events had been anything but normal, and they'd worn her out. She didn't know what time she'd be able to leave the office, but she was certain it wouldn't be before sundown.

Her tummy cried foul with another loud rumbling, and she stole a chocolate mint from a crystal bowl on Janet's desk. "Be good, and I promise I'll find some real food in just a little bit. First, I have to get that stupid report sent out."

She brought Janet's computer out of hibernation. Luckily, Janet had given Teisha her password which allowed Katy access to all her files. Otherwise, she'd never be able to pull off this assignment. It scared her to think this opportunity would either make or break her in Mr. Winward's eyes.

Before she started hunting down exactly what her boss wanted, she had to check one thing. She clicked on Janet's contact list and then the list of "B" names. Scott Beckstead landed close to the top. She clicked on it.

Right in front of her was Scott's work phone, cell phone, work address and the number for his assistant. There was a multitude of ways to reach him if she wanted to.

And she did...but she couldn't bring herself to call him at this very second. She clenched her fists in frustration. She pulled out her cell, typed in his personal number, and hit save. It was a first step. She might not have the courage to call now, but when she did finally garner it, she'd need his number.

She sighed and closed his information.

Maybe tomorrow. When things weren't so crazy.

A knock sounded on Janet's door, and Katy raised her gaze as Teisha walked in carrying a brown paper sack. The smells emanating from it raised the army in her stomach to a frenzied cry. Food.

Janet's assistant couldn't have been sweeter. "You didn't have to do this, Teisha. I'm quite capable of getting my own lunch." She glanced at the clock, noticing the time was closer to evening than noon. "Or make that dinner."

The woman huffed as she set the bag in front of Katy. "I didn't, and I know you are." At Katy's quizzical look, she continued. "This ain't from me, honey. Some hot-looking hunk of man dropped it by my desk and asked me to give it to you so he didn't disturb you." It was her turn to give Katy a questioning look. "You got something going on I don't know about?"

Scott's gesture nearly did her in. He'd taken the time to figure out what kind of a day she'd probably had, knew she'd been hungry before they entered the meeting, and even though she'd turned him down for a date, he'd sent her food.

What kind of a man did that?

The look on Teisha's face said she demanded an answer. "He's a…well, I just met him today. No, that's not true. I remember him from school, but we didn't run in the same circles."

"Uh-huh. Is that the whole story?"

"It is. I swear. He heard my stomach growl and was kind enough to think of me." Will had never done anything so thoughtful.

"Well, you must have made some kind of impression on him. Ain't many guys that will go out of their way like that for nothing. Though my Hector would." The woman turned and left the room, closing the door behind her.

Katy attacked the bag and pulled out a Styrofoam cup of soup. She lifted the lid, releasing more of the enticing aroma. Chicken Noodle. "Mmm…" Next, she pulled out a sweet-looking orange and then a wrapped sandwich. She peeked inside. Turkey on wheat. She peeled the wrapper back even farther and took a large bite.

"Oh, my God," she mumbled around the food in her mouth. She couldn't remember anything tasting *so* good.

Now that she'd had a bite, her thoughts reverted to Scott. He did not play fair. This was his subtle way of saying he might have backed off, but the game wasn't over yet.

What was she supposed to do with a guy like that?

Date him, a little voice whispered inside her head. *Definitely date him.*

CHAPTER FOUR

It was nearly nine before Katy reached her house that night. The drive home had been treacherous with patches of black ice lingering on the road, but she'd navigated it with only a few hair-raising slides.

She dropped her keys and purse on the first flat surface she came across as she made her way through the old farmhouse. Her coat fell to the couch. She wasn't quite sure where her red sweater and bra landed, but she'd worry about them later. By the time she reached her bathroom, she was left with nothing but her boots and panties, carrying only her cell phone.

She dropped to the edge of the tub with a tired sigh and turned on the faucet, adjusting the temperature to as hot as she could stand. It would take a great deal of heat to sink into her bones and relax away the craziness of her day. The scent of lavender permeated the air as she poured in her favorite bubble bath before leaning over to remove her boots while the tub filled.

She slid down a zipper and eased her weary foot out of its casing. She should have lost the boots hours ago while still at the office, but she didn't have a spare pair of flats with her that day. If she'd only known what might have transpired, she might have been better prepared. She removed the other boot, massaging the arch of her foot and then stood, allowing her feet a few seconds to become accustomed to a flat surface.

Her panties were all that remained, and she quickly dropped them and stepped into the soothing tub. It took a moment for her body to acclimate to the heat, and then she slowly sank to her neck.

She closed her eyes and sighed, letting each of her cares fall away.

All but one.

The vision of Scott smiling at her with that teasing, tempting look in his eyes haunted her. In the darkness behind her lids, she replayed the moment he'd kissed her in the elevator.

Scott Beckstead had kissed her. *Her.*

The one kiss she'd dreamed about back in high school, but knew would never come to fruition. Now it had.

More than that, he wanted to date her.

She retrieved her phone and punched in a number, grateful when a voice answered on the other line.

"I'm so glad you answered, Sienna."

Katy and Sienna had been best friends since elementary school. Their parents had grown up together, and she was pretty sure even their grandparents had known and liked each other.

"What's up, Katy?"

Just hearing the sound of her friend's voice calmed her. Sienna always was the voice of reason. "I had a heck of a day and just need to share. I started out wrecking my car because of this horrible weather. But that's not what really has me bothered."

She paused not quite sure how to phrase it. "I kissed Scott Beckstead."

Silence stole the line, and then Sienna laughed. "Good one, Katy. Is this one of those unbelievable ploys like using Hotty Scotty to take the emphasis off crashing your car?"

Hotty Scotty. She'd forgotten they'd used to call him that. "No, I'm serious. I slid into a dump truck outside the medical center. Then that bitch Nina unleashed her vicious tongue while we were in the elevator."

"Language, Katy."

Her friend's reminder stopped her. Many years ago, their parents had encouraged them to help each other not use cuss words. The thought that they'd held onto it all these years seemed stifling. "Sorry." Then she remembered how free she'd felt when Scott had encouraged her to speak her mind. "No, wait. I'm not sorry. She is a bitch, Sienna. She is."

"Uh, okay. I guess she is then, but maybe you could say it a little nicer or something."

Irritation nipped at her. "I don't want to. I want to call her a bitch. It makes me feel better."

"Fine. I can tell you're stressed. Let's move on to the rest of your story before you start spouting more obscenities."

Katy sat up in the tub. "Wow, Sienna. What happened to always being there for each other?"

"I'm here for you, Katy. I'm on the phone. I'm listening."

"Yeah, but you're not hearing me." Whatever the hell that meant. All she knew was she wasn't connecting with her friend like she normally did, and it added to her frustrations.

Another silent pause. "I'm trying, okay? I'm try-ing. Did you really kiss Scott Beckstead?"

A rush of exasperated air flew from her lungs. "I did. I was in the elevator with Nina, and she was taunting me about not getting another guy after I dumped Will, and Scott kissed me. I think to show up Nina, but I'm not sure." He'd assured her other-wise, but thinking about him telling her he'd wanted to kiss her was just….

"Wait. You dumped Will? Katy, what is going on with you? I thought you were hoping he'd give you a ring for Christmas and pop the question?"

She had said that, hadn't she? She must have been out of her mind at the moment. "I'm sorry, Sienna. I meant to call you this morning and tell you what happened with Will last night. I…he…I don't know. It just seemed like I was sentencing myself to a life of boredom if I married him."

"Are you hormonal or something?"

The absurdity of her friend's question made her laugh. "God, Sienna. I know it sounds completely crazy. Maybe I'm having my mid-life crisis early."

"Or maybe it's pre-wedding jitters."

"How can I have wedding jitters when I wasn't even engaged?"

"Psychotic mental breakdown, then?"

Her friend's joke eased her tension. "That must be it. Did I mention my boss eloped, too, and they put me in her position while she's away on her honeymoon?"

"That's good news, right? I mean, this could be your chance to get noticed."

Both she and Sienna had always been the quiet, good girls, the ones who were never seen because they faded into the background.

"It's a great opportunity. Mr. Winward put me on the construction committee for the renovations at the center."

"Cool."

"Scott Beckstead is the owner of the construction company. He's also on the committee."

"Did you really kiss him, Katy?"

"Yes."

"You're screwed."

She dropped her forehead onto her open palm. "I know. What am I going to do? He asked me out, too."

"Seriously?" Her friend's voice seemed almost disbelieving.

"What am I going to do?"

"You can't date him, Katy. You've heard the rumors. You know what he's like."

"I know. But he's *so* attractive."

"So is the Grand Canyon, but you're not going to jump off the edge just to see it better. Be professional. Be friendly. But don't get involved with him. You're the one who'll get hurt."

Sienna did a fabulous job of unearthing her fears. "That's what I'm afraid of. So stay away? That's what you'd do even knowing how gorgeous he is?"

"Don't get sucked in by his good looks, Katy. They'll fade after a few years, and you'll be left with the bad boy underneath who'll break your heart."

She paused for a moment, letting her friend's words sink in. She was right. Katy knew she was, but the exhilarating feelings she'd experienced with Scott were addicting, and damn it, she wanted him. "Okay. You're right. I can do this. I can be professional and nothing more."

"Good girl," Sienna responded. "I'm glad you're smart enough to think this through. I just have one question though. Was he as good as we always thought he might be?"

"Better." Katy closed her eyes and sank into the cooling water. *Sooo* much better.

The next morning, Katy found Nina hovering inside the front entrance when she arrived at work. She'd dyed her hair black and styled it in a trendy style that would have seemed out of place in their county, but it totally worked for Nina. Katy sent her a look heavy with loathing and continued toward the elevator. After yesterday's dressing down by Scott, she doubted the woman would have the nerve to confront her again.

She was wrong.

Just as Katy stepped into the elevator, Nina pushed in behind her. Unfortunately, they were alone. Tomorrow, she'd take the stairs.

"So how'd you do it?"

"Do what?" Get Scott to kiss her?

"Get a promotion? Lucy and I have been here way longer than you have."

"If you consider six months way longer."

"And we have higher job titles than you. One of us should have gotten that promotion."

Katy sighed and faced Nina head on, amazed at the thickness of her eyelashes. Had to be extensions. "First off, it's not a promotion. I'm only temporarily filling in for Janet while she's off."

"I heard she ran off with that guy, Pete, and they've decided to stay in the Bahamas permanently."

"Who said that?" As far as she knew, Janet intended to return to work. At least that's what Mr. Winward had implied.

"Jeffrey."

Mr. Winward's son? Katy was certain he and Nina were sleeping together, so she supposed it was a possibility that Nina could have learned new information through pillow talk. "Well, whatever. As far as I know, Janet's coming back."

"Don't lie to me. We both know she's not, and I want to know what you did to get the promotion. Did you go horizontal with Mr. Winward so you could go vertical?"

Like Nina hadn't done that with Winward's son? Katy narrowed her eyes in disgust. "Excuse me?"

"You know, trade favors with the boss?"

"I know very well what you're referring to. Just because you've used that tactic doesn't mean the rest of us don't have morals." The elevator dinged, signaling they'd reached the second floor. "Stay away from me, Nina. I have nothing to say to you."

"It's the construction guy, isn't it?" Nina called after her. "He's using his influence to help you get ahead."

Katy ignored her comment and continued toward Janet's office. She would not allow herself to be affected by Nina's jealousy. She just hoped the rest of the staff wouldn't listen to her, either.

⌒

Friday rolled around, and Katy's work week had gone from crazy to insane. By the time eight o'clock arrived, she'd had enough. Mr. Winward proved to be a very demanding and impatient boss, but he'd also been willing to hand out praise when she complied. Teisha was a god-send.

And Nina? She was still a bitch. She and Lucy were being quite vocal about the fact that Katy had been promoted instead of them. It hadn't mattered one bit that Katy had denied doing anything to get ahead. Fact was, Winward had selected her above the others. But she'd worked hard to prove herself to Janet, and Janet had every right to suggest Katy as a temporary replacement.

Didn't matter. People were talking.

With no snow hampering the roads, Katy made it to her hometown of Aspen in her usual twenty minutes. She thought of calling Sienna to see if she wanted to hang out, but her friend would only want to watch a movie or gossip about people at the community college where she worked.

Katy didn't want to talk. She'd heard enough useless chatter all week, and with the amount of nervous energy surging through her system, watching a movie sounded like a death sentence.

She slowed as the speed limit dropped from highway speeds to residential through the short span of Aspen's businesses. There wasn't much traffic, but considering the wide-open spaces of the rest of the town, some might consider it a more-congested area. If a person could even suggest that about a place with not a single stoplight.

She passed the town hall and Randall's Western Outfitters, the sign from the quaint coffee shop catching her attention. If she'd made it out of the office before seven-thirty, she could have stopped and grabbed a soothing latte. But they were shut down, along with the rest of the town. Everything but Swallow's Bar and Grill.

She eyed the packed parking lot of the local watering hole with renewed interest. She wasn't one to drink much and partying crowds had never been her sort of people, but the thought of getting lost in a dark room full of loud music tempted her. She'd never stopped in after work to socialize. Perhaps it was time.

Since it wasn't her crowd, not many would know her well. Chances of someone knowing her circumstances from work would be about zero since the medical center was in the next town, and the only person she knew that lived in Aspen and worked at the center was someone from the maintenance department. Fat chance he'd even care about the gossip mill in accounting or administration.

Her wounded car cruised into the gravel lot with no trouble at all, and luckily, she found a parking space near the entrance.

Her black skirt, lavender silk tank, and black jacket weren't exactly bar attire, but she'd decided the moment she'd pulled into the lot she didn't care. Wouldn't care about anything for the rest of the night. She would have a drink, maybe some food and let some of the town partiers absorb her restless energy before she went home and fell into bed. She could worry about work tomorrow when she'd rested and had a clearer head.

Her leather pumps crunched on the snow-crusted gravel as she headed toward the front door. When she tugged open the entrance to the bar, a rush of warmth and 80s rock music surrounded her and welcomed her inside.

CHAPTER FIVE

People packed the small tavern. Tables held the maximum number of occupants, and it would be hard to fit another couple on the dance floor. With winter upon them, there wasn't much else to occupy the fine citizens of Aspen. They could stay hunkered down in their homes, risk driving into Pinecone or Roosevelt for a greater selection of social activities, or go to Swallow's Bar and Grill.

Sadly, she'd usually chosen to stay home.

Katy eyed a corner of the bar where she was pretty sure she could squeeze in. She elbowed her way between two older cowboys, and one of them was kind enough to give his seat to her.

A young female bartender complete with ample cleavage and a cowboy hat approached her. She turned her pink glossed lips into a smile, flashing a cute set of dimples. "What can I get ya?"

Looking like that, Katy was sure the girl had earned some healthy tips from the men around her. "I don't know. I want something wild and exotic. What do you suggest?"

The girl nodded. "Needing a little excitement, huh? Something to break the monotony of the work week?"

Katy laughed. "Apparently I'm not the first to bring her troubles to the bar."

"Nope." The girl shook her head. "Happens all the time." She studied Katy. "You look like a Screaming Orgasm would fix you right up."

Boy, would it ever. "Bring it on."

The girl smiled. "Coming right up."

The bartender delivered a carmel-colored concoction with a pink umbrella clinging to the edge. "You look like the umbrella type."

She probably did wearing her office clothes. "Could be." She smiled and gave the girl a nice tip.

She swirled the wooden tip of her garnishment around in her drink a couple of times before slipping it between her lips. Sweet was her first impression. She took a tiny swallow. The creamy drink tasted more like a decadent dessert than alcohol. "That's really good," she said to no one in particular.

The grizzled cowboy to her right elbowed her. "I think you're supposed to drink it pretty fast." His deep voice and bushy mustache reminded her of Sam Elliott.

Katy drew her brows together. "Are you sure?"

He shrugged. "I've seen some of the youngsters in here do it. Up to you."

She glanced at the creamy drink again. "Okay, then. Here's to something." She lifted her glass. She didn't even know how to make a proper toast.

"How about here's to meeting strangers in bars and turning them into friends?"

"I like it. Here's to us." She drank it as fast as she could, the icy liquid giving her a brain freeze. "Sweet Mary, that's cold." She put her hands to her head trying to stave off the pain.

Her newfound friend laughed and slapped her lightly on the back. "Relax and let it work its magic. You'll be all right in a second."

She did as he suggested and in a few moments, the concoction settled into a blazing ball that heated her stomach and radiated outward. Her limbs loosened, and she let her shoulders drop, surprised at how much tension she'd held in them.

"Feeling it?" the older guy asked.

She grinned. "Oh yeah. This is good. I'll have another," she called to the waitress.

"You finished it already?"

Katy nodded, feeling pretty proud of herself. The girl shrugged and brought her another.

She downed it like she had the first one as a nice buzz settled over her. This time the cold didn't affect her head as much. "Bring me another."

Sam chuckled. "Uh, you might want to slow down just a bit."

"Sure, I'll get that for you. Give me a few minutes." The girl turned and headed to the other end of the bar. Katy squinted and leaned forward on the counter, suddenly feeling more comfortable in her chair. "Is that her ass peeking out the bottom of those short shorts?"

"Mmm-hmm." The cowboy turned his lips into a cocky smile. "Why do you think I picked this spot?"

Katy gave his shoulder a soft punch as sat back in her seat. "You're a dirty, old man."

"I may be. But if she's going to show it, I'm sure as hell going to look."

"I guess I would, too, if I were you."

"What the hell are you talking about? You did look."

A burst of laughter escaped her lips. "I guess I did." She was surprised how much she enjoyed the older man's company. "I don't think she wants to give me another drink."

"She probably doesn't want you puking on her bar. How about if I order a beer and sneak it to you?"

She giggled, feeling lighter than she had all week. "Okay."

The bartender delivered the ill-gotten drink and then shook her head a few minutes later when she caught Katy drinking it. The girl eyed Katy's new friend. "You two are going to have to find someone to drive you home if you keep it up."

"I've got it handled," Sam said.

A whisper of a touch caressed Katy's ear. "What are you doing in my bar?" a familiar voice asked.

Katy leaned back on her stool and half-turned, holding on to the bar for support. The devil who'd haunted her dreams all week stood behind her. "Scott." She turned farther, her knees bumping into Sam, her vision swirling along with the barstool.

The older man rested a hand on her bare knee as though to steady her. "Don't even try to steal her from me, Beckstead."

"She's already gone, Peterson." Scott turned Katy until she faced him and then helped her from her stool.

She wobbled on her heels, and Scott pulled her closer to him for support. "Whoa, those drinks were really potent." She blinked a few times and tried to clear her vision.

Scott snorted. "I think it's time for you to go home, Angel."

Sam whose real name was apparently Peterson stood along with her. "Maybe the lady doesn't want to leave."

Katy smiled at Scott. "We were having a great time. This is my new friend, Sam."

The older man raised a brow at her.

"I mean Peterson. And the bartender gave me screaming orgasms, and..." Wow, the music was really loud.

"Really, Becky?"

The girl shrugged. "It's a bar, Scott. We serve alcohol, and she wanted to blow off some steam. How was I to know she couldn't hold her booze? Besides, she looks much better now than when she walked in."

"It's true," Katy said, except for the fact the room was a little off balance. "I'm much better with my new friends."

Scott took her chin in his hand, forcing her to look at him. "Do you realize your new friend here is trying to get you drunk and hoping to take advantage of you?"

"No." She shook her head, not believing a word of it. She glanced at Sam, who smiled and gave her a sheepish grin. "Really?"

"You can't blame a guy for wanting to get to know a beautiful woman better."

"Just like you can't blame a guy for looking at a bartender's ass when it hangs out." She snickered.

Sam shrugged and smiled.

"You've been checking out my ass, Peterson?" Becky asked.

Scott tossed Katy's arm over his shoulder and placed a strong arm around her waist. "Come on. Let's get you home."

"Don't tell me you don't have the same thing on your mind, Beckstead," Sam challenged, and Katy glanced at her savior to read his expression.

"Difference is, I don't take advantage of drunken women."

That was too bad, Katy thought as Scott helped her to the door. He paused long enough to toss his keys to someone. "Follow me, huh?"

Katy couldn't see who followed them out the door, and quite frankly, she didn't care. Her bad boy, the one she should avoid at all costs, held her in his arms. The only place she really wanted to be.

"Which car is yours?"

She tried to focus, but the alcohol had snatched a good portion of her sanity. "It's the cute maroon Rio with only one headlight. I crashed it into a big truck. One of your trucks, I think."

"I believe you're correct."

"So sorry about that. I don't think I hurt it, though. Not your truck, 'cause it's so big."

"It's okay. We can talk about it later."

"I didn't really want to be at the bar," she said as he helped her into her car. "I just needed to do something different. Something wild. This week was hell."

He shut her door and walked around to the driver's side. "Why didn't you call me? If you need a wild time, I'm your man."

"That's what I'm afraid of. Hotty Scotty can steal your virginity in five minutes."

He shook his head and laughed. "I haven't heard that name since high school." He started the car and then turned to her. "Are you saying you're still a virgin, Katy?"

"No." She'd lost that back in college.

"Then I guess you have no reason to be afraid of me."

She thought for a minute. Everything he said made perfect sense. "You are so right. Why didn't I consider that before?"

CHAPTER SIX

Morning light teased behind her eyelids, but at the moment, Katy couldn't consider opening her eyes. She was afraid if she did, the brutal pain encircling her head would explode through her body.

She probably deserved it. There were enough memories tagging along with the ache inside her head to remind her of the prior evening. She'd wanted to unwind a little after her hard week, but she'd ended up completely unraveling and making a fool of herself flirting with a man old enough to be her father. He was kind of cute, though.

Then there was Scott. She couldn't even think about him right now.

She lay there for a while longer before someone pounded on her front door. "Go away," she mumbled. She glanced at her clock and found it well past ten, but there was no way she was dragging her sorry butt out of bed to see who wanted to bother her. She'd had enough bothering the past week to last her a lifetime. It was Saturday, a day that no one owned but her.

The knocking finally stopped, and she rolled over in relief.

"Hello?" a female voice came from the direction of the front door.

"Please, God. No," she whispered as she pulled the pillow over her head. Maybe her mother wouldn't notice the lump in her bed and leave.

"Katherine Eleanor Rivers. What are you still doing in bed?" Her mother jerked her pillow from her face, sending harsh morning light into her sensitive eyes. "Are you sick?"

"No, I'm not sick. I'm sleeping. I'm also an adult woman in my own home, and you have no right to come barging into my room like you did when I was a teenager. I gave you a key for emergencies only."

"How do I know this isn't an emergency? You didn't answer your phone or your door. How am I supposed to know someone hasn't snuck in here and murdered you in the middle of the night? I still don't think it's right for a young woman to live alone."

Katy snatched back her pillow and held it to her chest as she sat up in bed. "What did you need, Mom?"

Her mother shrugged as though offended. "Aunt Lana and I are headed into Roosevelt to do some Christmas shopping. I thought maybe you'd like to go with us."

She dropped her head into her palm, covering her eyes. She was such a bad daughter. Her mother only wanted to spend time with her. "I'm sorry, Mom. I have a horrible headache and don't really feel like going anywhere today." That included getting out of bed.

Her mom sat on the edge of the mattress, searching her daughter's face. "You don't look very well. Are you sure it's just a headache? You might be coming down with something." She placed a cool hand on her forehead. "You feel a little warm."

"I don't know. Maybe." Her illness didn't stem from a virus, but she couldn't very well tell her mother she'd gotten plastered at the bar the night before. Her mom would never recover from the disappointment. "I just feel like I need to rest today. This week was a tough one."

"I know." Her mother patted her hand. "But we're so proud of you for getting that promotion."

"It's not a promotion, Mom."

"That's not what I heard. Nelly said—"

"Mom." She held up a hand. "I know what the rumors are, but Mr. Winward said temporary, so that's what I'm going by until I hear otherwise."

"Fine, dear." Her mother stood. "You rest. I'll call later to check on you. Keep your phone turned on, or I'll be driving over here again."

Katy nodded. "I will." That would be one request she wouldn't forget.

Her mom hugged her and left.

She fell back on the bed, tucking her pillow beneath her pounding head. As she pulled the covers up to her chin, she realized, she was still dressed in her lavender silk shirt. Her black skirt, too. Sweet Mary. She still wore yesterday's clothes, and her mother hadn't noticed.

Somewhere, there was an angel watching out for her.

Her phone rang again, and she flailed a hand over to her nightstand to retrieve it. She slid her finger down the screen to answer the phone. "What did you forget, Mom?"

"I'm pretty sure I'm not your mother," a male voice responded from the other side.

Katy jerked the phone from her ear and took a moment to actually focus on the screen. *Scott-cell.* "Scott."

"It is. How did you know?"

"I recognized your voice." She wasn't about to tell him she had his number already programmed into her phone.

"Good. I like that."

She could picture him smiling that killer smile of his on the other end of the line. "How did you get my number?"

"You gave it to me last night." He paused for a moment. "Several times."

She groaned and closed her eyes, wishing the winter snow didn't reflect so brightly in her room.

"How are you feeling today?"

"Eh," she squeaked. "Maybe a little under the weather."

"Or maybe a lot."

There was no sense in hiding it. "Okay. A lot."

"There are two ibuprofen next to the water bottle on your nightstand. Take them. Wait thirty minutes. Then there's something I mixed up for you last night waiting in your fridge. Shake it and drink it all."

"What's in it?"

"I'm not going to tell you, but it will make you feel better."

"The last time I drank a concoction with unknown ingredients, I ended up like this."

"That's what you get for trusting the wrong people. Now, do what I say, and you can thank me later."

"Okay. Thank you so much." She'd drink anything if it would make her head stop throbbing.

"I mean it."

"I said okay."

"No, I literally mean you can thank me later. In person. You should be feeling like your old self about four o'clock. I'll be at your house then, and we're going to do something wild just like you wanted. See you then."

The line went dead. Katy looked at her phone, and sure enough, the call had ended.

She buried her face in her pillow. This day would kill her. She lifted long enough to find the pills and water he'd left for her. She swallowed them and prayed they'd kick in quickly.

Wild? What kind of wild did he mean?

A visual of him laughing after she'd called him Hotty Scotty surfaced from her hazy memories. She remembered them discussing her virginity and him telling her that since she'd lost hers, she didn't have anything to fear from him.

"Oh, God." She'd have to dig deep to face him after that discussion.

Katy made sure she called her mom at three to let her know she was feeling much better. A phone call now could save her a heap of trouble later. After that, she hit redial on Scott's number.

"You're not canceling on me," he answered. "I'll use blackmail if I have to, and trust me, after last night, I have plenty."

She laughed. "What happened to people saying hello?"

"Hmm…" His voice rumbled across the line in a sexy way that sent tingles through her. "Okay. Hello, Angel."

She rolled her eyes, but had to admit she loved the way he said it. "Is that how you talk to all the girls?"

"All what girls? You're the only one I've been thinking about."

He was good. Had he really been thinking about her all afternoon like she'd thought of him? "Enough of the sweet talk. It's not going to work on me."

"We'll see. If you're not calling me to cancel, then what's up?"

"This date that you've informed me of. Could you at least give me an idea of what we're doing?" She flung a hand outward even though he couldn't see it. "I have no idea how to dress."

His deep, rich chuckle came across the line. "I told you, we're doing something wild."

"I know that much, but what exactly?"

"Does that make you nervous? Not knowing what I'm going to do with you?"

"No." Yes. Every thought *she* had of them doing something wild started with both of them losing their clothes. She rustled up a cool composure in order to bury her thoughts. "Stop teasing me and give me a hint."

"Jeans and a warm coat ought to do. Warm boots if you have any. I wouldn't want your toes to get cold."

"We'll be outside?" Where could he possibly take her?

"I'm not saying anything else. See you in thirty minutes."

She glanced at the time as she clicked off her phone. She'd better scramble, or she'd never make it.

Scott arrived at her door promptly at four, unfamiliar nerves pricking him. Back when he and Katy had been in school, he hadn't been all that reliable. But he'd changed. He'd put that idiotic behavior behind him and was now a respectable business man.

He only hoped Katy would see it.

When she'd canceled their date earlier in the week, he'd been certain his past had caught up to him once again. There was an obvious chemistry between them, so he'd assumed she'd judged him based on his old reputation. Now, he wasn't so sure. Maybe he did have a chance with her after all.

He knocked on the door and waited. A minute went by, and she didn't answer. He couldn't imagine what would keep her.

He repeated his knock, a little louder this time.

She opened the door with a flourish. Her eyes sparkled with energy, and he was certain he'd never seen anything so beautiful in his life. "I'm so sorry," she said. "I'm not quite ready. Please come in." She hopped away from the door, one foot stuck in an unlaced suede hiking boot, the other only sheathed in a thick, gray sock.

He laughed at the sight. Her frantic disposition charmed him. "Need some help?" His gaze traveled upward, and he studied the way the little jewels on the pocket of her jeans flashed as she moved. He'd have a hard time keeping his hands off her.

"Just give me a minute. These boots are always so darn hard to get on." She sank onto a slightly worn brown couch and leaned forward to tie her boot.

He glanced around the small but tidy living room. "Nice place."

She looked up and grinned, her blond hair looking disheveled from her hurrying. "Thanks. It was my grandma's. I inherited it a few years back when she passed. I like to think she's happy that I'm here."

"I'm sure she is." He walked forward as she struggled to get her socked foot into the other boot.

He knelt down in front of her and pushed her hands out of the way.

"Ugh." She leaned back against the cushion. "I hate these boots, but they're the only warm ones I have."

He pushed up her pant leg and tugged on her sock. "You have to make sure your socks are snug to reduce the bulkiness."

"Is that all?" She rolled her eyes and snorted.

"I'm serious." He tugged her sock again, pretending to accidentally brush her calves with his fingers. Her skin was as soft as it looked. What he wouldn't give to kiss his way up her legs.

He stifled his lusty thoughts before he embarrassed himself, and he slipped her boot over her dainty foot with little trouble at all and tied both laces.

She sat up, looking amazed. "How did you do that?"

"I told you. Snug socks." He laced her boot and stood, holding a hand out to her.

She took it and stood. He didn't release her, but pulled her closer instead, needing her next to him. "I'm glad you decided to let me take you out. You won't regret it."

Her laugh reached deep into the heart of him. "Like I had a choice."

"You have a choice. You can always say no. I'm just hoping you won't."

"Okay, fine. After my disastrous attempt to live it up last night, I'm willing to try things your way."

"Good. I promise I'll bring you home in much better condition tonight." He gripped the belt loops on her jeans and tugged her to him. "I'm sorry..." He buried his nose in her soft tresses. "But you smell damn good."

"Thank you. It's..." She blinked as though she'd lost her train of thought. "Never mind. I'm glad you like it." She grabbed a turquoise ski coat from the back of the couch. "I guess I'm ready. Sorry I made us late."

"It's okay, Angel. There's no one where we're going that will mind if we're late."

"Why do you call me that? Angel?"

He straightened a piece of her hair that had gotten caught up in the masses. "Because you are. You remind me of everything that's good and right in this world."

She widened her eyes. "Okay, then. That's a little deep for a first date, isn't it?"

"Probably." He helped her with her coat. "I'll wait until we've gone out for a month before I call you Angel again."

She shook her head. "That's okay. I kind of like it."

CHAPTER SEVEN

Katy locked the door behind her as she and Scott left her house before turning toward his vehicle. Parked behind her tormented Rio sat an SUV similar to the one that had passed her that fateful morning. "It was you."

"What was me?"

"You're the crazy driver who went flying past me last Monday on my way to work. The roads were snow-packed, and you just flew right by me."

He shrugged. "Possibly. But there was never a moment I wasn't in control."

"How could you be? The roads were slippery. Just look at the front end of my car. I was driving super slow."

He grinned as he opened the passenger door of his SUV and waited for her to get in. "Oh, yeah. Now I remember. You were chugging along about five miles an hour. I'm surprised you made it to work before noon that day."

She gasped. "I hope you don't think I'm getting in your truck now that I know how you drive."

That earned her a deep, rich chuckle. "Don't worry, honey. I'll bring you home safe and sound. Besides, we're only going to be in my truck for a short drive."

He had her there. If she didn't go, she'd never know what kind of wild thing he had in store for her. "This better be good. The anticipation alone is driving me crazy."

"Really?" He seemed to like that. "I promise you won't be disappointed."

He drove at a respectful speed through Aspen and onto the main highway leading toward Pinecone.

"Are we heading into town?"

"Nope." He grinned, but kept his eyes on the road.

She loved it when he smiled. With his dark hair, eyes and goatee, he'd always intimidated her when he'd worn a serious look. But when he smiled, and his eyes turned all sexy, she melted. "Is it somewhere close to Aspen?"

"Kinda."

His sense of adventure was irresistible. "Who's going to be there?"

"Us and a few other souls."

"Anyone I know?"

"Doubt it."

The suspense was killing her, but she loved every second of it. "Come on. Give me a hint."

He gave her a sideways glance, his gaze traveling the length of her as though he was undressing her with his eyes. "You'll have to wait and see."

She broke eye contact with him, not wanting to give away how much he excited her.

He slowed and turned down a long road still covered in snow. He continued at the normal speed limit, and she bit her lip to keep from telling him to slow down.

He reached over and squeezed her hand as though he'd sensed her shift in mood. "Don't worry. My truck is great in the snow."

She dropped her shoulders and forced herself to relax. She'd wanted to live more dangerously. If the tempo of her pulse was any indication, she was well out of her comfort zone now.

At least she wasn't bored out of her mind.

Scott pulled through an open gate and up to a large white barn.

"You're taking me here?" For what? Showing her livestock wasn't wild and certainly wouldn't impress her.

"Gonna have to wait." He shut off his engine, his face alight with excitement. "Stay here."

Katy caught his enthusiasm as he exited the truck and headed toward the barn. What could he possibly have in mind? She supposed it didn't really matter what they did. She was spending the evening with a man who exemplified the word sexy. And hot. And irresistible.

This was not a good thing. But how could she resist? When he looked at her with that engaging smile, she was lost.

Maybe tomorrow she'd spend some time figuring out exactly what she wanted. For today, she belonged to him.

Two wide doors on the barn swung open. A moment later, two horses emerged, followed by Scott sitting in a sleigh.

Her heart took notice, and she climbed out of the truck, not caring that her boots sunk to her ankles in snow. "A sleigh ride? Are you kidding?" she called as she approached him. She couldn't bury her smile if she wanted to.

He halted the team of horses next to his truck. "Climb in and hold the reins while I close the barn."

He held out a hand to her. She grasped his gloved hand, grateful she'd stuffed her gloves in her pocket before she'd left. He'd said to wear something warm, so she'd tried to be as prepared as she could.

"It's gorgeous." Shiny gold adorned the sleek black sleigh that housed soft-looking, red seats. "Is it yours?"

He shook his head. "Nah. The horses are, but the sleigh belongs to Luke Winchester. I don't know if you remember him."

"Tall guy. Pretty well built. He was involved in some sort of relationship with Hannah Martin. I thought he got her pregnant or something."

Scott shook his head. "There were a ton of rumors going around back then, but none of them were true. Hannah made the whole thing up. But that's another story. Right now, we need to get going, or we won't make it there in time."

"Seriously? There's more?"

"There's far more than this. We haven't even started getting wild yet."

Her breath hitched in her throat, and she wondered if that was some kind of sexual innuendo. Maybe. Maybe not. If she considered his reputation, she was sure it had been. But he'd been nothing but kind and sweet to her. A true gentleman. So, was he teasing her with sexual comments or not?

He returned a few moments later to retrieve some blankets and a bag from his SUV before climbing up next to her. "Here, let's put this on the other side of you."

He leaned across her, arranging the bag between her and the side of the sleigh, forcing her to scoot closer to his side. Not that she minded. He settled a heavy quilt across her lap and looked down into her eyes. His warm gaze sparkled with excitement, and she couldn't help but return the gesture. He seemed too good to be true, and she wanted to pinch herself to make sure she wasn't dreaming. Maybe she'd knocked her head a little too hard during her accident and had been dreaming ever since. Perhaps the temporary promotion and Scott were both just figments of her imagination. Wrapped in her warm clothing, she couldn't find any bare skin to pinch. She bit her tongue instead, and a sharp pain spread over the surface.

Nope. All real.

"I think we're about ready." He sat beside her, his strong thigh nestled snug against hers. "Warm enough?"

Definitely. With the hottest guy in town sitting right next to her, how could she not be? "I'm good. Thanks."

He took the reins from her hands, and she slid the quilt so it covered both of their laps, her fingers tingling as they brushed across his jeans.

He smiled his appreciation and sent the horses on their way.

A cool breeze caressed her face as they traveled across the snow-covered field toward a rising ridge in the distance. Katy pulled up her hood to stay warm.

"Getting cold?" Scott tugged the quilt higher on her lap.

"Just a little."

He held the reins with one hand and wrapped an arm around her shoulders. Instant heat radiated through her.

"It's beautiful out here," she said. The evening sun shone across the white field reflecting off each snow crystal. "It's like we're flying across a field of diamonds. Thank you for bringing me."

"You're welcome, but I'm hoping this isn't the end of your surprises."

"Always the cryptic one, aren't you?"

"I like to keep people guessing."

"You do a good job of that. Never in a million years would I have thought you owned the construction company that was working on our building."

"Why not? Because I was such a screw off in school? People can change, you know."

Had her original thoughts about him been that transparent? "You're right." She shouldn't judge without knowing someone. "I admit I was a little surprised you'd turned your life around. A lot of people don't."

"Okay, I'll give you that. Some people aren't willing to put forth the effort to reach their achievements, whether they had a good upbringing or not. They accept whatever status quo they've been given and stay there."

She'd hit a sore point and done a fine job of botching their serene atmosphere. "I'm sorry. I didn't mean to come across as judgmental. You've done this wonderful thing for me, and I'm making it awkward."

"No, you're not." He shook his head. "I'm glad you're here. Obviously, you don't believe everything people say, or you wouldn't be."

She hoped that was true. She'd originally said yes because she'd developed a sudden thirst for flirting with danger, but she was getting to know the man behind the reputation and starting to like what she found.

"You might not believe this, but those of us with supposed stellar reputations also get shunned sometimes."

He snorted. "Right."

"It's true." She nudged him with her shoulder. "Just because a person got good grades doesn't mean they didn't like to have fun. Doesn't mean they didn't want to be invited to the parties, too."

"Who would have thought?" He nodded. "I guess I can see how that might be true. I guess we're both a couple of misfits."

He reached the top of a ridge and stopped the horses. They stood on a hill, a small valley spreading out in front of them before it rose again a good mile away. A small frozen pond sat squat in the center of the basin with pines and aspens growing in clumps around the edges. Dusk had forced away the harsh light of day, leaving the valley in shadow.

"We're here."

Katy glanced around, her breath clouding in front of her. "Where's here?"

"Good question." Scott looked around, nodding with satisfaction. "I guess you could say in the middle of nowhere, but if you're patient and keep your eyes trained down below, you might see something really wild."

Scott tied the reins to a hook on the side of the sleigh and settled back to watch the valley. Katy pulled the quilt higher up her chest.

"There's a thermos of coffee in the bag."

Katy shifted and found the thermos along one edge of the sack. "Good call." She poured a cup for both of them.

"Don't worry. I won't let you get too cold." He held his steaming coffee in one hand and wrapped the other around her shoulders again.

She had no doubt about that. She was pretty certain cold would never be a problem for her with him around. She settled against him, wanting to know more about how he'd gotten to where he was now. "What made you decide to go into construction?"

He tilted his head to the side and shrugged. "I was dumb and dropped out of high school. I ended up completely on my own. Then I picked up a job working for a guy framing houses. Joe Rogers. I never met a harder working man in my life. Or a smarter one. He more or less took me under his wing, taught me a few things, and convinced me life would be easier if I went back to school. So I did. I worked days and studied construction engineering at night. Socked away most of the money I earned. I started doing side jobs in addition to working for Joe. Bought me a few pieces of equipment. When Joe retired, I struck out on my own. I'm in my second year of business. My company's now in the black, and things are looking up."

"Winning the medical center bid had to be a huge boost. To your bottom line and to your reputation."

"You can say that again." He blew on his coffee and took a drink before continuing. "How about you? What made you go into accounting?"

She snorted and rolled her eyes. "It was a safe major. A versatile degree. Guaranteed to find a job. Besides, I'm kind of good with numbers."

"I think that's sexy."

"Numbers?" He thought she was sexy.

"Yeah. I like a woman with a brain in her head. Someone who can handle numbers and money is attractive. Maybe you could help me with my books sometime. I do most of the accounting myself, although I do hire a bookkeeper from time to time. But my records are a disaster. I'm sure the guy who does my taxes charges me triple because everything is a mess."

"Okay. Sure. There are lots of good computer programs out there that can really help. I'd be happy to help you get set up."

"Wait...there they are."

CHAPTER EIGHT

The hushed tone in Scott's voice brought Katy up straight in her seat, and she tried to follow the direction of his finger. "Who? Where?"

"Wolves. There's a pack of grays that frequent this basin during the winter. Right down by the base of those trees."

A shiver skittered through her, knowing the predators were so close. "I still can't see them. Which trees do you mean?"

Scott pulled her closer to him, leaning behind her, holding her to his chest. His warm breath brushed across her ear, sending another more potent tremble through her. He lifted his arm and pointed again. "Follow my finger." The sound of his voice mesmerized her. "See those three pines clustered together near the right edge of the lake?"

She nodded and leaned her head against his under the pretense of following his direction.

"There's another lone pine just to the left of them."

"I see it."

"Okay. Look down in the shadows at the base of the trees, and you can see them. Two adults and one smaller one. Possibly a half-grown pup."

One of the shadows moved, and she realized it was a wolf. Two similar forms stood close by. "I see them." Excitement pumped through her veins. "Friends of mine have said they've seen wolves in these hills before, but I've never had the opportunity to get into the back country. This is unbelievably cool. Do they know we're here?"

"Wind's blowing in our face, so probably not, but I doubt they'd approach us anyway. They'll wait for weaker prey, a young deer or an old one who's been left behind. They like to snack on deer that come to the river to drink. I brought a couple pair of binoculars, too, if you want a closer look."

Nice. "I'd love to see them up closer." She handed her cup of coffee to him and dug through the bag, her hand hitting a solid object. She lifted it, shock rippling through her at the discovery. "There's a gun in here."

"Sorry. Should have warned you. It's locked so there's no fear of it going off."

That was a relief. He didn't seem too concerned about the pistol, but she'd never touched a weapon like that before in her life and the experience was a little unnerving.

"The binoculars should be down on the left side of the sack in two smaller bags."

He tossed the contents of their cups into the snow and leaned across her, pulling the binoculars from the canvas sack. The feel of his hard body over hers was comforting and exciting at the same time. She hadn't realized how much she enjoyed having him so close. Will had never sent her heart racing just by brushing against her.

"Do you think we'll need the gun?"

He gave her a reassuring smile and shook his head. "Just a precaution. We're out in the wilderness. It pays to be prepared."

"I thought I was the cautious one, and you were the wild and crazy person."

"There's a difference between wild and stupid, Angel."

She supposed there was. She took the binoculars and held them to her eyes. "It's all out of focus."

"Tilt the edges down and in. That should make things clearer."

She did as he directed, and the trees suddenly came into view. The wolves were still kind of small, but she could definitely see them. "They look like dogs."

He chuckled at that. "What did you expect?"

She followed the movements of one, excited to see it approach another so that she now had two in her sights. "I don't know. I guess I thought they'd appear more vicious."

"Trust me. They're not sweet like puppy dogs. They're cunning predators who'd take you down if they were hungry enough and thought they could get away with it."

"Thanks for that. I'm feeling super safe at the moment. Maybe we'd better get that gun out of the bag after all."

He shifted, and she peeked from behind her binoculars to find him staring intently at her. "Don't worry. They'll have to go through me before they'd ever get a shot at you, and that is not going to happen, okay?"

The fierceness of his reply left her in shivers. "Okay," she answered, her word teetering on breathless. A rush of warmth flooded her. She had no doubt the guy who'd intimidated her with his dark eyes and devilish looks could protect her. The thought left her feeling very feminine and more than a little attracted to him.

She slipped back behind her binoculars, afraid if she didn't, she'd start fluttering her eyelashes like a silly fool. She located the pair of wolves again, and then circled the area, searching for the third wolf. It was headed back into the trees. She quickly located the other two, sad to see them heading in the same direction. "They're leaving."

"Looks like it. That's okay. I'm glad we spotted them. Sun will be down before long, and we won't be able to see them anyway." He removed the reins from the hook inside the sleigh.

"Are we headed back then?" She wasn't ready to go home, and he had not made one single move on her the whole night except to wrap an arm around her.

She wanted a kiss under the stars.

"I don't want you to get too cold."

"I'm not cold. Well, my nose is a little, but the rest of me is quite fine."

He quirked a sexy brow. "Yes, you are."

Warmth heated her cheeks. "Maybe we could watch the sunset. We're okay out here after dark, aren't we?" After all, she had her big, strong man to protect her.

"Yeah. I know this land like the back of my hand." He turned the horses around, facing them toward the orange globe hovering near the horizon. Slashes of white clouds cruised across the dark periwinkle sky, promising they'd soon claim the heavens.

She snuggled closer to him under the quilt.

He wrapped his arm around her again, tugging her close, making her heart thump faster. "I thought you weren't cold."

"Maybe just a little, but this is nice. Definitely warmer." She turned into him, slipping an arm behind his back, and rested her head on his shoulder.

A few minutes later the sun disappeared from the horizon, leaving them with nothing but a half moon to light their way. Stars in the sky popped out one by one, creating a show in the night sky.

"It's so peaceful out here. And just beautiful, isn't it?"

"It certainly is." He shifted in his seat, and the tension between them heightened. Something electric and strong replaced the friendly camaraderie they'd shared only moments before. "You should make a wish on one of those stars."

"Okay." She stared at him, not giving the heavens a second glance. Her wish was that he'd touch his lips to hers so that she might taste him.

He faced her, and she trembled. He slipped off his glove and ran a finger down her cheek. "Such soft skin."

"Thank you." She searched his expression, knowing where he was headed, frightened and exhilarated at the same time.

"Think we should head back?" He trailed a thumb across her bottom lip.

"No," she whispered, and then sighed as he dropped his head toward hers.

The moment his lips brushed across hers, her heart contracted as though holding on for dear life. Sweet Mary. She met his searching tongue, and the low-fire that had burned inside her during their evening erupted. The whiskers on his chin tickled her. He tasted of cinnamon, coffee and desire. And all those things she ached for since she'd become a woman.

A kiss from him would never be enough.

He seemed to sense her feelings and plundered deeper into the soft recesses of her mouth. Even as she accepted him, she yearned for more. He shifted her in his arms and leaned her across his lap, catching her head with the crook of his arm. Her position left her vulnerable to his sweet assault.

He stopped, allowing her to catch her breath. Her chest heaved as she studied his face in the quiet light. It might have been dim, but she was sure the passion that burned inside her was mirrored in his expression.

The start of a smile crossed her lips and slipped onto his as well. He cupped her chin and possessed her mouth again. Sparks more potent than anything she'd felt with a man flared inside her. Could she be that insanely attracted to him, or was the excitement compounded because he should be off-limits?

She didn't know, and right now, ah God, she didn't care.

When he finally stopped, she was a puddle in his lap. Her bones had melted, and any rational thoughts had been erased. She could stay like that forever if he'd keep kissing her.

He traced a finger across her tender lips. "I think we'd better head back. If we try to take this any further out here, we'll end up with frostbite. Besides, I never go all the way on a first date."

His statement coaxed a laugh from deep inside her. "Me, either."

"Common knowledge, Angel." He helped her straighten in her seat.

"Again with the assumptions."

"So what? You're saying you've had sex on a first date? Maybe I should rethink my plans for the evening."

"No." She tugged the quilt up under her chin to ward off the air that had turned frigid after he'd released her.

"No, what?"

"I've never had sex on a first date." Though she wanted to now.

He lifted the reins and urged the horses to head home. "See, common knowledge." He sent her a grin that set her insides to boiling again. "If you're not afraid to be alone with me at my house, I'd love to fix you dinner."

"Depends. Are you a good cook? I need to know what I'm risking my morals for." She couldn't resist the tease.

"Damn good. In the kitchen. And otherwise."

"I'll bet you are," she said, trying not to sound as breathless as she felt. "Okay, then. Take me home." She'd just tossed her first sexual innuendo, but he'd started it, and flirting with him had become her new addiction.

He shook the reins, sending the horses running at a faster clip. "Don't worry. In case you don't remember, we discussed the safety of your virginity last night and determined you have nothing to fear from me."

That's where he was mistaken. She might not be at risk to lose her virginity, but her heart was an entirely different matter.

CHAPTER NINE

B y the time they returned to Luke's barn, Katy was pretty sure her nose had turned into an icicle. A young man dressed in a warm winter coat and work pants came out of the barn just as Scott brought the horses to a halt. Scott helped her out of the sleigh, gathered his bag and slipped the kid a bill. Katy wasn't sure, but she thought it looked more like a fifty than a twenty. Scott led her to the passenger side of his truck and waited until she was inside before he closed the door. By the time he occupied his seat and started his SUV, shivers had claimed her body.

"Now, you're cold. I knew we stayed out there too long."

"I'm fine." She might be cold on the outside, but beneath her skin raged the fire he'd ignited.

He pulled his hand from his glove and reached over to touch her cheek. "You're freezing." He backed his truck around and headed down the snow-packed road to the highway. When his SUV was firmly on the cleared pavement, he accelerated and cranked up the blower on his heater. "It's not super warm yet, but it's better than outside."

She pulled off her gloves and leaned forward, holding her hands in front of the vents. "Feels good."

395

"Can't believe I let you get that cold."

"It's my fault. I wanted to stay out there."

"Doesn't matter. I should have known better."

She hated that he took responsibility for decisions that were partly hers. "Scott. I'm fine."

He eyed her, but didn't respond as he turned off the main road and down a long drive. Bright lights lit the two-story, dark gray rock home sitting at the end of the drive. She'd admired it many times on her way to work. "This is where you live?"

He nodded, a small smile of satisfaction turning his sensual lips. "It took me a while, but I'm happy with how it turned out."

"Happy? Are you kidding? It's breathtaking. You think numbers are sexy? I think a man who could build something this amazing is beyond sexy."

He grinned, his brows rising in a suggestive arch. "I like the sound of that."

The warm depths of his eyes coaxed the flirt from within her. "Maybe we *could* work a deal. I'll play with your numbers, and you can help me with a few things around my home."

"I'm all for working deals." His teasing, sexy smile twisted her insides. "Anything you need, just ask."

A few moments later, she stood in the entry of his comfortable home, grateful to have warm air to thaw her body. "This is just gorgeous. Seriously."

Beautiful wooden floors welcomed her inside. Several darkened rooms led off the entry way, and a stunning wooden staircase curved upward. The furnishings were a little sparse, but the place had so much potential. She inhaled, loving the new home scent. "I'm impressed. Did you do *all* the work?"

He unzipped her coat, pushing it from her shoulders. "Most of it. I hired an electrician and a plumber, but the rest is all me."

She focused on him as he pulled her jacket from her arms. "Are you trying to undress me or what?"

He stopped, a serious look on his face. "I'm trying to get you warm." He hung her coat in a closet near the front door and returned to her.

She smiled. "Ever the gentleman."

He snorted. "Now that's one I haven't heard much during my life."

"I'm finding that harder and harder to believe. I think you have everyone fooled with your bad boy reputation."

Interest flashed in his eyes. "You think so, huh?" He eyed her with a look that left her sizzling. "Maybe I really do want to get you out of your clothes."

A warmth rushed through her. Maybe she wanted that, too, although she'd never say it out loud. In her life, she'd never considered sleeping with a man the first time she was alone with him, but everything about Scott made her want to be as close to him as possible. She longed to pull him to her for another kiss. Longed to run her fingers over his biceps and down his chest. Longed to know what it would be like to make love with a man who made her feel so much more than anyone else ever had.

As he slid the scarf from her neck, she looked into his eyes. Immense attraction coiled around her, making it hard to breathe. The man she'd fantasized about all those years ago stood in front of her looking every bit as dangerous as he had then. She dropped her gaze to his lips, wanting him to claim another kiss. She focused on him, silently pleading for him to make a move.

Instead, he folded her scarf and handed it to her.

"Wait." The worry that she was about to miss an opportunity spurred her to action.

She stepped closer to him, hooking her scarf around his neck and pulling him to her. "You're not the only one who can flirt like that."

Surprised appreciation flared in his eyes. His reaction gave her the courage to continue.

She reached between them and unzipped his coat, desperately needing to lessen the barriers between them. "I think you need to take off your jacket, too."

It was only outer layers, but the way it mimicked a more sensual undressing was not lost on her. He stood immobile as she pulled his coat from him, watching her with a heated gaze, but not making a move. She knew he'd gone out of his way to treat her like a lady, but she didn't want that. She wanted to be treated like a woman. She wanted his touch, his kiss. More.

She placed her hands on the sides of his face and stood on her tiptoes, leaning in to him. She locked eyes with him until her lips touched his, and then she let her eyelids flutter down as intense heat roared through her body.

The first seconds of the kiss were under her control, but he quickly took over, his mouth growing more demanding. He snaked his strong arms around her, crushing her against him.

She slipped her hands beneath his flannel shirt, tugging his t-shirt from his jeans. Her fingertips burned with need when she came into contact with bare skin, and her sigh slipped between their lips. The intimate sound must have driven him to a higher level, too. He pushed her until she was caught between him and the wall, both immovable forces. He left her lips, pulling her hair to the side, placing scorching kisses along her neck, her throat. She tilted her head, gripping his waist as everything inside her turned hot and aching.

"Oh, God," she whispered, as she fisted handfuls of his hair, bringing him back to her for another fierce kiss.

"Do you want me to stop?" He was as breathless as she was.

"Uh-uh." She searched until she found the buttons on his flannel shirt. Each one easily popped open, increasing her anticipation. She'd been thinking about this moment for days, and now that she'd come this far, there was no way she could turn back. For all of the risky opportunities she'd passed on in her life, if she let this moment go, she'd regret it forever.

With his shirt unbuttoned, she tried to remove it, but it clung to his cotton t-shirt.

Scott stopped kissing her long enough to pull both over his head in a single, fluid move.

Sweet Mary. She had Scott Beckstead half naked. Each muscle and curve beckoned to her, and it thrilled her to know she was allowed to touch. It was obvious working construction kept him in top shape. Her eyes traced the glorious curves of his chest, and her fingers soon followed.

She sighed and leaned in, pressing her lips to a spot just beneath his collarbone, his flesh warm and smelling of spicy musk. She inhaled deeply before trailing several kisses upward to the indent where his neck met his chest. She flicked out a tongue, tasting him.

"Angel. You're killing me."

She lifted her face, finding his warm brown eyes had darkened to almost black with desire. Eagerness chased away her nerves. "I know we both never do this on a first date…" She ran her fingers down his bare chest.

"I really hadn't planned on seducing you tonight."

She met his gaze again. "Maybe *I'm* seducing *you*. I think it's about time I start living dangerously."

He lifted her chin, one corner of his mouth curving upward. "You're not this kind of girl. I want to respect that."

"Maybe I want to be. With you. Tonight. Is that such a bad thing?"

"Only if you won't hate me in the morning."

"Never." She pulled her sweater over her head and delighted in the way his eyes lit up. He ran a thumb over the curve of one breast before searching for her nipple beneath the veil of thin white silk. A sharp tingle exploded at his touch, leaving a deep ache within her. He leaned over, sucking her nipple through the thin fabric, and she wondered if a person had ever died from pleasure.

"Damn," he whispered. "I feel like I'm breaking the law."

"Don't put me on that pedestal. I don't like it there."

"Lucky for you, there's no way I can deny you. I'm not that strong."

Just to make sure, she reached behind her to unhook her bra.

He stilled her arms. "Let me, okay?"

She swallowed. "Okay," she said on a breath.

He stepped forward, eliminating any open space between them. His chest pressed against her bra, his stomach warm against hers. He looked down at her with a self-confident masculine gaze, a man sure of what he was about, and she thought she might orgasm from his look alone. His rough fingertips grazed the bare skin of her back. Instead of going straight for her bra, he pulled her tighter against him. "I love the feel of you next to me."

Her heart fluttered, but she couldn't respond. Words wouldn't form. Right now, she could only communicate in sensation and try to remember to breathe.

He tilted his head, leaning in toward her ear. Waves of tingles flushed through her as he sucked on her lobe and placed soft kisses in the hollow beneath. She held her breath as his hand moved up her back. A second later her bra went slack, her heavy breasts falling forward toward him.

Intense emotion blazed in his eyes as he trapped her gaze. With one hand, he slid the bra from her body and tossed it aside. He lifted his brows in a telling gesture before he devoured her bare skin with his eyes.

"Oh, Katy," he whispered as he wrapped his hands around her waist, traveling upward until he reached her breasts. He slid his hands forward, cupping her from beneath, dragging his thumbs across her highly sensitized buds.

He bent her across his arm, arching her back as he leaned in and captured her aching nipple. Instinct, need for release, caused her to thrust her breasts forward. She gasped and gripped his forearm, afraid she might lose her hold on reality and fall.

Delicious sensations raced between her breast to her core, leaving her hot and needing more. He continued to suck and tease her taut bud with his tongue, while he manipulated the other nipple into a burning peak. She tried to breathe through his sensual assaults.

He turned her, taking her hands and placing them on the wall above her head as though spreading her for a police search. His roughened fingers left a wake of powerful shivers as he dragged them down the sensitive undersides of her arms, back to her breasts.

She tried to lower her arms, but he pushed them back in place. "No. Don't move."

A ragged breath escaped her lips as she did as he commanded. Her heart raced faster. She closed her eyes, experiencing each touch, each sensation as he resumed his path down the undersides of her arms. He reached around, taking the full weight of her breasts, massaging them. Proof of his desire for her pressed hard against her bottom, leaving her unstable.

He dropped his hands to the waistband of her jeans, and she inhaled a sharp breath. He kissed her neck, nipped her shoulder as his fingers popped open her button. The zipper on her jeans let out a long, slow hiss as he lowered it. He worked the jeans over her hips, kissed her back and the curve of her waist as he pushed her clothing to the floor.

She stepped out of them.

His warm hands trailing across the bottom curve of her butt nearly undid her. He traced across her curves, over the lace of her panties. Sensation after sensation burst inside her as he spanned his fingers around and down the front of her hips, pulling her against him once again.

"I want to touch you," she whispered.

"Not yet."

He came from the side of her hip, slipping his fingers beneath the edge of her panties, and she stiffened in anticipation of his touch.

At her reaction, he paused. "Is this okay? Do you want me to stop?"

"Yes," she whispered. "No. Please don't stop."

It was his turn to suck in a breath. He traced his fingers across her mound, to the slick valley between.

Someone kill her now because she wasn't sure she could handle this much pleasure.

"God, you're sweet," he whispered as he slipped a finger inside.

She slid her hands down the wall, no longer able to maintain that form with her muscles softening beneath her. "Scott." Her world spun crazily out of control, and she needed him to hold on to. She turned, wrapping her arms around his neck as he claimed her lips in another passionate kiss.

He scooped her up, carrying her farther into the house, into a darkened room. He deposited her on a smooth leather couch, wrapping a soft cotton throw around her. "Don't go anywhere." The light from the foyer caught his features as he smiled. "This might not be when I'd planned to make love to you, but I'm a man who knows how to improvise." He made his way through the dark toward a fireplace and knelt on the floor.

Her heart flipped at his comment. "You'd already planned to make love to me at some point?"

He glanced at her over his shoulder, the muscles in his strong back contracting. "I've pictured it many times."

His answer stole her breath. "Were we good?"

"Damn good." The kindling caught fire and a warm glow filled the room. He walked back to her, a cocky smile on his lips. When he held out a hand, she took it. She wanted this so badly, but being with him like this still felt a little dangerous.

He dragged the blanket with them, spreading it on the floor in front of the crackling fire. With a firm grip, he pulled her into his arms, her breath vacating her lungs as he wrapped her in his embrace. "Mmm…" He laid her down on the blanket, following her to the ground as he gazed into her eyes. "You sure you want to do this?" He cradled her head in the crook of his arm, brushing her hair away from her face.

Renewed excitement built inside her. "Why do you keep asking me if I'm sure? Can't you tell how much I want you?" She ran her fingers over his cheek and into his hair. "I want this."

"You just seem too good to be true. You were always out of reach in school, you know?"

A laugh escaped her. "I'm surprised you remember me from school. You were popular, older, and couldn't have much use for a timid little sophomore."

"Trust me. I remember you. I have a very clear picture of you in a short blue skirt and a tight white sweater. First football game of the season. I couldn't take my eyes off you."

She smiled. "I remember. My mother had a fit about that skirt."

"I can see why. It gave me all kinds of wild ideas about you. I had my eye on you all night, but you were always firmly entrenched with your little group of friends. Besides, you were one of the *untouchables.*" He placed a heated kiss on her lips as though to remind himself he had full access to her now.

She ran a hand up the firm skin on his back, loving the feel of him beneath her fingertips. "What do you mean untouchable?"

"A good girl. Not one a guy could sneak out into the woods with and have his way. You were pure. Not for me. All the guys agreed."

"You talked about me?" She'd had no idea. She'd always thought she was too shy to attract attention. "What did you say?"

"I didn't say anything. Not about you. Not to those guys. But every one of them wished he could get close enough to you to steal a kiss or more if he could get away with it."

"Including you?"

"Trust me. I'd thought about it, but I'd never taint you that way. You were better than that."

"And look at me now. Not a good girl at all." She grinned.

He traced an eyebrow. "You're still a good girl. I can tell."

"But I'm sleeping with you on the first date."

"I do have a small problem with that. We should build a relationship first. That's the way respectable people do it."

He was serious. She laughed. "How do you know what people do behind closed doors?"

He lifted a shoulder and let it drop. "Guess I don't. Honestly, I don't really care what anyone else thinks but you. I want to make you happy."

"You already know how I feel." She tugged his head to her, kissing the man who'd never stopped haunting her dreams.

"I want this to be perfect."

"It is. This night couldn't be more wonderful." She dragged his hand to her breast and kissed him again.

He needed no further encouragement. He shed his jeans and boxers exposing every glorious inch of him. An electric thread of excitement curled through her in anticipation. Kneeling over her, he slipped his fingers beneath the elastic of her panties. She tightened her muscles as he leaned forward and kissed the skin between her belly button and the top edge of her underwear. The erotic gesture left her panting for more.

He slid her panties down her legs in a painfully slow way, his gaze flicking between her eyes and the part of her he'd exposed.

He grinned as he flung her panties behind him and crept forward over her body, sliding a hand up her legs, between her thighs. "Touching you is like touching heaven, Angel." He settled beside her, his hand seeking the center of her once again.

She ran a tongue across her bottom lip before biting into it to keep from moaning.

"You like that?"

She raised her brows in a show of unbridled passion and whispered, "Yes."

"How about this?" He spread her legs wide, massaging her mound before slipping two fingers inside her.

She gasped and bucked against his hand as a delicious shiver overtook her. "Yes."

He dipped his head, kissed the inside of her thigh.

She inhaled a surprised breath when she realized where he was headed. "Scott."

CHAPTER TEN

A moment of panic ripped through Katy. No one had ever been that intimate with her. She tugged on Scott's hair, but he gently pushed away her hands as he ran a tongue along her crease.

"Oh…my…God," she said on a ragged breath.

A wild current surged through her, singeing her with its raw power. She bent her knees, digging her heels into the soft blanket. He delved inside her, a whimper escaping her lips.

He had to stop. She couldn't take the intensity, the white hot passion that threatened to consume her.

She felt it coming. Everything she'd experienced that night had been leading her to this point, she realized. Her muscles contracted of their own volition as a blinding heat spread rampant through her body. She cried out as she went taut, held that feeling for a delicious moment, and then collapsed into a pool of satiated wonder.

He smiled as he scooted up next to her. He was the devil, obviously capable of stealing her soul.

"I've never…"

"Good." He gathered her into his arms, and she didn't resist. She knew at that moment, she'd never be able to resist him again.

She sighed and smiled as she laid her head against his chest.

"Don't get too comfortable. I'm not finished with you yet."

"Okay." Whatever he wanted, whatever he needed, she was at his mercy. But she needed a moment to catch her breath. No doubt, this sexy lover of hers would be relentless.

And she wanted him that way.

A naughty thought urged her forward, and she slipped a hand between their bodies, wrapping her fingers around his shaft.

Power pulsed beneath her touch, and an intense ache to take him inside rolled through her.

He pulled away for a moment, grabbing his jeans and fishing a condom from his wallet.

She wondered how often he'd opened that wallet for the same reason, but then pushed away the thought before it ruined her evening.

He slipped the sheath of latex over himself and settled between her legs. She relaxed, allowing her body to take his full weight. The solid length of him pressed against her apex, giving her a hint of what was to come.

He kissed her, hard, leaving her breathless. As he pulled back, she opened her eyes, finding herself trapped by his gaze, but not wanting to be anywhere else.

He pushed forward by slow degrees, sensations shattering inside her, around him. She kept her gaze on him until he filled her completely, then she arched her back and let her eyes close as she released a sigh of pleasure.

Sweet Mary. What was this intense thing she'd discovered with Scott?

He slipped out and then buried himself again, filling her with awe. Each stroke built toward the same powerful emotions she'd experienced earlier. She welcomed the waves of passion, craving more, and looked forward to the sweet release she knew would come.

He didn't hand it over easily. More than once, he let her get close before he slowed things. It wasn't until she begged for mercy that he gave it to her.

Several times. Over and again until Scott finally tensed. He plunged deep within her as he inhaled, holding himself above her in some kind of rapturous limbo. A fierce expression spread over his features before he collapsed on top of her.

"Ah, Katy-Angel." His shuddering sigh almost made her come again. He rolled to his back, pulling her against him, holding her in place with a muscled arm.

Contentment and something close to bliss flowed through her.

Katy woke the next morning buried in layers of brown and tan blankets in Scott's bed. She couldn't remember how many times they'd made love the previous night. Twice in front of the fire, not including when he'd...And two, no, three times after they'd climbed the stairs to his bedroom. Or maybe four.

She didn't know. Didn't care. All she knew was she couldn't have imagined a better place to find herself that morning.

Scott popped his head inside the door, met her gaze and grinned. "Breakfast?" He wore nothing but his boxers, most of his magnificent body available for her to feast on.

Her smile grew bigger as tantalizing scents filled the room. "You're spoiling me."

"It's what I intended." He set a tray filled with bacon, poppy seed muffins, and slices of aromatic oranges, complete with coffee on her lap and climbed in bed next to her.

She picked up a piece of crispy bacon and took a bite. Heaven. She held it out for him, and he gobbled up the rest, nipping her fingers in the process. She laughed.

He pulled off a chunk of muffin and stuffed it in her mouth. "Oh, that's good." Almond flavoring dissolved on her tongue.

He let her finish her muffin before he set the tray aside, except for the plate of orange segments. She took one and plopped it into her mouth and the citrus flavor exploded on her tongue. "Why does everything taste so good?"

"Sex," he said and bit the tip off his orange. She raised a brow as he encircled her nipple with it and then licked the juice off her.

A tight curling sensation wrapped around her insides, and she sighed.

He slid his strong arms around her and tugged her back down on the mattress. "It's Sunday. I think we should stay in bed all day."

His comment jerked her out of her reverie. "Oh, no." She pushed him back. "What time is it? I have to get home."

"About twenty to nine."

She squeezed her eyes shut. "Damn it." She sat upright and searched for something to cover herself with so she could get up. "I have to get home. My friend Sienna will be at my house at nine, and I have to beat her there."

"Call her and cancel."

She glanced at him looking ruffled and sexy lying back against his pillow. What she wouldn't give to have the whole day to linger in his bed with him.

"You don't understand. She comes over every Sunday morning, regardless. We usually get coffee in town, but if I'm ill or whatever, she still comes. It's like our girl time. I'd...I'd feel bad if I cancelled at the last moment." There was absolutely nothing around that would be useful as a cover. Her pillow. But that would be ridiculous. "Do you have a robe or something?"

"Uh-uh." He gave her a mischievous grin.

"I need to get up. Are my clothes still downstairs?"

"I expect they are." He rolled his eyes as though thinking. "Coat, sweater, jeans...bra are all in the foyer. I think your panties made it to the living room."

She widened her eyes at his teasing. "This is a serious matter."

He lifted his hands, giving her an innocent look. "I agree. You're free to gather your clothes, and I'll drive you home whenever you're ready."

She bit her lip, trying not to smile back at him. Her bad boy had surfaced again. "You're going to make me walk across the room butt-naked in front of you, aren't you?"

"You could stay in bed with me."

She tossed her pillow in his face in order to give herself a head start. She'd barely made it out of bed when his whistle followed behind her. At the door-way, she glanced back to find a huge grin on his face.

"Very nice," he called after her as she hurried down the stairs. She wanted to be angry with him for not helping her, but she couldn't. She was in too good of a mood.

She quickly gathered her clothes and headed into the great room to retrieve her panties.

He was dressed and downstairs before she finished. He helped her into her coat before donning his.

"I've changed my mind. You are not a gentleman," she tossed at him as he drew her into his arms.

He grinned. "Like I said." He leaned in, kissing her, swirling her thoughts until her smart comeback disappeared.

She sighed when he pulled away. "I wish I could stay."

"Me, too."

They didn't make it in time.

Clouds heavy with snow hovered overhead as Sienna stepped out of her little green truck. Scott pulled in to Katy's drive right behind her. Katy cringed as Sienna turned to see who'd arrived. Her eyes widened as she flung a long lock of straight black hair over her shoulder. Katy didn't need anyone to point out that her friend only did that when she was annoyed.

"Shit," Katy said under her breath. Instantly, she could hear Sienna warning her about her language. She really did need to watch it.

"What's the big deal? You made it here on time. It's not like she'll be pissed because you kept her waiting." Scott put his SUV in park.

A heavy breath fell from her mouth. She walked a tight line of not letting Scott know how greatly her friend disapproved of her being with him. "It's…you wouldn't understand."

He scrutinized her. "What? You don't want her to know you spent the night with me?"

She closed her eyes and tried to separate her anxiety from her feelings about their time together. "Thank you for a truly wonderful evening. Everything was amazing."

"Still trying to protect your reputation?"

"Something like that." She tightened her resolve and opened the passenger door, preparing herself for the fallout with Sienna.

"It's a bit late for that," he said as she shut her door.

She panicked when he followed her out.

He met her at the front of his truck. "I wish you'd let me get your door for you."

"Sorry," she said, her breath freezing in front of her. She glanced from him to Sienna, and he followed her gaze.

He stepped forward to her friend. "Scott Beckstead." He extended a hand. "Sienna, right?"

Her friend's wary gaze softened a bit, but didn't quite lose its sharpness. "Right." She shook his hand, and then looked at Katy expectantly.

"Uh…okay. I should get going," she said to Scott.

"Yeah, I'd better let you get to your girl time." He pulled her in for a scorching kiss that melted her toes and left her cheeks burning with embarrassment. "Call me later?"

"Yeah." She nodded and waited for him to get in his truck and leave. It gave her a few moments to compose herself before Sienna ambushed her.

When his SUV was well down the road, she turned to her friend. "Let's go inside. It's freezing out here."

Neither spoke until they were in the house and Katy had shut the door. "Want some tea?" she offered, knowing it was a futile diversion.

"What…was…*that?*" Sienna looked truly disgusted.

"Scott." Katy took off her coat and hung it in the closet, trying to ignore her friend's obvious disapproval.

"I can see that. I thought you weren't going to see him again." Her friend tossed her jacket on Katy's couch in a haphazard fashion.

"Obviously, I changed my mind." She headed into the kitchen. The moss green and lavender accents always had a way of soothing her.

"Obviously, you slept with him." Her friend tossed the barb with such attitude that Katy recoiled. She might as well have called her a slut.

Katy exhaled and grabbed her teapot from the stove. The simple routine allowed her a minute to plan her next words. "I don't really expect you to understand, Sienna. But I like him. And he likes me."

Sienna stood near the sink. "He's using you."

Her words stung like a frigid winter wind. She turned to her friend. "What if I'm using him?" After all, she'd been the one to instigate sex between them.

"I'm sure he'd like you to think so. That way when things don't work out, and you're left with a broken heart, it's your own fault." Something terribly ugly spewed from her cat-like green eyes.

"It's not like that, Sienna. It's…" How did she describe their relationship? There was certainly a

strong attraction between them, but was it just sexual? Could that be all he wanted from her? Maybe it
really was all she needed from him. "It just is what
it is. We've only begun to get to know each other. I
really have no idea where it will go from here."

"I thought you'd agreed it was best if you didn't
see him because of your job. If you break up, it's
going to make things really awkward."

Too late for that. Last night had completely
pushed them beyond the backing out gracefully
period. "Why are you so adamant about this, Sienna?
I understand you don't want to see me get hurt, and
I appreciate that, but you're starting to sound a little
bit too much like my mother."

Her friend stepped back as though Katy had
struck her. "That was rude."

Katy dragged a hand through her unruly hair.
She could only imagine what she must look like with
her bed head and wearing yesterday's clothes. Her
body was sore and stiff from her midnight escapades,
and all she wanted to do was soak in a hot tub. "I'm
sorry. I'm really tired."

"I can only imagine why."

"Really, Sienna? Is this where we want our friendship to go?"

Her friend clamped her mouth shut and then
blew out a breath. "You're right. I guess we're both a
little on edge. Maybe we should call it a day and try
again next week."

Now she felt like the worst person ever. "No."
She stepped forward to the one friend who'd always
been by her side. "I'm sorry. I'm getting bitchy. I
don't mean to."

"Language." Sienna rolled her eyes in a friendly
gesture that coaxed a chuckle out of Katy.

"I know you're worried about me, but I'm a big girl, capable of making my own decisions. Good or bad."

Sienna nodded. "You're right. I'm sorry, too. About the snarky comments and all. I just wish you'd reconsider the path you seemed determined to take. I know you like him, but all I see is heartache waiting for you at the end."

Katy nodded. "It could be heartache, Sienna, but at what point do I stop worrying about what could be and start living?"

Her friend shrugged. "I don't know. Better safe than sorry, I'd say."

That's what Katy had said all along, too. But suddenly "safe" felt more like a death sentence than actually living. "I'll think about it."

"I really hope you do. I think you'll find he's not worth it."

Katy nodded, not wanting to start another round of arguments with her friend now that they'd found a tiny spot of common ground. "How about we forget about Scott for now, and I'll make us some tea? I found this new mandarin orange green tea that's heavenly."

"Okay." Sienna seemed to relax, acting more like her normal self. "Something warm would be good. It really is cold out there."

Katy turned to the sink to fill her teapot with water. She sagged against the counter while she waited.

This was turning out to be far more complicated than she'd expected.

CHAPTER ELEVEN

Monday morning arrived far too quickly, and Katy felt less sure of what she should do. She knew Scott expected a call later in the day on Sunday, but she couldn't bring herself to do it. Too many conflicting emotions with no answers.

To make matters worse, Nina hovered at the reception desk as Katy entered the building. Her nemesis ended her conversation with the receptionist and headed toward Katy.

"Do not talk to me, Nina. Not one word." She punched the up button on the elevator.

"What's the matter? Bad weekend? No dates on the horizon?" She chuckled, making Katy want to punch her. "I asked around, and you aren't dating that guy. I heard he's with some girl named Jen." The elevator doors opened, and Nina stepped inside. "What did you do, pay him five bucks to act like your boyfriend?"

Her words were like a razor to the veins in Katy's heart. She froze where she stood and stared at Nina with enough venom to kill. "I said, do *not* talk to me. Ever again." Katy turned as the elevator doors shut, and she headed for the staircase. The stairs were better for her anyway.

She made it to Janet's vacant office and shut the door before her tears started. She grabbed a tissue and let them fall. Scott, her new job, the pressure from Sienna—it squeezed her until she thought she might implode. She shut her eyes and inhaled, searching for that calm spot inside her head. Another breath…and the tightness in her chest eased. One thing at a time.

Scott. Was he really seeing someone else? She couldn't be sure. She knew for a fact Nina would say anything to wound her. But Scott was a good-looking man, and it was hard to believe he wasn't dating anyone. Her tears threatened to start again, and she squashed the feeling. Sleeping with someone without really knowing him had its consequences. She'd recognized that fact going in. Maybe it was best if she didn't think about him right now.

It was Monday. She was at work. Her job had to come first.

She turned on the computer and waited for her programs to load. She clicked on the calendar, trying to not let the upcoming construction meeting bother her too much. She had reports she needed to complete before then, and she could remain professional. She would remain professional. All business. No emotion. She'd be fine.

Nine o'clock came way too fast. She should have stayed even later the previous Friday to make sure everything was in order for her meeting this morning. She would have been less likely to have stopped at the bar, and she could have avoided everything that had transpired in between. But by Friday evening, she'd had it, and Teisha had assured her there would be plenty of time Monday morning.

There *had* been time to get things in order, but no time to compose herself before she faced Scott.

She walked cautiously down the hall toward the conference room. Scott sat next to the seat she'd occupied at the previous meeting. She walked in, catching his gaze and sat on the opposite side of the table, as close to the end as possible. His lips turned upward, but she couldn't bring herself to return the gesture. All she could think about was Nina's cruel remark about Scott and a girl named Jen. She didn't want to believe it was true...but was it? When Scott's smile turned to a questioning look, she looked away.

She managed not to look in his direction for all of five minutes. When Mr. Winward walked in and took a seat, she snuck a glance at Scott. He watched her with a sober look.

The meeting seemed to last forever, but she was grateful she had all the information Mr. Winward required. For the majority of the time, she'd kept her gaze on the documents in front of her and only looked up when she'd been questioned or had given her report.

At the end of the meeting, her boss tapped his files in a neat stack and pushed up his glasses before glancing over the group. "I think that's just about everything unless someone has something else to cover."

"One thing," Scott said, and Katy turned her gaze toward him. "The amount shown for total expenditures on the radiology area is a little off from my figures. I'm wondering if Miss Rivers has included the built-in reception desk in her totals. We actually listed that in another area."

All eyes in the room turned to her, and she swallowed. "Yes, I believe those amounts were included. I'd have to pull the itemized expenditures to be certain."

"Would you mind doing that? I'd like to make sure we're both on the same page."

His message was cryptic, but she hadn't missed his meaning. "Of course. I can have that to your assistant later today."

"If it's all right, I'd like to have that information come straight to me. Please give me a call later, if you don't mind."

Mr. Winward raised his brows at her.

"Absolutely. I'll call as soon as I have it."

"That would be appreciated."

She held his gaze for a second longer and then looked away. If he kept this up, remaining professional would not be easy.

"Okay then. I'd say this meeting can be concluded." Mr. Winward's assistant slipped a paper in front of him. "Wait. One more thing. As most of you know, the annual Christmas Ball is coming up this Friday. It's especially important this year since we're planning to use the funds for the pediatric center upgrades as part of this year's expansion. I'm expecting all staff to attend in support of this event, especially those of us on this committee. Everyone good with that?" He glanced about the table. "Kevin?"

Katy's co-worker nodded. "Of course. My wife's excited to attend. She's thrilled that it's black tie so she can buy a new dress."

"Katy?" Mr. Winward pinned her with a questioning look.

"Uh…" She really hadn't expected to have to go. Usually only the administrative staff was required to attend, but she guessed she was now considered part of that group. "Maybe." She gave a hesitant smile. "I don't have a date yet." She prayed that excuse would get her off the hook.

"I'd be honored to take you, Miss Rivers, seeing as how I'd like to support this worthy charity but also don't have a date." Scott kept a straight face as he asked.

Once again, all the eyes in the room turned to her.

She forced a smile. "How can I say no to that?"

"Great." Mr. Winward seemed quite pleased with the turn of events. "Meeting adjourned."

Katy took her time gathering her materials from the table, hoping to have a chance to confront Scott. He seemed to have the same idea in mind, waiting for the majority of the people to leave the room before he addressed her.

"If you have just another second, Miss Rivers. I have one more question for you." Scott walked to her side of the table and waited for the room to empty. No one seemed to question why he might remain behind. When the last person left, he turned to her, but she beat him to the punch.

"What the hell was that all about, with your cryptic messages and forcing me to go to the ball with you?"

He shut the door before answering. "I could ask you the same thing. I thought we'd found something special, at least it was for me. Then I take you home and never hear from you again."

"It was one day that I didn't call. Not even a full day."

"So, you're saying you intended to call me today?"

"We're seeing each other right now, aren't we?"

Anger flashed in his eyes, giving him a menacing look. "Don't talk in circles, Katy. If this thing is over before it's even started, at least have the honesty to tell me."

She glanced away before focusing on him again. "I don't know what it is, all right?" She fingered her temples, searching for a way out of the mess she'd created.

"Is it because your friend caught you?"

She couldn't meet his gaze, afraid he'd see right through her.

"Is it because she caught you with *me*?"

She jerked her head up, realizing the moment she connected with his gaze she'd given herself away.

"You afraid I'll somehow soil your reputation?"

She stood, backing away from him. "Who is Jen?"

He flinched, his expression changing from one of irritation to...guilt? "Jen and I are no longer seeing each other. We haven't dated for months. It was never anything serious anyway."

Katy studied his features. She wanted to think he wouldn't lie to her, but how could she be sure?

"You don't believe me? You think I'm still the same guy I was back when? A player?"

She blinked, wishing she knew how to respond.

He turned, cornering her against the wall. "I'm not seeing anyone else, Katy. Just you." His voice dropped to almost a whisper, his features softening. "I hope."

Her heart knew the truth, and she wanted to reach out to him. To touch his face. To kiss him like she had the night before.

"I knew we were taking this too fast." He put a hand against the wall next to her ear and looked down, shaking his head.

"I'm the one who pushed it. If anyone is to blame, it's me."

He looked at her. "I should have listened to my gut."

The expression in his dark eyes tugged at her, reminding her of their evening together. Everything had been so perfect. Their sleigh ride to see the wolves. The way he'd been so concerned about her comfort. She had no doubt they wouldn't have slept together if she hadn't pressed things. She'd let Sienna's judgments and Nina's cruel words influence her opinion of him, when really, she needed to trust her instincts. Just because he'd tossed a little excitement into her otherwise boring life didn't mean he was what everyone else expected him to be.

There was still the work thing to consider though, but maybe that wouldn't be an issue after all.

She lifted a hand and touched his cheek. He placed a hand over hers and straightened.

"I'm sorry," she said. "I guess I got a little scared… and I handled this very poorly."

He searched her face, a small smile hovering on his lips. "Does this mean I get a second chance?"

He wasn't the one who should be asking. "Does it mean that I do?"

A sparkle lit his brown eyes, turning them a warm shade of mocha. "Only if we do it my way this time."

"What does that mean?"

"It means I'm going to tempt you and tease you until you can't stand it, and then still make you wait until we've dated the proper amount of time before we make love again."

"And how long would that be?"

"I guess we'll know when we get there."

His carefree manner brought a smile to her lips. "You think we can do that?"

He shrugged, a twinkle in his eye. "So, we have a date for the Christmas Ball, then?"

"Are you saying I won't see you until the weekend?"

He traced a thumb across her bottom lip, following it with a soft kiss. "Nothing wrong with taking it slow."

When she pouted, he laughed. "Trust me, keeping my hands off you is going to be a lot harder on me than it is on you."

She highly doubted that.

Tears pooled at the edge of Luke Winchester's eyes from laughing too hard, and Scott had to restrain the urge from all out punching his buddy in the face.

"Wait. Tell me again," Luke said.

Scott took a long pull from his beer before setting his bottle back on the bar at Swallow's. "Out of all the people I know, I would expect you to understand."

"Understand that you have Katy Rivers wanting to sleep with you, and you're telling her no? Are you crazy? You do realize you're now a legend, don't you? Every guy in town wanted to bag her, but no one had the balls to try because she was untouchable. You've conquered the unconquerable."

Luke might be an inch or two taller than him, but Scott packed a hell of a lot more muscle. "I should knock you to the floor right now for talking about her that way."

Luke started to laugh, but then sobered. "Hey. I'm just kidding."

"How would you like it if someone said something like that about Lily?"

His friend narrowed his eyes. "Watch it."

"Exactly." Scott hadn't wanted to toss Luke's cute new wife into the mix, but that seemed to be the only way to make his friend understand. "I'm just saying, watch it, too."

Luke turned, glancing at Lily who sat at a table with their friends, Milo and Anna. He looked back at Scott. "Sorry, man. I had no idea you felt like that about her. Honestly, I didn't even know you were dating."

"We've only been on one date."

"And you bagged her already? Man, you *are* legend."

"She's not that kind of girl."

Luke lifted a brow. "You sure? Maybe we had her pegged wrong all those years ago."

"Would you stop with the shit, already? I asked you over here to get your advice."

His friend held up his hands. "Okay. Sorry. What did you want to know?"

"How did you get Lily to not listen to all the gossip about you and Hannah? What made her trust you?"

"I don't know. I guess she was smart enough to trust her heart above everything else." He sized up his friend. "Does Katy have a problem with you?"

"I think she wonders if I'm still a fuck up. How do I get her to take me seriously?"

Luke seemed to mull over the question as he took a drink of beer. "I don't know. I guess just keep showing her the real you, and she'll have to decide for herself. We all know you've moved beyond your dumbass years. She'll figure it out, too."

"Thanks, dude." He rolled his eyes. "I knew I could count on you for some sage advice."

Luke laughed and headed back to his wife. Scott pulled the phone from his pocket and scrolled through his address book until Katy's number appeared. He stared at it, aching to call.

Distance makes the heart grow fonder.

The old saying circled around his mind for a few moments before he put his phone away. He needed to give her space. Give her time to miss him.

The Christmas Ball was only a day away. He'd see her then, and he'd do everything he could to win her heart.

CHAPTER TWELVE

Katy's pulse thrummed against her throat as she fastened the clasp of her teardrop zirconium necklace. She dropped her hands, brushing them over the sparkling jewels on her bodice, and down the folds of her silver gown. She loved it.

She'd taken a chance, ordering it online, but it fit her perfectly. She'd had her moment of panic Monday night when she'd realized she only had a few days and nothing to wear to the ball. But her perfect dress had arrived Thursday afternoon with still a day to spare. She'd ripped through the packaging, tugging the dress from its folds of tissue paper, and then nearly cried because she couldn't call her mother or her best friend to share her fun news.

But they'd never understand. They'd judge Scott and call her stupid for seeing him, and she couldn't handle their criticism at the moment.

She allowed herself a second to feel bad, and then she smiled. Scott would be there momentarily, and she'd dance in his strong arms and forget all her troubles. She glanced at the clock. Five minutes... and she didn't have her shoes on yet.

She fell to her knees, digging through the pile of shoes covering her closet, searching for her silver heels. She found one, but was interrupted by the doorbell. She growled and flung boots and flats out of her way until she discovered the second, and then she raced for the door.

Her heels nearly fell from her slack fingers as she stared at the vision standing on her doorstep. God, he was beautiful with his spiked hair, perfectly trimmed goatee and black tuxedo. "Wow," she said breathlessly, and he laughed. She did drop a shoe then.

He picked it up and handed it to her. "Are you going to invite me in?"

"Of course." She chuckled over her embarrassing behavior and took a step back. He looked so... impressive. She shut the door and turned to him. "You look very nice."

He crooked a brow and surveyed her with a gaze that left her sizzling. Taking her hand, he pulled her near. "And you are exquisite, my angel."

"Thank you." His obvious appreciation made her feel all the more beautiful. "I just need to put on my shoes." She held up the strappy silver heels.

"May I?" He took her shoes, leaving butterflies fluttering inside her.

She sat on the couch, and he kneeled in front of her. He lifted her foot, his roughened fingers sending tingles through the sensitive skin on the side of her arch. "One of these days, I'll be ready in time," she said, pretending his actions weren't as intimate as they seemed.

He slipped the shoe over her foot, his deft fingers working the buckle. As he lifted her second foot, he glanced up at her. "I don't mind in the least." A sharp dagger of desire pierced her heart. She knew in that moment why she'd pushed them that first night.

Every cell in her body begged to be closer to him.

She sighed as he finished and stood, holding out his hand to her. She stood, picked up her purse and her black satin coat, allowing him to help her into it.

"I'd make you bring something warmer for the ride, but my SUV is already heated."

"This is plenty warm. I'll be fine." At least as long as she had him by her side.

Scott kept the conversation light during the twenty-minute ride into Pinecone, and Katy was grateful. Their slight derailment earlier in the week seemed to be a thing of the past, and she hoped it would stay that way. She couldn't be sure there wouldn't be bumps in the future, but she didn't want to consider them now.

Scott pulled his SUV into the hotel parking lot, and Katy was surprised to see her company had provided valet parking. The event was always held at the biggest hotel in town. She was sure it would hardly be called a hotel by big city standards, but it was the only meeting space in Pinecone and the surrounding areas large enough to hold the event.

Didn't matter. Somehow Mr. Winward's assistant, along with whatever party-planning business she'd hired, had transformed the quaint little hotel into a magical winter wonderland.

Tiny white lights covered the stark branches of the trees, bringing them to life with warmth and beauty. Potted evergreens complete with crystal lights and silver ornaments lined the entrance into the hotel.

Scott exited his truck and walked around to her door. He held out a hand, helping her from her seat. It was as though she'd somehow been transformed into a princess, and he was her attending prince. He held up his elbow, and she took it, allowing him to escort her inside.

The more elaborate decorations had been saved for the interior of the hotel. Wisps of sheer white fabric floated down from the ceiling to piles of glimmering fake snow. More lighted trees, evergreen and bare branches, filled the corners of the ballroom, making her feel as though she truly were outside. The decorating committee had even managed to hang little lights from the ceiling, mimicking the night sky she'd shared with Scott on their sleigh ride.

The masterpiece was the large Christmas tree placed in the center of the dance floor. Silver satin ribbons cascaded down from a glittering bow at the top. Ornaments of white, silver and clear glass hung from the limbs while cherubic angels peeked from the branches.

"They go all out, don't they?" he whispered in her ear.

"Apparently so. This is my first ball, so I really have no idea what to expect. But I'm impressed so far."

"You can say that again."

The party had barely started, and people currently mingled as waiters with appetizers circled the room. More waiters carried sparkling flutes on their trays. One stopped and offered drinks to them. Scott looked at her. "No, I'm good for now," she said.

"No, thanks," he said to the man.

"I feel like I need to keep my wits about me for the moment. It's not going to look good if I get drunk in front of Mr. Winward."

"True. We all know what happens when you've had too much to drink."

She elbowed him. "Funny." She turned, hiding the smile that crossed her lips.

Dinner was a treat of prime rib or chicken marsala, complete with a succulent rice dish and chocolate mousse for dessert. She and Scott, along with several other people including Kevin and his wife, had been placed at Mr. Winward's table. Jeffrey Winward was also in attendance with Nina on his arm, but they'd been seated several tables away from them.

Katy couldn't have been more relieved. Nina's barbs would have ruined her evening.

Conversation mostly flowed without her input, although she'd been sure to compliment Kevin's wife on her beautiful dress. Scott held his own with her boss, talking politics and the particulars of what was taking place with the construction on their building.

She wasn't sure how she could have ever thought he might not be a man to be admired. He might not have made the best choices in school, but look what he'd achieved since then.

"Katy?"

She turned toward her boss.

"Make sure you get me the figures on what has to be spent from our building grant before I leave for Fiji right after Christmas. We need to make sure every dime of that money gets charged to the project, or we'll lose it. Work with Scott. I'm sure there are plenty of things he can bill us for before the end of the year."

Scott laughed. "You can count on me, James. And when you get to Fiji, make sure to visit the Naitasiri region, if you get a chance. And don't forget to present yaqona to the local chief."

Mr. Winward's cheeks pushed back in a rarely seen jovial smile. "My wife was spouting something about that. I guess I'd better pay attention." He shifted his gaze to Katy. "Why don't you take Katy out and dance? She looks a little bored sitting here listening to us talk."

She raised her brows, earning a laugh from her boss.

"Besides, if I had a date as pretty as yours, I wouldn't be talking to someone like me. Enough work's been done for now. Tonight, you should relax and enjoy."

"Good of you to remind me. I wouldn't want Katy to feel ignored." He stood and held out a hand to her. "Care to dance?"

"I'd love to." She carefully concealed her attraction to Scott as she stood and let him lead her to the dance floor. He slipped a hand across her back, his fingers warm on her skin, and held her hand with his other in a formal dance pose.

The strains of a waltz cascaded through the wintry scene, and he moved them around the floor with ease.

"I had no idea you knew how to dance."

He teased her with a smirk. "I had no idea *you* knew how to dance."

She snorted. "Good point."

"You think because I grew up in a small town that I have no concept of the finer things in life?"

"I'd be completely wrong if I did."

He grinned. "Damn right."

"You've obviously expanded your horizons much farther than I have. When were you in Fiji?"

"A few years ago. Mr. Roberts had been asked to give advice on a building structure there, and he invited me along with him. We explored the area a bit before we returned home."

"Again, you surprise me."

"Why? Because I know something about the world? Small town doesn't necessarily mean less educated."

"I know that. I grew up here, remember?"

"Then you shouldn't be so surprised."

"It's just interesting how a person can know someone her whole life, but never really *know* him. I remember Joe Roberts, but to me, he was the older man I'd see going into the hardware store. I never knew him beyond that. Never knew he was a world-traveler, or that he had that kind of expertise."

"You really need to get out of your protected little shell more often and start experiencing the life that's happening around you."

His words stung, but she couldn't get angry. "You're absolutely right. I feel like I've missed out on so many things."

"At least you're trying new things now." He twirled her. "See what's above us?"

She glanced upward to find a sprig of mistletoe hanging right above her head. Looking around, she found several more scattered across the ballroom ceiling.

"I couldn't. This is a work function. I couldn't."

He twirled her again, bringing her close to another sprig hanging near the tree. "Winward's across the floor, out of sight. No one's going to notice. No one's going to care."

He lowered his head to hers, his lips caressing hers with a whisper of a kiss. "See? It's all good."

She relaxed and gave a soft laugh. "Okay. You're right." She snuck another quick kiss, before she pushed him away. "Not quite the same as last weekend, but still good."

"Careful, Angel. You don't want to tempt me. You know where that leads."

She blushed, remembering the intimate things he'd done to her. "Maybe I do."

He shook his head and leaned close to her ear. "And they say *I* like to flirt with danger?" The deep timbre of his voice brought goose bumps to her skin.

She nearly tripped when she realized Nina and Jeffrey were dancing close enough to have seen her and Scott kiss, but thankfully neither seemed to be looking in their direction. "How about that glass of champagne now?" She was thirsty, and it was a good excuse to move away from Nina. "We aren't required to spend any more time in Mr. Winward's company, and I'd really like a taste before we go home."

He held out an elbow for her. "Whatever your heart desires."

The rest of the night passed like a fairytale. Scott didn't kiss her again, but he'd held her closer than would be appropriate for a professional relationship. She didn't care. For once, she just wanted to live for the moment.

He drove her home and walked her to the porch, waiting while she unlocked the door.

"Would you like to come in?"

A quick smile crossed his lips. "I'd better not."

She ran her fingers down his lapel, not wanting him to leave. "Afraid I'll seduce you and take you against your will?"

"It's been known to happen. At least the seducing part. Pretty sure it wasn't against my will, though." He took her chin, placing a soft but searing kiss on her lips. "Can I call you?"

Disappointment cycled through her because their evening was at an end. Then again, there was always the next day. "I was kind of hoping to ask you for a favor. I'd planned on picking out a Christmas tree tomorrow, and I need someone to haul it home for me. I could ask my dad, but…"

"You want a tree? I'll take you to get a tree. What time?"

"Two?"

"I'll be here." He placed another quick kiss on her lips and turned. When he reached his truck, he looked back. "Dress warm. Warmer than last time. Thermal underwear. Wool socks. Your turquoise coat will work fine."

"Again?" she asked.

He grinned. "Again."

Katy gave herself a goal of being ready thirty minutes before Scott was scheduled to arrive so that she could be certain she wouldn't keep him waiting. Sure enough, he rang her doorbell right on time.

She wore roughly the same clothes she'd worn on their first date with the exception of a different sweater, but she still couldn't shake the memory of each article of clothing as he'd removed them from her body.

Scott surprised her again. Instead of heading in to town, he drove her straight to his house.

She raised her brows at him as he opened the passenger door to let her out.

"Don't ask. You know how I roll. You'll find out when we get there."

He didn't lead her toward the house, but to the large garage sitting off to the side, instead. He lifted the door, and Katy's attention was snagged by a shiny Harley parked to the side. She approached the handsome piece of machinery, running a finger along the smooth black lines. "I should have known you'd ride."

He grinned, his eyes crinkling at the corners. "Wait until spring. I'll take you for a ride up in the mountains and show you the wildflowers. It'll be a day you'll never forget."

Her? On a motorcycle? A month ago, she wouldn't have considered it. "Promise?"

He stopped next to a covered mound and glanced at her. "Never doubt it. Give me the chance, and I'll take you wherever you want to go."

Her heart flopped as a happy grin spread across her lips.

"Okay, it was a little corny, but you get my drift."

She nodded. He meant what he'd said about wanting this to be a meaningful relationship. The only problem was, she had to reconcile him with those who didn't understand her new need to live. That would not be an easy feat.

He jerked the canvas off the mound, showing off a beautiful blue snowmobile.

"Seriously?" Riding in a slow-moving sleigh was one thing.

"You want a tree? You're getting a real tree. Those scrawny, half-alive things are not trees. They're former shells of trees."

He lifted the trailer hitch and pushed the trailer out the doorway. The thought crossed her mind that the show would have been much better if he hadn't been wearing so many layers of clothes so she could watch his muscles bunch and strain from his efforts. Did that make her shallow? She smiled. She didn't care either way. She enjoyed a nice display of muscle as much as the next girl, and the fact that she currently had a guy who liked to show off, worked out well for her.

The impressive machine rumbled as he backed it from the trailer, down into the sparkling snow that covered his yard. Next, he pulled a sled from the garage and hooked it to the back of the machine. He filled the gas tank, grabbed a tarp and some rope, along with a sharp ax and secured them inside the sled.

He pulled a few more items out of one of the many drawers that lined the side of the garage. "Hope you like the Steelers," he said as he tugged a black knit cap onto her head, tucking wayward strands of her hair behind her ears. "Cute." Black goggles followed and he nearly took off her nose, trying to adjust them on her face.

"I think I can do this." She fit the rubber glasses to her cheeks.

"I know. I'm just finding excuses to touch you." He didn't wait for her response, but pulled on an identical Steelers cap and goggles, though he left the goggles resting on his forehead instead of over his eyes. He had snow pants for them both, hers a little too big, but they'd provide the protection she needed.

The helmet he gave her fit better than the pants. He sat his helmet between his knees as he straddled the snowmobile. A second later, the engine growled to life. He tested the throttle a few times, making the sleek, mechanical animal roar even louder. His eyes glimmered with excitement as he met her gaze. "Ready?"

She stepped forward. Sweet Mary, what had she gotten herself into? She'd wanted wild and exciting? She'd definitely found it.

Her emotions jumbled, mixing anxiety with excitement, as she climbed aboard the machine and tentatively placed her hands on his waist.

"You're going to want to scoot a little closer to me."

She moved forward on the seat until she was an inch from him.

"Closer."

She exhaled and scooted until her crotch was flush against him.

"Mmm...that's perfect."

She had the distinct impression he was messing with her. "Do I really need to be this close, or is this just you wanting to touch me again?"

He laughed. "You already know the answer to that question." He throttled the engine again, before he lowered his goggles and slipped on his helmet. "Hang on tight."

CHAPTER THIRTEEN

The snowmobile moved, and Katy locked her gloved fingers around Scott.

He took them across open fields that sparkled under the afternoon sun. At first, he kept the machine at a respectable speed as he followed along a barbed wire fence. But once he cleared it, he opened the throttle, sending them rocketing over the glittering fields.

At the edge of a grouping of pines, he stopped long enough to detach the sled. "We'll come back for that in a while." Then they were off again.

An exclamation caught in her throat as he bounded over a hill, catching a small amount of air. When they landed safely, she released her breath and grinned. This was the wildest, craziest thing she'd ever done, and she loved it.

He slowed as they reached bigger slopes and turned his machine so that it angled up the incline. The snowmobile rumbled as he took them over a rise and down into another valley where he circled them around a field so many times she felt dizzy. At the edge of a lake, he stopped. She was almost certain it was the same spot where they'd seen the wolves the week before. He climbed off the machine and helped her off, too.

"Like that?" he asked, removing his helmet and lifting his goggles.

His question reminded her of what he'd asked when they'd made love. She smiled, wondering if he was thinking the same thing. "I loved it." She gave her head a slight shake. "It was insane."

He nodded, a self-satisfied expression settling on his features. "I knew you would. I think you have an untapped rebel hovering just beneath that good girl surface."

"Could be." She had to admit she was kind of proud of herself for stepping out of her comfort zone. "I think I'm starting to see the benefits of living it up a little bit."

"Hey, what good is life if you ain't living it? Might as well be dead."

"Yeah. I think I know a few people like that." She removed her safety gear and glanced at the pristine area filled with snow-covered pines that sat eerily quiet. She inhaled, filling her lungs with crisp, fresh air. "Isn't this where we saw the wolves?"

"It is. They were just beyond those pines over there."

Katy turned, seeing nothing but wilderness.

"If you look around, you can spot their tracks."

She widened her eyes as she glanced down, and sure enough, dog-like prints could be found throughout the area.

"Don't worry," he said, reading her thoughts. "With all the racket we made coming in, they've headed farther into the hills. They'll come back later when things quiet down."

She smiled. "I trust you to keep me safe."

"Good." He took two steps, covering the distance between them. "You can always count on that." He pulled her into his arms, giving her a scorching kiss. When he pulled away, she had to fight to catch her breath.

"I thought you were keeping the pace slow between us."

He shrugged. "Not much can happen out here, can it?"

"Smart of you." But there was always later. "If that's the case, I think I'll have another." She leaned into him, tugging his head down to hers. She matched the heat of his kiss and threw another log on the fire. This time he was the breathless one when they parted.

"Man, you sure know how to torture a guy." He shifted, adjusting the bulge in his jeans as he turned toward the machine. "We probably ought to go find your tree before you torment me any further."

She climbed on the back, scooting as far forward as possible, knowing it would tease him. Served him right. She shifted on the seat, creating friction between them. "Am I close enough? I wouldn't want to fall off."

He half-sighed and half-groaned. "Ah, Angel. You do have a devilish streak, don't you?"

"It's that rebel you seem determined to free. Better be careful. I kind of like it when she's around."

"Me, too." He revved the engine and headed out of the basin, back up to the ridge where they'd first kissed.

At the bottom of the other side, he slowed and located his sled. After he hooked it to the snowmobile, he began weaving in and out of groups of pines.

"See anything you like?"

She glanced at the pines, not really sure what she was looking for. Hunting for Christmas trees in the wilderness was a completely different story than lot shopping. "Maybe that one?" She pointed to a smaller tree sitting at the edge of a little grouping.

He stopped the snowmobile a few feet from it and climbed off the machine. He circled the tree, nodding. "It's a pretty one." He glanced at her. "You sure that's the one you want?"

Her heart lurched, her eyes frozen on the handsome man standing in front of her. "Yes. I think that's the one I want." God help her.

Scott removed the ax and approached the tree, his boots sinking into the snow with each step. He eyed it and took his first swing at the trunk. The sound of wood splitting echoed through the quiet. Again, he lifted the ax and swung.

Never in a million years would she have attempted to cut down her own tree, but Scott made it seem easy. A few more strikes and the tree tilted to the side. He gave the trunk a hard shove, and it toppled over.

"Woo," she called out, impressed with her muscled bad boy. "You are the man."

A wide grin curved his perfect lips. He grabbed the bottom of the trunk and dragged the tree toward the snowmobile, stopping long enough to clear out the tarp before he hauled his catch on top of the attached sled.

After he'd secured her tree to the snowmobile with the tarp and length of rope, she threw her arms around his neck, beaming a smile at him. "Thank you for chopping my beautiful tree. This will be my favorite Christmas tree ever." She knew that without a doubt.

He returned her smile. "I hope so." He kissed her nose. "Let's get it home. You're cold."

"Freezing." She pretended to shiver.

He eyed her with a suspicious look. "Uh-huh."

Katy had most of her boxes of ornaments and lights hauled into the living room by the time Scott had trimmed off the bottom of the tree and put it in a stand of fresh water.

She closed her eyes and inhaled the crisp pine scent. "That smells impossibly good."

"Told you. There's a difference between a fresh cut tree and one bought off the lot. Those trees were probably cut weeks ago." Scott eyed the evergreen. "Look straight to you?"

She checked the tree from different angles before she moved closer to him. "It's perfect." She put her hands on his shoulders, gazing into the deep brown eyes of the man who'd brought her so much happiness over the past few weeks. Who would have thought the bad boy from school would turn out to be so wonderful? She stood on tiptoe and kissed him. "Thank you."

He gazed at her down his nose, sending her heart rate galloping.

"Can you stay and help me with the lights? I could put on a pot of soup. My potato cheese is wildly sought after."

He studied her for a moment, his lips set in a serious line, and then the edges slowly turned upward. "I'd like that."

"Great." Happiness flooded her as she left him to string the lights while she went to peel potatoes. A couple of curse words came from the adjoining room as she chopped the last of the vegetables and slid them into the boiling water. She wiped her hands on a towel and walked in to check on Scott.

The second she saw her tree, her mouth went slack. "Wow." She blinked, checking out the perfectly lit pine. The bright-colored lights had been spread out uniformly over each branch. "After hearing you cuss, I expected to find a disaster, but you do amazing work."

"I had a few years of practice."

So many things about him continued to surprise her. "I didn't really picture you as the tree-decorating type."

He shrugged. "My mom wasn't up for much Christmas, so I always did the tree myself."

She stepped close to him and the glimmering tree. "What did she have against Christmas?" Her memories of the holiday had been nothing but happy.

He ran his fingers over some of the tips on the tree. "My dad left us Christmas Eve. Just up and walked out. I was eight at the time and didn't really understand what was happening." He ran his gaze to the top branches. "Sometimes as an adult, I try to figure out what might have been going through his head. Stress. Maybe he found someone else. I don't know. But everything changed that year. And of course, after he left, there was never enough money to do Christmas right."

He turned to her and snorted. "I'd drag out our little fake tree and decorate it, hoping to revive what we'd lost. She'd buy me a present or two if she could. Year after year, I'd keep hoping, but it was never the same. Once I was on my own, I realized it really didn't matter as much as I'd thought."

"Scott." Emotion clogged her throat. He did a pretty good job of camouflaging the heavy emotions scattered around them, but there was no disguising how deeply he'd been hurt. She touched his cheek, wanting to grieve his loss with him, but not wanting to make him feel worse. "I'm so sorry. That must have been difficult for a young boy to understand."

He nodded, his gaze fading to a far away spot. "It is what it is." He focused on her. "There's no changing it. I'm sure there are people worse off than I was."

"Are things better with your mom now?"

He gave her a puzzled look. "Katy, my mom died when I was sixteen."

Back when he'd barely entered high school. No wonder he'd acted out. Alone in the world and not even an adult, yet. She tilted her head. "I don't remember that." She should have with their town being so small.

"Grocery store clerk hit by a semi-truck speeding through town?"

She brought a hand to her mouth. "Oh, my God." Her parents had talked about that accident. The whole town had whispered about the woman's son and what would happen to him. That was before Katy had gone to high school, before she'd gotten her first real glimpse of him.

She'd been so wrapped up in the drama of her life that she hadn't really given it a second thought. Now here was the tragedy, ten years later. Quiet tears wet her eyes. "I don't know what to say."

"I didn't tell you to make you cry." He thumbed a tear from her cheek. "In fact, I'm not sure why I told you at all. I kind of prefer to keep that in the past where it belongs."

She looped an arm around the back of his neck, pulling his head to hers until their foreheads touched. She met his fractured gaze. "I'm so sorry. I wish I would have known you better then. Wish I could have cried with you. Wish…" She shook her head, overcome by emotion. She wrapped her arms around his waist and held him tight.

He crushed her with a hug, burying his face in her hair.

They stood like that for a few moments until he pulled away. He dried her tears again, searching her eyes, and giving her a tender smile. "It's okay. Really. I feel sad sometimes when I think about her, but the best thing I can do is live a good life. It took me a few years to figure that out, but I like to think she'd be proud of who I am now."

"Stop." She sniffled. "You're just going to make me cry worse."

"Okay." He held up his hands. "Sorry." He studied her for a moment, a deep tendril of some unnamed feeling burying itself inside her. "How about you feed me instead? I'm starving."

She exhaled an emotion-tainted breath, a measure of peace taking its place. "That, I can do."

Katy placed the last ornament on the tree. The crystal snowflake she'd found in Yellowstone caught the red fire burning next to it, scattering a pattern of crimson light all around. "What do you think?"

For the past hour, Scott had handed her the colorful, mismatched ornaments and gold ribbons, letting her place them on the tree. Now, he watched her with an interested gaze that sent a band of desire coiling through her. "Beautiful."

She rolled her eyes, trying to pretend their lighthearted teasing hadn't suddenly taken a sharp, unexpected turn toward intense. "You're such a flirt. No wonder all the girls wanted to get close to you."

"There was only one who kept my attention. One I've never been able to forget."

Desire tightened inside her. "Not me." She tried to laugh, to lighten the moment, but his declaration sparked a memory inside her. There had been many times during school when she'd caught him watching her with a serious gaze. At the time, she'd thought it was because they'd been so opposite, and she was sure he and his friends had made fun of her.

"Yes, you." He advanced toward her, something dark and a little dangerous flickering in his eyes.

A quick, excited breath filled her lungs. He looked as though he'd like to devour her, and the sudden, very masculine move made her feel deliciously hunted.

She put a reflexive hand on his chest. A corner of his mouth lifted in a sexy grin that mesmerized her. "Scott," she said, his name escaping on a breathy whisper. She wanted to get close to him again, but his seduction had come out of nowhere this time, surprising her and delighting her at the same time.

Before he could answer, music erupted from her pocket, her phone singing the tune that announced her mother was calling. She closed her eyes and shook her head in disbelief. "It's my mother. If I don't answer, she'll come over."

"So answer it." He wrapped his hand around the one she had pressed to his chest, forcing her to fish out her phone with the other.

447

She narrowed her eyes but grinned as she pushed the green button. "Hey, Mom." She tried to take a step back, but Scott held her tight.

"Hi, honey. Your dad and I are headed back from Pinecone. I thought we'd stop by and drop off the snow shovel your dad picked up for you."

Scott slid her hand over the hard curves of his pecs. Solid muscle met her fingertips, and she flexed, wishing she could dig her fingers into his bare skin. He dragged her hand farther, holding her fingers out, sucking them into his mouth. Sweet Mary.

"Katy? Are you there?"

"Uh, yeah, Mom. That's fine. I'll be here." She clicked off her phone without saying goodbye and tossed it on the couch behind her.

Before she could say another word, Scott yanked her back to him, possessing her mouth with a demanding kiss. She tried to catch her thoughts, but they'd been left outside the swirl of hot need that suddenly owned her. She curled her fingers into his hair as his tongue danced against hers.

He fisted her hair, tugging her head back as he moved his heated kisses to the sensitive curve of her neck.

"Scott," she whispered, breathlessly. "We have to stop. My parents will be here in like twenty minutes."

"Twenty minutes is a long time," he said as he slipped a hand between them and cupped her breast.

She inhaled. "I thought you wanted to wait." She closed her eyes on a sigh as a tremble rocked her.

"Ah, God. My resistance is running low, Angel. I want to be good for you, but even a good man can only stand so much, and you and I both know I'm not a saint."

"I think you're perfect." She tugged his head toward her and branded him with her kiss.

"If I was perfect, I'd stop. Maybe we *should* stop," he said between kisses.

"That's not going to happen," she responded, tracing her fingers over the strong curves of his shoulder. "Maybe we could hurry." She jerked his t-shirt from his jeans and tugged it over his head, baring him to her will. She skimmed her tongue over the shoulder she'd just uncovered. Hard muscle rested beneath the smooth surface of his skin. She folded her fingers around his biceps, enjoying the strength that rested there.

"We could definitely hurry." He wasted no time removing her sweater. Her bra was off before she realized he'd had his hands behind her back. His fingers were rough, greedy on her breasts. He cupped her with his large palms before he dipped his head. A raspy groan escaped his lips as he sucked her into his mouth.

She gasped, arching backward. He barely had to touch her, and she was wet for him. She jerked at the button on his jeans. "Take me now. I've got to have you, and we don't have long."

He growled as he tugged her jeans down. Her panties followed, and he bit the black lace thong while he removed his pants.

"You're so bad," she laughed, pulling her underwear from his lips.

He grinned.

He had a condom on in less than a minute, before he pulled her back into his embrace. Her naked body melted against his. *This* was what she wanted. She reached between them, circling his rock hard steel with her fingers, reveling in the fact he would be inside her soon.

He gripped her hair, tugging her head back, ravaging her mouth with his. Ragged breaths escaped them both.

"I want you."

"Shit," he hissed, obviously affected by the heated currents that shot between them.

She pushed him back onto the couch, straddling him even as he sat. She positioned him and slid over his hard, heated sex, her body accepting every inch until he was deep inside her. Her breath rushed out in a contented whisper. "Oh, God."

A laugh rumbled through. "Damn, you feel good. Feel free to push me around like this any time."

Wicked pleasure rolled through her. "Oh yeah?" She wet her lips. "You like this?" There was something about Scott that left her feeling like the sexiest woman alive. She lifted her hips and then impaled herself again.

He closed his eyes for a brief second, a look of intense gratification flashing across his face. Then his dark eyes met hers. "You're teasing me."

A smile tickled her lips. She leaned forward, brushing a nipple across his upturned mouth. He caught it with his tongue, sucking her hard until her inner muscles clenched.

"Yeah, baby. I like you tight around me," he whispered, rocketing her close to an orgasm.

She lifted again and took him deep inside her in a desperate search for what lay just beyond her grasp. He seemed to sense her need and wrapped his large hands around her hips, helping her move. Each descent onto his thick shaft increased the friction and pace between them. She moved above him, her breasts rocking with their rhythm.

"Go, Angel. Go," he whispered, watching her expressions intently.

"Oh, God," she cried. She clenched, wrapping her arms around his neck, holding on while the power of their love-making ripped through her.

When the intensity subsided, she sat back, a soft laugh slipping from her lips.

"Enjoyed that, did you?"

A hint of embarrassment heated her cheeks. "Yes, I did." She'd never used a man to pleasure herself like that before.

"Good," he growled and pulled her down on the couch. "Cause now I'm going to have *my* way with you." He covered her with his hard, naked body.

His spoken intent sent a shiver racing through her. There was no way she could deny him. "What are you going to do?"

"Hmm...Maybe this." He drew a finger along her sensitive folds, and she closed her eyes in ecstasy. "Or maybe this." He shoved the steel length of him inside her.

Her eyes flew open on a gasp. He was hard and deep and so big. She wrapped her legs around his waist. He slid out and buried himself again. "There's nothing sweeter than this, Katy."

She shook her head, agreeing with him. "Nothing," her voice came out as a husky whisper. She cradled his face in her hands and kissed him.

"Hold on to me."

Before she could question what he meant, he rolled to the floor, taking her with him.

"What are you doing?" she said with a laugh.

"I couldn't get a good enough hold on you up there."

She looked beyond his head, the multi-colored holiday lights from the tree twinkling, adding to the magical atmosphere. She smiled as he claimed her again, riding her until the lights faded into a blur of hazy intensity.

Sensation after sensation pushed her closer until she reached the precipice. Before she fell off the edge, she grasped his shoulders. A second later, hot gratification ripped through her, constricting her muscles. She hung on until he stiffened, his gaze locking with hers as his expression shifted from one of something akin to pain to supreme satisfaction.

"Ah, God, Katy. I—"

He stopped and shook his head before he rolled, pulling her close to him.

She lay panting against his chest, unable to believe the things he could make her feel. In that moment, she knew she could never get enough of him. If they ended up together, it wouldn't matter how boring life got, with him around, she'd always have this. She lifted her head.

A cocky smile hovered on his lips, happiness shining from his eyes. "Damn, you're good."

She snorted. "Me? You mean you. I've never felt—"

Her doorbell chimed through the house, spearing her with a sharp panic.

Chapter Fourteen

Katy pushed off Scott and was on her feet in a second. "Sweet Mary," she whispered. "I forgot about my parents."

"Shit." Scott jumped up, too.

Their clothing littered her living room floor and furniture, and she lunged for her shirt. It tangled in her hair as she dragged it over her head. She could live with a few missing strands.

She and Scott gathered the rest of their items.

"Go in the bathroom." She waved him away. "Wait," she called as she grabbed his boots. "Don't forget these."

"Sorry." He slapped a fat kiss on her lips before he took his shoes and hurried down the hallway.

She watched his tight butt as he left, wishing she could ignore the doorbell and devour him instead. With rushed movements, she shoved her feet through her jeans and tugged them up before burying her bra and panties under one of the pillows on the couch.

Her mother knocked again and called her name. If Katy didn't have that door open in two seconds, her mother would use her key.

She fingered combed her hair, glancing in the mirror hanging in her entry way. Lord help her. She looked like a ravaged woman with flushed cheeks and kiss-swollen lips.

She could only hope her mother wouldn't notice.

Katy swung the door wide, hoping the crisp winter air would sweep in and clear away any last traces of what she and Scott had been doing.

"What took you so long?" Her mother studied her with narrowed eyes, a bright red snow shovel perched in front of her.

"I was in the kitchen. Had to dry my hands."

"Your hair." Her mother reached out, but Katy quickly dragged her fingers through her strands again.

"I've been cooking."

Her mother turned and looked over her shoulder. "Whose SUV is that in your drive?"

She tried to put on a calm smile. "That would be Scott's. He's in the bathroom, I think, but why don't you come in, and you can meet him." As her mother passed, Katy glanced outside. Her parents' car sat idling, the headlights still glowing. "Dad not coming in?"

"You know how he is around strangers."

"Yeah." Katy waved and closed the door. If her father stayed in the car, then her mother wouldn't hang around long, and there'd be less chance she and Scott would get busted.

Scott picked that moment to walk down the hall, looking as put together as he had earlier in the day. Not fair, but at least he didn't look as though they'd just engaged in unadulterated sex.

"You must be Scott." Her mother gave him a warm, genuine smile, and a small measure of relief sank into Katy's bones.

"Scott, I'd like you to meet my mother, Eleanor Rivers."

He shook her hand. "Very nice to meet you, Mrs. Rivers."

"Oh, please. Call me Ellie." She sent Katy an impressed smile, as if to say Katy had struck gold with him.

"Mom, this is Scott Beckstead."

The smile slipped ever so slightly from her mother's face. "Beckstead? Your parents weren't Bryce and Melanie Beckstead, were they?"

Scott stiffened as a chill spilled over the room. "Yes, ma'am. They were."

Her mother nodded and then tried to lift her falling smile, but failed. With just a few words, happiness slipped from the face of Katy's world. "Well, I won't keep you. I just wanted to drop off this shovel for my daughter."

"Okay, Mom." Katy took the gift and set it aside, sending her mother a look of hurt and disappointment. She never would have believed her mom could be so cold to someone's face. Resentment cried out inside her, but she couldn't voice her opinions. Not in front of Scott. From the stoic look on his face, Katy knew he'd read her mother quite well.

Katy marched to the front door and opened it, shaking her head at her mom. "How could you?" she whispered.

Her mother spread her mouth into a thin line. "Do you know who he is?" Her mom's whisper wasn't so quiet.

"I'll be right back," she called to Scott and pulled her mother outside with her. She turned on her, rage blocking out the chill of the night. "Yes, I know who he is, and I can't believe you'd treat him like that."

"You could do *so* much better."

"You don't even know him. What about all that bullshit you used to tell me about not judging others?"

"Watch your mouth, Katy."

Katy took a deep breath and closed her eyes.

"His father was a no-good drunk who deserted his family," her mom continued. "His mother wasn't much better. This boy that you've let into your home spent a lot of time in juvenile detention. He's not the one for you."

She couldn't stop her mouth from dropping open. "Wow, Mom. I never thought there'd come a day when I'd be embarrassed by your behavior, but I am. For your information, Scott is not a boy. He's a man. A man who has overcome some difficult obstacles and made something out of himself during the last few years. I'm sorry if you can't see that."

Her mother shook her head. "I'm sure he's a nice person, but a little below your status, don't you think?"

She stared at the woman who'd raised her, wondering how she'd never seen this side of her before. "I think you should go now. This conversation is over."

"Fine." Her mother turned and started down the steps. "But you're on the edge of making a huge mistake. I hope we've raised you well enough that you can recognize it before you're in too deep."

Too deep? Words burned on Katy's tongue. Right now, she'd love to tell her mother exactly how deep she'd been with Scott moments before her mom brought her high-and-mighty attitudes to her door.

But that wouldn't serve anyone.

Katy stood on the porch, watching her mother get in the car and her parents leave. She could only imagine the scathing conversation spewing from her mom's mouth, and she could picture her dad rolling his eyes in response. At least her father was a reasonable man.

When her little street was quiet once again, she sagged against the porch railing. Soft, fluffy snowflakes tumbled from the midnight sky as though sprinkling peace all around her.

The door behind her opened, and Scott emerged. He placed her coat over her shoulders, and she turned, finding him tucked inside his jacket as well. "You okay?"

She whipped out her brightest smile. "Yep."

"I'm sorry."

"No." She shook her head. "You have nothing to be sorry for."

"I've caused you problems with your mom."

She stepped to him, slipping her arms inside his coat, locking her hands around his waist. Warmth and strength infused her. "You've done nothing but make me extremely happy."

He smiled, but the gesture didn't quite reach his eyes. "I should go."

"No, you should stay." Forever.

⌒

When the alarm on Katy's phone sounded, she tried to roll, but found Scott's strong arm holding her snug against his warm body. She smiled and squirmed from his grasp, reaching for her phone that rested on her nightstand.

Ugh. Sunday morning. Sienna would be there in an hour.

She slipped back under the cozy blankets, Scott tucking her against him. He ran a possessive hand over her hip, along her rib cage before cupping her breast. Her nipple tightened, sending a shiver through the rest of her.

"I have to make a call," she said, laughing as the hard length of him pressed against her bottom. The man had an insatiable appetite, and she found she loved that about him.

"Hurry." He nipped her shoulder before nuzzling his way along the curve of her neck to kiss behind her ear.

She dialed Sienna's number, knowing her friend wouldn't be happy about her canceling. "Hey Sienna," she said when their lines connected. "I'm so sorry, but I'm not going to be able to meet this morning."

"Why not?" Her friend paused. "Don't tell me you're at *his* house again?"

Recently extinguished irritation from her mother's visit flared. She was so tired of her friends and family trying to box her in. Scott was a good man, and she would not be made to feel guilty for whatever was blossoming between them. "Actually, he's in *my* bed this morning," she said, letting a little of her annoyance show.

"Great." Her friend's disgusted sigh only angered her further. "You need to wake up, Katy, and see that he's no good for you."

She shifted higher in bed, trying to put a little distance between her and Scott so he couldn't overhear Sienna's ugly words. "You have no idea what you're talking about."

"I know enough to know he's not worth ruining our friendship."

Hurt penetrated deep inside her. How could her best friend not listen to her and not give Scott a chance when he was obviously important to Katy? "Is that what's happening here?"

"You tell me."

"Wow, Sienna. I can honestly say I never expected this."

"I don't know why not. I'm your friend." Sienna's voice turned cajoling. "You can't believe I'd sit by and watch you flush your life without trying to stop you."

"Don't you think you're being a little extreme?"

"No, Katy. I don't. I talked to your mom last night, and we're both worried about you."

Scott's body stiffened behind her, and she knew he was probably getting the gist of her conversation. She rolled, caressing the stubble on his jaw, smiling into his concerned eyes. Her friend had basically given her an ultimatum. Scott or her friendship. "I'm going to have to think about this and call you later." She hung up the phone without waiting for a response.

She had no intention of mulling over her choices. She'd made her decision, and he was right in front of her.

The moment she put her phone back on the nightstand, he hauled her to him, rolling her, and burying her beneath the strength of his warm, muscled body. She laughed and wiggled, but he held her firm. He pinned her hands against her pillow as he settled between her thighs.

"I'm causing you trouble." He said it jokingly, but Sienna's and her mother's reactions no doubt bothered him.

"Only this kind of trouble." She rubbed her ankles on his shins. "And I like it."

He studied her, a warm glow burning behind his worried eyes. "I don't want us...this to make you unhappy."

She grinned. "Do I look unhappy?"

"You know what I mean."

She pulled a hand free from his grasp and traced from his temple, down his cheeks and over his lips. "I feel like I'm finally living my life, and I've never been happier. For years, I've done what's been expected. I've lived for others." She lifted off the pillow, pressing her lips against his. "Now, I'm living for me." She ran her fingers down the warm, firm skin on his back. "This is what I want. You are what I want."

He paused for a moment before his lips curved in a wide grin. "Me, too."

Scott placed the cue ball in front of the tight triangle of colored balls. He stepped back, aiming his cue stick and then took his shot. The white ball careened into the others with a loud, satisfying crack, sending them scattering in different directions. The red and yellow balls vanished into holes at the edge of the pool table.

"Now I know why you skipped English all those years ago and played pool instead." Luke glanced up from beneath the brim of his ball cap.

"Why's that?" Scott grinned at his friend.

"So you could kick my ass."

"That's what I thought you'd say." Scott tipped back his bottle of beer, letting the cold liquid slide down his throat. He'd rather be snuggled up with Katy than hanging out with Luke on a Saturday afternoon at Sparrow's, but she'd gone into Pinecone to put in overtime hours, trying to sort through some accounting mess someone in her office had created. He hated that the stress from her job was partially due to the construction project, but he respected her work ethic.

"Where's Lily today?"

"Ten ball in the side pocket." Luke took his shot, the ball barely missing his intended target before it rolled back toward the center of the table. "Shit." He stepped back. "She's off gallivanting with her girlfriends. They're doing some last-minute Christmas shopping."

Christmas was less than a week away, and all he'd found for Katy was a gorgeous hand-blown glass figurine of a wolf. He'd spent most of his free time with her and hadn't done any shopping. "That's probably what we should be doing."

"I'm done with my shopping, dude. Did it all online." Luke eyed him over the tip of his cue stick like he was some kind of superior being because he didn't procrastinate.

"What did you end up getting her?"

"A bunch of stuff. She's going to love this emerald necklace I found. It should keep me out of the dog house for a while."

Scott snorted. "Lily's too sweet to put you out, even if you did deserve it."

"Ha. She may look sweet, but trust me, she's got a temper."

"Yeah. I remember that time at the bar when she took down Hannah."

Luke laughed. "That's my Lily." He narrowed his gaze at Scott. "What about the girl you've been seeing?"

"Katy? I don't know what to get her."

Luke puffed out his chest. "It's my experience that there are two things that will lead you to a woman's bed…er, her heart. Doing chores or buying her expensive jewelry, with jewelry seeming like the better option. If you like her so much, why don't you buy her a ring?"

Scott rolled his eyes and rubbed the short whiskers on his chin. "I think it's a little early for a ring." Though he'd actually toyed with the idea.

"Who says? Didn't take me long to figure out I wanted to spend my life with Lily, though I was a bit of a dumbass and almost lost her." He caught Scott's gaze. "Don't do what I did."

"I don't want to scare her off."

"If she loves you, she won't be scared. Besides, you could always go for a long engagement."

He nodded, wishing he could feel happier about the whole thing.

"But…" Luke lifted his brows.

"No buts. Not really. Just her mom's not enamored with the idea of her daughter being with me."

"Damn reputations will kill you every time." Luke shook his head and smiled.

He knew Luke was joking, but he couldn't return the gesture. "It's all fucked up."

"What does Katy say?"

"She doesn't care what anyone thinks."

"Then what are *you* worried about?"

"I care, damn it. I don't want her sacrificing anything for me. It's not right. I don't want her regretting that she's with me six months down the road when she realizes her family is important to her, too."

"Maybe you should give her a little credit. Maybe her family just needs some time to get to know the real you, and she knows this about them. Stop thinking in black and white, and give life a chance to happen."

Could it be Katy wasn't the only one who needed to start living?

Luke shook his head. "Like I said, don't be a dumbass. If you love her, tell her. Give her a damn ring that will knock her off her feet."

CHAPTER FIFTEEN

A knock on Janet's office door startled Katy, but she breathed easier when she recognized the familiar face. "Mr. Winward. What are you doing here on a Saturday?"

"I could ask you the same thing." Her boss didn't look the same dressed in jeans and a sweater instead of his suit. He actually looked like…a real person. It was weird. Disconcerting.

"It's these expense reports for everything we've spent since January. Some of the figures weren't jiving, and I want everything in order by Monday's meeting."

He nodded, seeming pleased. "I appreciate that, Miss Rivers." He sat in the chair opposite her. "I'm actually glad you're here. There are a couple of things I'd like to discuss with you."

Her chest tightened. He had always been fair, but he still intimidated the hell out of her. "Uh, okay."

"First off, I'd like to commend you for the fine job you've done. I might forgive Janet for leaving like she did since everything has worked out so well."

She smiled despite her nerves. "Thank you. I've appreciated the opportunity."

"You've done more than appreciate, you've excelled." He intertwined his fingers. "I don't know if you've heard the rumors, but Janet's not coming back."

"She's not?" She widened her eyes. Nina and the others *had* spoken the truth.

"No. Apparently, she's damn happy with her new husband, and they intend to relocate somewhere warmer."

Katy couldn't help but smile. Janet was living her dream.

"I'm now tasked with finding her replacement, and I'm seriously considering you."

She'd wondered if this was where he'd been leading, but she didn't dare hope. "I don't know what to say. I...I...would give it my all, Mr. Winward. I'm dedicated to seeing our company prosper."

"I know you are, Miss Rivers. Your performance speaks volumes. There's just one problem." He shifted in his chair. "Scott Beckstead."

"Scott?" She frowned. "I don't understand."

"I've been informed that you have a relationship with him." He paused. "A sexual relationship."

Her face heated a hundred degrees. "I, uh..."

"I recognize this is an unorthodox question, but I need to know about any conflicts of interest before I could consider promoting you."

"Yes. I do have a relationship with Scott. It's a recent development." She swallowed, wondering who'd been talking about her and Scott. They hadn't totally hidden their relationship, but they hadn't flaunted it, either. It had to be Nina. She must have seen them kiss at the Christmas party after all.

"I see. I was afraid of that. With the millions of dollars that we're spending on this project, I believe the board will have an issue with your relationship."

The potential consequences of his statement hit her like a bitter, winter wind. "So, you're basically saying it's my promotion or Scott?" Could he do that?

"At least for the duration of the project."

"That's a good eighteen months."

"I'm sorry, Miss Rivers. I realize my timing is not the best, with Christmas right around the corner and all, but I need to move on this. The board is pushing for a replacement. You certainly won't lose your job if you continue this relationship, but, in good conscience, I'm not sure it would be in the best interests of the company to put you in this position. It wouldn't be fair to the stockholders, and quite frankly, it wouldn't be fair to you."

"I've always done my job well. With never a hint of anything irresponsible or illegal."

"I agree. I can still put your name before the board, but with this issue, I'm sure they'll shoot you down."

Hot tears pushed from the backs of her eyes, but she held them in check. "I understand. May I have some time to think about it?" This was not happening.

"Of course." He stood. "I won't meet with the board until Tuesday." He gave her a consolatory smile. "Regardless of your choice, thanks again for your dedication."

He left, closing the door behind him. She blinked, her tear ducts suddenly dry. She didn't need time to think. What she needed was answers.

She was pretty sure Scott felt the same way about her as she did him, but she had to know for certain.

⌒⟩

Wild, excited heartbeats thumped against Scott's chest as he pocketed the diamond ring and exited the jewelry store on the corner of Main and Canyon in Pinecone's thriving business district. It only covered two square blocks, but plenty of bustling shoppers ducked in and out of stores, not bothered at all by the fluttering snowflakes that were determined to give everyone a white Christmas.

The phone in his coat pocket vibrated, and he pulled it out, hoping it was Katy saying she'd ended her day and wanted to spend the evening with him.

He was surprised to find James Winward's name and number flashing at him instead. "James?"

"Scott. I'm glad I caught you. There's something I feel compelled to discuss with you even though I'm wondering if I should."

"What's going on?"

He released an anxious chuckle. "I'm being selfish here and completely overstepping my bounds by calling you, but I need to talk to you about Katy."

"Katy?"

Winward covered his issue with wanting to promote Katy, and the problems he faced. "I know this is none of my business, but I like her. She has real potential, Scott. I'd hate to see her blow her future on something superficial."

Superficial. There was nothing shallow or insincere in the way he felt about Katy. But could he let her give up her future for him? Would that be another thing she'd regret? "Have you talked to Katy about this?"

"I did."

"What did she say?"

"She asked for a couple of days to think about it."

Winward's reply sucker-punched him in the heart. "I see." If she needed a couple of days to think about things, then she wasn't certain about him at all. "I'm not sure how I can help, James. This really has to be her choice."

The CEO of the medical center sighed. "I was afraid you'd say that. Like I said, I'm being selfish and influencing people when I shouldn't. I hope you'll forgive me."

Scott ended their call and pocketed his phone. The ring he'd just purchased burned against his hip, mocking him for his absurd idea.

Katy couldn't believe she was actually looking forward to starting a new work week. She hadn't been able to connect with Scott all weekend other than a quick phone call, and she couldn't wait to see him at the Monday morning construction meeting.

The hour between eight when she arrived and their nine o'clock meeting crawled by. This would most likely be her last time to sit on the committee. She was certain after she spoke with Mr. Winward and gave him her decision, he'd remove her from her position.

She didn't care. She'd known that she couldn't pass up this opportunity to see what lay ahead for her and Scott. But beyond that, she'd also come to some other conclusions.

This was her life. She was tired of living up to others' wants and expectations. Yes, she might be giving up a chance to move up the ladder, but she couldn't believe this was the only opportunity she'd have to use her talents. However, it might be the only chance she'd have with Scott, and she was determined to own her life.

She arrived at the meeting five minutes early.

Scott walked in ten minutes late, his coffee cup and files in hand, a solemn look on his face. "Sorry to be late," he said to the group. He sat and pulled out some papers without giving her a cursory glance.

The quiet meeting room roared around her. Something was wrong. Something was *very* wrong.

The meeting dragged on forever, and Scott did not look in her direction one time. It was as though someone had skipped ahead a few chapters in her book without letting her know what had happened.

Her phone vibrated. She didn't want to get in trouble for reading emails during their meeting, but she felt compelled to look at it. She tucked her phone between her and the edge of the conference table before checking her messages.

There was a text message. From Scott.

She glanced at him, but he kept his gaze on Winward.

She opened the text. Scott wanted to meet in her office right after they finished.

At the conclusion of the meeting, Scott was the first person out the door. She jumped up and went after him.

"Hey." She caught his jacket sleeve, tugging him to a stop. "Would you like to tell me what's going on?"

The troubled expression in his eyes disclosed more than she wanted to know. "I don't think we should discuss this here."

"Discuss what?" She couldn't go another second without an explanation.

He looked past her, down the hall, as Katy heard voices behind her.

"Let's go to your office."

Katy led him to Janet's office and shut the door. She turned to him. "Scott, I don't know what's going on, but you're scaring me."

The look in his eyes turned tortured. "I never meant to hurt you, Katy."

Oh, God. "But you're going to anyway, aren't you?" She put a hand on a bookcase to steady herself.

"This isn't going to work." His words were like arrows pulled from a quiver as he stared straight at her. His weapons pierced deep into her heart.

Pain swelled in her throat, choking her. This was not how she'd pictured things going between them. She'd been certain he'd felt the same way about her. How could she have been so wrong?

It took her a moment before she could speak. "Why?"

He turned toward the window, presenting his back to her. "I don't want to go into it, Katy. I'm sorry I didn't tell you sooner."

"Sooner? Have you been thinking about this for a while, then?" Had her mother and Sienna been right? Had he been using her? Worse, had she been making a fool of herself this whole time, thinking she'd stumbled across something really special?

He released a weighted sigh and turned to her. "I'm sorry, Katy. I really thought I was ready to take this to the next level, but it turns out I'm not."

She studied his face, looking for any sign that might hint he wasn't serious. She found nothing but a blank slate of granite. "Oh." Bitter emotions welled inside her. She couldn't believe she'd been so wrong about him. But she obviously had been, and it hurt to look at him now. "Then I guess you should go."

"I..." He pressed his lips into a hard line, and she could tell it was difficult for him to speak. But obviously easier than keeping their relationship. "I should go."

He turned and hurried out the door.

Katy stared at the spot he'd occupied only moments before, her heart a bleak, empty shell. A tear formed and ran down her cheek. Then another. Then more, as her grief swallowed her.

She'd never recover from the hole he'd left in her heart.

CHAPTER SIXTEEN

Several hours later, Katy had composed herself into some semblance of who she'd been before. At least on the outside.

Maybe all those years of living safely had been the wisest choice. She'd certainly never had to endure pain like this before.

She headed out of Janet's office and through the maze of cubicles, passing by her old desk. The four half-walls might not have been the choicest office space in the building, but she'd managed to work there just fine. Several of her co-workers eyed her with envy as she passed. They thought she had it made. They hated her for what she'd accomplished, when really they had no right.

No matter. They'd learn the truth after the holiday.

She reached the administrative suite and entered the quiet sanctuary. Winward awaited her decision.

One of the men directly under Winward passed. She smiled, but he barely gave her a nod. Funny, but it didn't seem to matter which side of the fence a person was on. There were those on both sides who were miserable. Position, money even, obviously didn't make a person happy.

It was up to each of them to ensure their own happiness. How had she not realized this? Getting Janet's job wouldn't fill the empty spots in her life.

What made her happy was the knowledge she was free to live her life as she chose. If nothing else, Scott had given her this.

She nodded to Winward's assistant as she passed. "He's expecting me."

"Yes, Katy. Go on back."

Winward sat in his chair much like he had that first day he'd summoned her to his office. It was amazing how much had changed in her life since that fateful day. One thing she learned was that Mr. Winward was a person like everyone else with wants and needs, and yes, an ego the size of Texas.

Her boss looked up. "Katy. Have a seat. I'm guessing you have an answer for me."

"I do." She inhaled and let the weight on her chest carry the air away, knowing she didn't really have a choice in the matter, not if she wanted to enjoy her life. "I can't accept."

Mr. Winward's eyebrows shot upward. "Are you sure?" He blinked a few times. "This is a huge salary increase for you, Katy. Promotions like that don't come along very often in a person's life."

She folded her hands to keep them from shaking. She couldn't believe she was actually turning him down, either, but she had no doubt it was the right choice. "It's not that I don't want the promotion, Mr. Winward. I do, and I know I would do an excellent job for you. It's the conditions of the offer."

"Scott."

"Not so much Scott, but the fact that I'm giving up control of my personal life to my job. I'll happily give you eight or more hours a day, but when I walk out that door, I need to own my life. I'm sorry this puts you in a spot. I understand the whole conflict of interest thing and certainly understand why you can't promote me if I don't agree to your terms."

Her boss shook his head. "This is all very interesting, Katy. I heard a rumor this afternoon that you and Scott had already decided to call it quits, so why not just take the job?"

Damn gossip mill. "Like I said, Scott really isn't the point. I refuse to give up my freedom for my job. If it's not Scott, it may be something or someone else down the line."

He studied her for a moment, then shrugged. "If that's your decision, then there's nothing much I can do."

Her stomach sank as she rose. "Thank you for understanding. And thank you again for the opportunity." She walked across the plush carpet toward the door and stopped. "If you don't mind me asking, Mr. Winward. Was it Nina Compton who told you about my relationship with Scott? I'd just like to know who I shouldn't consider a friend."

"I appreciate your question. Whenever you're in business, it's good to know who your friends are and who your enemies are. But no, it wasn't Nina. The information actually came from my wife. She works with a friend of yours at the community college, and you came up in a casual conversation one day."

Bile rose in her throat. "Oh. I see." That was no casual conversation, and Katy had no doubt Sienna had sabotaged her on purpose. "Thanks again, Mr. Winward. Please keep me in mind if any other positions come open."

"Will do."

By the time she made it back to Janet's office, everything was tinted a bright shade of scarlet. She picked up her phone and dialed Sienna's cell. "You'd better answer, because if I have to see you in person, you may not live."

Her friend answered on the second ring. "Katy. I'm glad you called. I've been wondering if you're okay."

Sure she was. She knew the kind of destruction her words could cause and was probably curious about the fallout. "Of course I am. Why wouldn't I be?"

Awkward silence crept across the line. "I don't know. I guess, of course, you'd be fine." The tone of Sienna's voice might as well have been a confession.

"I did have an interesting conversation today."

"With Scott?" There was that, too.

"No, with Mr. Winward. Apparently, you work with his wife."

"Winward?" She paused for a moment as though thinking. "I suppose that could be Glenna Winward."

"Cut the crap, Sienna. I know what you told her about me and Scott. And I know you did it to sabotage my relationship with him."

More silence. "I did it for you, Katy. To keep you from getting hurt. You didn't have a relationship with him. He was just using you."

"How the hell would you know that? You don't know him at all."

"We both know what he's like."

Heated blood hammered through her veins. "This makes me sick, Sienna. You make me sick. You don't know Scott, and I obviously don't know you as well as I thought." She had to hang up. "I sincerely hope you were trying to protect me, and this didn't come from some jealous seed growing inside you. If you did it out of love, there may come a day we can be friends again, but right now, I can't talk to you anymore."

She hung up the phone and grabbed her keys. She'd had all she could take. She'd managed to lose a friend, a promotion, and worse, the man she loved all in one day. Add into the mixture that it was two days before Christmas, and she had the perfect reason to want to escape her life.

If she wasn't worried she'd run into Scott at Swallow's, she'd stop by and get totally smashed.

Katy called work the following day and let them know she was taking some personal time. Most people would only work a half day anyway on Christmas Eve, and she couldn't stomach watching everyone gloat at her losses. Nina would be the worst.

It was after nine when she rolled out of bed, her head pounding like none other. She'd had a restless, tear-filled night, and she was certain the pain she felt now was worse than her hangover.

She cursed when the doorbell rang before she'd had time to pour her first cup of coffee. She really should watch her language, she thought as she trudged to the door. It wasn't like her to have such a potty mouth, but sometimes, it felt so damn good to toss out a cussword. Like damn. She said it aloud, just because she could.

She peeked out the window to find Sienna's gold Taurus parked in her drive.

"Damn." She slid the deadbolt and unlocked the door, a burst of icy air rushing in as she opened it. "I don't have anything to say to you."

"Please, I need to say something." Her friend stood before her, eyes wet and swollen, a wretched look on her face.

She wanted to slam the door, but she couldn't do it. "Fine. But only because you look such a mess."

Her friend wiped her eyes as new tears started to fall. "I am a mess. A horrible mess." Her voice trembled, and Katy actually felt sorry for the woman who'd been her lifelong friend.

Sienna took a deep breath before continuing. "You're right, Katy. What I did was wrong. *So* wrong."

She nodded, but didn't interrupt.

"I was jealous." Sienna rolled her red-streaked eyes. "Who am I kidding? I am jealous. It's always been the two of us who've hung out together, and then suddenly, you get a cool promotion and a hot guy, and all in the same day. I felt like all the exciting things were happening to you, and I let it get to me." She exhaled a shudder. "I did tell Glenna Winward. Oh, God." Her tears fell faster now.

Katy's anger faded and pity occupied the space. "I thought we were friends. Why would you do that to me?"

"I don't know. It was such a stupid thing." A nasally sound accented her words. She walked into Katy's kitchen, and Katy followed. Her friend grabbed a tissue and blew her nose before continuing. "I'd run into Lily Winchester at the market, and she brought up Scott and you. She'd heard that Scott intended to propose. She knew we were friends, and she wondered if he'd already popped the question," she said in a rush of misery.

Katy sagged against the counter, shocked. "He was going to propose?"

"He hasn't?" She glanced at Katy's left hand, her brows rising. "Oh, God. Now I've ruined that, too."

Katy shook her head, dazed, only part of her recognizing the utter misery on her friend's face.

"You were a friend, Katy. I was a wretched, jealous beast, and I'm so, so sorry. I know I can't ask you to forgive me, but I had to apologize. I had to tell you the truth."

He'd intended to propose. Tears filled her eyes now, too. She held open her arms, overcome by emotion and unable to speak. Sienna walked into her embrace, and she held her friend tight. "Thank you for telling me this," she whispered.

Sienna pulled away, sniffing back more tears. "I'm sorry I've been so horrible."

She nodded. "We've been friends forever, and I guess it's about time we admit we're just as human as everyone else. We're allowed to make mistakes. In fact, if we're not out there trying things, making mistakes and learning from them, then we're not really living, are we?"

As far as she could tell, she'd made a huge blunder taking Scott at face value. He'd lied when he'd told her he wasn't ready to be serious, but she knew without a doubt he'd done it because he loved her.

A swelling ball of happiness warmed her insides. He loved her. And she loved him.

And she knew the perfect way to show him how much she cared.

There was just one thing she needed to take care of first.

Katy pulled into the familiar drive. Her parents would be surprised to see her. They were expecting to meet with her later at her Aunt Lana's house for their traditional Christmas Eve party. But, as her mother was soon to find out, things would be different this year.

Her boots made tracks in the newly fallen snow glistening on the sidewalk. Just like she was making new, unpredictable tracks in her life. But, deep down in her soul, her decisions felt good.

She opened the door, preparing herself for the worst, but hoping for the best. Her mom acted out of love, not spite.

A pile of gifts sat next to the front door. Offerings to take to the party. Placing them by the door was another tradition her mother had started after the year she'd forgotten all the presents. Katy smiled at the memory.

She found her parents in their bedroom, her father sitting on the handmade Christmas quilt that covered the bed and her mom spraying on perfume.

"Katy?" Her mom managed to sound surprised and worried at the same time. "What are you doing here? It's Christmas Eve. You should be getting ready for the party."

Katy sat on their bed. "I'm not going this year."

Her father furrowed his brows.

"Why on earth not?" Deep concern lined her mother's forehead.

"Mom. Dad. There's something I need to say, and I really need you to listen and to hear me, okay?"

"Sure, honey." Her dad scooted closer and took her hand.

She'd always been grateful for the quiet, steady support her father had offered her. Her mom stepped forward, too, giving her a measure of comfort.

"I'm in love."

The sharp intake of her mother's breath set her back on edge. "Not that Beckstead boy."

"Mom." Katy stood and took her mother's hand. "This is where the listening part comes in."

"Eleanor." Her father sent her mother some sort of silent communication, and Katy smiled. Her parents had been talking like that since she could remember.

Her mom looked between her husband and Katy. "Fine." She took a seat next to Katy's dad.

"I do love him, Mom. I know he's not the doctor you were hoping for, but he's a successful business owner. He's kind, and so, so sweet to me."

Her dad smiled, but her mother didn't look convinced.

"Look, I know you love me. If you could see how happy I am when I'm with him…If you'd just give him a chance, I know you'll see what a wonderful person he's turned out to be. Yes, he had a rough time when he was younger, but I think that's what helped make him the man he is today." She paused, searching her parents' faces. "Please give him a chance."

"Katy—"

"Mom. You and dad have had this wonderful relationship with each other. I feel like I could have that, too, with Scott. Just give him a chance before you label or condemn him?"

Uncertainty hovered on her mother's face.

"Of course, Katy," her father answered.

Her mom glanced between them both again before she sighed. "What can I say? You're right, Katy. If you care about him, I should give him a chance." She nodded. "It's not that I have anything against him. It's just I've always wanted the best for you."

"I know." Katy held out her arms, and her mom stood and hugged her. "Thanks, Mom." She glanced at her father. "Dad."

He nodded.

"What are the chances we could get both of you to come to Christmas dinner tomorrow?" her mom asked.

Katy's grin formed in her heart and spread to her lips. "I'm going to say the odds are pretty good." Or at least she hoped and prayed that they were.

CHAPTER SEVENTEEN

S cott sat alone in front of his television, suffering through a dim night of searching for ways to pass the time until he could crash in bed. He'd skipped over *A Christmas Story* and *It's a Beautiful Life*, instead opting for his DVD of *The Expendables*. Nothing like some serious violence to take his mind off losing Katy.

Luke and Lily had invited him to their house to celebrate Christmas Eve. Normally, he would go, but he just wasn't in the mood this year.

His phone rang, and he eyed it with a wary expression, knowing Luke wouldn't give in until he said yes. His heart stopped and then raced forward at an alarming pitch when he saw Katy's name on his screen.

Damn it.

He shouldn't answer. He was at his weakest right now, and it wouldn't be a good idea to talk to her.

He let it ring a couple more times before he succumbed to her call. "Hello."

"Scott, I need you."

His brain tried to warn him against falling for her sweet voice, but his heart sang louder. "Are you okay?"

ASPEN TRILOGY

"Not really. One of my pipes burst." Her voice
sounded panicky. "I can't get a hold of my dad or
anyone else. Would you please come help me?"

"Of course." How could he ever refuse her? "I'll
be right there."

Despite the snowy roads, he made it to her house
in record time. He knocked on the door, toolbox in
hand, and this time, she answered right away.

She didn't look as panicked as she'd sounded
earlier.

"Which room? Kitchen or the bathroom?" The
delicious smell of something cinnamon caught his
nose.

She bit her bottom lip, a look of uncertainty
wavering in her eyes.

"Katy?"

"I lied."

"What?" With his initial spurt of adrenaline
now fading, he recognized the soothing strains of
Christmas music playing in the background, and
the way all of the lights in her living room had
been dimmed allowing the Christmas tree to glow
brighter. "You don't have a leak?"

"Not in my pipes." She gave him a trembling
smile. "But maybe in my heart."

He took a step back, knowing she'd tugged him
down a slippery slope with her words. He needed a
moment to fully process what she'd said. "You lied?"

She moved closer to him, placing her hand on
his cheek, watching him with her green eyes. "You
lied, too. You said you weren't ready to get serious,
but you were."

He stared at her, not knowing where she'd gotten her information, but unable to deny the truth.

"I was going to ask you to marry me, Katy, but I love you too much to let you ruin your future."

Her lips twisted into a smile even as tears formed in her eyes. "I'd like *you* to be my future."

"What about your promotion?"

"I turned it down. Even though you ended things. I've learned enough from you to realize I want to own my life. I'll give my all while I'm at work, but I control the rest. I can't work in a position where I'm held captive twenty-four hours a day." She placed her lips on his in a soft kiss. "I won't be told I can't love you. Even if I tried, it wouldn't work."

God, he loved her. He set down the toolbox and snaked his arms around her. He held her in a tight embrace, burying his face in her fragrant, blond tresses. Everything in the world was right as long as he held her against him. "Ah, Angel. I can't live without you, either." Unable to deny himself any longer, he claimed her mouth in a passionate kiss.

She laughed, breathless when he finally pulled away. "I love you, Scott."

"I love you, too." He dug in his coat pocket. "I have something for you."

Her eyes grew wide. "It's…"

"I don't know why I brought it. I guess subconsciously I was hoping." He handed the silver wrapped package.

"You're going to make me cry again." She put a hand over her mouth, but still took the package from him. Her fingers shook as she opened it, and he couldn't help but smile.

When she opened the jewelry box, she looked at him with tear-filled eyes. "It's breathtaking."

"You're breathtaking." He pulled the diamond and platinum ring from the box. "Will you marry me?"

She nodded, happy tears spilling from her eyes. "Yes."

He slipped the ring on her finger before tugging her to him, giving her another powerful kiss.

"I cooked you a turkey," she said between kisses. "And baked you an apple pie. All of the things you said you missed about Christmas."

"I thought something smelled good." He possessed her lips again. "But you smell better."

She chuckled. "I need to pull the pie out of the oven before you devour me, or it will be ruined."

"Deal." He took her hand as they walked into the kitchen. "I'll help, but you can be sure you're the first thing on the menu for me." His heart expanded twice its size and life suddenly became more valuable than it ever had been before.

He'd found the woman of his dreams, and he would never let her go.

The End

CHAPTER ONE

April Sandoval walked up to the rundown little house in the outskirts of Salt Lake City and paused on the porch. Two golden lilies had forced their way through the thick weeds that claimed most of the space in the overgrown garden next to the crumbling cement steps. Her cousin had always seemed like the meticulous type when they'd been growing up, but almost three years had passed since she'd last seen Jessie. April had changed since then. Perhaps her cousin had, too.

That was the only reason she found herself outside Jessie's door—to see if time really did heal old wounds.

She took a deep breath and rang the doorbell. She'd expected to hear the chime echo from inside the house, but there was no noise. She waited a moment, and then with a closed fist, she pounded on the door.

A minute later, the sound of locks clicking tightened April's already tense nerves, and she sucked in a breath as the door opened.

The sight of her cousin standing in a stained t-shirt and worn flannel pants surprised her. Jessie had pulled her hair back in a messy ponytail and wore no makeup. However, the thing that really shocked April was the tow-headed little boy Jessie held in her arms. He gazed at her with a combination of curiosity and shyness as he clutched a ragged brown teddy bear. She guessed he had to be about two years old.

"April." Jessie smiled. "Thank you for coming."

April returned the gesture, knowing her lips had curved more with uncertainty than with happiness. "I was really surprised to get your call. I had no idea you were living in Salt Lake, too."

Her cousin stood back to encourage her to enter the house. "I left about a month after you did. I needed a change of scenery."

April walked inside, noting the barrage of scattered toys littering the worn carpet. The smell of a house closed up for too long permeated the air, and April repressed the urge to ask if she could open the windows and let in the fresh summer breeze.

Dirty lunch dishes had gathered on the coffee table in a pile that obviously needed attention. Perhaps her cousin ran a daycare as a way to earn income. That would explain the child and the clutter. April sat, poised to make a hasty exit if things went south.

Jessie followed her to the couch and sat next to her, setting the little boy on the floor. "Sit down here for a few minutes and play, okay?" He wrapped a possessive hand around her cousin's leg, still staring at the newcomer with bright blue eyes framed with dark, thick lashes.

"He's adorable." April envied his mother, whoever she was. For the longest time, April had looked forward to having a child. She'd been certain she and Seth would have been married by now and quite possibly would have started a family. But Jessie had ruined all of that.

"Thanks." Jessie hugged the little boy, and April was certain her eyes couldn't have grown any wider.

"He's yours?" She blinked, processing the information. "I didn't know you'd had a baby. No one in the family said anything."

Jessie's smile faded, and April noted the dark circles and pale skin that aged her cousin's face. "I didn't tell them."

"*What?* Your dad doesn't know?"

The slender woman shook her head. "I don't want him to know, either. You have to promise me you won't tell anyone."

April hesitated before finally agreeing. It would be hard not to mention it to her sister or parents, but she'd respect Jessie's wishes. It was her cousin's news to tell. April understood why Jessie might not want her alcoholic father to know, but April's mom had always been a mother figure to her cousin. She'd be thrilled for Jessie. Although, she'd be sad to see her in such a worn-down state. "What's his name?"

"Your name is Danny, right?" Jessie smiled with pride when she said it. The little boy buried his face against his mom's stomach.

"Hi, Danny."

He peeked at her, grinned, and hid his face again. After a second, he looked again and held out his teddy bear to her. April took it, gave it a hug, and then handed it back to him. His smile widened, his bright eyes flashing with sweetness.

"Is his daddy here?" April asked.

Untold pain lit her cousin's eyes and spread outward across her face. "No," she whispered and shook her head.

"You're raising him on your own?" Maybe that was why the house was in shambles. April hadn't had any personal experience, but she could imagine a little one would take a lot of time and energy.

Her cousin swallowed as tears gathered in the corners of her eyes. She opened her mouth to answer but shut it again as the tears rushed down her cheeks.

The sight of Jessie crying erased the uncertainty and spurred the seemingly never-ending supply of compassion April had been cursed with. She put an arm around her cousin's shoulders. "What's the matter? Did he leave you?"

Jessie wiped the tears from her face, glancing upward as she gathered in a shuddering breath. "He's never been a part of Danny's life."

A vile stroke of suspicion whipped through April's mind. "Danny's not...Seth's, is he?"

"No," she quickly answered. "I really don't want to talk about that time in our lives if it's okay with you. Let's leave it in the past."

"I'd prefer that, too." She had to admit Jessie's answer brought her a tremendous amount of relief. "I'm sorry you have to raise Danny alone. It must be tough. How can I help you? Do you need money?" After the awful way Jessie had treated her through their high school years and afterward, she'd deserve it if April walked right out the door, but obviously Jessie had been beaten down by life and needed help.

Jessie half-laughed and half-cried. "I'm so broke it's pathetic, but money isn't going to help me now."

April drew her brows together, not understanding. "Then what will help?"

"You."

She shook her head in confusion. "How?"

Her cousin licked her dry, cracked lips. "I'm dying, April. I have a rare type of leukemia."

The cruel hand of fate gripped April's throat, making it hard to speak. "Can't the doctors do something? Chemo or radiation?"

A sad smile turned Jessie's lips. "They've tried. Everything." She took April's hand, hers feeling cold and thin. "I can't fight this anymore."

Alarm triggered inside her. "You have to, Jessie. For Danny's sake."

"I have, April. Trust me."

"There must be *something* the doctors can do. He needs his mother."

"He needs *a* mother. Someone who will be there to love him through his life." Her voice broke as painful regret streamed from her eyes. "But God has decided that person won't be me."

"Momma." Fear radiated off the little boy as he pushed to his feet and tugged her elbow.

Jessie gathered him into her arms as she cried. "It's going to be okay, honey."

An older woman with a tight gray bun and kindness wrinkled on her face approached from the kitchen. "Danny? Would you like a cookie?"

April was surprised to find there was another person in the house.

The little guy looked to his mother for reassurance and approval.

Jessie did her best to smile. "A cookie? For Danny? That sounds pretty good. I wonder if it's your favorite, chocolate chip."

Danny grinned and nodded.

"Okay, go with Mary then and get your cookie."

The little boy nearly tripped in his haste to get to Mary and the promised treat.

Jessie wiped her eyes while April tried to think of something, *anything*, to say to her frail cousin.

"I want you to take him, April."

A rush of panic filled her. "Me? I—I couldn't. I don't know how to be a mother." She always figured when the time came, she'd have nine months to figure it all out before she'd be expected to perform.

Jessie smiled. "You're the best person I know. You have so much love in your heart. I know it's a huge responsibility, but you've always wanted kids, and I can't imagine leaving Danny with anyone else."

Her cousin's words sucked the air out of her lungs. She forced in a breath. "There has to be someone better."

Jessie placed her hand over April's. "Please don't let what happened in the past come between us now. There was a time we were like sisters."

Until Jessie's petty jealousy ruined everything.

"If you don't take him, the state will contact my father. If he refuses, Danny will become a ward of the state. I don't know which would be worse. Either way, he'll have no one," she ended with a whisper.

April put a hand to her mouth as though it would keep her heart from being ripped out. A mother? Her? "Can I take some time to think about it?" She stood, the world spinning around her.

"I just need a minute." Without waiting for Jessie's approval, she walked out the front door.

Her little blue Toyota sat parked along the curb in front of Jessie's house. She could stumble down the stairs, get in her car and leave. This wasn't her nightmare to solve. Jessie had been an absolute bitch to her before April had left for Salt Lake.

She'd wanted April's job, April's boyfriend, basically April's life.

But Jessie was obviously no longer her malicious cousin. Time and fate had taken care of that. And that little boy was as innocent as they came.

She dropped onto the top step, her bottom hitting the warm cement as her conscience kicked in. How could she walk away? Jessie's father was a drunken bastard. He couldn't take care of Danny, and what kind of monster would put a baby in his hands anyway? April had seen the marks he'd left on Jessie. As a child, April hadn't been able to stop it. As an adult, she could prevent little Danny from becoming another victim.

The other option would be to let him become a ward of the state. Surely, there were plenty of good people out there aching to become parents.

Her fears kicked up. What if he didn't get good parents? What if they hurt him? What if he didn't get the love he needed?

She dropped her face into her hands. "God," she said the word on an exhale before she straightened. "Am I ready for this?"

The door opened and closed behind her. Jessie slowly lowered herself onto the step next to April, a soft sigh escaping her cousin when she reached the sitting position. "Some days..." she whispered.

April glanced at her, the bright sunshine intensifying the wear and tear on her cousin's face.

"This is my last summer," she said, her words slashing at April's heart.

A swift, unexpected death was a blessing, she realized. "I'm sorry, Jessie. I can't imagine how hard it must be to be in your position."

"It would be a lot easier if I knew Danny would be okay."

The guilt. April wanted to scream at her, to yell at how unfair it was to be put in this situation. But if circumstances were reversed, she knew she'd do anything to make sure her child had a safe and happy future. "How long?"

"A few weeks if I'm lucky. They've sent in hospice to help me. Mary will be here until the end."

April tried to swallow but couldn't. "I'll do it." Her heart thundered. "I'll raise Danny like he's my own." She could practically hear the compass of her life switching directions.

"Really? I could never thank you enough." A sob escaped her lips, and she threw her arms around April. "He's my most precious thing."

"I know." April didn't quite get her words out before she started crying, too.

CHAPTER TWO

Two months later…

April gripped the steering wheel of her Toyota as she drove down the main street of Aspen, Utah, her headlights capturing the hanging baskets of autumn chrysanthemums. At the moment, only the street lights kept the road from being completely deserted. Everything, even Sparrow's Bar and Grill had been buttoned down for the night.

She'd planned it that way. She didn't want any-one to know she was back in town until she was ready for them to know. It only took one person to see her cruising along Main Street to ignite the rumor mill. As it was, when her news finally leaked, she'd start an explosion of gossip.

She was prepared for that but on her terms. It was the cost of having family support, something the last two months had taught her she couldn't live without if she was going to be the mother Danny deserved.

Her mom hadn't questioned her late night arrival. She'd happily agreed to leave the lights on and, of course, the door would be unlocked. April had given them very limited details on what had taken place during the last few months of her life. All they knew was she was bringing home a little boy.

Several minutes after passing through town, she turned down the dusty lane that led to her mom and dad's house. She had to have traveled this road thousands of times in her life. None of them seemed as momentous as this.

She parked the car alongside her father's old red pickup, the feeling of being home comforting as well as generating a massive amount of anxiety. She grabbed the overnight bag from her passenger seat and slung it over her arm before quietly shutting the car door.

Danny roused only slightly as she lifted him from his car seat in the back. He sleepily wrapped his arms around her neck and laid his head on her shoulder, his soft breath whispering against her ear. Her heart tightened. Something in her soul smiled every time he latched on to her. His mother had called him precious, and there was no doubt he was. Difficult and ornery at times, yes, but also sweet and loving, and there wasn't a day that went by that she wasn't grateful she'd been graced to share his life.

She draped his blanket over his head to keep away the evening chill, the gravel crunching underfoot as she covered the area between her car and the house. Inside, she quietly headed through the darkened kitchen toward the hall, knowing each inch of her childhood home by heart.

Without warning, she stumbled into something hard, knocking it over and causing it to bash against the wall with a loud, resounding noise. Danny stirred, and April paused, trying to figure out how to get around whatever had fallen in front of her without tripping and waking Danny.

Her parents' bedroom light came on, and her mom stepped into the hall. "What in tarnation?" Her mother's southern accent was more prominent than usual.

Her father stumbled out after her, his salt and pepper hair sticking out wildly like it always did after his head hit the pillow.

The light and her mother's voice woke Danny, and he began to cry.

"It's me, Mom." April glanced down at her feet, cursing the bag of golf clubs scattered on the floor. Since when did someone in her family golf?

It took April a good hour to settle Danny back to sleep. She gently placed him on her old bed before quietly creeping out of the room.

The clock on the kitchen wall read a quarter after two, but her mother sat waiting for her at the table. Some things never changed.

"Where's Dad?" April asked.

Her mother's face still held a youthful glow, and she kept her hair dyed auburn to cover the telltale signs of age that might give away her secret. "He went back to bed. Said you appeared to be alive and well, so your story could wait until morning."

Smart man, her father. April sat in the chair next to her mother and met her serious gaze. She released a heavy breath. Not once in her life had she disappointed her mother, and she was deathly afraid this would be her first. "I don't know where to start."

She should have told her mom the day she'd agreed to adopt Danny. But it hadn't been that easy. She'd ended up moving in with Jessie to give Danny time to adjust to her and to give her cousin as much time with her son as possible. But then there had been Jessie's burial to handle, and Jessie didn't want the family to know. Danny had been a handful. He'd missed his mother desperately, and April had spent most of her time taking care of him. So much so, she'd finally left her job before they fired her. And now here she sat, two months later, ashamed that she hadn't included her mother.

"Is this the little boy you told me about?"

She nodded, bracing for the worst. "I adopted him. After my friend died."

"He's *your son*?" Her mother's green eyes pierced April so deep she thought she'd break. "Why didn't you tell me?"

Heartbreak registered on her mom's features, leaving April with a weighted ball of guilt she wasn't sure she could carry at the moment.

"I'm so sorry, Mom. It happened so fast. I was overwhelmed when she asked me, and then she was dying, and then Danny needed me constantly. I thought about calling so many times..." Her tears broke through, and she sniffed. "But I knew I needed to be strong, and I can't do that with you around. When I see you, I break, and I just want to crawl into your arms and let you hug me."

Her mother's piercing gaze had been tempered by tears as well, and she held open her arms. "Oh, baby. Come here."

The heavy emotions of everything she'd been through with Jessie and Danny came pouring out as her mom hugged her. She told her mother as many of the details as she could without giving away Jessie's secret.

"What do you plan to do now?" her mother asked as she swept away her own tears. "This is a very nice thing you've agreed to do, but do you truly understand the responsibilities of taking on a child? How will you afford it? Babysitters can be very expensive, not to mention all the other costs."

"I know, Mom. I was hoping we could stay here for a while." She knew her mother wouldn't refuse her. "I've decided I want to raise Danny in Aspen where he'll be safe and around family. I'm sure I can find a job and an apartment without too much trouble, but we need somewhere to stay until I can get back on my feet."

"Of course, April. You both can stay as long as you need to. It will give me and your dad a chance to get to know our new grandson."

"Thank you." April leaned over and hugged her mom again. "I want you to know you're the reason I decided to adopt Danny. Everyone needs someone like you to love them. I fell in love with that little boy, Mom, and I know in my heart this is the right thing to do. "

A week was too long to stay hidden. She'd had her time to settle in, and now she needed to reclaim her space in Aspen. The firestorm of speculation and discussion would happen, so she might as well get it over and done with.

Early autumn sunshine rained down on April's car as she drove toward Rumors Coffee Shop. She'd stop there before she headed to her sister's house at the opposite end of town.

Rumors had been built after April had moved to Salt Lake, but her mother and sister constantly raved how they now had their own version of Starbucks. April had missed stopping in when she'd last been in town at Christmas, and she was curious about it now. Besides, her mom had tipped her off that the owner was looking for someone to cover the afternoon shift. It might not be the best-paying job in the world, but it was a start, and that's all she needed.

Surprisingly, Main Street was crowded with trucks bearing the Beckstead Construction company logo, making it difficult to park directly in front of the coffee shop. She eyed the construction site as she helped her son from the car. The workers had nearly finished framing in the walls. She wondered what kind of business would inhabit the space once it was finished.

New businesses were rare in her hometown, but as the nearby cities grew bigger and bigger, she supposed it was only a matter of time before strangers recognized her little gem of a town and wanted in on the action, too. She just hoped Aspen wouldn't grow too big, too fast.

Danny held tightly to her hand as he made the big step up onto the curb. "Trucks," he said with a wide grin, his attention snagged by the various pieces of construction equipment. She redirected her son, and passed by the decorative hay bale stacked with pumpkins before entering the coffee shop.

Except for the pop music bouncing off the sunny walls, Rumors was empty despite all the trucks parked outside. "Hello?" April called out.

Noelle Parker entered from the back room, her lips breaking into a smile. "Oh, my God. April

Sandoval. I keep asking your mama when we'll see you again. It's about damn time." Her blond hair was a little longer than when April had last seen her, but the warm personality remained the same.

"Hi, Noelle." She walked to the end of the counter and gave the woman a hug. They'd been enemies in junior high and then suddenly friends in high school. A mutual friend had forced them to get to know each other, and they'd realized they actually liked each other. Life threw some funny curveballs, for sure. "I'd heard you'd opened a coffee shop. It's adorable."

"The coffee's great, too. Wait until you taste it." She widened her eyes when she finally noticed the little boy clutching April's leg. "Who's this?" Noelle asked in a singsong voice as she knelt down to Danny's level.

April blew out a silent breath. "This is my son, Danny."

Noelle stood, her eyebrows lifting until they disappeared beneath her bangs. "*Son?*" Her gaze flew to April's left hand, and she immediately felt the burn of being an unwed mother.

Another moment passed. She was certain Noelle was calculating the time since she'd left town and comparing it to an estimate of Danny's age. "I don't mean to pry...but he's not Seth's, is he?" she whispered, though they were alone.

"No," she answered a little too quickly. She knew that would be most of the townspeople's reaction, and she'd already grown defensive against it. "I adopted him." She kept the rest of the arrangement details to herself, not wanting to add extra kindling. "But living in the city is hard with a little one, so we decided to move home, huh Danny?"

He turned his angelic smile on her, melting her heart once again. There had been many days right after his mother's death when April had feared she'd never see him smile again, but time had helped them both move on. "Cookie," he said and pointed to a chocolate chip cookie in the display case.

"Would you like a cookie?" Noelle asked, glancing at April. "If it's okay with your mom?"

April agreed. It took the simplest things to make a two-year-old happy. If only life could be that simple for an adult. "I just stopped in for a moment to say hi. I'm headed to Caroline's after here. She hasn't met Danny, yet."

"I'll bet she's excited." Noelle worked the steamer behind the counter.

April's stomach twisted. "I haven't told her much about him." She really should have been more forthcoming with her family. She glanced down as Danny happily munched on his cookie, ignoring the two adults talking above him.

"Oh." Noelle gave a knowing nod, pouring the contents of her concoction into a cup and handing it to April. "Should be interesting."

"Yeah. I'm hoping she'll listen before she judges." She took a sip of her drink. "Oh, this is good." Chai-tea lattes were her favorite.

"Told you." Noelle gave her a confident smile. "Caroline's pretty level-headed," she said, continuing their first conversation. "I think you'll be okay."

April glanced at her watch. She was supposed to be at Caroline's in ten minutes. "Before I go, I want to ask about the afternoon job my mom said you had available."

Noelle's smile blossomed. "You'd be perfect. It's yours."

"Really?" April mirrored her expression. "That seems a little too easy."

"Why? I already know you're dependable and friendly. Most of my customers know you and love you."

"Okay, then." She extended her hand, and Noelle shook it. "I can start as soon as you need me." It wouldn't pay the same wage she'd made in Salt Lake, but it was a start. Between that and Jessie's life insurance policy money, she should be able to make a decent life for her and Danny until something that paid more came along.

"Great." A hint of a shadow crossed her friend's face. "I wish I could offer you more hours, but I'm still struggling to get the café firmly out of the red."

The bell on the shop door chimed, stealing their attention, and in walked three construction workers complete with dust-covered boots and grease-streaked t-shirts. Before April could react, her gaze collided with the most amazing blue eyes. The same eyes that had haunted her for the past three years.

ABOUT THE AUTHOR

Cindy Stark lives with her family and a sweet Border Collie named Boo in a small town shadowed by the Rocky Mountains. She currently writes romantic suspense and contemporary romances.

To find other books by Cindy, visit her website at www.cindystark.com